ACCLAIM FOR CHARLOTTE BINGHAM

The Kissing Garden
'A perfect escapist cocktail for summertime romantics'
Mail on Sunday

Love Song
'A perfect example of the new, darker romantic fiction
. . . a true 24-carat love story'
Sunday Times

'A poetic and poignant love story'
Sunday Post

The Love Knot
'The author perfectly evokes the atmosphere of a bygone
era . . . An entertaining Victorian romance'
Woman's Own

'Hearts are broken, scandals abound. It's totally addictive,
the sort of book you rush to finish – then wish you hadn't'
Woman's Realm

The Nightingale Sings
'A novel rich in dramatic surprises, with a large
cast of vivid characters whose antics will have you
frantically turning the pages'
Daily Mail

To Hear a Nightingale
'A story to make you laugh and cry'
Woman

'A delightful novel . . . Pulsating with vitality and deeply
felt emotions. I found myself with tears in my eyes on
one page and laughing out loud on another'
Sunday Express

The Business
'A compulsive, intriguing and perceptive read'
Sunday Express

'Compulsively readable'
Options

www.booksattransworld.co.uk

FRIDAY'S GIRL

Charlotte Bingham

BANTAM BOOKS

LONDON · TORONTO · SYDNEY · AUCKLAND · JOHANNESBURG

FRIDAY'S GIRL
A BANTAM BOOK : 0553817930/9780553817935

Originally published in Great Britain by Bantam Press,
a division of Transworld Publishers

PRINTING HISTORY
Bantam Press edition published 2005
Bantam edition published 2006

3 5 7 9 10 8 6 4 2

Typeset in 11/13pt Palatino by Kestrel Data, Exeter, Devon

Bantam Books are published by Transworld Publishers,
61–63 Uxbridge Road, London W5 5SA,
a division of The Random House Group Ltd,
in Australia by Random House Australia (Pty) Ltd,
20 Alfred Street, Milsons Point, Sydney, NSW 2061, Australia,
in New Zealand by Random House New Zealand Ltd,
18 Poland Road, Glenfield, Auckland 10, New Zealand
and in South Africa by Random House (Pty) Ltd,
Isle of Houghton, Corner Boundary Road & Carse O'Gowrie,
Houghton 2198, South Africa.

Printed and bound in Great Britain by
Cox & Wyman Ltd, Reading, Berkshire

Papers used by Transworld Publishers are natural, recyclable
products made from wood grown in sustainable forests.
The manufacturing processes conform to the environmental
regulations of the country of origin.

For my favourite Sunday Painter

This novel is set in Victorian England.

FRIDAY'S GIRL

Chapter One

Just because you are poor does not mean that you are dirty, although it has to be said, soap never having been cheap, that you might have a bit of trouble keeping clean. Certainly no one could have felt the impact of dirt more than Edith that morning, and no one could have looked poorer. Indeed her skirt and blouse, her apron and cap, could not have felt more depressing to their wearer had they been prison clothing decorated with small distinguishing arrows. What was more, after the weekend the floor of that particular part of the Stag and Crown seemed to be inches thick in dirt from the street and spilled beer from the bar, not to mention pieces of dropped food; and at the edges of the tables and chairs lurked that worst of all worsts for the dedicated cleaner – grime.

Grime is not dust, not light and grey, but dark and slimy, and it is shifted with difficulty, as anyone who has tried to remove it knows. Luckily Edith had strong arms. They might not be thick and round like those of her stepmother, the second Mrs Hanson, and she might not have short, stubby fingers like hers, but since the time of her father's remarriage she had been set to work as a general dogsbody at the old coaching inn whose gardens bordered the rolling acres of Richmond Park. This meant that from the age of ten Edith's slender arms had been toughened year by year, until now, at the ripe old age of sixteen and a half, she found, perhaps unsurprisingly, that she could lift and shift with the best of them.

Not that she did not still always feel sickened by the state of the inn floor every Monday morning, not that she did not sometimes feel that she would like never to see a scrubbing brush or a pail of water ever again, of course not. A shining floor may be life-enhancing for those who tread across it, but it is rather less so for those who have the duty of cleaning it.

This particular Monday morning, however, she felt even brighter than the piece of floor she had just scrubbed so dutifully. The reason for her inner exuberance was that she had risen an hour before the rest of the maids, and several hours before her stepmother, in order to steal out, all alone, into the royal park to enjoy the sight of the blossom, to embrace the air and to admire the deer moving stealthily between the old trees and across the carefully tended acres of what she considered to be a little piece of heaven, before bolting back to her duties.

16

'You're looking like the cat that got the cream. What you been up to, then?'

Edith had pretended not to hear the brewery man, and had run down the kitchen stairs with her bucket to fetch more clean water before she would be forced to tell the truth. For it was true, she knew that she did look happy. After all, who would not look happy after escaping into the park of a fine May morning, enjoying an hour away from the smell of stale ale and the heat of the cooking, not to mention the ever-present dread of hearing her stepmother's sharp voice?

The kitchens were alive with activity and steam, with large joints of meat being brought in on bare shoulders and huge pots being stirred, and maids running in and out with dishes from the dining rooms; and that was all before the hall boy started getting under everyone's feet because he was waiting for his well-earned rind of crispy bacon, and his cup of milk.

Edith ran to the scullery and then back through the kitchen, hoping that when she reached the upper rooms again the dreaded brewery man would be gone. None of the young maids liked the brewery man, for the good reason that he was notorious for taking more than a passing fancy to anyone who stood in his way for more than a few seconds.

Happily, as she walked cautiously into the main thoroughfare of the public rooms Edith saw at once that he was gone, and she had resumed her scrubbing before she heard something else:

not the uneven gait of the departing brewery man, but the quick light step of someone she instinctively knew was different.

It was an iron rule at the Stag and Crown that none of the female servants were allowed to look customers in the face. This was because Edith's stepmother was quite sure that it led to nonsense, and Mrs Hanson always said that any nonsense from Edith, or anyone else, and they would all end up in the workhouse along with a great many of the others who had been dismissed from her service.

The continuous threat of the workhouse hung over the Stag and Crown in the same way as an early summer haze had hung over the park that morning, except that unlike the summer haze it never lifted to reveal beauty or serenity, only fear and panic. Nor was Edith, despite being the only daughter of the owner, able to escape it. She too felt the shadow of it, the fact of it, its cold welcome always waiting, almost a certainty, almost a reality, to those who did not work hard enough or long enough, who were impertinent, or did not realise their good fortune in being employed by Mrs Hanson at the Stag and Crown.

But fast as all the servants ran, and hard as they all worked, it seemed that Mrs Hanson could never, ever be content. Edith had long ago recognised that contentment was not in her stepmother's makeup. It was not part of her nature. There was no doubt at all, at least in

Edith's mind, that if her stepmother ever had the misfortune to find herself feeling happy, she would very likely lose her reason. It would mean that she had nothing about which to inwardly rage, about which to become hourly infuriated, or constantly irritated. It would mean that her husband and sons, not to mention her step-daughter, would lose their fear of her. It would mean that she would have to appreciate every-one's efforts to make her happy, instead of drawing attention to herself by her constant demands. If she were happy and content, her life would be meaningless.

On the other hand, in sharp contrast to her own open discontent, Mrs Hanson always seemed to be on a mission to make sure that everyone else realised their own good fortune.

'The sooner you recognise how sinful and ugly you are, the sooner you will content yourselves with what God has given you, and the more gratefully you will accept your lot in life,' she would say to Edith and the other maidservants, which often had the unfortunate effect of making some of them so downhearted that they left the Stag and Crown and took up other occupations, the most popular being prostitution. Walking the streets for a living brought in quick money, but all too often an early death.

Little wonder therefore that as the early morning visitor to the inn paused by her metal bucket, Edith had no trouble keeping her eyes bent on the bright, clean tiles she had only seconds before scrubbed back to their original blue and green and white and cream glory.

'I hope I am not too late for a good breakfast?' the visitor said to the hall at large.

Edith kept her eyes cast dutifully down, staring now at the visitor's beautifully shod feet. They were the slender feet of a gentleman, and what was more and what was better they were not muddy, so they were not ruining her precious floor, but actually enhancing it. They were a May morning of a pair of feet, and they were very welcome to her floor.

'I said, I hope I am not too late for a good breakfast, hmm?'

Edith, knowing that Mrs Hanson was never around in the early hours of the old inn's busy day, slowly lifted her head, and found that the face into which she now dared to look was as unusual as the feet at which she had been staring moments before. It was a startlingly handsome face, and this despite the fact that it was bearded. Any facial hair, even side-whiskers, was, in the view of persons such as Edith's father and his friends, synonymous with a lazy sort of fellow, a fellow who did not, or would not, make time of a morning to use a proper cut-throat razor. Facial hair was only worn by men who would harbour newfangled ideas, ideas to which her father's customers would be about as attracted as they would be to fleas in a cat. Worse than that, they made a gentleman look foreign.

Looking up from her kneeling position on the

floor, Edith was so distracted by the fascination of his face, which was almost too handsome for its own good, that, quite against her will, she found herself staring at him for far too long, just as earlier she had stared at the deer moving quietly around her in the park.

Perhaps everything might have been all right if the visitor had not widened his eyes. And if those same dark brown eyes had not travelled over Edith's still slender childish figure, and if he had not put out a hand to her shoulder, and tapped on it with some authority, forcing her to respond.

'Stand up, do,' he commanded, and then he gently placed a hand under Edith's chin and moved her face from one side to the other, murmuring over and over again, *Stunning.*'

He held her chin in his gloved fingers with such confidence that Edith felt it was not the first time he had done such a thing. Finally, he let go of her face with evident reluctance, and turned towards the main room where breakfast was still being served, letting out a sigh of such huge contentment that Edith felt she could have been some sort of buried treasure he had come across while out walking, which must now be put aside in favour of a more practical consideration, such as eating.

The moment was over, thankfully unobserved by anyone else, and he went in to breakfast without saying more, taking off his gloves and rubbing his hands together at the smell of the bacon cooking and the sight of the kedgeree and the ptarmigan, and every other dish laid out for the delectation of their customers. Edith returned to her floor-scrubbing with renewed vigour. She knew the stranger should not have touched her, and yet she could not help feeling glad that he had. The truth was – her father being distant and unaffectionate to a degree – no man had touched her since she was quite small and her grandfather was still alive. She suspected that it would have meant nothing to the elegant bearded gentleman, and yet, much against her will, she could not help realising that it meant a great deal to her.

Normally she did not appreciate her father's customers. They might be conventionally dressed, but they had the upsetting habit of running their fingers over whatever part of Edith's body they could safely reach without attracting attention to themselves.

'It is no one's fault but your own if a customer takes liberties,' Mrs Hanson was fond of saying to the girls, with a strange, cruel little smile. Her expression at those moments was the very opposite of the look that so often came over her face when she was speaking of the Almighty. That expression was always one of proud complacency.

Mrs Hanson believed in God, and she followed Christian practice, attending every service at nearby St Peter's, whether it was for the churching of women, or the burying of customers. She was certain that she was protected not just by the success of her husband's thriving business, or the excellence of the brewers' ale, but also by the unseen approbation of God. This unshakeable belief in God's approval left her free to behave exactly as she wished once she had stepped outside the portals of the great grey church that dominated the end of the road. So it was with the memory of her stepmother's voice proclaiming the guilt of any servant who allowed a customer to take liberties that Edith returned to her work, scrubbing with all the renewed energy of a prisoner determined on reducing a life sentence.

She had just reached the last, large, square tile when she again heard his voice.

'Would you mind turning round for me, Miss . . . ?'

Edith started to turn, but as she did so she heard the familiar swish of the silken-skirted Mrs Hanson approaching, and her stepmother's equally silken voice saying in the tone she always used for customers, 'May I be of help, sir?'

'You certainly can, ma'am,' Edith heard the man's voice asserting, as she turned back to her bucket and cloths. 'You most certainly can. You can tell me who this beautiful girl might be.' He pointed across the tiled hall. 'Yes, and you can tell me how she comes to be employed in this dreadful fashion, cleaning floor tiles on her hands and knees, when paintings of her face and form should be adorning the walls of every house in the kingdom.'

'Who could that be, I wonder? Of whom could

you be speaking, sir? I see no beautiful creature, sir, I see only a young maid and her bucket.'

Mrs Hanson's voice was rising in amazement, and although Edith did not look at either of them she felt quite sure that her stepmother must have been staring across at her as if she was some sort of necessary evil, like the leavings from the kitchens, which were always donated to the local hospital.

'That beautiful young creature over there cannot be a maid, ma'am. She is surely an angel sent down to remind us of paradise?'

'But you can't mean that person, surely?' Mrs Hanson pointed at Edith, who had finally finished cleaning her last tile and was standing up, preparing to pick up her bucket and scuttle off towards the busy, teeming kitchens. 'You can't mean that person there?' Mrs Hanson was trying hard to keep real astonishment from her voice. 'That person is – *Edith*,' she finished, reluctant as always to add 'my stepdaughter', which, in the circumstances, and given Edith's poor appearance, was perhaps understandable.

'Come across, please, mademoiselle, do, if you would not mind?'

Edith put down her bucket, and did as she had been ordered by the stranger, and as she raised her eyes once more to the startlingly handsome face with the dark hazel gaze she could not help feeling a second, more highly charged, frisson of excitement.

*   *   *

Celandine stared up at her professor's face and as usual felt a great deal more than a frisson of impatience. Mr Brandt sported a neat beard such as every teacher in the art department of Munich university seemed to wear, and since at that moment his face was reflecting unshakeable boredom, his mouth beneath the hirsute upper lip was also drooping downwards, a perfect matched set.

'Fräulein Benyon, your choice of subject is, if I may say so, lacking in depth and maturity. When given a free hand you will always return, will you not, to the domestic? However, if you must return to the domestic,' he continued quickly, observing that Celandine was about to interrupt his brief dissertation, 'if you *must* return to the domestic, could you not make it something more – shall we say – *elevating*?'

Celandine stared up at him from under her own dark curled fringe of hair, which framed her heart-shaped face and large grey eyes in such a way as to almost over-emphasise the liveliness of her expression, an expression which at that moment – eyes widening, lips parted – gave every indication of bursting into voluble protest.

'I find subjects such as these just as elevating as anything classical or religious, Herr Brandt.'

'A maid peeling apples is domestic,' the professor said, sighing. 'A goddess holding an apple, the apple symbolising love, *that* would be elevating.'

'But only, surely, Herr Brandt,' Celandine said,

tightly, 'only if the goddess and her apple had a title such as . . .' She stopped and thought for a few seconds before going on. 'A title such as "Insidious Cupid Calling on Diana While she is at her Toilette Finds to his Consternation that she has Already Eaten of the Apple". In these modern times the *titles* of paintings, and of course their *frames*, are far more important to art dealers than the paintings themselves, are they not, Herr Brandt?'

The professor shook his head in despair. Fräulein Benyon was not wholly European, being, as he now knew, the single issue of a French provincial painter and an American mother; she could not therefore be expected to have the same attitudes as the rest of his comfortingly male class of students.

'Classicism is what is important, Fräulein, classicism, classicism, classicism, copying, always copying, the great masters.'

'Certainly, Herr Brandt, but remember that at some time or another students do have to *produce* something, rather than *re*-produce everything.'

Her professor pointed across the studio to the rest of the art class. 'These gentlemen are working on paintings that spring directly from the classical tradition, Fräulein. Can you not observe how much deeper their work is than yours?'

Celandine stared in fury around the atelier. The young men had now broken up into groups and were smoking and talking, admiring each other's works, most of which she was quite certain would be dutiful evocations of biblical subjects, or adaptations of scenes from the ancients.

'What are you doing now, Fräulein?'

'I am packing up my paints and brushes, Herr Brandt, and I am leaving you and your students to the ancient world.'

Herr Brandt struggled not to look relieved, but then, remembering that Celandine's mother, the docile Mrs Benyon, was always so prompt at paying the fees, he quickly suppressed his feelings.

'I hardly think – I hardly think that is necessary, surely, Fräulein Benyon?'

Celandine stopped in the middle of her task and stared up briefly at the art teacher, an indignant look on her face. 'That is why we will never see eye to eye, Herr Brandt,' she retorted. 'You are always *hardly* thinking, while I wish to study under someone who will *wholly* think.'

Back at their comfortable lodgings, Mrs Benyon stared first at her daughter and then at the hackney cab driver who was carefully placing Celandine's canvases and other paraphernalia in the hall of their rented apartment.

'You are leaving Herr Brandt, did you say, dearest? You are leaving Herr Brandt's studio, before the end of the present term?'

'I certainly am, Mother.'

'But why, dearest?' Mrs Benyon's heart was sinking even as she asked, because finally she always knew why. 'You seemed to be so happy there, so much happier than when you were in Amsterdam. And, well, we are all so happy here in Munich. At least I thought so, dearest, really I did.'

Mrs Benyon could not prevent herself from wringing her hands together as she watched the inexorable chaos that was now invading the hallway. Unmoved by her mother's obvious distress, Celandine sighed with unusual vigour and followed the driver back down the stairs and outside to the courtyard. There she paid him handsomely before turning to go back up to the apartment.

'Is there nowhere we can find you where you can be happy with your art teachers? Why have you left the good Herr Brandt?'

'Why have I left Herr Brandt, Mother? I have left his atelier because I have to tell you that one more day in that smug all-male establishment and I would have committed suicide or – worse – murder.'

Mrs Benyon wiped a lace handkerchief across her forehead, and then promptly waved it in front of her face. She only imperfectly understood her daughter's quest for perfection, and she certainly did not understand her outraged impatience with Herr Brandt, who seemed such a nice young man, always so polite and assiduous in his attentions to the ladies when he came to one of Mrs Benyon's Thursday afternoon At Homes.

By now they had both made their way to the

main salon, and Mrs Benyon was able to sit down rather suddenly.

'I have to tell you, Celandine, whatever you may think of poor Herr Brandt, I myself am most reluctant to leave Munich, dearest. I have made so many, many delightful friends and acquaintances.'

'You must stay then, Mother dearest. You stay here with Marie, while I leave in search of some new place to live and work. I cannot stand a moment longer of Herr Brandt and his ancient world.'

'But where are you going to go then, dearest? Where can we find you something more satisfying for your talents?'

Celandine hesitated. 'I was thinking about it as the cabbie brought me back here. It seems to me that I must go to France, Mother. I am going to go to France, where I should have gone in the first place, France, the mother country of my father, your beloved husband. I don't understand why I did not think of it before, really I don't.'

Mrs Benyon seemed to take this as well as any American mother could be expected to take such an announcement. She had fallen in love with Celandine's father, a widower with a small daughter, while he was visiting her own parents in Boston, having been commissioned to paint a family portrait of the Benyons and their dogs.

Jacques Delors Benyon had been a tall handsome man with the sad air of someone who had been robbed of his happiness at too young an age. Helen was the youngest daughter of a well-to-do family, and her parents had been less than happy at her determination to marry her French painter. Finally, however, they gave their consent, not to mention a handsome dowry from which Helen was able to draw a substantial income to this day.

'To France for the reason of? What I mean to say is, why go to France especially? I have lived in France, as you know, dearest, and it can be singularly difficult for an American girl, really it can. Everything so different.'

'It seems if I want to progress I must go to France in search of that fast-disappearing – as far as the art world is concerned – soon to become mythical, place, the modern world, Mother.'

'But I did think, dear, that this time, here in Munich—'

'They do not understand a woman painter here in Munich either, Mother, any more than they did in Amsterdam. In fact, if we searched all of Europe, I truly do not think that, even now, there are many ateliers that accept that women can and will paint. Yet . . .' Celandine stopped, making a small determined fist of her right hand. 'Yet I will not be put off. I am determined to find some place where they do accept that women can paint, and what is more will paint what they, women, want to paint, which is somehow a reflection of their own sensitivities, their own understanding of life, their differences from the all too masterful male sex. I am not interested in painting huge canvases that take seven or eight years to complete, with titles that take seven or eight minutes to repeat. And that, Mother, I am dearly afraid, is that.'

The expression on Mrs Benyon's face was close to tragic. First it had been Holland, and now Munich, but everywhere seemed to be the same, nowhere near what Celandine needed to progress in the way she so wished. The thought of giving up yet another comfortable apartment was not a welcome one.

'Well, whatever you think, dear, whatever you think. But where shall we go in France? I suppose we could go to Avignon and rent somewhere near your half-sister Agnes, dearest? I suppose we could do that. But, as I have often reminded you, Avignon is very hot in summer, and quite cold in winter. Even your father – whose birthplace as you know it was – only went there for the last months of spring and early summer.'

'No, I don't want to go to Avignon, Mother. I think we must go to Paris.'

'Paris? But your father, rest his soul, never approved of Paris, dearest, you know that. He thought of it as being degenerate, and decadent. He thought Avignon far more beautiful, more artistic in every way.'

'I read that Paris is changing, that it is fast becoming the centre of something very lively, a new art movement. I feel sure that Father would approve.'

'And I feel sure he would not. When in France

31

your father rarely wished to move more than a few miles from Avignon, and only then so that he could hurry back to re-appreciate its splendours before returning to America in the fall.'

'That may be so, Mother, but although I hope I will always respect Father's memory, I really would like to go to Paris, and what is more, with your permission, of course, I think we *should* go to Paris.'

'Oh dear, are we quite sure we should?'

Mrs Benyon managed to look distressed and startled at the same time. Distressed at the idea that they would, yet again, be packing up their trunks and moving on, and startled that Celandine was using such a firm tone with her.

'Quite, quite sure, Mother. I have to try to find another art teacher, and even if I should not, at least there is the Drawing Room at the Louvre where, when I am not studying, I can go to copy.'

'But I thought that was why we were leaving Munich, because you *dislike* copying so much?'

'We are leaving Munich because copying is *all* that I am doing here. I must try to find another art teacher, someone who will not treat me with such very overt condescension. There surely must be such a person in Paris? The French, since the Revolution, are in the forefront of advanced ideas in everything, are they not?'

Celandine smiled at her bewildered mother to alleviate the determination behind her words. Her mother stared back, heart sinking at the idea of the packing, the rearrangements, the adjustments, and breaking the news to Marie, who was, Mrs Benyon was quite certain, currently carrying on an increasingly interesting affair with a boy who worked in the building opposite.

'Very well, dearest, if you insist. It does seem most awfully troublesome, but if you insist we must go to Paris, to Paris we will go.'

Mrs Benyon sighed and turned towards her bedroom, her mind already preoccupied. *Paris*,' she murmured as she made her way decorously towards the heavily curtained room with its dark club-footed furniture and its large ornate pieces of china set about in vast cabinets. *Paris*,' she said again as if trying out a new name for someone just born. 'Paris.'

She stopped repeating the name of the French capital when she felt first a dart and then a small shudder of excitement. Paris, after all, whatever Celandine said, was the city of both gaiety and sin. It was the place where kings and princes headed when they wanted to indulge in every, or any, kind of vice. The place where the chefs of the Italian-born Catherine de Medici had taught the French to cook, a fact, her husband had used to joke, that the Parisians now preferred to forget.

On the way to her bedroom Mrs Benyon came upon her maid sewing by a window overlooking the street which also conveniently overlooked the building opposite.

'Oh dear, Marie, I have a little bit of bad news, I am afraid.' Mrs Benyon hesitated before continuing. 'I think you might be going to be a little put out at what I have to say, Marie. I am afraid we are going to have to leave this apartment – we are going to leave for Paris as soon as is perfectly possible, because my daughter, Mademoiselle Celandine, is still not happy with her art teacher.'

Marie stared at her American mistress, and her eyes grew dark with sadness.

'But, madame, we have hardly arrived in Munich, no? We have not yet unpacked the paintings for the *petit salon*, and now we have to go away again. *Enfin!*'

'I know, I know, Marie.' Mrs Benyon tried not to look flustered. 'And I have to tell you that I too am most miserable at this news.' She paused. 'But what can we do, Marie? We must accompany Mademoiselle Celandine. She cannot be allowed to travel on her own to Paris. We must chaperone her while she pursues her studies. I have no alternative.'

Marie said something very French under her breath, which owing to the maid's obvious distress Mrs Benyon decided to ignore, even though she understood it really quite well.

'Mademoiselle Benyon is very spoilt by Madame, madame,' she said, this time out loud.

Mrs Benyon nodded slowly and sadly. It was undeniably the case. 'Very true, very true, but even so I will make the necessary arrangements, Marie.'

Marie nodded, her expression tragic. For the

first time in her life she was in love with a beautiful young man, and now she must leave him. God, having smiled down on her from heaven, was now frowning. It was hard, very hard.

The name of the stranger who had come in search of breakfast at the Stag and Crown was Napier Todd. Edith's stepmother repeated it to Edith's father as if it was the name of some strangely foreign beer that she very much hoped he was not going to order for the inn.

Harold Hanson looked up from his meticulously kept account books and eyed his second wife, the mother of his two sons now away at boarding school, with his usual reserve.

'Who did you say it was, my dear?'

Mrs Hanson stared at her husband from the door of his business room with her usual mixture of impatience and inner fury. Somehow Harold always seemed able to invest whatever he did with a peculiar importance, an importance that she knew for some reason she was not able to invest in the myriad tasks that she herself undertook on behalf of them both.

'He *says* his name is Napier Todd,' Mrs Hanson repeated.

'Is he a regular, my dear?'

'No, he is not a regular, Harold. If he was a regular I would not be standing repeating his name to you, would I? He has been here the past three mornings, but despite that he is most definitely not a regular – far from being so, now you come to mention it. He lives somewhere quite other.'

Harold's eyes flickered back to the all-important columns of figures, the pounds and ounces of foodstuffs ordered and paid for, the pints and fluid ounces of the drinks. Somehow his books of accounts, the meticulous record of his financial transactions, always proved more satisfactory to him than the day-to-day business that took place at the Stag and Crown. If he glanced at his books, he could not see wastage. If he turned the pages he could see profits and more profits, and the dizzying amount of con-sumption that, thankfully, occurred at the usual festive times. What he could not see was the boots boy lounging about the scullery, or the cook selling off precious lard at the back door, instead of keeping it for use in his own kitchen. He could not see the maids skimping on their dusting duties. His books were tidy, ordered, filled with solid information with which no one could tamper, over which no one could lounge or laze. Two pennies added to four pennies made six pennies, and no argument. All of which meant that he was now staring at his second wife, the present Mrs Hanson, with unconcealed reluctance.

'Perhaps you should show him in here, my dear. If he is not a regular, it should not take very long. If he wishes to complain I shall listen to him as courteously as is my wont, I do assure you.'

'He does not wish to complain, Harold, far from it. No, he has quite another intention.'

'And what might that be?' Harold's eyes had returned to the page of his accounts book which was now being turned, presenting him with the gloriously heartwarming sight of a blank sheet already neatly ruled, waiting for his profit and loss accounts to be annotated across its virgin surface.

'What might be *what*, Harold?'

'What might be his *intention*, my dear?'

'To marry your daughter, Harold. To marry Edith, of all people. His eye has been caught by Edith, who as we both know is not what I would call a beauty. Quite a plain Jane, poor child, is your daughter Edith.'

Harold's eyes now swivelled from his favourite sight to one that was rather less appealing to the landlord of the Stag and Crown. He stared at his wife.

'He wants to marry my daughter?' he asked, a blank look coming over his face, as if he was finding it hard to remember whether or not he actually had a daughter. Having reassured himself of this fact, he frowned deeply, staring ahead of him in a great effort of concentration, as if conjuring up Edith's image was more than difficult, it was almost impossible.

'Yes, Harold, your daughter. Edith Hanson? Your daughter, remember? She is the only child of your first wife, who died when she was run over by the tram when walking in—'

'I can remember my first wife's sad demise, my dear, without any help from you.' Harold removed his spectacles, slowly, and very deliberately folded them up and placed them in a case to the side of his ledgers. 'But I fail to see who would wish to marry our Edith, most especially if he knows that the poor girl has no dowry.'

'Oh yes,' Mrs Hanson stated as if she were imparting surprising news. 'He knows she has no dowry, but he is still more than keen.'

'How do you know, my dear?'

By now Harold too had started to look keen, something which Mrs Hanson had quickly noted.

'For the simple reason that he told me so this morning. This is his third visit to the Stag and Crown, Harold. He knows that Edith has no dowry. He wishes to marry her, and take her to live with him in his house in the Cotswolds, it seems, where, as I understand it from him, he is apparently attempting a new style of country living, less autocratic, less patrician.' Mrs Hanson paused, frowning, suddenly realising that the idea of a country house run on democratic lines did not sound at all nice to her. However, realising she could do nothing about democracy as practised in the Cotswolds, she continued, after a few seconds, 'As I understand it, he will also provide her with the use of a small town house, albeit only rented and in Kensington. There are studios, it seems, within these houses, and many of his kind live there, pursuing their occupations in different ways.' She paused again. 'He is a painter, you see, Harold. A painter of some means, and he thinks Edith a beauty, would you believe? Edith. Edith of all people! Edith a beauty.'

Mrs Hanson was managing to make her step-daughter's being a beauty sound about as likely as Harold's becoming king of England.

'My dear!' Harold gave his wife one of his rare smiles, as he suddenly realised that he did not care if the man was a painter or a dustman. 'What a thing! Someone wants to take Edith off our hands, what a thing! With both the boys away at those expensive boarding-out schools, it is God smiling on our affairs, no doubt of it.'

All at once Harold could see the sense in his interviewing the gentleman in question and as soon as possible, before he changed his mind. He had long found being a father to a girl a most particular nuisance, but, seeing that he had no wish to provide for her future, had also long ago resigned himself to the idea that his only daughter would have to continue to work for him in a menial capacity in order that she would not prove a drain on the family resources. But now, wonder of wonders, manna from heaven, it seemed a man of some substance had been found who wanted to take the sixteen-year-old off his hands. In all honesty he could not wait to meet the fellow. After all, a maid could be replaced, but the thought of being able to get his daughter off his hands, and what was more married and away from the paternal home, out of sight and therefore out of mind, was more than a blessing, it was a miracle.

He turned to his chair and plucked his coat from the back of it. His wife, knowing her place, immediately fussed around him, removing imaginary pieces of fluff from his sleeves, and dusting his shoulders quickly with her small, pudgy hands.

'Remember who you are when interviewing this painter, dearest. You are Harold Hanson, a man of substance, no different from him.'

'Do I need to be reminded of that, Aurelia?'

'No, dearest, of course not. I only make mention of it because, although the gentleman in question is only a painter, he has the manners of a member of the aristocracy. However, he is certainly not titled, I do know that.' She paused and smiled. 'We both know that if he were a member of the aristocracy he would be trying to buy Edith, not marry her!'

Mrs Hanson gave a short laugh, and then, her duty done, she hurried to the door and down the corridor to where Napier Todd was standing surveying a still life of dead birds laid out for plucking, not to mention hares hanging from hooks.

He nodded towards the painting before turning to Mrs Hanson. 'Strange for such a talented painter, as this fellow undoubtedly is, strange that his only desire seems to be to spend as much time as possible depicting nature red in tooth and claw,' he murmured. 'Look at the poor hare, friend to everyone, enemy to no one, yet look at him here, would you? Poor creature strung up like a piece of rubbish on a string, a tribute to man's appetite for ugliness and destruction.'

Mrs Hanson, who rarely glanced at the paintings on the walls of the Stag and Crown except to run a finger down their frames to make sure that they were properly dusted, had no idea what their visitor was talking about, and so, in the absence of any maid to take care of the formalities, she merely nodded and beckoned Mr Todd to follow her to her husband's business room. 'Mr Napier Todd, dearest,' she murmured discreetly from the doorway.

Napier Todd entered Harold Hanson's business room with a sense of destiny, a sense that a door, and not just the door of the landlord's business room, was opening to him. Art and the Muse were about to place their hands in his, and because of this he was sure he would be able to lead the way to a new heaven on earth.

'My card, sir.'

Since the card was properly engraved, and proclaimed that Mr Napier Todd was the possessor of two goodish if not sparklingly smart addresses, Harold smiled at his visitor. It was not a vastly welcoming smile, but it was a cordial acknowledgement all the same.

'Would you care to be seated, Mr Todd?'

'I won't, thank you, sir.' Napier Todd, tall, bearded, slim and formally, if artistically, dressed,

41

stood in front of Harold and pulled at the signet ring on his right hand, but he did not smile. 'I am here, sir, to ask for the hand in marriage of your daughter, Edith.'

Harold, who would really rather have preferred to have been able to sit down, found himself standing instead, and since he was shorter than his visitor he also found himself staring up into Napier's bearded face in a fashion that he did not find wholly enjoyable. Most unfortunately for Napier Todd this meant that Harold was staring fixedly at that part of his visitor's face of which he could not possibly approve, namely his dark, foreign-looking beard.

'You are aware, sir, that my daughter Edith is all too young for marriage, and has no knowledge of the world, outside the Stag and Crown, that is? Her poor mother passed away some few years ago, and the present Mrs Hanson has struggled to bring her up as best she may, but since Edith was not a clever girl at her books she was forced to take her into service in this place, rather than have the discomfort of seeing her led astray, as so many of those of her sex, also alas possessed of a lowly intellect, so often are.' He paused here before continuing in a changed tone. 'However, the present Mrs Hanson having brought Edith up in such a manner, I can only say with some pride that my daughter has turned out a model of beauty and virtue, as you have no doubt noted, or *you* would not be here, sir.'

Napier Todd said nothing. It was difficult for a

man like himself to imagine setting a beloved daughter to work in such a place as that in which they were now standing. On the other hand, since he was a bachelor, and had always had servants, he was quite happy to accept Harold Hanson's view of his daughter, and of his second wife's virtuous struggle to turn her into someone respectable – and indeed anything else – just so long as he could whisk the girl off and marry her as soon as possible.

Harold Hanson stared at the handsome stranger in front of him. He would not and could not explain, naturally, that nothing would give him greater pleasure than to get poor Edith off his hands before she grew any older. She might be another useful pair of hands at the inn to her stepmother, but to her father the employment of a nubile daughter as a maid was an embarrassment. Besides, although Aurelia always insisted that she was plain, that what with her red hair and bright green eyes she was almost a freak, to her father her colouring alone was a constant reminder of the days when he was young and foolish and loved Edith's poor, beautiful auburn-haired mother devotedly. With her death had come a darkness that had never lifted.

Napier stared at Harold Hanson. What *he* could not and would not explain, naturally, was that he had been going through a lengthy and tedious period of artistic sterility, a period during which he had toiled for weeks on end to produce canvases of which he could be proud, only to realise that he was once more artistically becalmed. For some reason, Edith's upraised face, the startling colour of her eyes and hair, had set him afire, and he knew at once, as the light fell on her features, that his painterly ship was once more about to set sail on the artistic ocean. The only trouble was that this slip of a girl who had freed him from his gaol was not just young and startlingly beautiful, but a member of a bourgeois family that would not give her up as easily as a poor working-class man who might willingly have sold her to him for the price of a clutch of paint brushes, just as an aristocrat would have sent her to him with a huge sigh of relief and a considerable dowry. Folk such as the Hansons were different. They were middle class and respectable, and so for Napier it was marriage or nothing.

Even now, unsurprisingly, Harold Hanson was getting down to the thing that affected him most, namely money. He was dreading that the negotiations would fail, that he would once more be left with Edith on his hands, and that, not wanting to let her loose to bring trouble to their door, they would have to go on employing her at the inn. He approached the whole matter in the same manner as he would any other business.

'She has no dowry, sir.'

'That is no matter, sir. I have enough money of my own. A handsome income from a trust means that I live well enough, I do assure you.'

'She will come to you as she is, sir.'

44

'That is how I want her, sir.'

'Very well, sir. You may have my daughter's hand in marriage.'

'Thank you, sir.'

'When do you want to marry her, sir?'

'As soon as possible, sir.'

'Have you asked her, sir?'

The two men stared at each other, the idea gradually dawning on them that no one had yet thought to ask Edith.

'No, I have not, sir.'

'In that case, I suggest that you do, sir. As I have said, Edith has never been one for her books, but she must be allowed her say.'

Napier stared at his future father-in-law. He could not explain that he did not wish for a wife who read books; he wanted a wife who would inspire him, whom he could mould. He had always avoided marriage, searching in vain for something which would be both inspirational and desirable, and that he was sure was what he had found three days earlier at the Stag and Crown. If he had to marry Edith Hanson, which she being so young he obviously did, then so be it. But married or not married, what he needed more than anything was not a wife, but a muse.

Celandine looked around her. Their new Paris apartment was light and airy, and everything that she could possibly desire. Not only that, but it was in such a convenient position that she was able to walk both to the Louvre and to the private studio into which she had been accepted as a pupil. Her mother too could walk to the smartest shops and gaze in the beautiful if simply arranged windows, occasionally allowing herself the luxury of entering the boutique of her choice and buying herself a longed-for pair of gloves, a new evening arrangement for her hair – all feathers – or a pretty velvet waistband to add new interest to an old gown.

Since their arrival in Paris Celandine had been filled with the sense that her life was just beginning. This was not just because she had, to her delight, been accepted by the studio of Pierre Laurent, but also because the vibrancy of the city, the beauty of its buildings, the brilliance of its architecture, had become part of her every waking moment.

She would always remember her first walk towards the left bank, crossing the Pont des Arts, walking down the rue de Seine towards the Ecole des Beaux Arts. The sun was just beginning to set, almost imperceptibly, so that the pale blue of the sky was turning to that particular faded pink that always seems to be so busily creating a fairytale atmosphere at the start of a spring or summer evening.

Once the bridge had been crossed she passed under a dark archway spilling over with the darkly vast figures of tramps spread about the paving, their bearded faces emanating the un-mistakable smell of wine.

'Ah, mademoiselle, how these tramps smell 'orrible!'

The maid's voice coming from behind her had been filled with disgust, but Celandine had ignored her. The left bank of Paris might be unfashionable as far as the rich and tonnish were concerned, but it was a Mecca for artists. Once the Seine was crossed there was a sense of being beckoned towards a bubbling cauldron of aspiration and learning, of artistic endeavour and intellectual thought. Each old winding street into which they turned seemed to promise to lead them to some new discovery, some fascination that could be explored at a later date.

Finally Celandine had turned towards home and away from their tentative explorations, but with such reluctance that it had seemed to her, as she walked back across the only bridge in Paris over which no horse or vehicle was ever allowed to pass, that she might actually be leaving a part of herself behind.

The natural excitement she felt, a few days later, when she entered Pierre Laurent's studio evaporated on meeting the man himself. To say that Monsieur Laurent was a disappointment was to say the least. Besides, as had been the case in Munich, there were no other female students in the studio. There was no one else, young or old, who had to cope with long dresses that looked either too dowdy in the street, or too glamorous to be worn in a working studio.

47

Celandine found herself, once more, quite alone in an all-male world.

Yet again she found herself reluctantly having to cope with the sudden shouts of laughter, the ceaseless gossip and chatter, and the equally ceaseless smoke that made her hair smell. Her mother always complained when she returned home that Celandine reeked as if she had just descended from a public tramcar, so faithfully did the stench of the studio accompany her back to their apartment.

So it was that in those first few weeks in Paris, despite the presence of her mother and Marie, Celandine found to her consternation that she felt as isolated as she had ever done. She could not even admit as much when she returned to the apartment, for her mother had busily turned it into a haven of domestic prettiness, setting it about with cushions and flowers, ornaments and peacock feathers, with her own particular artistry, as well as mastering the difficulties of the kitchen, which had somehow become more onerous now that Marie had been forced to leave Munich.

'Is that you, dear?'

Mrs Benyon was stitching at her needlepoint frame, seated by the open window above the elegant courtyard over which all the apartments looked.

'Yes, Mother.'

'Did you have a good day, dear?'

The exchange was always depressingly the

same, and, hovering by the door, Celandine always knew exactly what would be said next.

'Do not come too far into the room, dear, whatever you do. We do not want the perfume of the flowers to be affected by the odours of Monsieur Laurent's studio, do we? Go straight to your bedroom and change. Marie will take your clothes and air them.'

'Yes, Mother.'

As she tottered towards her dressing room at the end of every day Celandine would only ever admit to herself just how played out she actually felt. It was not the constant struggle to get better at her drawing, to compete with the noise and chatter which seemed to be an accepted part of a working Parisian studio; it was the deep artistic depression she was experiencing, a depression that she knew stemmed from the growing realisation that she really was no better off in Paris than she had been in Munich. She was still a freak, a young woman struggling to become a professional artist, not content like so many of her contemporaries to sit at home executing polite water colours.

Night after night Celandine found herself unable to compose herself for sleep, instead lying awake and staring at the ceiling, tussling with the idea that she really should give up any idea of trying to be a painter. And it was worse when she had to succumb to the weekly visit to his studio of Monsieur Laurent himself.

How she dreaded the moment Laurent stood

in front of her work, knowing only too well as she did that the fog under which she had been daily struggling was soon to be lifted, only to be replaced by a black cloud.

Laurent was a fussy little man with a stiff moustache, both sides of which he kept carefully waxed. It was his custom when about to pronounce on his pupils' work to stand back from the canvas with one hand raised, straight black eyebrows twitching, lips pursed, silent as the grave for a full minute. What seemed like hours, but was probably actually only seconds, would pass, while Celandine waited for him to say *something*, at the same time aware that it would probably take a miracle to prompt him to do anything more than murmur phrases which amounted to little more than bored condescension, in a purposefully hopeless voice.

'*Tiens*, but whatever have we here, *enfin*, mademoiselle?'

The opening remark was always the same, and, probably because she was the only woman in the room, it seemed to Celandine that following his inevitable opening remark all chatter around the studio would stop, that just as Monsieur Laurent opened his rather too full lips to pronounce on what he thought to be the faults in Celandine's work, a silence would fall. It was as if everyone in the great, dark-panelled atelier, with its upper balcony where visitors, potential buyers, but more often dealers, were invited to drink and smoke, had fallen silent. It was a silence that always brought Celandine nothing but embarrassment.

After he had finished trying rather too obviously to find something to say about Celandine's work, ending up, more often than not, damning with nothing but faint praise, Monsieur Laurent would finally shrug his shoulders more than a little hopelessly and give a small sigh, before moving on to the next student.

As he moved smoothly on to another easel it seemed to Celandine that the other students would turn to each other and shrug their shoulders, the expressions on their faces indicating that really, whatever Monsieur Laurent thought of their work, just to glance at Miss Benyon's canvas was to find themselves feeling sympathetic to their professor. The young American woman chose such trivial subjects – domestic interiors, her mother sewing a piece of lace, the maid cooking – well, really, what *could* someone like Monsieur Laurent say?

Sometimes, at the end of one of the professor's visits, when she had heard him discussing every other student's work in depth, Celandine would stare at the palms of her hands, noting with vague interest the nail marks caused by trying to control her inner fury, before quickly pulling on her gloves. Then she would cram her hat on the back of her head and set off home, unable to communicate her inner despair to anyone, knowing only that she was beginning to share Monsieur Laurent's opinion of Celandine

Benyon's talent. It was small, it was trivial, it was hardly worth the canvases upon which she daubed.

'Not off to the Louvre museum again, dear?'

'That's right, Mother.'

It was Saturday and rather than stay in and watch her mother doing needlepoint and pouring tea for friends, Celandine had packed up her drawing books and pencils and was slipping out of the apartment.

'What I do not understand, Celandine dearest,' her mother continued quietly, turning away quickly so as not to risk contradiction, 'what I am finding very difficult to understand is why poor Herr Brandt should have been always so out of favour when we were in Munich, most particularly because he was continually asking you to copy so much from the ancient world, when now we are in Paris all you yourself seem to want to do is to go to the Louvre on your own and copy the old masters. I mean, surely this is the same salad as before, dearest, just a different dressing?'

Having had her say, Mrs Benyon was gone from the hall so quickly that Celandine had no time to explain that copying in the Drawing Room of the Louvre was very different from being *made* to copy day after day, with no chance of expressing your talent, as she had been in Munich. She closed the front door behind her, consoling herself with the thought that even should she have been able to explain her mother would not have been very interested, for what was really at stake was the fact that Mrs Benyon was irritated that Celandine was not staying for one of her mother's much treasured At Homes.

Not that the guests who came to the apartment were without interest. Nowadays, thanks to letters of introduction from friends in New York, her mother's visitors could include such diverse characters as a Russian countess, a relative of the queen of Spain, and a lady from the Latin quarter who was rumoured in private life to dress as a man and smoke a pipe, but, perhaps in deference to her hostess, arrived in a perfectly acceptable afternoon dress, only slightly marred by her carrying a walking cane and sporting a pair of men's black and white spats on her feet.

Celandine walked determinedly off in the direction of the Louvre. She knew how much her companionship meant to her mother, but to have to stay to take tea and make polite conversation with her mother's visitors was sometimes more than her daughter could bear. She sighed inwardly. She would never be the sort of daughter a mother like Helen Benyon wanted. She was too like her father, too fascinated by her art, too determined to make something of herself, something that was not to do with either fashion or marriage, and they both knew it.

Celandine entered what she always thought of as the *portals* of the Louvre museum – for such a cathedral to art and the ancient world could not, surely, only boast doors – with her usual feeling of excitement and made her way rapidly to the Drawing Room, where she knew she would be able to settle herself contentedly for the afternoon. Once away from the increasingly dreaded confines of Monsieur Laurent's studio she seemed to be able to find her centre once again, and draw much needed confidence from the feeling.

She stared at the old master she was attempting to copy, and started to settle herself to her work, searching for that particular moment of creation when all sound and outside movement was cut out, but for some reason not finding it. She looked up, frowning, and gazed round, only to find that a young man on the other side of the room was staring at her in the same manner as she had been staring at the old master in front of her.

She immediately turned back to her work, attempting to ignore him. But the moment of concentration still eluded her. Against her better judgement she looked up once more, only to see that he was still staring at her and, worse, that his pencil was moving swiftly, his eyes dropping now and then to his sketch book. The wretch was only drawing her!

Chapter Two

Edith paused to look at herself in the rust-dotted mirror outside the servants' lavatory. Inside she could hear two of the other maids giggling. They were quite sure that she was about to be hauled over the coals by her father, and they were not alone. Edith too was quite sure. Why else had she been summoned to his business room, after all? She attempted to swallow away the near-hysterical lump that seemed to have grown up in her throat. What had she done wrong?

She let her mind wander back over the past weeks. She had not been caught up in any of the day-to-day domestic scandals that were regular, almost banal daily occurrences at the inn: kitchen boys found stealing mutton chops or sausages, customers trying to become intimate with maids, barmen caught swilling beer when they should be selling it. Employees were always being dismissed on the spot, only to be promptly re-hired, either because their tears or pleas were convincing enough to move Mr or Mrs Hanson to give them a second or third chance, or – more to the point – because it was the weekend, and no one else suitable could be found to take their place. As far as all that was concerned Edith knew that her slate was clean: she had worked hard and long, to the point of exhaustion; she had not annoyed any of the cooks, or succumbed to any temptations. So why was she being summoned?

Now, eyes lowered, she made her way to her father's business room. She could think of no particular reason why she was going to be punished, but the memory of previous punishments, when she was younger, was never very far from her mind. Her father could be ferocious when roused to anger. His was not a hot fury, but a cold rage, far more terrifying than anything more undignified or flurried, the normal kind of plate-throwing tantrum in which one of the cooks might occasionally indulge.

The door handle in front of her slid in her nervously warm hand as she turned it, but she persevered as her father's voice called her into the room. She walked slowly towards his desk, towards the familiar sight of his ledgers, his ink well and his long quill pen. As always her eyes fixed on the centre of her father's waistcoat, around the area of his watch and chain, and then raised themselves a little higher as she heard him say in his distant way, 'Ah, Edith – there you are: yes, of course.'

Since her mother's death he had always

greeted Edith in this way. It made her feel as if she was something that had been forgotten, something someone had left out by mistake, as if he really meant to be saying, 'Ah, Edith, she is gone, but you are still here?'

Unfortunately for him, in many ways, Edith was still there, a leftover from his previous marriage, a permanent reminder of the woman he had once loved, a mirror image of the first Mrs Hanson.

'Edith, this gentleman wants to speak to you.'

Another voice spoke. Edith recognised its dark, velvet timbre, its rich resonance, so different from her father's light, precise tone. 'May I put the question to Miss Hanson?'

Edith gave the owner of the voice, the tall, handsome stranger who had walked into the inn and interrupted her housework, a brief look as he turned to her father.

'Yes, of course.' Her father sounded almost bored, as if he had already undergone the whole proceeding and already knew the outcome.

'Miss Hanson, with your father's permission, I would like to ask for your hand in marriage.'

Dumbstruck, Edith stared up into the brilliant eyes, the handsome bearded face, taking in the carefully tied cravat, the beautifully cut clothes, and for a second it seemed to her that she stood at the gates of paradise, that she must be going to faint with joy. Marriage was not something that she had ever contemplated for herself, since London servants stood very little chance of being married, but she knew from paintings what marriage looked like. It was white, and it was orange blossom, and it was beautiful. She could find no words, having no idea what to say, unable to overcome the habit of years, which was not to speak to a customer unless to direct them to the dining room or the bar.

Her father, seeing that his daughter's brilliant green eyes had become huge in her small face, felt he should prompt her to a reply.

'Would you like to marry this gentleman, Edith dear?' he asked, trying to sound affectionate, which he had realised in a rush could be important if he really was to get Edith off his hands.

Edith nodded slowly.

'Well. No more to be said, then. The matter is settled.' Harold Hanson turned to Napier Todd. 'Just need to name the day.' He moved swiftly towards his desk with its neatly stacked leather-bound accounts books.

'As soon as possible, sir,' Napier told him, his eyes never moving from Edith's face and form, her hair pinned up tidily under her cap, her service dress clean but stark.

Edith found his gaze thrilling, which was only natural since it told her that he already knew her body, in every way. She quickly looked away, realising that although it was wonderful to be the object of such interest, she could not meet his eyes. She knew that if she tried, she might faint.

'Well now, Edith, I think it would be oppor-

tune for you to leave us now. Quite opportune,'
her father repeated, and nodded his dismissal.

Edith could not wait to leave the room. She
closed the door quietly behind her, leaving the
two men together, and walked quickly away.

It was not until she reached the servants'
quarters again that the full implication of
what had happened hit her. She had not been
reprimanded, she was not even going to be
punished – she was going to be married.

'I heard you was in for it, Edie.'

Becky Snape peered anxiously round the door
that led down to the kitchens, her blonde hair
escaping flirtatiously from beneath her maid's
cap, her large cornflower-blue eyes reflecting her
fascination with trouble.

'That's what I heard, that you was in for it
proper and good; good and proper, like.' She
sounded concerned; Edith had always gone out
of her way to make Becky's life easier, especially
when the poor child first started at the Stag and
Crown and like all the youngsters was being
horribly bullied by Mrs Hanson. Edith had even
insisted on taking the blame for some of Becky's
more juvenile errors, knowing that Mrs Hanson
would not quite dare *swipe* Harold's daughter in
the same way she would have done the young
Becky Snape.

'I thought I *was* in for it, Becky,' Edith agreed.
'I really did think I was,' she repeated solemnly,
unable nevertheless to stop her own large eyes

from shining, and her face breaking into her always warm and generous smile.

Becky stared at her. 'So what was it you was in for it *for*, then?'

'I'm in for – I'm in for being married, Becky, that's what I'm in for being. I'm in for being married.'

Edith stared at Becky, the idea only now sinking in. Her strange-coloured eyes widened so much that Becky found herself staring into them, wondering what it was they reminded her of so particularly.

''Ere, you just drunk a jug o' Mr Bancroft's best ale with your breakfast?'

'No, Becky, I haven't, although I don't blame you for thinking that I might have.'

'Yer what, then? Yer in for what?'

'I told you, Becky, I'm in for being married.'

'Oh, you are, are you? And I'm off to be a cloistered nun, I am.'

'No, it's true, Becky. I'm . . .' Edith paused. 'I've been spoken for today. By a gentleman caller. He wants to marry me, and that means I'm leaving here soon, to be married. I am to be married,' she finished slowly, quite suddenly smitten by the truth of her own words.

'I know it now. You been up these last nights drinking the bottle ends with Willy Bancroft by the back door, haven't you, Edith Hanson?'

Edith shook her head. 'No, Becky. It is true. No word of a lie. I am going to be married. I really am going to be married.'

'Very well. So what's his name then, this man you're going to marry? What's his name when he's at home?'

It was Edith's turn to stare. 'Never you mind,' she said, a little too quickly even for her own ears. 'That's my business.'

Becky's eyes narrowed. She knew Edith well enough to know when she was being evasive. ''Ere, you don't even know his name, do you, Edith? You don't know the name of this gentleman what wants to marry you, that's how real your marriage is. You don't even know his name.'

'Of course I do,' Edith lied. 'But I'm not telling you, Becky. Of course I know the name of the man I am going to marry. Why wouldn't I know his name, if I'm to marry him?'

Becky's fingers shot out and twisted the flesh on the top of one of Edith's hands, which happened to be resting on a nearby door handle. 'Go on, tell out, if you know his name so well, then. Tell out the name of your intended, *Miss* Edith Hanson.'

Despite the pain, Edith continued to smile, determined not to give in. 'No, I will not tell you the name of my fiancé, Becky Snape, not if you were the last person on this earth I wouldn't. After all, Becky, you might pinch him the way you're pinching me, mightn't you?'

Becky grinned. 'Yah, I might at that, Edith. Yah, I might well do just that.' She stopped her flesh-twisting and changed her tactics. 'When

61

will you tell me then, Edie?' She looked purposefully forlorn, small and defeated, which did not really wash with Edith, who, fond though she was of Becky, knew she was up to just about everything. It was her way.

'I will tell you on my wedding day, so you won't have to wait long, Becky. My wedding day is sure to be quite soon, and if I'm allowed I'd like you to be my bridesmaid.'

Becky stared as Edith turned to go, and the expression in her eyes was one of incredulity mixed with dawning hope. 'I could be your – bridesmaid? Edith Hanson, get on! Be your bridesmaid, go up the aisle behind you, and wear flowers in me hair like a proper lady? Get on!'

'No, it's true, Becky. I shall ask for you to be my bridesmaid. If I'm to be married, you can be with me and hold my bouquet. I shall insist on it!'

The actual date of Edith's wedding was dictated by the wait for the special licence, this in its turn being dictated by the impatience of both the bride's father and the bridegroom-to-be. It was applied for as soon as was perfectly possible while the rest of the servants waited in disbelieving suspense, unable to credit that young Edith had been spoken for, and not by the delivery boy, or the brewery man, but by a proper gentleman.

Mrs Hanson was possibly the most bewildered of everyone at the sudden turn of events regarding her stepdaughter, and perhaps because of this she still expected Edith to work right up until her big day. There was no talk from her step-mother of what Edith should wear, or what she might be given in the way of a trousseau, so, perhaps realising, somewhat belatedly, that something was required, her father took Edith aside.

'I think you should go shopping for a gown,' he announced a week before the chosen date. 'I will stand by whatever you choose, for Mother, I know, will select something tasteful for you.'

Because it was her day off Edith had already washed her long auburn hair and brushed it out, instead of pinning it back. Mrs Hanson looked startled when she saw her stepdaughter hurrying towards her clutching her old, thin, grey cloak around her – though not as startled as the pro-prietor of the discreetly smart local dress shop when he saw how poorly clothed was the young girl being presented to him for a bridal gown. He was not used to dressing servants.

For once in her life Mrs Hanson looked what she must have been feeling, namely embar-rassed.

'This is my stepdaughter, newly arrived from the provinces,' she said, by way of polite ex-planation. 'She is to be married next week.'

Mr North smiled at the young girl standing beside her stepmother. She might be too thin, she might be wearing clothes that frankly he fully intended to see burnt within the next few minutes, but even so he was not surprised that she had been picked to be someone's wife, for, despite her drab appearance, her odious step-mother, and her pale cheeks, she was truly stunning.

Mr North could appreciate that Edith Hanson's long, richly red auburn hair and bright green eyes were her most startling attributes, and that the shape of her pale-skinned face with its perfectly set eyes and straight nose was actually classical in its appeal. But the main attraction, and one that could not be missed, was the mouth, the lips of which were full and curved, giving her an air of involuntary voluptuousness.

'Follow me, Mrs Hanson.'

Despite himself Mr North had to pretend to be deferential to Mrs Hanson, not just because she was a regular customer, but because she regularly entertained the ladies of the neighbour-hood to private luncheons at the Stag and Crown: luncheons at which Mrs Hanson, with equal regularity, wore her best silk and satin gowns, all of them purchased at *Charles North of Paris, London, and Vienna*. The ladies in question, having viewed their hostess's fashionable frocks, very promptly made a beeline for Mr North's premises; for whatever her faults, Mrs Harold Hanson was a handsome woman, who looked very much the part in pintucked gowns of a discreet hue.

'Miss Bagshaw?'

Although Miss Bagshaw was standing ex-pectantly by the large cheval mirror in the palely lit salon ready to leap into action, alert to the need for sales, Mr North nevertheless clapped his hands with authority, so that not only Miss Bagshaw but her two young assistants sprang to attention with almost soldierly respect.

'Bridal gowns, Miss Bagshaw, bridal gowns.'

Miss Bagshaw could not help looking startled. Her eyes went from Mrs Hanson to Edith and back again, and for the briefest of seconds Mr North could see that she was wondering if the bride was the older of the two women rather than the pathetic, drably dressed young girl with the startlingly coloured hair standing beside her.

'My *step*daughter is marrying next week,' Mrs Hanson announced to the startled vendeuse, but she said it in such a way that Miss Bagshaw was quite able to imagine that she had not previously ever had much to do with this stepdaughter in her thin grey cloak and poor shoes. 'She is marrying Mr Napier Todd, the famous portrait painter.'

The occupants of the salon stared at Edith with some interest. A portrait painter, while not a belted earl, was nevertheless perfectly respectable. After all, Her Majesty the Queen regularly entertained such people, and it was well known that some of them stayed for months at a time at Balmoral, painting portraits of everyone from Her Majesty's daughters to her beloved dogs.

However, if the older people in the room were only mildly impressed by Napier Todd's credentials, Edith was profoundly stirred. The fact that her husband-to-be was called *Napier*

Todd and not John Smith was exciting enough, but the fact that he was a *portrait* painter was more than exciting, it was enticing. It meant that Napier Todd was not just a businessman like her father, but someone who painted famous or perhaps even aristocratic people, like those she had sometimes glimpsed riding or driving through Richmond Park, their matching teams of greys or bays pulling them through life with an ease which, to a humble maid such as Edith, seemed unimaginable.

'There is very little time to prepare, all so sudden,' Mrs Hanson continued, giving the kind of tremulous smile that was intended to invite immediate sympathy.

'Would you care to step this way, mademoiselle?' Miss Bagshaw asked Edith.

It was Miss Bagshaw's wise custom to use a smattering of French to her customers, if only because it tended to reassure them of the fashionable standing enjoyed by the Charles North salon. Besides, she had discovered over the years that customers addressed as either 'madame' or 'mademoiselle', for reasons even she herself did not fully understand, would respond better to her guidance, the inference being that she must have spent time in a Paris salon.

Edith looked at her stepmother, who nodded briskly, and led the way to the room reserved for fittings. There Mrs Hanson left her, and beckoning to Miss Bagshaw walked the vendeuse a little way further up the main room. 'She will need new *sous-vêtements*,' she murmured discreetly, and Miss Bagshaw, understanding immediately just what was needed, hurried off in the direction of the lingerie cage.

It was not difficult to choose the right style of underwear for one so young and slim, but it was hard to find enough of the undoubtedly tiny size that was required. Her selection made, Miss Bagshaw hurried past Mr North, who was approving a parade of white dresses being unveiled by her two assistants. Mr North eyed the armfuls of camisoles and silk stockings piled high in the vendeuse's arms, and sighed inwardly with relief. His brother-in-law ran just such a business as his own, but he had no Miss Bagshaw upon whom he could rely. No one who could sum up a size with one glance and come up with exactly the right measurements of a customer, no one who could flatter with the perfect, carefully placed remark, no one who could soothe his feelings at the end of a long day like his own Miss Bagshaw.

'In here, Mademoiselle Hanson.' Miss Bagshaw opened a door to a large well-lit changing room into which Edith passed, followed by the vendeuse, who then deftly closed the door behind them, thus shutting out the second Mrs Hanson. 'You may place your own undergarments here, mademoiselle.' Miss Bagshaw held out some discreet sheeting, and laid a selection of underwear on the banquette behind

67

them. 'Then I suggest that you try this, and that – and this other.'

She stood back, eyeing Edith with interest, testing her figure against her own choices.

'I dare say we will have to tighten the corset more than it has ever been tightened, but it will greatly enhance your trousseau if we get the undergarments right from the start, and boneless corsets,' she stared at Edith's young figure with vague despair, 'boneless corsets such as you are obviously wearing, however healthy, will never do that.'

Edith dutifully removed her undergarments, her boneless stays (complete with suspenders), thick black stockings, and white flannel petticoat, and wrapped them carefully in the piece of sheeting provided.

'We will not be needing those again,' Miss Bagshaw announced with some relief as she started to place a boned corset around her and quickly and expertly tighten the laces, whipping the threads through the eyelets with such dexterity that before Edith knew it her body had been transformed from that of a slip of a girl to a fashionable, womanly 's' shape.

As soon as she had seen the sheen of the silk underwear and stockings that Miss Bagshaw was holding out to her, Edith had been unable to wait to feel the smooth, subtle texture against her skin. She knew just how sensuous it must be after the scratchy woollen stockings and stuffy petticoat to which she had become all too used.

'If Mademoiselle would raise her arms.'

As she secured the suspenders to the stocking tops Miss Bagshaw sang out what was happening to Edith, as if Edith could not see herself in the looking glass.

'Fashion dictates that we draw the eyes to the back of the silhouette. This is what the crinolette petticoat will do for Mademoiselle: it will concentrate the eyes on the back of Mademoiselle. The bustle, or *tournure*, as we call it in France, is most effective, even when worn under the heaviest materials.' She smiled at Edith, who was trying not to look bewildered. 'Do not fear, Mademoiselle Hanson. All will be revealed when we bring in the dresses.'

This time it was she who clapped her hands to indicate to one of the assistants that she could bring in the first of the costumes that Mr North had decided might be suitable for Miss Hanson to wear to her marriage to Mr Napier Todd.

'May I?' Miss Bagshaw carefully twisted Edith's hair around her own hand and placed it in a net snood to keep it from interfering with the dressing. Then she and her assistants, having pulled on white gloves and with the aid of expertly handled wooden sticks, scooped up the first of the gowns selected for the bride-to-be and lowered the silk dress over Edith's now fully bustled silhouette.

'*Et voilà*,' she murmured. Smoothing the fabric over the bustle cage with gloved hands, she nodded to the older of her assistants and murmured, 'Button hook!'

Not wanting to spoil the surprise of what she knew was her transformation Edith gazed at the ceiling as the tiny silk-covered buttons were expertly done up with the precious hook. Eventually satisfied that Edith was looking as good as she could perhaps ever look in the immensely draped dress with its rear interest, Miss Bagshaw removed the snood, re-dressed Edith's hair into a large piece of ribbon so that the emphasis of both her head and her rear view were beautifully co-ordinated, and slowly turned Edith towards the mirror. Then she stood back, her head on one side, ready to be critical, but nevertheless undoubtedly pleased.

Edith gazed at herself. The person her large green eyes saw reflected in the dressing mirror had nothing to do with the person with whom she had grown up. Her hands might be a little too rough – a sad legacy of years of carbolic soap and rinsing cloths in cold water – but there was nothing else about the young girl now staring at her reflection that could be so described. The young lady in the mirror was taller than Edith remembered. Courtesy perhaps of the crinolette petticoat, this beautiful girl was slender, not thin, and yet her silhouette was not without shape. The collar of the cream satin dress was frilled, showing off her long neck and bright hair, and looped back to set off neat ears. The three-quarter-length sleeves ending in a lace frill pointed up her slender arms, her long, ringless fingers with their tapered nails.

'Shall we?' Miss Bagshaw beckoned to Edith to follow her.

Edith turned reluctantly from the young woman in the mirror, trying to put aside the feeling that she needed to be introduced to the person there reflected, for she was certain she had never met her before.

Miss Bagshaw flung open the door that led back into the main salon from the fitting room.

'Mrs Hanson, Mr North, may I present to you – Miss Edith Hanson. Or perhaps it should now be Miss Edith *Handsome*!'

Edith would never forget the look on Aurelia Hanson's face as she stared at the vision that her stepdaughter had become. She was plainly horrified by what she saw, and not just horrified, but affronted. She was made indignant. She even reddened as if she had been insulted, as if Edith had been transformed not only into a beautiful white swan, but to someone quite improper.

She turned to Mr North.

'Oh, I don't think so, do you, Mr North? I don't think so at all. This gown is far too sophisticated for someone so young – would you not agree?'

Miss Bagshaw's lips tightened, and she pulled herself up and shook her chignoned head as if she had heard someone swear. Mr North's mouth twitched, and his lips too tightened.

'I am not really very sure that we can agree about that, Mrs Hanson,' he said with sudden firmness, after a small pause. 'I doubt it very much.' He cast a superior look at Mrs Hanson, a look that showed sudden despite for this provincial woman with her uppity manner, and at the same time he turned towards a pile of discreetly placed magazines. 'I think you will find here, for instance, in this last copy of *The Season*, I think you will find the original description of what we ourselves would certainly term a very simple, rather unsophisticated dress described—' He snatched up the relevant fashion journal, and started to flick through it at great speed. 'Ah yes, we have it here. I thought so.'

He placed a pair of lunettes, hastily produced from his waistcoat pocket, on the bridge of his nose.

'Yes, we have it here. *A silk gown from the Master of Paris, Monsieur Worth, undoubtedly perfect. A gown that will show off the youngest and most unsophisticated bride in a way to satisfy the most exacting of tastes. Demure is the word.*' He looked round at Mrs Hanson as he said it. 'Demure,' he repeated. '*Demure and appealing in every way, leaving nothing for the bride's mamma to do except to pick fresh orange blossom for the headdress and bouquet on the morning of the wedding.*' He closed the magazine sharply. 'I do not think we can argue with *The Season*, which is after all the organ of fashion, Mrs Hanson.'

For the first time in her life, Edith saw that someone was standing up to her stepmother,

72

perhaps for the first time in *her* life, and she could not help finding it a delightful sight.

Mrs Hanson swallowed hard; she even licked her lips, mercifully briefly, as if she was aware that her mouth had become suddenly dry. She searched within herself for a few seconds for words that might combat the accolade accorded by the fashionable journal to the vision presented by her stepdaughter, still standing in front of her, and could find none.

'Of course we can look at some other choices against which Miss Hanson could set this first one,' Mr North finally offered in the seconds of silence that had followed his reading from the journal. 'Bring the draped muslin with the ruched ribboning,' he commanded Miss Bagshaw, who was staring at him with proprietary pride.

'Very well, sir.' Miss Bagshaw nodded to one of her assistants to do as Mr North had commanded, and turned back to Edith. 'If Mademoiselle Hanson would like to follow me?'

Edith, who had long grown accustomed to her stepmother's sharp tongue, followed Miss Bagshaw back to the fitting room, and, not long after, the two young assistants hurried in carrying more dresses. Miss Bagshaw smiled at Edith in the dressing mirror, thinking that she must need to be comforted after such a disappointing reaction.

'The first one is always the right one, believe me, Miss Hanson. You will walk up the aisle in the first one.'

There was so much to-ing and fro-ing after that, with Edith appearing and reappearing at well-timed intervals in gowns of wildly differing styles, that Mrs Hanson, dizzy and confused, which was perhaps what was intended, finally flung in the towel and turned to Mr North with pleading eyes.

'What would you say, Mr North?'

'I would say the silk with the three-quarter sleeves and the frilled collar,' Mr North announced, having first thrown a small triumphant glance in Miss Bagshaw's direction. 'Most definitely the silk. And now Miss Bagshaw will fit Miss Hanson with some new day dresses.' As he spoke, Mr North made sure to roll up Edith's servant dress in such a way that Mrs Hanson could not help noticing it.

Mrs Hanson half rose from the duenna sofa upon which she had been seated, the expression on her face that of a woman who was finding herself in a bad dream.

'Surely we should be going? If the bridal dress is chosen, that is the end of our task, surely?'

Mr North shook his head. 'The trousseau, Mrs Hanson, we must not forget the trousseau,' he murmured, and he smiled. 'Please allow me to ask the maid to bring you a nice glass of ginger wine and some sweet biscuits. We shall be quite a while yet, you may be sure.'

Inside the fitting room, Edith, now clothed in a demure two-piece, complete with hat and gloves, one of many such outfits that would go to

74

make up her trousseau, smiled at Miss Bagshaw.

'I would like to bring my little friend Becky Snape to be fitted as a bridesmaid,' she murmured. 'But I do not have enough money to buy her anything new. In fact I have so little money, it would be impossible to buy her anything more than a petticoat or a new pair of stockings.'

'I will lend your friend something, mademoiselle. We sometimes do this.' She smiled in the mirror at the beautiful young girl standing before her. 'We sometimes do this for people we like.'

A few days later Becky was brought to Mr North's salon, and delivered into Miss Bagshaw's expert hands.

'I dunno, I dunno that I should,' Becky kept protesting. 'Cook said that Mrs Hanson had a fit when she heard I was to be yer bridesmaid, Edith, really she did.'

'Mademoiselle?'

Becky turned slowly back to Miss Bagshaw. She had never heard French before, let alone been addressed in it. 'Ye-es?'

'Miss Hanson has chosen you to be her bridesmaid, so that is how it has to be, mademoiselle. You understand? You are not to be the only one, you know. Two of my assistants are also to attend Miss Hanson. We have some lovely dresses for the purpose, and you will be given some lady's underwear without charge.'

When the underwear duly arrived, as it had done for Edith, Becky stared first at it, then later at herself in the mirror, astonishment in her eyes.

''Ere,' she said, after a few moments. 'I could get used to this!'

On the day of the wedding, Edith's father did not look in the least impressed by either Edith or her gown, which, as predicted by Miss Bagshaw, was indeed the one that Edith had tried on first. He was far too worried about his own appearance to bother much with that of his daughter.

However, if Edith felt disappointed by her father's muted reaction to her transformation, the rest of the servants certainly made up for it. As she walked slowly down from one of the best bedrooms, reluctantly loaned to her by Mrs Hanson for the purpose of changing, Becky and the other bridesmaids following her, the servants stood at the bottom of the wide oak staircase and allowed their mouths to drop open in astonishment. Since the arrival early that morning of Miss Bagshaw and her assistants, there had been total concentration on the bride-to-be, beginning with a long longed-for bath – a copper placed in front of the fire and filled from cans – and ending with the placing of a bouquet of orange blossom in her hands.

'Edith Hanson, you look beautiful,' one of the younger maids murmured, trying to reach out to touch her gown for luck, but Miss Bagshaw was there before her, smacking the eager fingers away from the precious cream silk.

'Be off with you all,' she said, although in a

kindly tone. 'Back to your pots and pans and dusters and pails.'

The three identically dressed bridesmaids stepped into the hackney carriage that was to follow the bridal coach. Seeing them, Harold frowned, and before stepping forward to join his daughter he took Miss Bagshaw aside.

'Are the bridesmaids coming at extra cost, do you know?' he asked anxiously.

Miss Bagshaw gave him a tolerant smile as she took his silk hat and quickly buffed the edge with the small brush that she always carried on such occasions. Surely only Harold Hanson could ask such a vulgar question on the morning of his only daughter's wedding?

'No, sir, they are here courtesy of Mr North. It seemed a pity not to make some sort of occasion of it, particularly since there has been so little time for us all to prepare in the kind of style for which you might have otherwise wished,' she told him, a look of innocence on her face.

But if Miss Bagshaw sounded lightly sarcastic, Harold Hanson seemed to be unaware of it, for he merely nodded, and giving every appearance of being reassured he climbed into the bridal coach to seat himself beside his daughter. Miss Bagshaw leaned into the carriage after him and handed him his brushed top hat.

'I will be following with Mr North in the hackney behind the bridesmaids',' she told Edith, 'so wait for me, outside the church, so that I can adjust your gown.'

Edith smiled. Miss Bagshaw closed the door, and nodded to the coachman, and the be-ribboned carriage set off for the church, which was so near that it made the use of the carriage seem almost ludicrous to everyone except Mr North and Miss Bagshaw, who had a firm rule when it came to the dressing of brides: as far as they were concerned, either their clients arrived looking immaculate, fresh from the hands of the Charles North salon, or their custom was refused.

After all, as Mr North was very fond of point-ing out, their bridal wear was immensely popular. A Charles North bride had to look fresh, dainty, and immaculate, not windswept and mud bespattered.

Edith walked up the aisle, one gloved hand on her father's arm. For a second she imagined that everything was going to change and that in a few minutes she would be working like all the others back at the inn, instead of walking up the church to the sound of an organ playing, with no one telling her to go back to the Stag and Crown and get her bucket and mop.

All at once, even before her father and herself reached the top of the aisle, she could see her future husband. He was dressed as a man of fashion – black coat, tall silk cravat with a pearl pin, highly polished boots, the whole fandango. It did not seem possible that this elegant creature was about to become her husband, and she his wife.

Edith smiled up at the vicar's round, reddened

face, feeling vaguely disappointed that he did not look more like the saints in the stained-glass windows that surrounded them, before turning to Napier. As she looked up at him through her bridal veil, happiness of a kind she had never known before flooded through her. Napier Todd was so handsome, and the expression in his eyes so kind, that she knew at once that she had to be the luckiest girl in England. She was getting married in a silk dress to the sound of an organ playing, with the smell of orange blossom scenting the air, and what was more and what was better, she was in love.

With a sudden giddiness Edith at last recognised what she was feeling. Of course, she was in love! And why would she not be? What young woman would not find it easy to feel passionate about this tall, handsome man with his pretty mouth and darkly intense eyes, who even she realised could not take his eyes off Edith's face now that her veil was lifted?

They took their vows with quiet intensity, but when Napier slid her wedding ring on to her finger and Edith looked down at it she felt she did not, could never, deserve the joy that she was feeling.

The bridal breakfast was held back at the inn, and was everything that it should be. Harold – feeling great relief that not only had the bridesmaids been fitted out courtesy of Charles North, but happily the cost of the breakfast could be put down in his accounts books as entertaining influential customers – was now quite able to smile down the table at his second wife. He knew he had laid on as good a spread as could be wished for, and since his new son-in-law, aside from his best man, had invited no other friends, the whole affair was proving really very satisfactory. He rose to his feet to make his speech.

'I am very proud to be able to say that giving away my daughter Edith, the only child of my poor late wife . . .' Here he paused for a few seconds to remember his poor late wife, which turned out to be a mistake, since at the mention of his previous union his second wife found it incumbent on her to clear her throat in a rather too marked manner. 'Where was I? Ah yes, my poor daughter Edith, left as an orphan, except for myself, of course. Not that my dear wife, the second Mrs Hanson' – he once again smiled down the table with unusual warmth at Aurelia, who, seeing that all eyes were upon her, smiled back as best she could – 'not that the second Mrs Hanson has been backward in coming to my aid in bringing up my poor motherless daughter. It was not easy to raise a daughter, as you can well imagine, what with the temptations of the present day, not to mention the pits into which orphaned children, bereft of their mothers, can fall. Mrs Hanson had her work cut out, you may be sure. Nevertheless I think we must all agree that she has done a fine job, and will continue to do a fine job, if and when Edith should need her in the future. Married life can prove thorny, however good the intentions of those caught up in its broil. So now, I really must pause to raise my glass to the bride and groom. Before too long I will have to be about my duties, but until then I hope all of us present will continue to enjoy the blessings of this table. The bride and groom!'

They all raised their glasses to Edith and Napier, but Edith, who had been constantly distracted by the looks of the maids waiting at table, had hardly heard her father's speech, being all too aware of the wonder in the faces of her former colleagues as they busied themselves with the placing and replacing of the dishes. Would any of these girls, in their crisp uniforms and stiff collars that chafed so infernally at the neck, ever marry? Edith knew that they must be asking themselves the same question, even as they scurried backwards and forwards. They must also be wondering what kind of lucky star had allowed Edith to be scrubbing the floor when Napier Todd had come into the inn that Monday morning.

'Imagine you, you of all people, waltzing off with a gentleman the likes of him,' Becky murmured as she changed out of her loaned bridesmaid dress and back into her maid's clothes, before in turn watching Edith change into her going-off costume of brown silk with blue-spotted velvet trimmings and cream lace ruffles.

Edith shot her an anxious glance and then

smiled at her with sudden, almost nostalgic affection from under her ostrich-trimmed hat.

'Goodbye, Becky. You must come and see me in my new home in the country, when you can. Come to tea with me. I hope you will.'

'I shall miss you so, Edith – really I shall. You're the only one 'ere what's been kind to me, I know that.' Becky burst into instant tears.

'Don't cry, Becky dearest. We'll see each other again, really we will. I shall make sure of it, truly I shall.'

Edith patted Becky on her thin shoulder and hurried off to the top of the stairs, which led down to the hall and the small party waiting below to wish the newly-weds luck on their going-off.

In the smart carriage that was taking them to the station, and so on to the honeymoon, which was to be spent at Napier's country house, Edith turned and smiled at her bridegroom. It was a smile full of love and expectancy, full of hope for the future. Napier too smiled, but his smile was filled with something quite different.

Napier's smile was one of adoration, of worship. He took one of Edith's newly gloved hands in his and raised it to his lips with such reverence that Edith, for some reason she could not name, found her heart contracting with a vague kind of fear. She knew that she did not know her bridegroom, that she still only thought of him as some kind of knight in shining armour, but now she realised, looking at his still bent head, that it would seem he did not know her either, for if he did, he would surely not be kissing her gloved hand as if she was some kind of grand lady?

'Napier?'

He raised his head, and as he did so Edith realised she had not called him by his Christian name before, but that, so little did she know him, she would not have been surprised if she had heard herself addressing him as 'Mr Todd'.

'Yes, Edith?'

'Where are we going to, may I ask? I mean, to where exactly are we going?'

Edith's voice, untouched by years of being treated as a servant, was as light and refined as the day her mother had met her death so suddenly. She was not so naïve as not to know that this was reassuring to them both, but in the confines of the cab her voice had all of a sudden assumed an unreality, and she knew exactly why.

When she had seen her mother for the last time she had been dressed in a beautiful street costume such as Edith was now wearing. Quite a different fashion, of course, but nevertheless, Edith realised with a rush, she must have looked and sounded just as her daughter did now.

Edith remembered her mother turning and kissing her hand to her ten-year-old daughter. *I will not be long, darling, not long at all.*

But she had been. She had been for ever.

Edith turned away from Napier and stared out of the carriage window into the busy afternoon outside, at the streets always filled with steaming horse droppings, mud and stale vegetables, not to mention poorly dressed people tramping along not knowing where they were going, and, worse, not caring. From such sad figures her gaze transferred itself to smart carriages that were passing their own, to ladies carefully lifting their street dresses before crossing the roads, to the carters' horses with beautiful brass fittings on their bridles, to coal being delivered outside the station, to other hansom cabs stopping to let their passengers alight, and she was filled with the kind of sad, nostalgic longing that so often accompanies intense happiness. Today at least her mother might have been proud of her. She might have helped to choose her trousseau, she might have calmed her nerves, prepared her for the days ahead – days and nights, the thought of which was already making Edith nervously aware of her innocence as far as the marriage bed was concerned.

'Oh, Napier, do look. It has been made into a bower!'

He had just handed her up into their private railway-carriage, which was beautifully arranged with flowers in holders on the wall, and a bucket with wine, not to mention silver salvers covering who knew what delicacies to keep them from starving on the journey to the country.

'Did you arrange this, Napier?'

'I asked for it, dearest, if that is what you mean.'

'It is all so pretty. You are so clever.' Edith turned to thank her new husband, and raising her face to his she quite spontaneously kissed him, discovering as she did so that Napier had the prettiest mouth. His lips were not large, but nicely plump, and his mouth curved up at the corner, even before he smiled.

He did not return her kiss, but smiled and lightly touched her cheek.

'I should so love you to remove your hat . . .' he murmured, his voice seeming to Edith to be throbbing with intensity.

It was Edith's turn to smile, and she put up both hands to her hatpin to oblige him, but Napier immediately shook his head.

'No, dearest, no. You must not remove your hat now. It would be letting yourself down in front of the railway staff if they saw you bare-headed. Besides,' he touched her cheek lightly once again, 'besides, I want to save that moment for myself, for when we are alone.'

Edith's heart raced as she saw the expression in his eyes, and she felt quite faint as she knew that he was looking at her as if she was no longer wearing her beautiful brown silk travelling costume with its cream lace ruffled sleeves and long brown gloves. He was looking at her as he had looked at her on the very first day he had seen her, the day he had walked into the Stag and Crown, when she had been scrubbing the Monday morning floor, and he in search of a decent breakfast.

It was as if he knew exactly how she was made, exactly how she was modelled; as if he already knew her intimately, which perhaps, being a portrait painter, he did. Perhaps that was what happened when a painter fell in love with you. Perhaps he knew you, heart and soul, long before he took you in his arms, long before he spirited you away from your father and stepmother to some new, strange land where you would love each other for eternity.

Edith was no stranger to the taste of wine. From the time Aurelia had decided, really rather conveniently, that her stepdaughter was too stupid to do anything except help to clean, and run errands, the older servants had given her the ends of wine bottles to sip, if only to keep her warm, or to help her sleep. She therefore took the glass Napier offered her only too thankfully. It had been a long day, and she knew it would not do to fall asleep or look tired. The wine revived her spirits. More than that, she could tell Napier was almost relieved that she was quite as ready as he to drink wine and lift the covers off the serving dishes, and nibble at the refreshments so thoughtfully provided.

'Tell me about your country house, Napier. I cannot wait to meet it.'

The expression in Napier's eyes changed from quiet passion to one of warm intensity.

'Such a pretty way of putting it,' he said, smiling. 'For of course one does *meet* a house, or it *greets* you; there is always an introduction from one side to the other. Of course there is.' He dwelt on this notion for a few seconds before continuing. 'Helmscote Manor was first built by my father, but has been remodelled by me, with the help of Basil George Canford, a pupil of the great Augustus Welby Pugin. We both have a passion for the Gothic style, and not just the style but also the *principles* of Ruskin and his acolytes, the modern ideals of home and hearth.'

Edith did not know who this Augustus Pugin could be, but she looked suitably impressed. She had certainly never heard anyone talk about ideals. Ideals were not something discussed by anyone at the Stag and Crown, where conversations had always centred round money, profit, and very occasionally that dread of all dreads – loss of regular custom.

'Edith.'

There was a long pause, as Napier's look continued to become steadily more intense.

'Edith, nothing matters more than the principles of art, bringing about the kind of warmth and the humane ways of living that have come about since the Industrial Revolution, since the population abandoned the countryside for the cities. Each man in himself, as we know, is equal to his fellow, but no man is more equal than the man who works with his hands: the labourer, and the artisan. The artisan fulfils God's purpose by putting his God-given talent to carving or modelling, to the making of beautiful objects that are to be used every day, objects that we must never, ever take for granted – wooden spoons, carving boards, pitchers and beakers; just as the artist is put on this earth to glorify such things in his work.'

Edith's heart sank as she realised that she did not really understand what Napier was talking about. It all seemed a little far-fetched to her, but of course she could not say as much to Napier, whose eyes were shining with fervour. She tried to imagine the kitchens of the Stag and Crown being inhabited by people who constantly reverenced their implements. She found herself struggling for a few seconds with a mental picture of Cook and her cohorts glorying in the lively shape of their wooden spoons, before using them to beat the kitchen boy about the head. She thought of the maids, and in turn tried to imagine them admiring the form of their buckets, rather than moaning about the freezing temperature of the cleaning water. In both instances she failed, but realising it was not the moment to ask for further enlightenment on this subject of the worship of ordinary things, she smiled at Napier.

'It sounds very – religious.'

Napier leaned forward and kissed her now ungloved hand. 'It is religious, my dearest girl, it is exactly that. How clever of you to say so. It is entirely religious, and that is a further beauty of the Gothic style, which others, and of course I myself, naturally, find so irresistible. The Gothic style can easily incorporate religious paintings and stained-glass images from the Bible; they never look out of place. At Helmscote Manor you will see we have been able to use them with great effect.'

The wine had not made Edith feel as dizzy as Napier's ideals, artistic and otherwise. She put her glass down carefully on the receptacle provided, and gazed out of the window for a second. She was beginning to feel that she had not married so much as joined a monastic order, which she had to admit was a strange feeling. But as she turned back to Napier, she was instantly reassured by the look of passion in his eyes. She smiled at him. She could not wait to reach his house and be greeted by it, to see all his ideals put into practice, not to mention his paintings.

'I am so looking forward to being in your studio with you, Napier,' she told him.

Napier breathed in suddenly with an intensity that was almost startling. 'And I cannot wait for you to be in my studio with me,' he murmured.

Edith looked at him, warmed by the wine, and the knowledge that she must be the luckiest girl in the world. She knew now that she was longing to arrive at Helmscote Manor and to be taken to their rooms. To say that she felt she already worshipped Napier, and could not wait to give herself to him, was to say the least.

The eagerly anticipated sight of the house waiting to greet her was finally something of a disappointment. It could hardly be anything else, since they did not arrive at the gates of the house until dusk, so Edith could only see the lights of the hall spilling out over the dozen or so stone steps outside, and nothing really of the house itself, except two towers to the side, and a black and white timbered first floor.

However, after Napier's eulogy about his artistic ideals, it was no surprise to find that the front door was carved in a classic Gothic shape, and that there were two or three rounded archways beside it which did indeed give the house a cloistered, monastic air.

'Welcome to Helmscote, Mrs Todd. I am Mrs George, Mr Todd's housekeeper. My husband is Mr Todd's estate manager. You will meet him later.'

As she recited her obviously well-rehearsed greeting Mrs George executed a magnificent, and doubtless equally well-rehearsed, curtsy. Edith put out her hand to thank her, appreciating all too well the fuss and furore that must have preceded their arrival, the anxiety of keeping the fires stoked up, and the difficulty of preventing the flowers from drooping in the heat that those same fires were so busy providing, while in the kitchens the food would be having to be put on back burners, for the train had been late, owing it had been said to a suicide on the rails.

'I do wish Mrs George would not do that,' Napier muttered under his breath, turning away and frowning as his housekeeper arose from her deep curtsy.

'Shall I show Madam to her room?' Mrs George continued, smiling with pride as she saw the appreciation on her young mistress's face as she took in the brightly burning fire, the flowers in their huge and complicated arrangements, and the gloss and glitter on every object in the simple but stylish hall.

The brass vases seemed to be smiling down at the polished oak furniture, gaily determined to use the old, seasoned wood to see their reflections. The colours of the stained-glass windows, high above their heads, were muted in the early evening light, while at the same time undoubtedly welcoming the illumination coming from the vast wooden candelabra high above, as a performer might welcome the warm glow coming from the footlights.

'Those are my ancestors,' Napier told Edith, as he saw her staring up at the coloured glass. His voice became confidential. 'My father had them designed when Garter king-of-arms confirmed that through my great-grandmother on my father's side we are descended from King Edward and Queen Philippa, and of course our Anglo-Saxon ancestry is reflected in the Gothic style here. I always think, without my knowing it, that this must have greatly influenced my attraction to the teachings of Ruskin and my present thinking.'

He looked around him once more as if to reassure himself that his mentor, the genius Ruskin, the philosopher and thinker, would approve of his hall and his kinship with medieval kings and queens, and sighed with contented gratitude that he was once more at home.

Edith followed Mrs George, her eyes taking in the order, the beauty, and the cleanliness of everything that surrounded them. The rush matting in the corridors, the oak furniture, every handle, every sconce seemed to her innocent eyes in some way to reflect Napier's personality.

'It is all so beautiful.' Edith turned to the housekeeper, her eyes sparkling in the gaslight of the bedroom, her whole slender young body exuding confidence and happiness.

Mrs George nodded. 'This house was built for Mr Todd the elder, Mr Napier's father, and it is not just beautiful, it is also practical,' she said, and she pointed proudly to the ventilation system.

'I hope I will be able to be of practical use in the kitchens—'

'And I hope you will not,' Mrs George rejoined crisply. 'You are here to be decorative in the morning room and the drawing room, Mrs Todd. We don't want you busying yourself in the kitchens, making your hair and your clothes smell, do we now?'

For a second Edith looked taken aback, and seeing this the housekeeper continued in a more kindly voice. 'If you don't mind me reminding you, madam, you're naught but a bairn. Hardly had time to flutter, let alone fly, and here you are a married woman. You've been snatched from the cradle, we can all see that, and for that reason you don't want to keep worrying about the kitchens and the running of the place. That's my business. Yours is to please the master, and that I am quite sure you will,' she ended, staring with concentrated appreciation at Edith's brilliant auburn hair, which she was now shaking out as she removed her going-off hat.

'You are quite right, Mrs George. I do see that. And how very silly of me to even mention the kitchens. Of course you have been running the place for probably as long as I have been in this world. Why on earth would you need me under your feet?'

She laughed, and Mrs George turned away, looking relieved. She had to get that one sorted out before they all started running into trouble. After all was said and done a house had to be run on certain lines, like the railways with their main lines and their branch lines, and if there was any kind of confusion there would be crashes. She had seen it happen.

'I have arranged for you and Mr Todd to dine alone tonight, madam,' Mrs George murmured discreetly. 'Now I will have one of the maids bring up a tub and place it in front of the fire, for I am sure you will not want to bath the way Mr Todd is in the habit of bathing. On the balcony outside his dressing room, and in freezing water!'

'No, you are quite right.' Edith pulled a little face. 'I wonder why he does that?'

The expression on Mrs George's face could only be described as purposefully blank.

For her first dinner with her husband at Helmscote House, Edith chose to wear a pale green taffeta evening gown, bought second-hand from Mr North, on the recommendation of Miss Bagshaw, who had whispered to Edith that it had once belonged to 'a Countess of A'.

As she dressed herself, Edith remembered with gratitude how Miss Bagshaw had been assiduous in the extreme in providing a proper trousseau for her. For some reason that Edith could not understand the vendeuse had gone out of her way to provide her young customer with everything she could possibly want for her new life.

'And do not, I beg you, Miss Hanson, as I can see you are about to do, do not fret that your father will be infuriated by the accounts that will be sent to him,' she had told the astonished Edith as she packed the treasured items in tissue paper, adding with a calm smile, 'I have managed to lose a great many of your trousseau costs in your stepmother's summer wardrobe, not yet paid for, and in other ways too, to be sure.' Seeing Edith's very evident embarrassment, she placed a cool hand on her arm to reassure her. 'I may be speaking out of turn, but I judged it only fair, after all, for I dare say you have never once been paid for all your years spent scrubbing the floors at the Stag and Crown?'

They had stared at each other for a few

seconds as Edith realised that Miss Bagshaw must have known all along that she had been dressing for her wedding one who to all intents and purposes was a mere maidservant. Somehow the expression on Miss Bagshaw's face had been so serious, so solemn, so weighty, her mouth pulled down into such a funereal expression, that the moment had toppled over into charade, and they had both ended up in fits of laughter. And of course it would have been difficult for Edith not to have seen the rough justice in Miss Bagshaw's accounting, for it was true that she had worked at the Stag and Crown all through her adolescence with no payment beyond a feeling of gratitude that she had a roof over her head.

Now, of course, as she stared at herself in the dressing mirror, Edith was more than grateful to Miss Bagshaw, for she could see that not only must the Countess of A have had great taste when she first ordered the gown in which, with her new personal maid's help, she herself was now standing, but so must Miss Bagshaw.

The green silk set off Edith's auburn hair, white skin, and green eyes to perfection, and certainly the overskirt in patterned green and gold velvet did nothing but enhance the general effect, as did the short matching taffeta train. The bodice was cut so as to show exactly the right amount of what Miss Bagshaw would often discreetly refer to as Edith's *décolletage*. In other words, there was just enough of Edith's curves on view to be appealing, but not so much as to be an embarrassment.

Edith turned sideways to view the train and the bustle effect at the back, realising as she did so that she looked not just beautiful, but grand, so of course as she set off from her new bedroom to dine with her new husband her green eyes were sparkling and her head of hair – which Miss Bagshaw had taught her how to pin with a couple of expert twists to the top of her head and the aid of a few combs – looked as lustrous as it had ever done.

'Madam looks beautiful,' the maid that Mrs George had sent up to help her murmured, but she turned away from her as if the sight of Edith looking so stunning was more than she could bear.

Edith walked carefully down the highly polished oak stairs to the hall where Mrs George was waiting to show her into the dining room.

Here two maids, dressed in rustic skirts with crisp white aprons over the top, hovered anxiously, waiting to do whatever was asked of them. The food was beautifully produced, and served on a mix of pewter and wooden platters. It was simple but delicious, and quite different from anything to which the servants at the Stag and Crown might have ever been used.

'Everything from our own soil, dearest, imagine that,' Napier told her, smiling with satisfaction.

He himself was dressed in an artist's silk cravat

and a black frock-coat, and looking so handsome that Edith could not take her eyes off him. She found little difficulty in hanging on to his every word all through dinner, even if every other sentence seemed to start with the word 'Ruskin'.

Dinner at last at an end, and Edith having left Napier for the required time with his port, they made their way once more to the upper floor, to the great bedroom that Edith now realised with a rush of joyous excitement they were going to share. Despite the fact that it was a vast oak four-poster, seen through the connecting doors of her dressing room, Edith thought the bed looked most inviting, although the linen drapes on the posts were so strangely patterned that she felt sure they must have been designed by someone like this Ruskin person.

Edith changed into her frilled nightgown in a state of great excitement. She loved Napier so much she knew now that she longed to give herself to him, although what exactly the giving and receiving would entail she had no real idea.

Eventually Napier appeared, carrying a wooden bed stick at the centre of which was a large, chunky, tallow-coloured candle whose light spilled out generously over the rustic furnishings of the room. He trod quietly and discreetly across the rush matting that covered the polished oak floorboards towards the bed where Edith was lying against carefully arranged pillows, her own candle already blown out. With a mounting sense of excitement, eyes open,

Edith felt the mattress beside her dip, and then eventually, after some few minutes, the last of the light in the room disappeared as Napier turned and extinguished his vast candle with the aid of a snuffer.

There followed a long silence, before Edith heard Napier murmur, 'Good night, my dearest dear.' And then, eventually, came the sound of his gently sleeping breath rising and falling beside her, a sound that seemed strangely magnified owing to the deathly quiet of the countryside, and the dense, unrelieved darkness of the room.

Edith turned on her pillow and stared at the long, masculine back facing her, before turning back to stare once more into the black of the night, her carefully arranged auburn hair still massed behind her on the pillow, the frill of her nightgown touching her small, rounded chin.

After some long time of waiting and listening to Napier's steady breathing, inevitably Edith felt the cold tears of disappointment begin to slide down her cheeks, and eventually the salt of those same tears on her lips, as they coursed with increasing rapidity down her young face. Yet so silent was her emotion, and so successful her suppression of it, that Napier was able to sleep on, oblivious of his bride's sorrow.

Chapter Three

Celandine sighed and put down her pencil.

'Mother dear! Do try to sit still, won't you?'

Mrs Benyon nodded abruptly. She was finding it increasingly difficult to sit poised with her sewing by the window, and if the truth be told that was not all she was finding difficult. She was finding Celandine a great deal more difficult than she had found her in Munich. The girl was silent at times when her mother would prefer her to be talkative, and talkative at times when her mother would prefer to be allowed some peace.

Mrs Benyon was beginning to find traipsing round Europe after her painter daughter some-what of a trial. She would only just have made friends in some new neighbourhood – settled down to a delicious set of interesting and lively relationships – when, at Celandine's say-so, they would have to up sticks and go somewhere else. She was hoping that she could now settle down to life in an easy-to-run apartment in Paris, but she could not help fearing that her hope would soon be shattered.

'Hold the sewing nearer to your face, if you would, Mother.'

Celandine, enlarging spectacles poised on her nose, leaned forward, frowned and then began once more to apply her pencil.

'How ever many of these preparatory sketches do you have to do, dear?'

'A great many, Mother.'

There was a long silence during which Mrs Benyon silently bemoaned the fact that she was not actually allowed to stitch, but only to look as if she was stitching. She felt it would be less of a strain if she could actually sew, instead of just posing with a needle and thread held up to her face. She wondered if she could say as much to Celandine, and then realised that such was Celandine's utterly selfish artistic resolve, it would make very little difference if she did pluck up the courage to complain. She resolved instead to speak about something else.

'Your sister is coming to Paris next week, Celandine. Do you think you will be able to spare some time to take her shopping, and to the opera?'

Inwardly Celandine sighed sharply. She wanted to tell her mother not to speak about anything, but above all not to bring up the subject of her married half-sister, for just the thought of her half-sister made Celandine's heart sink to her boots.

'Of course I will be pleased to take Agnes shopping and to the opera, Mother,' she lied, none the less managing to sound as pleasant as possible. 'But I'm sure she would probably be far happier going with *you*.'

Agnes, the sole product of Jacques Delors Benyon's unhappily short first marriage to a beautiful young French girl from Avignon, was a great deal older than Celandine. She had married a provincial doctor at a very young age and borne him two children. Celandine, the product of her father's second marriage, had finally had to concede that, despite all her efforts, she could not find favour with Agnes. Aside from being violently possessive of their joint father's memory, Agnes tended, for some illogical reason, to be just as possessive over her stepmother as she was sentimental about the mother she could hardly remember.

'I am sure Agnes would like you to take her shopping, Celandine.'

'I hate to disagree with you, Mother, but I am quite sure that she would not. I am quite sure that she would prefer to go with you.'

Mrs Benyon put down her sewing. She was tired. She was tired of posing for Celandine. She was also tired of trying to reconcile Celandine and Agnes.

'I must go and see if Marie is doing what she should,' she said, rising, putting her sewing aside, and thankfully removing her spectacles.

Celandine was left staring moodily at her

drawing. It was better than it had been, but not as good as it should be. She stood up and went to the salon window.

Outside, Paris was busying itself in its usual way, horses, carriages, and beautifully dressed women hurrying through the street below, enjoying the warm weather, their lighter clothes, the idea that soon they would be leaving Paris for their country houses. Why did Agnes have to do the reverse of what everyone else did? Why could she not go to the country in June? Why did she have to come to Paris? Paris was always empty of everyone except the concierges by the end of June.

After lunch Celandine would go to the Louvre, if only to get away from her mother, and the thought of Agnes arriving from Avignon. If only Celandine did not know exactly how she would be, exactly how the visit would progress, exactly what Agnes would say and do.

First of all Agnes would look Celandine up and down, and no matter what she was wearing would make it plain from her look that she did not in any way approve. No one ever wore anything that Agnes liked, it was just a fact. Next she would bustle towards Mrs Benyon and throwing her arms round her would kiss her as if she had not expected to see her ever, ever again.

The next victim would be Marie. Agnes loved to flatter the maid with her attentions, her enquiries after her health. She would ask tenderly after Marie's parents, her nephews, even her godchildren, before exclaiming over the arrangements in the guest bedroom. The apartment, the flowers, the food, everything would be commented on and praised, causing everyone to sigh inwardly with relief, for Agnes pleased was always a very pretty sight. Unhappily, however, as Celandine well knew, this would be the calm before the storm, for as the days of her visit progressed, Agnes would gradually make it quite plain to one and all that there were things that were not right, things that she, Agnes, could make right.

Her eyes would seize on a cushion which it would turn out was definitely *not* the right colour to go with the curtains. Next it would be a casserole that was always made *much* better at her house. After which it would transpire that a wine was far too heavy to go with the casserole and Marie too slow serving at table. She would then discover that really Mother had taken to wearing fabrics that were too drab for her colouring, and Celandine a street dress that was by far too ordinary.

All in all, whether she had been staying with them in Europe or America, once Agnes had departed back to Avignon Celandine and her mother would always be left with the realisation that their life, which they had only days before found pleasant and well ordered, was in fact chaotic and in bad taste, something which could, of course, not be said of Agnes's own dear home life. For, as all of Avignon must know by now,

Agnes's children were perfect, her husband was perfect, her house was beautifully run, and as far as taste was concerned – well, taste actually began with Agnes.

'Where to now, dearest?'

Now that lunch was over Mrs Benyon found herself looking Celandine's street dress up and down, as she waited for the inevitable reply.

'Back to the Louvre, Mother. I really have to set myself to work longer hours these coming days, you know. The term is finishing, and all the studios will soon be closing down for the summer, so I must take advantage of the remaining time.'

Mrs Benyon nodded before deciding to take ruthless advantage of Celandine's departing figure. As the door to the street started to close behind her daughter, she said, 'You know, I have just received another letter from Agnes, while you were changing, Celandine. It appears that not only is she coming to stay, but she is also bringing the boys with her. For a fortnight.'

The door opened again, very, very slowly.

'Both the children? For a fortnight?'

Mrs Benyon nodded slowly. 'Yes, both of them,' she agreed, trying not to sound as depressed as she felt.

'Will that not be a trifle tiring for you, Mother?'

They both knew from Celandine's tone that as far as the prospective visit of her half-sister was concerned she was already counting herself out.

She could just about tolerate Agnes, but her two sons were, to put it bluntly, almost unbearable.

'I am sure that Agnes will want to take them out and about – to the Bois de Bologne, the Bastille, the . . . Louvre. *You* could take them to the Louvre, Celandine.'

'Oh, I do not think that they would at all enjoy the Louvre, Mother,' Celandine said, far too hastily, even for her own ears. 'It would be very . . .' She paused. 'It would be all too confining for them, really it would. What I cannot understand is why Agnes would want to come to Paris in the summer, least of all bringing two boys, at a time when everyone else, with the single exception of ourselves and the mice, is fleeing the place.'

'It seems,' Mrs Benyon held up her latest letter and stared at it a little hopelessly, 'it seems that she longs to see us all.'

Celandine frowned. It did not sound in the least like Agnes, but if Celandine was to get any drawing done *at all* it would be best to seem to accept this notion.

'I dare say you can get her to see reason, and not stay for a full two weeks, Mother. We are after all hoping to rent somewhere in the country, despite its being so difficult at this time of year, with everything taken.'

Mrs Benyon nodded. The door closed. She stared at it for a few seconds. She never could understand why Agnes, who was her husband's daughter, was so attached to her. After all, she

105

was only Agnes's stepmother. It was, well, almost unnatural.

Celandine was about to burst through the doors of the revered Drawing Room at the Louvre museum before she remembered, just in time, to tiptoe into the still, silent atmosphere. She was so preoccupied by the ghastly thought of Agnes and her boys coming to stay that she hardly noticed who was in the room, but crept to her familiar station feeling as if she had been pursued all the way from the apartment by the Furies, which in a way she had been, for she was sure that the Furies of *thought* could be as destructive as the wretched creatures themselves.

Before starting work she always sat quite still, calming herself, trying to find her spiritual centre. Only after this did she pick up her pencil and start work. On this occasion she had only just finished praying for inspiration, and had not yet picked up her pencil, when she became aware that someone was staring at her. She turned slowly to see the tall, dark young man who had only the day before been guilty of the same behaviour drawing her again.

She frowned at him. He smiled. She dropped her eyes and picked up her own pencil. Really, it was too much to find, yet again, that she was acting as some stranger's model. She turned back to her drawing, frowning, at the same time realising that she was powerless to do anything about it. After all, anyone could draw anyone, or

106

anything, for that matter; permission was not needed. It was a fact that so long as she was seated at her work she could find herself acting as an involuntary model for anyone else in the room and would be powerless to do anything about it. Her frown lightened as a novel thought occurred to her. It was an idea that should have come to her long before, and, when all was said and done, hardly original. She moved her drawing stool slightly, and directing her gaze across the room at the young man she smiled openly at him before picking up her own pencil and starting to draw *him*. After all, two could play at this lark.

As she turned to face him, and started to sketch what she saw, Celandine quickly discovered that the face was actually quite worth a study. First of all it had that all-important mark of intelligence, a high forehead, from which the thick dark hair was swept back, and the nose, though large, was straight and set above a nicely shaped mouth. But what dominated the whole was the eyes, bright and humorous, but at the same time questioning as if the owner had seen something on the horizon to which he was quite determined to draw near before too long.

After half an hour during which Celandine finally found herself concentrating less on her subject than on the vase beside which he had been sitting, she heard a voice behind her whispering, 'That's far too flattering.'

'Forgive me, but this is private.'

'Nothing is private about my face, made-moiselle. My face is for the world to see, I do assure you.'

'Tit for tat then, sir. I have been subjected to your pencil for far too long. It is only fair that you, in your turn, should become my victim.'

They were both whispering, but Celandine's whisper was as indignant in tone as her model's was quietly humorous.

'Yes, I do see that, but nevertheless your depiction is far too flattering.'

'Shsh.' A tall, well-dressed man with black hair seated nearby raised a mocking eyebrow in their direction before turning back to his drawing.

'Sorry, Alfred – I forgot you have such poor concentration that even a leaf stirring can break it.' The young man executed a small, equally mocking bow, before turning back to Celandine. 'Come and have an ice cream or coffee with me, please? We can argue better in a café.'

Celandine knew her mother would certainly not approve of her going to a pavement café, so of course the invitation was simply irresistible.

'Oh, very well,' she whispered back.

Outside he put up a large umbrella against the light, early summer rain and walked care-fully along beside her, keeping her on his inside, shielding her from the mud and debris that was flying near the edge of the pavement, not to mention the all too present gentlemen's *pissoirs* that dominated the sides of the roads.

'Have you been in Paris long, Miss . . . ?'

'Benyon. Celandine Benyon.'

'Those sound to be French names.'

'My father was French, my mother is American.'

She smiled briefly up at him. It was a challenging smile and they both knew it.

'And you, monsieur?'

'Well, as I dare say you might have guessed, I am English, and Irish. Or Irish and English, depending on where I am at the time of speaking.'

Celandine carefully lifted her skirts as they approached a road crossing. 'And your name is?'

'Sheridan Montague Robertson.'

'How do you do, Sheridan Montague Robertson.'

'How do you do, Celandine Benyon.'

He stepped in front of her briefly as they came to a bustling roadside café. 'Pierre? Pierre?' He looked round, clapping his hands lightly.

'Monsieur Robertson—' The waiter was at his side in a moment.

'A table for two, Pierre.'

Sheridan nodded at the money in his hand, and Pierre, quite obviously well used to the routine, took the money with practised ease and showed him to a table from which he deftly removed the notice of occupation, concealing it in the pocket of his *garçon*'s apron. A look of quite false concern came into his eyes as he pulled out two chairs for Sheridan and Celandine.

'Your usual, monsieur, coffee and ice cream for two?' he offered.

'You know me too well, Pierre,' Sheridan told him, as the waiter scribbled on a piece of paper.

'You obviously come here quite often, Monsieur Robertson.'

Sheridan smiled a smile that seemed to Celandine to be meant to be enigmatic but which she felt she could interpret all too easily. The waiter had been too practised in his greeting, too assiduous in his attentions. It was immediately obvious that this was Mr Sheridan Montague Robertson's lair, somewhere he could lure young artistic ladies of his acquaintance.

'To be there when the sun is up, to be there when the moment is right, to be there when love strikes, but most of all to know it, that is the secret of life,' Sheridan announced to Celandine as he quickly stepped in front of the waiter and pulled out the rounded back of the café chair for his companion.

'That is a quotation from someone?'

'From no one. It is just my belief.'

Celandine decided to ignore this. 'Well now.' She stared across the table at Sheridan's bulging artist's bag. 'You have seen my drawing of you; it is only fair if I see your drawing of me.'

'I do not know you well enough, Miss Benyon.'

'If you know me well enough to draw me, then you know me well enough to let me see the result of your efforts. After all, you have the advantage of me.'

Sheridan frowned. 'I do?'

'Yes. You have been working on your drawing

a great deal longer than I have been working on mine.'

'Oh, very well.' Sheridan bent down and produced his sketchbook. 'It will probably reveal more of me than it does of you,' he said, smiling, and at the same time flicking through his drawings until he came to it. 'Ah, here we are.'

Celandine found her heart sinking just a little. After all, if he made her look more plain than she felt herself to be, or more cross than she knew herself to be, it might be difficult to eat an ice cream in front of him, but rather more easy to tip it into his lap. So it was with some apprehension that her eyes dropped to the page in Sheridan's sketchpad to see herself as Sheridan Montague Robertson saw her.

Later she found herself creeping into the apartment, hoping against hope that no one would be about. She paused, listening, only for her heart to sink, not simply at the sound of feminine laughter from the salon but also at the sound of other voices – and not just any voices, but boys' voices. Her heart sank at the realisation that Agnes's sons had arrived, bringing with them not just their mother, but also their conviction that the world had to stop for them, or else they would know the reason why.

She walked quickly down the corridor, hoping to get to her bedroom before seeing Agnes, and passing on the way the chaos of what was obviously a very recent arrival. Her half-sister's portmanteaux, opened, with dresses already draped over the bed; her nephews' suitcases, their toys already set about the floor; cups of milk on trays, half-eaten biscuits left on the dressing table so carefully laid out by Marie.

She hurried into her own room. It was too terrible. They had only just received Agnes's letter, and yet here she was. Celandine sat down hard on her bed. The weeks of summer in deserted Paris seemed to stretch ahead of her in an acre of unrelieved boredom accompanied, without any doubt, by the inescapable sound of Agnes's voice. She could see herself walking in the Bois de Bologne, not having a moment to sit and draw, being forced to admire the boys, endlessly and pointlessly – while listening to her sister talking the kind of trivia to which Celandine found it so difficult to respond. It was as if they were thinking and speaking entirely different languages, which of course they were.

Not that Celandine imagined that art was more important than the bringing up of children, or being the wife of a provincial doctor, for of course she could quite see that, certainly as far as Agnes was concerned, it was not. It was just that she found it impossible to speak that particular language, a language that centred on vague rivalries over children's achievements, or husbands' monetary success.

Agnes on the other hand could not be expected to be in the least fascinated by a conversation which examined the new influence of the

Japanese style on French painting, or to become exercised over whether being rejected for exhibition by the all important *Salon* – the great grand arbiters of French artistic taste – could in reality be construed as a backhanded compliment, for Celandine was only too aware that Agnes had always considered her half-sister's art to be faintly absurd.

'Women artists, as everyone knows, can never sell a painting, for everyone knows that a man would never wish to hang a painting signed by a female on his wall. He would know that to do so would be to invite ridicule from his friends, and suspicion from his wife.'

At the memory of this warning, repeated by Agnes on all her previous visits, Celandine's stomach contracted. It was difficult enough having a half-sister at the best of times, but having Agnes as a half-sister was a dire warning never to marry, for it seemed to Celandine that everyone who married became like Agnes.

Whenever Agnes came to stay with her stepmother and sister, which she regularly did, Celandine had noted that in her half-sister's presence everyone was finally reduced to a dull, accepting silence. It was shaming, it was embarrassing, but it was the truth. Neither Mrs Benyon nor Celandine possessed the kind of moral fibre that could summon enough energy to fight Agnes's unending criticisms, silent or otherwise, or even her sometimes quite open spite.

It was always the same sequence of events.

Agnes would arrive full of bonhomie, looking, and quite obviously feeling, radiant – in sharp contrast to Mrs Benyon, who, long before the visit, would have become pale with exhaustion and anxiety from constantly wondering what, if anything, would or could please Agnes. It was not that Celandine's mother was a weak character, it was just that Agnes seemed to exert some sort of awful power over her when she willed the older woman to stand up and fight for herself, something which Mrs Benyon, for her own reasons, resolutely refused to do.

Dinner on the first night of Agnes's visit was, more often than not, cheerful. Everyone determined that things would be different *this* time, that *this* time Agnes would not find fault, that Marie's choice of menu would be perfect, that the wines accompanying the food would be at just the right temperatures, and the cheese *à point*.

Today, it was a warm evening and Marie and her newly hired acolytes issued forth from the kitchen with the *hors d'oeuvres*, a plate carefully arranged with mixed delights, varying from olives to specially prepared cold meats and hard boiled eggs stuffed with mayonnaise and chopped parsley. A slight breeze was blowing the dark dining-room curtains. Outside, the Parisian pigeons cooed on the rooftops of neighbouring buildings. In the courtyard below there was a low murmur of voices; probably a party of people from some neighbouring apartment going out to dinner. For a fleeting second Celandine felt a dart of envy. How nice it would be to be going out with a party of friends rather than sitting waiting for Agnes to help herself from the proffered plate, while Marie's youngest protégée reverentially offered her the appropriate serving spoons.

The spoons were taken up; they hovered over the large blue and white patterned plate, only to be finally lowered after only a few seconds. All eyes followed Agnes's hands as she helped herself to a mere half of an *oeuf mimosa*.

'Is that all you are having?' Mrs Benyon's eyes registered frozen fear. Such summary rejection on the first evening was unusual, even for Agnes.

Agnes gave her well-practised pained smile.

'That is all I can manage, really. I have to watch my *avoirdupois*.' She looked across pointedly at her stepmother's burgeoning figure. 'My darling husband does not like me to gain weight. He thinks it so bad for the heart. Besides, the *hors d'oeuvres* in Avignon is unsurpassable.'

Celandine looked across the dining room at Marie, whose face was a picture of suppressed fury. Noting this, Celandine, when her turn came, quickly helped herself to something of everything.

'Gracious me, Marie,' she called across the table to the infuriated housekeeper. 'This looks so good I am afraid I shall be coming back for more.'

She saw a bead of sweat appear on her poor mother's upper lip, which Mrs Benyon wiped away with her heavy linen napkin, before she too carefully helped herself to a liberal amount from the serving plate.

'Celandine is right, this looks *so* good,' she murmured hopelessly.

Agnes made a point of toying with her egg half, staring at it in a concentrated way as if she was quite sure that the egg was probably Chinese and very old, or the recipe imperfectly executed. After which, since the others were busy eating, she stared round the room at the furnishings.

'What a pity you could not rent a more elegant apartment, but I dare say you left Munich so quickly, in such a hurry, that you were forced to take the first one offered to you,' she murmured as she sat back to watch her stepmother and sister still gamely attacking what was on their plates. 'The Countess de Charbonne de Molinaire, whom I shall be calling on some time during my visit before she leaves for her château at St Cloud, now *she* has a beautiful apartment. Really beautiful. Not dark like this, but full of light, and of course the furnishings are *ravissants*.'

Agnes always pronounced the French word for ravishing in a particular way, splitting it into three very separate syllables: *'ra – viss – ant'*.

Celandine avoided looking at either her mother or Marie, principally because she still had so much on her plate that she knew if she did not carry on eating they might all still be at table at midnight. Nevertheless the exaggerated pronunciation, the bored sigh as the other two women, already suitably chastened by Agnes's implied criticism, fell to silently chewing their way through each course to the accompanying sound of Agnes's feet moving, restlessly and audibly, under the table – it was all so horribly predictable.

Celandine sighed inwardly, and very heavily. Agnes's attitude was already so hostile. The prospect of a whole fortnight of such behaviour held about as much attraction for her sister as being flung into a bullfighting ring without cape or sword. Course after course, in the French tradition, now followed, all of it only picked at with exaggerated fastidiousness, and without comment, by Agnes. Finally, after the coffee had been taken into the main salon, the dining-room door was slammed with awful finality.

Mrs Benyon's eyes flew to Celandine's. Marie never slammed a door behind her. It had never happened before, not even during a visit from Agnes. Marie was meticulous about such matters. They both immediately suspected what such a sound might mean: that unless Celandine followed her out to the kitchen and placated her, Mrs Benyon would shortly lose her devoted maid-cook-confidante, upon whom she depended for so much companionship and comfort.

'Marie . . .'

'Mademoiselle?'

The dialogue inevitably began with Marie handing in her notice, which Celandine accepted, before telling her that the dinner had been above reproach, each course more marvellous than the last. Celandine, a food lover, carefully commended the choice of sauce to go with the beef, the exquisite taste of the *haricots verts*. Every aspect of the dinner was gone into and carefully praised. The dialogue inevitably ended with Marie rescinding her notice, and Celandine retiring to her bedroom with a pounding head, for what with the food and the wine, with Agnes and Marie, with her poor mother taut with nerves, the whole experience had been horrid.

The following morning Celandine bathed and dressed at some speed, and bolted out of the door without seeing either Mrs Benyon or Agnes, for the thought of having breakfast with Agnes and her boys was tantamount to torture.

Once outside she fairly ran down the street, pausing only when she came to the corner of the road, where she slowed down. It was as if she was being pursued by Agnes's ego, an ego as large as the Louvre museum, but unfortunately a great deal less interesting.

The whole of my life I have had to contend with Agnes's ego, she silently told the already bustling street. *Agnes, always Agnes! I want so much to love her as I should, but I can't because really—* She stopped suddenly as she found herself standing outside the café where she had enjoyed ice cream and coffee with Sheridan Robertson the day before. *I can't love Agnes*, she went on, speaking silently to herself, imagining each word being slowly articulated, *I can't love Agnes because – she – does – not – love – me*. The realisation, as well as perhaps a possible solution, sank slowly into her head, before seeming to make its way down through her whole body. *How silly of me! Of course! I can't love Agnes because she – does – not – love – me. Or Mother. She possibly does not even like us, now I come to think of it. So why does she come and stay with us?* Because *she doesn't like us. It's her way of making sure that we feel unsure, lowered in our opinions of ourselves.*

A voice spoke behind her, but since she was still so preoccupied with her own thoughts it was a few seconds before she turned.

'So, you too come here for breakfast?'

It was Sheridan, busily lifting his artist's hat, his smiling face exuding what, even after such a short acquaintance, Celandine realised was his own particular form of warmth and exuberance. As if he too had been up much earlier than usual, and as a reward had found out the secret of life.

'Mr Montague Robertson.'

'Miss Benyon.'

Celandine wanted to look serious, already concentrating on the day ahead, on the study of, as well as the copying of, the old masters in the Drawing Room, but instead she found herself smiling, and a great deal more broadly than she would have thought possible after an evening with Agnes and her barely veiled contempt.

'You are here for breakfast? How civilised.'

He stepped back to allow Celandine to go ahead to the table at which they had previously sat, and which, yet again, had the 'occupied' notice on its top.

Sheridan nodded towards it, and the waiter carefully placed the notice on another table.

'I have them under my large painter's thumb here,' he confided, as they both sat down. 'Now, for your breakfast you will have the same as me, no?' He did not wait for Celandine to reply. 'You will have yards of black coffee and a brioche and butter with honey, *n'est-ce pas*?'

Celandine shook her head firmly. 'No.' She looked up at the waiter. 'I will have a bowl of hot chocolate and a *petite baguette* with no butter, no jam. Just on its own.'

The waiter nodded. 'For Mademoiselle then, the breakfast of *les enfants*,' he noted without sarcasm.

Sheridan frowned. 'A child's breakfast? Now what does that say about you, I wonder?'

'It could say that I am in a particularly childish mood.'

'Or it could say that you are in need of comfort.'

'That is quite true.' For a second Celandine looked so thoughtful that Sheridan would have liked to take her on his knee.

'I am glad you looked more cheerful when I drew you,' he told her, opening his newspaper and glancing at the headline.

'You made me look far too pretty.'

'I did not make you look anything, Miss Benyon, I drew you as I saw you, I do assure you.'

'You drew me as you saw me, and I drew you as I saw you.'

Sheridan raised his eyes from *Le Figaro*. 'You made me look too intelligent – no, you did,' he went on before Celandine could protest. 'You made me look as if I was the sort of fellow who could understand *Le Figaro*, which I know very well I cannot. I follow five words in ten in written French, whereas my spoken Frenchy is perfect.'

To distract herself from the concentrated look in her companion's eyes, Celandine reached down into her artist's bag and took out her drawing book.

'One should never talk at breakfast,' she told him, 'particularly not to a person who is trying to improve his French.'

She nodded at the newspaper a little in the manner of a schoolteacher encouraging her pupil to re-apply himself to his homework, and started to draw him once again, this time while he was too busy reading his newspaper to pay much attention. She became so engrossed in her work that the arrival of her hot chocolate and baguette seemed to act as nothing more or less than an interruption.

Nevertheless they were both hungry, and ate their individual breakfasts with relish, but as soon as Sheridan had finished, safe in the knowledge that no one around them would understand what he was saying, he started to fantasise about the customers at nearby tables.

'Don't look, but the man of round girth who

arrived just now, he has just had a quarrel with his wife.'

'How do you know?'

'I know because he has just taken out his bad mood on Pierre.'

'How do you know *that*?'

'Because Pierre has just pulled a face behind his back.'

'What have he and his wife quarrelled about, do you think?'

'Well now, I would say that she has accused him of infidelity, which he has of course hotly denied. He is still incensed, but as soon as Pierre brings him coffee and croissants, he will calm down, and when he has calmed down – despite his undoubted innocence – unfortunately the idea of infidelity will have started to take hold, have some undeniable appeal for him. He will start to think, *Well, if I am to be accused of this, well, I might as well be hung for a sheep as a lamb.*'

'How do you know all this?'

'Very easily. To begin with he came into the café in a hurried manner, and pulled out his chair without waiting for Pierre. Then he scowled around him after he had finished ordering.'

There was a long pause.

'Ah, now,' Sheridan said with justifiable triumph. 'Just as I said he would, he has just seen you, and his eyes have turned as bright as the lamps in the Place Pigalle. Not only are they lighting up, but they are dwelling lingeringly on you.' Sheridan looked at Celandine, all false innocence. 'He must like dark hair and large eyes, not to mention a slim waist, and hands with long tapered fingers. He must like a young woman to look intelligent, and to dress in a way that does not attract too much attention to herself, but is stylish enough to make her a good subject to draw.' Satisfied that he had made his point, Sheridan returned to *Le Figaro*.

'Do you sympathise with him, with the husband?'

'I do *not*,' Sheridan told her, lowering the newspaper again and suddenly sounding more Irish than he quite intended.

'Oh, do you *not*?' Celandine asked him, relieved to be able to mimic him.

'No, I do *not* sympathise with him, and neither do I sympathise with his wife.'

'For the reason that?'

'For the simple reason that, if we are right, and I am quite sure we are, then the wife *has* behaved badly, because she has allowed herself to voice suspicions for which she has not the slightest evidence. He, on the other hand, having had his male pride dented, is now looking around him as if her silly accusations can justify his behaving in an even sillier fashion. As if her jealousy can, in some way, free him. So, no, I do not have the slightest sympathy with either of them. Pierre?' Sheridan folded his newspaper and waved to the waiter. 'I wish to pay, Pierre!'

'You wish to pay, Monsieur Robertson? *Enfin*, then I know you can have no French blood!'

123

Pierre took the money proffered to him. 'Only an Englishman *insists* on paying!'

'Pierre, I have told you a hundred times. I am an *Irishman*. From *Ireland*.'

'You are from Iceland?'

'No, Pierre. Not Iceland.' Sheridan rolled his eyes mock-furiously to indicate to Celandine that it was an old routine. 'I come from Ireland. Ireland where there are no snakes and the shamrock grows – and no, you can't put your *sauce vinaigrette* on it . . .'

'You don't sound Irish,' Celandine said, collecting up her things. 'You sound English to me, except for just then, when you did sound Irish.'

'That is because you are an American, Miss Benyon. Americans sound Irish to the English, whereas the Irish sound English to Americans.'

'I think you may have something there.'

They strolled past the table occupied by the Frenchman about whom they had only just finished speculating. The subject of their fantasy immediately raised his eyes all too appreciatively to Celandine.

'I told you,' Sheridan sighed, once they were safely past his table. 'I am never wrong about behaviour. As soon as you are out of sight, he will probably try to join that other young woman at her table.'

'I think you're quite wrong about him. I think he is probably single, and very lonely.'

'He was wearing a wedding ring.'

'How would you know that? When we passed

him he had only removed one of his gloves. His wedding-ring hand was still gloved.'

Sheridan stopped and stared at Celandine. 'I was quite sure that I had caught you out. No, sorry, I had *hoped* that I had caught you out, but it seems I have *not*.'

'No, you have *not*.' Celandine mimicked his Irish intonation once again. 'Besides, there is no reason, surely, that I should not prove to be as observant as you, is there?'

Sheridan thought for a moment. 'Well, no, I suppose there is not,' he agreed, but the look in his eyes became wary.

Celandine walked ahead of him, her slender body moving gracefully between the tables, Sheridan following, until they found themselves on the pavement, at which point Sheridan started to walk on her outside.

'I do hope you are not an active member of some sort of suffragist women's organisation,' he stated, a little plaintively. 'So many young women I have met in Paris lately turn out to be furiously involved with something very fierce to do with the sisterhood of women, and – of all myths – freedom. It quite makes my head spin when they talk, really it does.'

Celandine shook her head. 'American women have no need of such things,' she told him grandly. 'We are already far more liberated than European women. Why, my mother told me only the other day that when an Englishwoman has her purse stolen and the theft is reported to the police, the purse must be reported as being the *property of her husband*! An Englishwoman today does not even own her own purse! She is therefore no better than a slave, for like a slave she owns nothing, has nothing she can call her own.'

She shrugged her shoulders expressively as if to say that she was very glad that she was not English, and as she did so, Sheridan stopped walking.

'I am so glad to hear that you have no need to be fanatically inclined, because in that case you won't object to what I am about to do. Wait here for a second, if you would not mind?'

Celandine did as he asked, staring round her at the blue sky, at the people passing, at the old buildings, and feeling an inconsequential rush of happiness. She knew that somehow everything in her life was about to change, but just for that minute it was quite still, full of the kinds of colours that morning brings before too many people are about, before the pulse of life started quickening and blurring the beauty around her. And then Sheridan thrust a bouquet of flowers into her hand.

'Happy birthday!'

Celandine stared from the flowers to him, and back again. 'Gracious, but how beautiful. Thank you! They are beautiful. But – you must know, I have to tell you – it is not my birthday.'

Sheridan placed his panama hat at a rakish angle. 'As far as I am concerned today is most definitely your birthday,' he stated with authority. 'And tomorrow, and the day after. That is the kind of person you are meant to be. I am sure of it. From the first moment that I started to draw you in the Louvre, I knew you to be the kind of person who should have a birthday every day.'

They walked along, smiling at each other. Celandine looked from him to the flowers and then up at him again, and down at the flowers. She did not know why he had bought her such a beautiful bouquet, but she sensed that to ask him would spoil both the fragility and the delicate sensuality of the gesture; that it would take away from the gaiety of the morning if she said anything more.

And so they progressed, in happy silence, until they came to the Louvre museum, and the true business of the day began.

When Celandine returned to the apartment much later, it was teatime, but not just any teatime, one of Mrs Benyon's At Home afternoons when ladies called, took tea, engaged in serious, vaguely intellectual conversations or lighthearted chatter, depending on their characters, and after not more than twenty minutes left to call on some other lady also holding an At Home on the same day.

Celandine did not like tea, nor did she enjoy wearing a smart afternoon dress and pretending not to be bored, but, having missed out on the doubtful delight of lunching to the sound of Agnes holding forth on life in Avignon, she knew that it was her duty to help her mother out.

She changed into something more demure, more suitable for taking loathsome tea, and was approaching the door of the main salon when Agnes's voice, long before Celandine had entered the room, started to float towards her.

'As I said to the Countess de Charbonne de Molinaire on my last visit to Paris, there are very few pieces of porcelain that I would wish to acquire now. Meissen of course, and Limoges, but not all of Limoges, and nothing would induce me to buy English pieces. They are so lacking in delicacy. Always dogs or peasants, or cows. They seem to love cows. Not deer, if you please, but cows!'

She laughed delicately, but not delicately enough to stop at least two of the visiting ladies immediately replacing their teacups, standing up and walking to the side of the salon where they had placed their parasols. The mention of a cow had offended their sensibilities. No one could think of a cow without thinking of its udders. As one woman they picked up their parasols and with restrained gratitude excused themselves to their hostess.

Celandine watched, struggling with the anger she was feeling on behalf of her mother. Poor Mother, as always when Agnes was around, had acquired a moist upper lip, not to mention a flushed face.

'Oh dear, you too are going, are you?' she asked more than a little hopelessly, as, after all too short a moment, two more ladies collected their parasols and took an abrupt leave of Mrs Benyon.

'Oh dear, Belle-mère, I hope I have not said something I should not?' Agnes asked, after glancing around the now empty salon.

Celandine bit her lip, and half closed her eyes. The very fact that her half-sister seemed to take delight in every now and then addressing her stepmother in French as 'mother-in-law' always vexed Celandine.

'Why do you not tell her that you are not her *mother-in-law*, Mother? It would be more natural for her to address you as "Maman".'

Celandine and her mother had retreated to Mrs Benyon's dressing room, where Celandine now found herself speaking in an infuriated if hushed tone to her mother.

'Celandine, dearest, what does it matter? As your darling father would have said, "What does it matter in the scheme of things?"'

'It matters because she is deliberately trying to upset you.'

'Oh, no, I am sure you are wrong. I would not say that, not for one moment, Celandine, dearest. Really not. Agnes is very kind-hearted. Think how she moved heaven and earth when I was ill last year, bringing her husband to my bedside. So considerate.'

'You were only two kilometres apart at the

time, Mother, and he got your diagnosis all wrong.'

Celandine sighed inwardly. It was quite useless to expect her mother to accept that Agnes was actually quite spiteful, and, in truth, not only was it useless, but it was not really her concern. Agnes was her mother's stepdaughter far more than she was Celandine's half-sister.

Perhaps it was this feeling of impatience that gave Celandine the courage to broach the next subject, a subject that she knew might not prove to be very popular with her mother.

'Mother—'

'I do hope that those ladies did not leave so quickly, those ladies who called on me this afternoon, I do hope they were not *offended* by Agnes's mention of . . .' she lowered her voice, 'her mention of *la vache*?'

'No, I am quite sure they did not mind Agnes's mentioning a cow in the drawing room,' Celandine said, lying. 'Besides, it was not as if you mentioned the animal, Mother. It was Agnes, not you.'

'I suppose that's true, dear, but they did leave rather swiftly – after only five minutes, which is unusual, even for Paris, do admit.'

Her mother picked up her lace handkerchief and waved it a little in front of her face in the manner of a fan. Celandine cleared her throat and quickly changed the subject, realising that she could take ruthless advantage of the confusion her mother was feeling.

'Mother, you – er – know there is a summer school in Brittany? I have mentioned it to you before, I think. Well, I was hoping that I could join it, if you remember, but then I found that it was all booked out. But now it seems that there is one place left, after all, and that I *can* go, in the company of this other girl I have met at the Louvre. We could go together and we will be painting in the new manner, outside, *en plein air*, they call it. Do you think I might go, Mother? I do feel it will do my style so much good. This other girl, you see, has the same ideas on art as I have, so it would be very beneficial.'

Happily for Celandine her mother was not listening, being too busy worrying about whether or not Agnes's mention of a cow at an At Home had put up backs.

'The mention of *la vache*, well, it is not usually done to mention it in polite circles, I feel. But I dare say Agnes does not realise how very sensitive Parisian ladies can be. It is not that a cow is sacred in France as it is sacred in parts of India, it is because it is a very common word, and, as I understand it, a word that can be used in a pejorative way. That is why it is never mentioned *dans le salon*, in polite company. Still, I should have thought that dear Agnes might have known that; except of course the genteel perceptions of Society are very different at Avignon, as I remember.'

'So it will be all right if I do go to Brittany for the summer school there, Mother?'

'Yes, of course, dearest. Much better that you should get out of Paris, and besides it will free another room, which might be very useful. I did not tell you, dearest, that Agnes's dear Tomas is coming to stay at the apartment next week. It seems he is able to join the boys and Agnes here, and they will be able to make sorties of an educational kind. It will be lovely for them all, I feel, to have the freedom to come and go as they wish.'

Celandine immediately felt a mixture of relief, guilt and anger. Relief that her mother had agreed to her going to the summer school in Brittany, guilt because she had turned Sheridan into a girl she was studying with, and anger that Agnes and Tomas were about to take Mother for their usual ride. She knew very well that, comfortably off though her mother might be, she could ill afford to keep taking Agnes and her family out to restaurants and paying for them to go on excursions, but that undoubtedly was what she would be required to do, since Agnes was adept, if not masterly, at playing on Mrs Benyon's feelings, managing somehow to make her stepmother feel guilty that her father had remarried.

'So I really can go, can I, Mother?'

'Of course you can go to your summer school with your friend, dearest. Much the best, as I said.'

Mrs Benyon continued to wave her lace handkerchief in front of her face, which was

132

probably just as well because it meant she missed seeing the look of excitement that came into her daughter's eyes. A young horse being let out into acres of spring grass could not have felt more joyous than Celandine at that moment.

Happily it did not take her long to pack up for her departure to the summer school, which was fortunate, for by tackling everything at the gallop she could avoid the reality of what she was doing. She was taking herself off to Brittany with a single man. If anyone found out she would probably become an outcast, although Sheridan had assured her there were going to be so many other students travelling with them that there could be no suggestion of impropriety on anyone's part.

An overpowering feeling of running away from home, of throwing off all care, suffused Celandine as, hardly more than a day later, and followed by a deferential porter, she walked with Sheridan towards the already crowded train. Heads were hanging out of the windows and beckoning to *'Sheree'*, as some of his fellow students endearingly called him.

'Viens ici, Sheree!'

Celandine thought she could already sense that they were a grand crowd as she stepped into the carriage, followed by Sheridan and the luggage.

'I say, what a capital idea to bring a picnic breakfast,' he enthused as Celandine was carefully handed up her final piece of luggage, a large picnic basket crammed to the top with items of delicious food provided by the ever-solicitous Marie. 'The train stops at various stations on the way to Cancale, but I have to admit I have only to hear a train whistle blow and I become overwhelmed by a prodigious hunger.'

Celandine started to take off the gingham cloths with which Marie had covered the top of the picnic basket. Evidently she had, with some sixth sense, anticipated catering for more than just two girl artists, for the basket was full to the brim with luncheon boxes, themselves crammed with everything from freshly baked rolls to baguettes filled with little pieces of chocolate or ham, and ripe tomatoes, bought from the market that morning, along with more fruit and chocolate and hot coffee.

Nor was Celandine the only person to have brought a picnic from home. Everyone except Sheridan seemed to have thought of bringing something, so that when a great cheer went up as the train eventually pulled out of the station there seemed to Celandine to be a veritable mountain of food in their carriage. Somehow, even so, the chatter increased, and the compartment was soon full of the robust sound of opinions being exchanged.

'Soon we will all be *en plein air*, painting the sea and the sky, and our longing to be one with everything in nature, to make our art as natural as nature, will start to be assuaged.'

'Hark at him!' Alfred Talisman, the tall, handsome, darkly bearded man who had shushed them in the Drawing Room of the Louvre, now winked at Celandine. 'You should have seen him last year – struggling to keep his canvas on his easel. *En plein air*? Thank heavens we *were* in the open air, my dear, for the language was enough to shock an army sergeant.'

Sheridan rolled his eyes at Celandine. 'So who is going to volunteer to buy the picnic lunches on the station?'

Celandine stared back at him. 'Who is going to – buy – *luncheon*?' she asked.

Sheridan peered into the basket. 'Yes, luncheon, because there certainly is not enough here to keep us going, is there, Alfred? Robert? Tom?'

If Celandine had imagined that Sheridan and his friends were teasing her, she was mistaken, for when the train finally steamed into a station around the time of *déjeuner* all three young men jumped off the train, disappearing for a full ten minutes, and only climbing back on board as the train doors were starting to be slammed.

'Gracious, I thought you might have run off—'

Sheridan, his arms full of small boxes, said, 'Quick, take one before I drop them all. There's one for each of us.'

This time the individual picnic boxes were filled with food which could be eaten from the dishes: hot pastas with meat fillings, salad on

135

the side, and small bottles of wine, followed by fresh peaches and small sweet biscuits.

'This is the life, eh?' Sheridan smiled across at Celandine.

She nodded. It certainly seemed to be.

It was evening when they finally arrived at their destination: an old inn in the middle of a village near Cancale.

'Everyone stays at Chez Cécile. Principally because she loves parties and doesn't care what time of the day or night we come in or out, or whom we bring back. She is not only a great lady, she is a great tradition, aren't you, Madame Cécile?' he added as a large lady dressed entirely in black, with only a spotless white lace-trimmed apron to relieve it, sailed into view.

Sheridan gaily kissed the plump, beringed hand held out to him, as Celandine submitted to being given a piercing look from two small, dark brown eyes.

'Ah, very pretty, Monsieur Sheree, very pretty indeed. You 'ave your old room, and you too, Tom, and you, Robert, and Alfred. All of you, upstairs and wash, please! Dinner is at eight o'clock and I do not want to have to tell you to change. Please. Clean shirts, clean hands, for you are not our only guests this evening! I will send Raoul with the rest of your suit-cases.'

Madame Cécile winked at Celandine as she turned away. It was an all-embracing wink that said that since they were the only women

136

present they would have to stand shoulder to shoulder, ranged up against the men-boys.

Celandine, quite tired but still very happy, followed Sheridan up the stairs to the landing.

'Ah, here we are.' He opened a door to a prettily decorated small sitting room, off which was a bedroom, and, turning, smiled at Celandine. 'Now, which bed do you want, my dear?'

Chapter Four

Edith stared across the room. If she had imagined that her new married life would be full of delightful intimacies, fresh discoveries and raptures of a kind of which she had never even dared to dream; that her honeymoon would be spent in loving her new husband, getting to know him in every way, then she was already sadly mistaken. Her arrival at Helmscote, at a flower-filled house with the fires lit and every possible comfort on hand, might have seemed dreamlike, but what followed over the next few days had been more and more bewildering.

Each morning Napier would rise early and disappear back to his dressing room where, as Mrs George had first indicated to Edith, he would take a freezing-cold bath in a tub set out on the balcony outside the French windows, after which he would walk briskly around the extensive grounds on his own. His strict instructions to Edith in the first days and weeks of her marriage were always to stay in bed until her personal maid, Betty, came to bath and dress her.

It rapidly became a strict routine. Napier would arrive back promptly at nine o'clock from his walk and appear, unsmiling, at their bedroom door ready to escort Edith down to breakfast in the back dining hall. Edith did not have to be told that she must always be ready and waiting on the stroke of the stable clock; she knew from the brooding expression in Napier's eyes that this was expected of her. She also knew that she must look like the wife of a well-to-do personage, but that her morning dress must not be too elaborate, her hair must be simply arranged, and she must have some sewing ready in the morning room, before whose fire she should be prepared to sit and stitch.

But first she had to face communal breakfast in the dining room, where everyone who worked on the estate sat down together. At the start of the meal Napier said grace and the workers sat shoulder to shoulder in silence, waited on by the household staff, who eventually joined them at the long tables.

Breakfast at Helmscote was therefore a strange ceremony, most particularly for a young bride, and one which Edith had already started to dread. The meal, while quite obviously an attempt at democracy, turned out to be, in essence, formal to a degree. Following Napier's begging the Lord, on everyone's behalf, to accept their gratitude for what was before them, the meal began, but because they were eating in front of the master of the house no one actually cared to open his mouth except to put food in it. It was as if the coming together with their master and mistress made all the workers on the estate fall into self-consciousness; indeed, it seemed to Edith that they were always looking round at each other, noting each other's table manners, perhaps afraid that they might get bad marks if they were to fall below some imaginary, self-imposed standard.

From her very first morning Edith had not been able to resist making the comparison with the jolly, hail-fellow-well-met carefree breakfasts of the servants at the Stag and Crown, where it was not unusual for the younger ones to play practical jokes on their elders – changing the sugar for salt, or leaving out the tea from the pot, and other harmless japes. Once grace was out of the way, everyone at the Stag and Crown had swapped stories and told jokes, gossiped and made plans. In contrast to the estate workers at Helmscote they were all able to relax, even though the time they had off to eat was all too short, and they all detested Edith's stepmother. Never mind that the work was hard: when they breakfasted the servants of every age at the old inn made sure to enjoy themselves.

Edith's eyes now travelled round the bedroom. Soon she knew she would hear Betty's discreet knock on the outer door, and then see the black outline of her uniform as she lit the bedroom fire prior to bringing in the copper bath. It was strange to be helped to do something you had always been in the habit of doing for yourself. To have someone hand you each of your silk stockings, to have her brush and arrange your hair for you, do up your clothes, and finally pull your dress into place, twitching and adjusting it before standing back and giving you an approving look. It was as if you were a doll, not a young woman.

This morning it seemed was to be no different. The handing over of the soap and the sponge, the wrapping of the carefully warmed bath towel around Edith's long-limbed body, prior to her stepping carefully out on to the thick, warmed bath mat. It was all so ritualistic, and yet in its way mesmerising. Edith found her mind went into a passive mode, as if she had been drugged in some way, and by allowing the maid to wait on her she had somehow, she did not quite understand how, herself become subservient.

This morning, having allowed herself to be dried, and handed a set of new underwear, Edith waited for Betty to bring her the corset, the horsehair-based bustle, and all the other accoutrements that were necessary to the building of the fashionable dresses that she now wore with such enjoyment. No such items were offered her. Instead, Betty carefully undid some closely wrapped clothing which she had taken from the large, beautifully inlaid wardrobes in the adjoining dressing room.

'What are these?' Edith stared down at the

long, diaphanous garment made of green silk, with floating panels, like nothing she had ever seen before.

'These are for Madam. This morning we are to go to the studio.'

Edith turned and stared at the maid. 'We? You are not coming, are you, Betty? You mean *I* am going, don't you?'

'No, I mean we, madam – I take you to the master's studio, and I arrange you,' Betty said with such sudden firm authority that Edith realised at once that the maid had been through this ritual before, perhaps with other girls.

She stared down at the long gown with its panels and scarves. She had no idea why it filled her with panic, but the fact was that it did: the kind of suffocating panic with which her maid's uniform, when she first wore it as little more than a child, had filled her. She adored the clothes chosen with such care by Miss Bagshaw. She loved hearing the gentle swish-swish of the short trains that fell from her bustle as she crossed rooms or went down corridors in the evenings. The truth was that the wearing of her new, fashionable clothes was one of the real joys that her marriage of a few days had so far brought her.

'Where are you going, Mrs Todd?'

Edith was pulling her dressing wrap round her in a swirl of panic. 'I am going to find Mr Todd, Betty.'

'Mr Todd is not in the house today, madam.'

142

Edith turned slowly, and she knew immediately from the look in her eyes that the maid would think it more than passing strange if the new Mrs Todd was to demand of her, Betty, where her husband might be. After all, Edith was meant to be not just his wife, but the mistress of the house.

'Oh, yes, yes, of course. He told me last night. I quite forgot. It had escaped my mind.'

'The master will be waiting for you in the studio this morning. Waiting to give you breakfast. You are breakfasting together in the studio this morning, remember?'

Edith stared at Betty and then dropped her eyes. She had no idea where Napier's studio might be. She had been so panicked by his attitude to their marriage – the passion in his eyes leading to nothing at all at night, or at any other time; so much did it not correspond to anything she had tried to imagine that marriage might bring – that she had never once thought to ask to see his studio.

'If you stand still I will arrange the gown the way Mr Todd has told me it should be arranged.'

Why had Napier not asked her himself?

The question went round and round in Edith's head as her eyes travelled to the gown, which she already knew she was going to detest. It had little or no shape, except for the wretched panels and the voluminous sleeves – at least she thought they must be sleeves, since they both ended in a gold and green brocade trimming.

Betty was now moving towards the dress with all the determination with which Edith's step-mother had moved towards her maid's uniform six years before.

'If you stand over there, by the window, madam, it would be easier for me to arrange you according to the master's wishes.'

Edith moved towards the window as directed, and after a few seconds the maid followed her with two dressing sticks holding the gown, which she gently lowered over Edith's head.

She had no idea why, but as the silk slid past her face it seemed to Edith that it smelt of carbolic soap, of dust and grime and mud, reminding her with a sudden, convulsing violence of her mother's death, and the ensuing days and weeks which had ended with her being ordered to work in the inn. She felt a suffocating tightening of her throat as a lump came into it and tears threatened, tears that she determinedly fought, only for them to threaten once more. She hated to be made to wear something!

'If Madam would hold out her feet, one by one? I have some beautiful slippers that the master wants you to wear with your gown.'

Edith could hardly see her feet for the emotions that were swamping her slender body, but when she was able, with one great shuddering sigh, to defeat the shaming tears and send them on their way, she could see at once that Betty was right, the gold embroidered slippers were beautiful. Yet Edith knew, even as she stared down at the delicately embroidered Oriental slippers, that she hated them. She hated them as much as she hated the gown, as much as she hated Betty's dressing her in something Miss Bagshaw had not helped her choose.

'Now if Madam would sit down, I will dress her hair as the master wishes it to be dressed.'

Hairbrushes of the softest bristle at the ready, Betty approached her mistress.

'Mr Todd wants your hair to be arranged as loosely as possible.'

The brushes moved through Edith's long, auburn hair with a steady sweeping motion.

'A hundred strokes to make it shine,' Betty murmured appreciatively as she continued the rhythmic brushing.

In her new role as Mrs Napier Todd, and to go with her new clothes, Edith had taken to wearing her crowning glory swept back into a magnificent chignon held in place with two tortoiseshell combs presented to her on her wedding day by Cook and the other servants. It was a style that she hoped suited her delicate features, seeming somehow to enhance her clear green eyes, straight nose and full lips, the almost alarming red of the hair setting off her pale, pale skin.

Now Betty parted the waist-length hair with a comb, and brushed one side to the back and the other to the front, twisting the latter slightly to allow it to fall down over the loose cut of the already detested gown.

'If Madam would now stand up?'

Betty lifted the back of the gown as Edith stood up and carefully removed the dressing stool upon which Edith had been seated. Then she stood back to admire her handiwork, walking round her model and finally sighing with some satisfaction. It was a sigh that gave Edith the feeling, once again, that Betty had carried out her husband's orders before.

'I think the master will be pleased with this,' the maid murmured. 'The gown is something he had made some time ago. It was a silk he had seen in France, a beautiful colour that had caught his eye, in Paris, I think. But he never did find a use for it.' She walked round Edith, who stood stock-still, her heart beating a great deal faster than was natural. 'I do think that the master will be pleased, that he will realise that the use he has found for the gown is perfect. Come to the dressing mirror, madam. I think you will agree that it looks perfect.'

Edith walked towards the cheval mirror that Betty now placed in the middle of the room, and saw a new person walking towards her. She was statuesque, a model of beautiful arrangement, not a modern young woman, not a young wife, but someone unearthly.

Edith stared at the saint-like figure in the mirror. Was this how Napier wanted her? Unbound, uncorseted, the outline of her body showing through the silk? Was this how he desired her? She stared at herself as hope rose within her. If he wanted her like this, well then, so be it, she would dress like this for him. If he wished her to look like some sort of medieval angel, or a saint depicted in some ancient mural on a chapel wall, if that would make him desire her as a wife, then she would try with all her heart to like the silk gown, the gold slippers, and the tumbling hair.

She turned towards Betty, and away from the mirror.

'I just need a harp,' she said, trying to smile.

It turned out that Napier's studio was one of a pair of old stone barns across the courtyard from the house. It was a dark morning with rain pouring, so Betty took up a large black umbrella and held it over her mistress as they made their way quickly towards the refurbished building with its tall, Gothic windows and large porch light swinging and glowing despite the weather.

To walk into the studio was to walk into another world. For a second Edith stared around her, wondering at the smell of oil paints and spirits, at the stacked canvases, their faces, like naughty children, turned to the walls. So this was where Napier worked? This huge wooden-floored room with its tall windows, carefully placed – she would subsequently discover – to bring him the best of the northern light. There were a number of large mahogany easels set about the room, all holding paintings, some finished and some unfinished, only one large one quite blank.

'Give me your cloak, please.'

Napier, dressed for painting in a high-necked shirt with a silk cravat at his neck, already had the look of an artist at work. Edith saw at once that she should be prepared for him to appear distracted, but it seemed that he was far from being so. He walked towards her, his face cold and detached.

Edith stared at him in some trepidation, unsure as to whether he would like how she looked, since she certainly did not. She clasped the top of her cloak, unwilling to let it go, while Betty deserted her to walk quietly away towards a service area at the back of the studio.

'I am not sure—'

But Edith did not have time to register any personal doubts about the green silk gown, because Napier's hands closed over her own, gently forcing her to release the tight hold that she had on the top of her cloak.

He took the cloak from her, using an expert sweeping hand to gather its long folds, and marched it, as if it were a person, towards a bench upon which he flung it. Then, taking her hand, he walked her into the middle of the huge room and circled round her, saying nothing.

Edith would never forget how she felt during those minutes. She had no idea whether what her husband was seeing pleased him or not, but she had every idea of how *she* felt.

As Napier walked round her, Edith, always generous to a fault in everything, struggled in vain not to feel humiliated. It was somehow odious to be left standing in the middle of a room, her hair falling down her shoulders in what she knew her stepmother would call an 'unkempt manner', a shapeless gown clothing her, a silly silk scarf draped round her neck – for no particular reason that she could see – with her husband walking wordlessly round her, staring at her with cold detachment as if she was an object in a shop window.

To make matters worse there was Betty of all people, a far from disinterested witness to all that was happening. Since she herself had been in service Edith was well aware that while Betty might pretend she was only interested in laying a breakfast table for them, putting out white linen napkins and glittering silver knives and forks which somehow contrasted rather oddly with the beautifully fashioned, obviously handmade pottery and hand-beaten pewter plate, in reality she would be spying on the scene taking place in the studio.

Edith's heart sank, for she was not so stupid that she did not realise that Betty would not be able to wait to get back to the servants' hall and tell them all about Mrs Todd's having to stand as still as a statue while Mr Todd paced round her wordlessly, assessing the spectacle of his wife dressed in a Biblical gown, trying to sum up whether or not she was going to prove to be an inspiration. Servants always love to gossip. Edith knew, if only because she had been one.

'First we must breakfast.'

Napier put out his hand and led her to the table. Edith followed him dutifully and sat down. He still had not said what he thought of her in his choice of gown.

'Do you have an appetite?'

Edith heard her own voice replying 'No', seemingly coming not from her, but from far away in another part of the room.

'Try to have an appetite,' Napier commanded her, frowning, and he reached forward and placed some ham on a plate for her. Seeing her look of despair, he touched her gently on the arm to encourage her.

It was the first tender gesture that he had made towards her for some time, and, as was perhaps intended, it had a particular effect on Edith. It made her tremble. It also made her long, not to ask him, but to beg him to tell her what was wrong with her that he had not touched her. It made her long to ask him if she pleased him more in this eccentric form of dress than in the pretty gowns and costumes that she herself so loved. But he turned away so quickly, applying himself assiduously to the sumptuous breakfast being brought to them by Betty, that the moment passed, and Edith, her eyes fixed to her plate, set aside her longings and tried to eat the home-made porridge richly heaped with clotted cream, the home-cured ham and the other accompaniments. Napier ate heartily, but not so heartily that he did not spare a moment to appreciate Edith's efforts.

'You will need to eat if you are to sit to me for the long hours that I intend – and no prattle, please. I want none of your girlish chatter.'

Edith nodded. She had been brought up to be seen and not heard, so she knew her place. She just had never thought that you had to go on knowing your place after you were married; that the role of dutiful daughter and maid was merely to be swapped for the role of dutiful wife and model.

It had not occurred to Edith – as why should it – that painters posed their models. She had somehow formed the idea that every artist worked from real life, so that if she saw a painting of a man ploughing a field she had always imagined that the artist had seen a man ploughing a field, and painted him. Now, as Napier wheeled a harp towards her, and sat her down on a gold-painted chair against a black drape, she realised in a rush that not only was she to pose with a harp, as she had somehow suspected as soon as she saw the voluminous gown, but she was to pose as *someone else*.

As Napier showed her how he wanted her to hold her hand, she realised with shock that paintings were not real at all, that the people in them were just dressed up to seem to be other than themselves, that they were all just pretending.

As Napier started to mix colours on his palette,

Edith gazed round the studio at all the different objects, feathers and flowers, mirrors and hats, pieces of silk, busts of Roman emperors or Greek gods – she would not know which. What she did know was that she was just like them. She was just an object waiting to inspire Napier. For the next few hours she really might as well be made of marble.

She struggled with this thought until another more cheerful one followed it. Of course! Napier only wanted her to wear such a horrid dress and have her hair arranged about her shoulders as if she was going to bed because he was *not* painting Edith Todd, his wife, but some sort of saintly girl with a harp; perhaps someone from the Bible, or a favourite book, but someone quite other, no one to do with Edith herself.

She realised that it might take hours and days and months for the painting to be finished, but she resolved not to mind, because if she could help Napier achieve his painting in every way, once it was finished she could go back to being his wife, not his model, and he would surely feel then that he could love her as a husband was meant to love his wife? As Edith loved him, with all her heart.

She turned at a sound behind her, just in time to see Napier opening both the large double doors which led back to the courtyard.

'I need a good breeze, a nice draught, to make the material move,' he called to her from the open doors.

Edith turned back as Betty passed in front of her.

'You're one of the lucky ones, Mrs Todd. Believe me, some of them have been made to pose in the snow.'

Celandine would always remember the way Sheridan had laughed at the expression on her face as, following his gleeful announcement that they were to share rooms, she turned smartly on her heel and started to make her way back to the door of the suite with every intention of going straight downstairs and asking Madame Cécile for another set of rooms.

'Oh, if only I could have drawn you at that moment,' Sheridan teased her later when she came downstairs to join them in the restaurant at the side of the small hotel. 'The shock on your face!'

He stared at her and for a moment it was his turn to look shocked, for Celandine had changed from her travelling clothes, and was now looking magnificent in a dark blue two-piece with a high collar and deep lace cuffs. It was not an evening dress but it was excessively pretty. She had restyled her thick, dark shining hair to go with some new tortoiseshell combs found in a small boutique off the rue de Rivoli, so what with her white skin and green eyes, her tall figure and tiny waist, it was little wonder that not only Sheridan but every other man she passed gave her a second glance, glances which it has to be said she hardly noticed, for it was not in her nature to pay attention to flattering looks.

'You were very lucky I had left my umbrella downstairs in the hall. You only narrowly missed being hit over the head with it,' Celandine told him, while the men all rose from their seats at the supper table as she sat down.

'Would you really have hit him?' Alfred asked her with a sly look, lighting his pipe, seemingly impervious to everyone else's sensibilities as he puffed acrid smoke all over the table while Sheridan refilled their wine glasses.

'Of course. That is what an umbrella is for.' Celandine smiled. 'As is a parasol, naturally. But an umbrella is best, because it's heavier.'

'How many people *have* you hit with your umbrella, Miss Benyon?' Tom asked.

Celandine thought for a moment. 'Well now, in Munich I hit a man who had just beaten his dog, and I have to tell you I hit him hard. The man ran off, and I was able to take the poor hound home, bath him and feed him, and we soon found a new home for him. So that was good.' She paused, looking round with some satisfaction at her all-male audience. 'And then in Avignon one day there was a robbery at the grocer's store – that time I managed to put out the end of my umbrella and trip up one of the young thieves. So you see an umbrella is not just to keep the rain off. Oh, no, like the parasol, it is very much a lady's best friend.'

'How magnificent!' Tom looked round, first at

154

Celandine, and then at Sheridan. 'Miss Benyon is obviously so fearless, gentlemen, we can all feel quite safe on the beach tomorrow. No matter what occurs, we know we have Miss Benyon and her umbrella.'

Celandine smiled, and leaned back against the hard wood of the bench. As she did so, as if at a signal, the men started to talk and drink, which allowed her to fall silent, and gaze around the rural Breton dining room with its walls smoked over the centuries to a saddle-leather brown, its dark furniture and white tablecloths, its red and white checked napkins, its bar with its many wooden racks filled with bottles of many hues. She gave a small inward sigh of contentment. Chez Cécile was everything she had hoped it might be. It was smoky, it was filled with painters eating, drinking and talking. The waiters and waitresses emerged from the kitchens and moved swiftly around the tables as they called out the names of the dishes they were bearing, waiting for swift hands to pluck the air, for the gloriously tasty dishes to be greeted with delighted smiles as they were set down at the relevant places.

Since Celandine had no desire to join in the wrangling conversation that Sheridan and his friends were enjoying, she found she was happy sitting and watching everyone around them. Happy to take in the rising smoke, the emptying glasses, the black and white tiles of the floor, the flickering candles that played inconstantly, impishly, over the men seated about the dining room. Happy to try to catch the exchanges and the banter between the Breton waiters and waitresses and the many diners, all of them in some way or another students or enthusiasts of the summer school.

A few minutes later the menu lists were presented to their table, and they all gazed in excitement at the large, sloping pale blue-mauve writing that described the dishes of the day, imagining the culinary delights that would soon be winging their way from the small, hot kitchen with its blackened woodburning stove, and even blacker skillets and pans, which could be glimpsed for a few tantalising seconds as the waiters and waitresses pushed in and out of the swing doors.

At that moment Celandine felt that exquisite frisson of delight that comes from having an unexpected experience thrust suddenly upon you. She was only too happy to embrace this new scene, to wonder at its variety, to take in the warmth and delight of those who, having laboured in the open air at their easels, were now relaxing in each other's company.

'What's the matter?' Sheridan broke off his conversation to turn to Celandine. 'Have you just seen someone you know and don't like? Or are you just fainting from hunger?'

'I don't understand.' Celandine found herself quite against her will chewing her lip in suppressed anxiety. 'I really don't understand.'

'You've lost colour—'

'Have I?'

'Yes.' Ignoring the rest of the table, who were still wrangling over some finer point about the new square brush technique that was proving so popular at the summer school, Sheridan leaned forward and murmured, 'You have gone quite pale. Do you feel unwell, Miss Benyon?'

'No, no.' Celandine quickly sipped some wine. 'No, of course not. Who could feel unwell in such a place? No, it's not that. It's just—'

'Yes?'

'It's just that I've suddenly realised why Madame Cécile gave me such a look, almost of – almost of *shock*, when we first arrived.'

'She gives everyone deep looks, that's Madame Cécile.'

'No, she gave me a deep, sharp look, and I wondered why.'

'Tell me why, Miss Benyon. If you tell me why, I will immediately tell you why not.'

'It was because I am the only woman here. I am the only woman painter here,' she repeated in a low voice, looking around.

'But of course.' Sheridan smiled. 'That is why I wanted you to come to summer school. I want more women to become painters, so many that in time it will become quite commonplace to see women at summer school, as why should it not? There are far too few women painters, and those that there are . . . well, you know; their talents are really not appreciated. I thought if you came here

157

it would set an example to other women, show them that it is possible to come here, on your own, and not feel out of place. Besides, Madame Cécile needs our patronage,' he ended jokingly, indicating the room, which was full to bursting. 'We must help her. There are far too many rival establishments springing up round here and around Cancale. After all, she was the first to encourage the summer school.'

Celandine was about to say something, but she stopped herself, because really it was too late. She had lied to her mother that she was going on a course with another female student, but only because she had been quite sure that there *would* be other female students with whom she could quickly become friends. But there were none. If her mother knew she was in Brittany, a woman alone among dozens of males, she did not know what she would say.

She looked down at the wine in her glass and then up into Sheridan's reassuringly calm eyes.

'Well, I dare say it doesn't matter,' she said, shrugging her shoulders.

'Nothing matters if your heart is set on it. Is your heart set on it?'

Celandine said nothing.

'Well, is it?'

'Of course, it must be, or I wouldn't be here.' Celandine dropped her gaze to the menu. 'Gracious, I don't know about all of you, but I am so hungry I think I will start with the *crevettes*.'

'And I too.' Sheridan nodded. 'And after?'

Celandine shrugged her shoulders, lightly, but there must have been just a hint of despair about her, because Sheridan leaned forward and whispered, 'Don't worry, Miss Benyon, there will be others of your sex coming along soon; if not this summer, next summer; no doubt of it.'

Celandine smiled, not really believing him, but realising that she had little alternative. She tried not to think of Paris, of her mother, of Agnes beetling back to Avignon with news of her sister's going off to Brittany, quite on her own, without a maid, in company with a clutch of disreputable art students – for in Agnes's eyes all art students would be disreputable.

'You don't need to call me Miss Benyon,' she told Sheridan, realising in a rush that such formality in the reality of their new situation was really extraneous.

Sheridan smiled. 'Very well, Celandine—'

Hearing this, Tom, his long blond hair flopping into his eyes, leaned forward.

'I say, can we all call you Celandine, Miss Benyon?'

'Of course.'

'Even me?' Alfred Talisman's eyes, perhaps made more brilliant by his short crisp black hair and neat black beard, looked questioningly at Celandine.

'Yes, even you, Alfred,' Sheridan agreed, leaning forward to block Alfred's view of Celandine. Alfred promptly leaned back and talked to Celandine behind Sheridan's back.

'Are you sure?'

'Of course.' Now Celandine too leaned back and smiled at Alfred. Not to be outwitted, Sheridan leaned back once again, whereupon Alfred, refusing to capitulate, stood up, his long, lean frame towering over the table.

'Sit down, Alfred Trelawney Talisman. The *crevettes* are arriving, and not even you can eat *crevettes* standing up.'

Alfred lowered himself once more, but not before he had smiled his dark smile at Celandine, knowing he had made his point to the only girl in their midst. Sheridan was not going to be allowed to keep Celandine to himself.

Before Edith had married she had dreaded the coming of nightfall. As darkness crept further and further towards the old inn the noise in the bar and restaurant grew and grew, and the hurrying maids would trip over each other's feet in their weariness, before falling exhausted into their iron beds in the attic rooms in which they were housed – rooms that were either too hot in summer, or too cold in winter.

Now it was different. Now, as the early summer light eventually faded, and Napier's brush at last grew still, and Edith was thankfully allowed to stand up and unfreeze her limbs, dusk had become her friend and ally. As Betty had already hinted, with the doors open, despite the summer weather, the old stone barn was arctic.

Once she was released from Napier's artistic

160

aura, Edith would hurry back to the house and lie under a quilt on her dressing-room bed, waiting for life to come back to her body, waiting to become a human being once more rather than a frozen inspiration.

She often thought back to her life at the Stag and Crown. If it had been hard, it had at least been hard in a way she could understand, and one to which she had been used, which was more than could be said for her present lonely existence. Apart from anything else, and for reasons she could not herself quite understand, she was finding it almost unbearable never to be allowed to see the painting for which she was sitting; not knowing how she was being represented, she felt, in some strange way, as if she might be going to be humiliated, as if the moment she did see the painting she would become the person depicted, vapid, unrecognisable. And then too the silence, upon which Napier insisted when he was working, made her feel as if she was quite alone in the world. The hush in the studio was so endless, lasting for what seemed to be days, not hours, that it made even the sound of Napier's brushes moving across his canvas seem unnervingly loud.

One evening, as she lay willing the warmth back into her frozen body, Edith heard a knock at her dressing-room door. Hoping, as she always did, that it might be Napier, she quickly sat up, her auburn hair tumbling around the top of her tightly held wrap.

'Who is it? Do you want to come in?'

Disappointingly it was not Napier. It was Mrs George.

'I thought I should call to tell you that poor Betty has been taken ill, I'm afraid, taken ever so poorly, so I have come to help you in any way you might wish.'

Edith stared at Mrs George. Despite Napier's frowning on such undemocratic behaviour, the housekeeper still insisted on curtsying to Edith whenever she passed her.

'That is very kind of you, Mrs George, really it is.'

'It is the least I can do for you, madam, after such a tiring day.'

Mrs George came to the side of Edith's bed and, seeing her hands clutching her wrap around her, reached forward and gently took one, as a doctor might who is intent on taking a patient's temperature.

'My, my, but your hands are as frozen as our pond in winter,' the housekeeper announced in a shocked voice. 'What has Mr Todd been doing to you?'

Edith tried not to look embarrassed as the older woman rubbed hard on first one white, cold hand, and then the next, until at last the faintly blue look to them had disappeared.

'Thank you so much. That is so much better.' Edith smiled her warm, kind smile at the older woman, who frowned in return.

'I shall ask the master why he is not still

lighting a fire in his studio. That is ever such a cold room, that is, even in summer. I know all about that room,' she went on. 'I should do, seeing as I sat to Mr Todd when the studio was first completed. I was but frozen mittenless, before even an hour was out. Well, finally, even though it was summer, I made it my business to be in there before him, and I laid the fire myself, I did, before he could think of why not; and a lot quicker we got on after that.'

'He has to have the doors open, to create a draught to blow the silk scarf back towards the backdrop.'

'Oh, he does, does he? Well, we'll see about that, ma'am. Dear oh me, artists think we are all of us made of stone, they do really. When I was sitting to him, I remember, he did not like that fire being lit, but in the end he was pleased, because he said it gave me rosy cheeks. Then, of course, the paint was hardly dry when he sold the wretched thing – to Mr Rosebery, I think it was. Lives up near Stowe, and a right gamey, mutton-whiskered old gent he is, so what he would want with a picture of yours truly sitting with a basket of apples and a dead rabbit at my feet, heaven only knows. But he paid Mr Todd good money for it, I fancy, because he was off to Paris the next minute, thank the Lord, leaving me to go back to what I do best, what he pays me for – the running of his blessed house.'

She looked down at Edith and tucked the quilt tighter round her, a worried frown on her face.

'Seeing as your teeth are still chattering, I'm going to light your dressing-room fire for you, my dear, really I am. There's one thing about stone houses that no one tells you and that is they may be warm in winter when the fires are lit, but they're that freezy-cold in summer when they're not.'

'I'll help you—' Edith struggled to sit up.

'You'll do nothing of the sort. You'll lie right where you are until such time as your teeth stop chattering.'

'I used to be in service, you know,' Edith confided suddenly, as the older woman took spills from the spill box on the chimneypiece preparatory to lighting the fire with them.

'Oh, you did, did you? Well, you're not in service any more, madam, you're young *Mrs Napier Todd* now, and as such you'll oblige me by leaving the fires to us, while you get on with being a wife to Mr Todd and the mistress of Helmscote. We agreed that the first evening of your arrival.'

Edith closed her eyes. For no reason she could think of she could feel tears welling, possibly because Mrs George was being kind to her. She had always found that if people were kind to you when you were having a bit of a difficult time of it, it made you feel sorry for yourself. She remembered how Cook had taken her under her wing when her mother had died so suddenly, and how hard it had been not to give way to her sorrow.

Soon the fire was warming the room, and the shaming, weakening moment had passed, leaving Edith, eyes open once more, staring up at the reflections of light on the ceiling, still too cold and tired to do anything except wonder, as she did every evening now, if after a day posing for Napier she would ever, ever feel her limbs again?

'I know how you feel, that is all I meant to say,' she explained.

'Of course you do, but you would anyway. You're not the sort to not know how someone feels, we all know that,' Mrs George agreed, coming back to Edith's bedside and staring down at her. 'Now you just lie down and enjoy some rest and warmth. I'm going to come back in a short while with some warmed towels, because no one should be as cold as you are on a warm summer evening, Mrs Todd.' Mrs George tiptoed to the dressing-room door, opened it, and repeated quietly but vehemently to herself before closing it, 'No one!'

It transpired that Betty was going to be indisposed with a 'cold' for fully nine months, but since it seemed that she had been engaged to a Mr Tyler for over ten years, her marriage, although taking place very rapidly after the announcement of her indisposition, did not, it seemed, come as much of a surprise to anyone at Helmscote.

'Just as well that Betty has been made an honest

woman of at last,' Mrs George announced, some few days later, her small brown eyes somewhat narrowed. 'Any more of that John Tyler's dithering and I dare say her father would have taken a shotgun to him, and all the village knows it.' She sighed and looked down at Edith, who was at last beginning to enjoy her statutory pre-dinner rest, so necessary to her thawing out after a day in the studio. 'I don't know, I don't know, really, Mrs Todd. Maids! Well, you must know, seeing as you've been in service yourself, or so you say, bless you. They are either indisposed, about to be indisposed, or running off to some city where the poor creatures have some ridiculous idea they will be better paid. Still, at least Betty is a married woman now, and won't be a nuisance no more.'

She left Edith's side to put another log on the fire and set items of her underwear to warm on a towel rail in front of the flames.

'You'll be wishing for me to hire you another maid, won't you, madam?'

'No, really, Mrs George, thank you, I don't think that is necessary. I can manage quite well, really I can.'

'No, you can not manage, Mrs Todd,' came the robust reply from the fireplace. 'By no means.' Mrs George paused in her turning of the warming garments. 'In all honesty, seeing that you can't and shouldn't manage without a personal maid, I would suggest that until we find some-one suitable, I should double as housekeeper and

166

personal maid to you, Mrs Todd, just for the time being.' She smiled, perhaps to temper the commanding tone she was using.

'Will I always need a maid, Mrs George?' asked a sadly resigned young voice from the bed.

'Every lady has a personal maid, Mrs Todd, you know that. But we can make do, as I say, until such time as we find a suitable replacement for Betty.'

'I understand. Well, I dare say you're right, Mrs George.'

Edith closed her eyes. She was gradually coming to realise how little she knew of Napier's feelings on any subject, let alone herself. Today for some reason he had seemed even more remote than usual. He had been totally distanced from her, as if she was a stranger brought into his life at certain points, only to be taken out again at others; just a dressed-up doll of a person, not a human being at all. She had a growing feeling of despair which she was finding impossible to conquer, a despair born out of the gradual realisation that try as she might to sit to him the way he wished, she was not proving to be inspirational. It just might be that she was not only not desirable as a wife, but also a failure as a model, and this being so she saw little hope in the future.

Perhaps Mrs George sensed Edith's despair because she was being more than usually solicitous, fussing about her as if she was ill, staring down at her lying on the bed as if the buxom housekeeper was a doctor and Edith her wan-faced patient.

'I will get a warm flannel for your head. It seems to me you have the air of someone about to have a migraine.'

'Why do you think that?' asked Edith in a faint voice.

'You have less colour than usual.' Mrs George bustled out of the room, trying to keep her feelings of inner fury from showing.

It seemed to her that had she not been the housekeeper at Helmscote she would have told the poor pale-faced young girl lying in that bed to pack in her marriage and run back to her mother, if she had one. But since it seemed she did not have a mother, and since Mrs George needed to keep her position at Helmscote as much as anyone else, she found herself daily fighting her worry for her poor young mistress. It was not just her pallor, the shivering fits to which she succumbed, it was her voice. If there was one thing of which Mrs George was sure it was that the voice reflected the state of someone's heart, and this being so, young Mrs Todd was certainly sick at heart.

Edith opened her eyes briefly as she heard the older woman leaving the dressing room, and the door shutting quietly behind her. The movement of her long-lashed lids as she closed them again was so slight that they might have been the wings of a butterfly.

Day after day she had climbed into her floating

silk costume to sit holding the wretched harp. Day after day she had sat, feet frozen, hands frozen, as the draught from the open doors turned the stone-built studio into an agony of cold, despite the summer weather. If she shifted her position on the gold-painted chair by so much as an inch, Napier would throw his paint-brush across the room, sigh, and stalk off to the back of the studio to light a cigar. As the air grew heavy with the scent of his smoke, there would be a long, frightening silence, a silence that seemed to suggest to his model that he was struggling within himself not to throw something at either her or the painting. Eventually he would return, and Edith, having taken advantage of his momentary absence to move a little in her seat, would resume her rocklike position.

As the days passed, agonisingly slowly, Edith came to realise just what her future might be going to be, and in facing the reality of her life the person she once was seemed to be dying, little by little.

Every day was always the same as the students of the summer school prepared to set off to the beach: arms and bodies waving and bending in search of the inevitably missing bundles of brushes, pencils or pads; endless strapping of easels and canvas bags. Indeed, the prepar-ation of the male students took so long that by the second week of the summer school, Celandine, who was always ready and waiting first, her dark hair tucked up under her straw hat, her hat ribbons tied securely against the sea wind, had started to resign herself to the inevitability of the daily wait for the men to organise themselves. She knew it would be a waste of precious energy to grow impatient, so she fell instead into the habit of leaving out her sketching stool from her own paraphernalia, and determinedly setting to draw the scene before her, a scene which it had to be said was affording her increasing amusement. However, the very fact that they knew they were being sketched naturally slowed everyone up, but since she was the only girl present none of the men appeared to mind, willingly holding their positions for her until such time as the rudiments of her sketch were finished.

'That is very good, Celandine,' Alfred remarked shyly one day, as he stared approvingly over her shoulder at the drawing. 'You have me off to a T. Even my father would recognise me, and I haven't seen *him* in years; and as for Tom and Sheridan, they look quite as chaotic as they undoubtedly are. You have a light touch. Not something that can be learned, as you doubtless know. You either have it or you do not have it, as I always tell my young pupils.'

Celandine turned and, catching the mildly astonished look in his eyes, she smiled. 'It's only a sketch – I should do it in water colour first really, but I couldn't be bothered to unpack everything again.'

'Art is too difficult for anything to be "only a sketch" – whether it's a cobweb in the early morning, a red cloak on a far dark horizon, or all of us preparing to go to the beach. We can allow life in the form of other people and most particularly posterity to laugh at our poor efforts, but we ourselves must take care to take what we do seriously, no matter what.'

Celandine stared up at the quiet intensity in Alfred's face. 'We must talk about this some more at lunch,' she murmured.

Before Alfred had time to reply Sheridan appeared from nowhere and stepped un-apologetically and quite purposefully between Alfred and Celandine.

'Time to move off,' he announced, as if every-one was not already doing just that. 'You're lunching with me at the café today,' he told Celandine. 'I marked your dance card yesterday, if you remember?' He turned and frowned at Alfred's retreating back, as Celandine shook her head.

'You did nothing of the sort. You did not even mention luncheon, Sheridan Montague Robert-son.'

'Well, I have now,' Sheridan stated, still frown-ing after his friend. 'Besides, Alfred must have bored you into the ground over the past few days with all his ideas, surely?'

Celandine moved away from Sheridan. Really, he was becoming possessive of her in a way that she did not really welcome. She

171

wanted to be free to pick and choose her company.

'Let's hope that the wind has died down a bit today,' she murmured to no one in particular.

The wind had indeed died down enough to allow them all to work, at least for the first few hours, without having to keep retrieving either their hats or their easels from the sand dunes into which the summer school settled themselves with such hope every morning and afternoon.

The principle of painting in the open air might have caught Paris by storm, but the reality of it was that canvases were constantly being flung on to their faces, and easels, and indeed sometimes painters, off their legs. Celandine had found that she was certainly learning some new and interesting words, in several languages, for her artistic companions, forgetting there was a lady present, seemed to swear constantly and easily, as easels swayed and sand blew into and on to everything.

At midday, as grey clouds gathered and wind and rain whipped round the corner of some nearby rocks and flung themselves at his easel, causing it once more to topple over, Sheridan pushed his straw hat firmly down round his ears and started to pack up, cursing and swearing as he did so.

'Painting in the open air is one thing, but painting in this is enough to make a bishop swear,' he yelled above the sound of the increasing storm.

172

His words were not lost on the rest, but seeing the white tops to the waves out at sea, the deserted beach, and the ship on the far horizon, they all pulled their hats down and their collars up and remained locked in position, staring from the soon to become raging sea back to their canvases in excited fascination.

'Remember Turner lashed himself to a mast to paint,' Tom yelled to Sheridan's departing back.

'I dare say, but if he had known that today the Café Florence's *plat de jour* was scallops in a creamy sauce served on a buttery parsley purée of *pommes de terre*, accompanied by a crisp dry white wine, he would have unlashed himself within seconds and done the decent thing by them,' Sheridan murmured, half to himself and half to Celandine, who had also, regretfully, decided to pack it in, and was following him across the dunes back to the edge of the village.

She put up her faithful umbrella against the rain, and together they clung to it as they bent their heads against both the increasing wind and the rain, finally arriving thankfully at the café, which was already filling up.

'I am no good at storms,' Celandine confessed. 'The idea of detailing all those white tops to the waves makes me seasick before I have even begun.'

Sheridan gave his infectious laugh, perhaps delighted by her honesty, but perhaps even more delighted by the delicious smells coming towards them from the kitchens. The two of them quickly took their seats at a corner table, well away from the bump and bang of the service door.

'Just how hungry can painting make you?' Celandine asked dreamily after demolishing a plate of scallops and several glasses of white wine.

'There is no greater hunger than the vulpine appetite of the artist arriving at table for his lunch or dinner.' Sheridan smiled, and allowed his free hand to touch Celandine's, which was resting on the table. She did not react, but nor did she move her hand, preferring instead to ignore the contact rather than hurt his feelings. 'What were you talking to Alfred about this morning before we left?'

'Nothing.' Celandine pulled a small face.

'Nothing, eh? Now that is a grand subject.'

'Yes, it is, isn't it—'

'I don't like you talking to Alfred Talisman about nothing. It is far too big a canvas, especially in the early morning.'

'He's been hurt, quite badly, by his father, I think. That is why he is so reticent.'

'Well, so have I! I have been hurt by my father. He died when I was quite young. And you don't confide in me as much as you confide in him. I must confess it is making me jealous.'

'Well now, what is that supposed to mean?'

'It is supposed to mean that it's making me jealous.' Sheridan took a long sip of his wine. 'You must know that I suspect that Alfred is entertaining feelings for you, and I won't have it, because I fell in love with you first,' he continued

174

in a low voice. 'You know very well I have been in love with you ever since I drew you in the Louvre. I won't let anyone else be in love with you, not the way I am.'

Sheridan's free hand was no longer placed beside that of Celandine, it was now covering it. Celandine looked away.

'I don't want anyone to be in love with me – I really don't. I don't like the thought of love, or being in love, or anything to do with it. I only like the thought of art—'

'What about the art of love, then?'

'Love in art would be all right,' Celandine returned, 'but anything more is so tangled. People in love are always moaning and losing their ideals in a welter of emotion that has nothing to do with real life. People in love do not notice life, only each other. No, I don't think love is for me.'

Sheridan sighed. 'Well, isn't that a bit of a pity, since I *am* in love with you, and have been ever since I sat drawing your lovely face in the Louvre museum that rainy afternoon – what now seems a hundred years ago.'

Celandine smiled. They had both presented each other with their drawings. Sheridan's offering was far better than hers, and he knew it. It was plainly sensual, startlingly so, despite the fact that Celandine was fully clothed and even wearing a hat. She decided to change the subject.

'I shouldn't even be here in Brittany, you know that. If my mother knew—'

'If your mother knew I want to marry you she

would be like all mothers, thrilled to the marrow at the idea of a wedding.'

'But you don't seem to understand. I don't want to be married either.'

'You have to marry, Celandine. Not to marry would be to waste your talents as a woman. You have to marry to be truly appreciated.'

'I don't mind wasting my womanly talents, whatever that might mean, I just don't want to waste my artistic talent. Artistic talent lasts, beauty does not.'

'Whoever told you that was not telling the truth. Beauty lasts for ever, because it comes from inside, whereas talent, my beautiful Celandine, is only as good as whatever you did yesterday, and that *is* the truth.'

'I don't want to be married. My half-sister is married and she is essentially very dull.'

'She would have been dull *un*married, surely?'

'Maybe.'

Seeing that he was gaining ground just a little, Sheridan took Celandine's other hand in his, and shook both gently up and down as he went on, at his most persuasive.

'Just supposing you could be both beautiful and talented? Supposing you married someone who allowed you to be both, and loved you into the bargain, would not that be paradise?'

'Didn't anyone tell you, paradise was lost by Eve tempting Adam, leaving us only with real life?'

'When I've finished here,' Sheridan continued,

ignoring her, 'I am not going back to Paris, except to pack up, and pay my rent. No, I propose to go to England, to Cornwall, to Newbourne, where I was last summer.'

'Why Cornwall?'

'The light in Cornwall is just like here; it is perfect for painting in the open air. Why don't you come with me, Celandine? We could share a studio, be part of something new and special, a new realism that is starting to happen in European art. I want to take everything I have learned in Europe back to England, perhaps eventually set up a school at Newbourne. Myself and some like souls, we all want to get away from the studio, away from painting men and women in the heroic or Biblical mould. We want to paint real people, working people, depict faces that are worn and torn, not painted and varnished and glowing with unreality.'

The expression in Celandine's eyes changed. 'I know just how you feel—'

'No, you don't,' Sheridan interrupted with sudden passion. 'I know you don't know how I feel, because if you did you would not, *could* not, go off on walks talking the hind legs off that wretch Alfred Talisman every morning!'

'Oh, we're not back to that, please say we're not back to that.' Celandine sighed and looked away and then back at Sheridan. 'Alfred is very intelligent. I like talking to him,' she said slowly. 'I am only trying to draw him out. He is so shy and sensitive.'

177

'So am I! I too am shy and sensitive, but I have overcome it,' Sheridan protested. 'Do you realise what you put me through when you walk off with him, deep in some conversation about that all-embracing subject – nothing?'

'We only talk about the principles of art, about painting, Sheridan. Nothing that could not be overheard by your maiden aunt, I promise you.'

'Talking is often considered, quite rightly, to be more intimate than lovemaking,' Sheridan stated sulkily.

Celandine banged the table lightly with a small fist. 'I won't have anyone telling me whom I may or may not talk to,' she protested. 'I am a free spirit.' She pointed towards the windows of the café. 'I have to be as free as the birds on the shore out there, or I will die.'

'I insist once again, Celandine, talking is more intimate than lovemaking. For the past few days you have done nothing but take yourself off down the coast walking and talking with Alfred. It is maddening me, and you know it. You know how I feel about you; you know how passionate I am about you. I don't want you going off for walks with Alfred Talisman.'

Celandine shrugged her shoulders. 'That is my affair, surely?'

Sheridan, perhaps seeing that he was getting nowhere at all, leaned forward and kissed her on the lips, in full view of the waiter, who was at that moment approaching their table with a tray of coffee.

'*Ah, vive l'amour,*' the waiter murmured approvingly as he placed the coffee pot in front of them. '*It so often follows after a good lunch, n'est-ce pas?*'

Celandine was so shocked by Sheridan's behaviour, most particularly since it was so public, that she was overwhelmed by a violent wish to slap his face, and slap it hard. The only thing that actually saved Sheridan from public humiliation, that prevented Celandine from administering a stinging reply to his audacity, was not the fact that Celandine had never been kissed on the lips before, nor the fact that the waiter had seen the kiss, but the effect that it had on her.

In those few seconds, even as she pulled away from him, Celandine knew that she had been admitted to a magic circle outside which nothing really mattered.

It was surprisingly easy to return to the old inn and creep up the stairs to her room. As Sheridan and Celandine inched open her door, from all over the small hotel could be sensed the feeling that siestas were the order of the day. Of course, what surprised Celandine more, was how easy it was to make love. How quickly clothes came off and laces were undone, and how her long, dark hair seemed to take on a life of its own, unwinding itself with unnatural ease from combs that had been carefully placed only hours before.

And if she had often wondered what the

attractions of love could be, now her mind and body wondered no more, for they were greater than she could ever have imagined.

In the light that filtered from behind the deep red curtains their bodies seemed to take on a dark fascination of their own; so much so that by the time Sheridan was leaving her to rest and sleep under the thin French quilt, stealing out of her bedroom to his own, it was with a smile of such radiant happiness that, had it been night, he would have had no need of a torch to light his way.

From the bed Celandine watched the door shutting behind his slim, handsome figure, and was startled to find that she felt as if she already owned it.

Chapter Five

They were painting on the beach, and it was their
first really perfect day, a day so beautiful that for
once everyone was silent. Not even Sheridan
had spoken for some hours so intent was he,
like everyone else, on capturing the scene before
them: the sea, the sunlight on the water, the blue
sky. Celandine had just started to wonder what
she had done to deserve such happiness, in love
and surrounded by artists, watching the sunshine on the water, the children in their floppy
hats and pretty dresses paddling on the edge of
the still cold water, the frilling of the waves
reaching towards the beach, when she heard a
sound she had come to dread. It was unmistakable, rising insistently, imperiously, above the
sound of the sea, the quiet happy calls of children
looking for shrimps in the rock pools behind
them, the murmur of grown-ups gossiping to
each other in their deck chairs – Agnes's voice.

Celandine turned, unable to believe that it was
actually her half-sister calling to her.

'Agnes?'

The word came out as a quavering horrified question loaded with uncertainty, as if she was a blind person who could not recognise the figure of her sister standing at the top of the beach staring down to where Celandine and the others had been, until that moment, quietly concentrating.

'Celandine – will you please come here?'

Agnes's question, unlike Celandine's, held no uncertainty.

Years of jumping to, years of being the much younger sister, years of seeing her mother hurrying towards Agnes in answer to her querulous demands, meant that Celandine, to the astonishment of the other painters, immediately put down her brush, rose from her stool, and walked quickly up the beach.

'What are you doing here, Agnes?'

'What are *you* doing here, Celandine? That is what I am here to ask.' Agnes took Celandine by the arm as if she was some sort of naughty schoolgirl and pulled her towards her.

'It has been reported by someone at the hotel that you have been behaving like a – slut! Dragging the family name through the mud.' She nodded towards the group of artists. 'And where is the lady friend whom you were so anxious to go away with, may I ask? Where is your regard for your poor widowed mother, for our father – who had he been alive would undoubtedly have had a heart attack should he have read the letter that your mother received? It is nowhere. You have, I repeat, dragged the family name through the mud. Your mother sent me to bring you home, at once.'

Celandine shook herself free. 'I am not coming home, Agnes. I am not one of your children to be dragged off the beach when you decide. I am here, painting, in company with my fellow artists. I am not coming home, not for you, not for anyone. I don't know why you came here. You could have saved yourself the journey.'

'I came here on behalf of your poor mother, who wanted me to bring you back.'

'I don't and won't come back until I am ready to do so, Agnes.'

Agnes crossed herself. 'May God help you, Celandine. You are in grave sin.'

'If I am, then that surely is between myself and God? Nothing to do with you, Agnes.'

'I have come to save you from yourself, Celandine.'

Celandine stared at her sister. She knew that even if Sheridan and the others could not actually hear what was going on, they must know that whatever was being said could not be amicable.

'You should not have come here, Agnes, really you should not. You must go back. Tell Mother I am perfectly fine, and I will be coming back when I said I would, not before.'

'Mother insists.'

'Mother cannot insist, Agnes, as well you

know. Thanks to my father I am independent.'

'Do you really think you are, or could be, independent?' Agnes looked at her pityingly. 'Do you think you could live on the tiny annuity Father left both of us: pin money, not enough even for a new hat? Or is it that you think your paintings will make you rich?' She laughed.

It was the laugh that confirmed Celandine's determination to do exactly as she wished, no matter what.

'I shall come back when I have finished the course, and not before. Now goodbye.'

She turned and went away down the beach, back to her easel and her painting, back to her fellow artists.

Sheridan allowed only a few seconds to pass before he was at her side. 'What happened? Tell me what happened. Who was that fury who suddenly appeared before us as from a nightmare from Hades?'

'My half-sister Agnes.' Celandine's mouth set determinedly, but her eyes were full of despair. 'Someone from the hotel wrote to my mother and said that I was – you know, that I had been seen with you. Someone must have seen us, Sheridan, one of the servants.'

Sheridan took her hands. 'Never mind. We have done nothing of which we need to be ashamed. Love is not shaming, it is beautifying.'

Celandine nodded. Part of her wanted to believe him, but another part of her knew that her mother would not share his view.

*   *   *

'How could you!'

Mrs Benyon never raised her voice. She was always the proud possessor of a low tone, barely speaking above what most people would call a murmur, unless to Marie, and even then she would never raise her voice, only ever over-enunciating her words, aspirating her Ts and Ss, in a supreme and worthwhile effort to make her wishes plain in a mixture of French and American, a form of expression which seemed to satisfy both maid and mistress.

Now, thank goodness, Marie was nowhere to be seen. Celandine was quite alone facing her mother, still in her travelling dress.

'You lied to me, you lied to me, you lied to me.'

Celandine stared at her mother. She loved her with all her heart, and normally she would have hated to think she had really hurt her, perhaps for the first time in her life, but she had to be truthful. She could not spare her mother's feelings, at least not at that moment, because she now knew she loved someone else even more than she loved her mother.

'Yes, Mother, I did lie to you, but not in the way you think.'

'In what way then, pray?'

Mrs Benyon's hands were trembling and she put out one of them to the marble hall table to steady herself.

'I did not lie to deceive you, I lied to put your mind at rest. I was going to the summer school

185

with a friend, and I did think, as he told me, that there would be other females there. I felt the lack of female company, as a matter of fact,' she went on, frowning slightly. 'Men on their own are really quite – male; as a matter of fact, quite, quite male. But there were no other females there, which was a shame, as I say. However, I learned a lot, really I did. Painting in the open air is not as easy as everyone here in Paris would have you believe. You become such a victim of the weather—'

Mrs Benyon looked momentarily bewildered, before quickly returning to her theme.

'You were seen by Monsieur Declos – behaving like a common street walker, in a restaurant of all places, kissing in a restaurant, and then he wrote to me here. One of the servants at the inn – they too saw you with a man, and not in a restaurant – upstairs!'

Celandine now remembered a familiar face looking up at her as she left the restaurant so hastily that day with Sheridan, but she had no time to take her mother up on the point because Mrs Benyon was busy undoing the strings of her precious drawing folder, looking as if she was quite sure that the contents would be found to be non-existent, as if she was sure that Celandine had escaped to Brittany merely to make love, not to draw. She thrust the folder towards her daughter.

'Let me see what you learned, and if what you learned is worth deceiving your poor widowed mother for. Show me all this famous work that you accomplished. Show it to me, I say!'

Celandine opened the leather folder, but in such haste that most unfortunately a drawing of Sheridan fell to the floor. She watched in horrified fascination as her mother picked it up and stared at it. It was not a drawing that any daughter would want her mother to see, and it was certainly no surprise when she felt a stinging slap across her cheek and heard her mother's now distanced voice.

'You are no longer my daughter. You will leave this house at once. I never want to see you again.'

Sheridan was relaxing in front of the floor-length windows that gave on to the inner courtyard of his lodgings, listening to the Paris pigeons calling to each other, watching the occasional visitor crossing or recrossing the cobbled enclosure, when he heard a knock at the outer door. Putting down his glass with some reluctance he strolled across and opened it, expecting perhaps the early return of one of the other lodgers, or one of the other students from the summer school, already bored with their own company, coming to seek his. Instead he saw Celandine, still in her travelling dress.

'Celandine?'

'May I come in?'

'Of course, come in at once.' Sheridan seized her by the hands and pulled her into the hall, but Celandine turned back to the door.

'I'd better bring my luggage in,' she said in a resigned voice. 'It is, after all, all I have.'

Between them they dragged her luggage into the hall, and then stood looking at each other as if neither had any idea what to do next.

'Come in, come in. I have opened a bottle of wine.'

Sheridan was tactful enough not to ask any more questions until they had both sat down and he had poured her a large glass of comforting red wine.

'Mother has thrown me out. It appears I am no longer her daughter.' For a second it seemed to Celandine that Sheridan looked unsurprised.

'She was angry?'

'When people tell you that you are no longer their daughter it usually means that they are not very pleased.'

They both laughed suddenly, almost hysterically.

'I keep wondering who might have seen us together. Surely not just a servant? Anyway, why should they mind? They would be more likely just to come and ask for money in return for not saying anything, surely?'

'I believe someone we know from Avignon saw me being kissed by you.' Celandine smiled. 'I dare say I need go no further.'

'But young people do kiss each other. A great deal, as it happens.'

As if reminded by the delicious memory Sheridan leaned across and kissed her once again, with sudden passion, and then stood up and walked up and down the room for a minute or two quite obviously deep in thought, which Celandine recognised was not really like him. Sheridan liked to react to events, not plan them.

'This makes no difference,' he finally announced. 'It only means that we marry earlier rather than later, by special licence, or some such. We shall be married in Cornwall.'

'Cornwall? *Cornwall?*'

Celandine hoped she did not sound as appalled as she felt. To leave Paris for Cornwall, which she certainly did not know and was not quite sure she wanted to know, appealed to her not at all. Bad enough to be thrown out of her mother's house, to have the lasting image of Agnes appearing just after her mother had slapped her, smiling at her discomfort, taking Mrs Benyon's hand and leading her away, sobbing. Bad enough to have been punished so heavily for falling in love with Sheridan, but to be told that now she was to be taken to an alien land, as far away from the sophistications of Paris as it was surely possible to be, was really more than a punishment, it was a life sentence.

'Yes, darling, we're going away to Cornwall. I have a small allowance from my father, enough for us both to live, albeit not extravagantly.'

Celandine stared at Sheridan. She loved him, she realised that, and with all her heart, but Cornwall sounded far more foreign to her than either Paris or Munich.

'I understand that it rains all the time in Cornwall, Sheridan.'

'It rains a great deal, I grant you, but to make up for that there is the light. The light is exactly similar to the light in Brittany. It is clear, translucent, brilliant. Spring comes to Cornwall long before the rest of England. It is on its way shortly after Christmas. You will delight in it. Nature sends the daffodils ahead as messengers. Oh, Cornwall is a miracle of beauty, believe me. The flowers in the hedgerows, the wild pounding seas, the pebble beaches and white sands, they will be our inspiration, my darling.'

Celandine sensed that this was not the moment to remind Sheridan that he had told her that it was the working people, the fishermen and their women, who were going to be his inspiration. Instead she smiled.

'I expect it will all turn out for the best,' she said, unable to keep the doubt from her voice.

'Turn out for the best?' Sheridan stood her up and swung her round and round. 'Turn out for the best?' he repeated. 'My darling Celandine, it is going to do more than turn out for the best. It is going to be delightful. The moment you set foot in Cornwall you will sense that it is holding out its arms to you, waiting to embrace you, as I am now.'

He took her in his arms, but Celandine promptly stepped back out of them, putting out her hands to his shoulders, holding him off.

'I can't stay here, Sherry. I only came to tell you that my mother had thrown me out, not to stay. I must find lodgings nearby. The concierge, everyone here, they would not like it if I stayed. It would upset them.'

Sheridan smiled down at her with passionate tenderness. He appreciated how she felt but it did not stop him, would not stop him, kissing her.

As for Celandine, Sheridan's ardour reminded her that whatever turn her life took next, it would surely be worth it.

The days spent in the *pension* seemed to crawl by, and her room felt just as a prison room must feel. It was narrow, and cramped, and the washing facilities were of the most primitive. Celandine tried not to think of the heartbreak she had caused her mother, of how her reputation was now destroyed, of how she would never be able to return to Avignon, where her parents' friends and relations would think of her as a fallen woman, for really, what was the point?

At last they were on their way, catching a train that would take them to the coast once more. And all the time there was Sheridan, nonchalant, carefree, looking about him first in the train, and then on board the ship, as if he knew exactly what happiness lay ahead of them, as if he could see no possible problems, smiling gaily at her, at the white-topped waves, at the other ships and boats, at the blue sky, sketching her happily, looking up still smiling, until he saw how pale Celandine had turned.

'Oh, my poor darling.' He flung his sketch-book down and ran to her aid. 'Being sick is such a martyrdom,' he murmured as he held her head.

Celandine lay back against the bench on which he had carefully helped her to lie down, and stared up at the sky above her, a sky that now seemed to be dipping and diving into her face, the morning sun as bright as it had ever been, making her feel dizzy. Tears rolled slowly down her cheeks as she realised her plight. Alone in the world, without anything but the smallest of allowances left to her some years before from her father's estate, cut off from her family, never to see her mother again. Everything seemed suddenly hopeless until she felt Sheridan's hand on her forehead and his handkerchief wiping her cheeks, a look of such devotion on his face that her tears turned from sorrow and sickness to relief.

'I am so sorry to be causing you a fuss, Sherry.'

She tried to smile and failed, but Sheridan made up for her failure with his own smile, before he kissed his elegant index finger and planted it tenderly on her lips.

'Don't fret, my darling. We will be in Cornwall quite soon. You will love our lodgings at Mrs Molesworth's house, where I stayed last year, really you will. But first we must go to

Rosewalls, Aunt Biddy's house. We can be married from there, and you will never have to go on a wretched boat again.'

Minutes later, leaving her dozing in the sunshine with his coat over her, he sat down on his camp stool, and despite the rocking of the boat and the screaming of the seagulls overhead he started to sketch the coils of rope and the other passengers, humming happily to himself as he did so.

Celandine opened her eyes for a second, but seeing Sheridan already happily engrossed, she quickly closed them again. Of one thing she was quite sure: she was in love with a man with a golden nature.

When they finally reached Cornwall, the coastline was obscured by mist, which meant that Celandine, although grateful in the extreme to put a foot, if not two feet, on dry land, was unable to observe the beauty of the harbour.

And it was raining.

Sheridan, who had stayed briefly with his Aunt Biddy at Porthrowan the previous summer, was anxious to marry as soon as possible, his anxiety being based on Celandine's resolute refusal to live with him as his mistress.

The matter had arisen in Paris, during her sojourn at the down-at-heel *pension*. Celandine had been firm in her resolve.

'I may be a fool to love you, Sheridan, but I am not such a fool as to want to live with you except as your wife. Besides, who would want me after, except as his mistress? No one.'

'There would be no *after*,' Sheridan had assured her, a little too blithely.

'Women do not win at love, Mr Montague Robertson, and you know it.'

'In that case we will most definitely go and stay at Aunt Biddy's at Porthrowan. She will help us to be married. She is very practical. And very romantic. She has never married herself, you see.'

'Doubtless that has helped her stay romantic?' Celandine suggested, straight-faced.

Sheridan laughed. 'Doubtless, my darling, but nevertheless it is to Aunt Biddy we will go.'

And so they arrived, still in pouring rain that flooded the narrow pavements and washed through the roads outside Aunt Biddy's neatly kept house overlooking the harbour at Porthrowan. The sea was pounding against the harbour walls, anchored boats huddled together in brightly painted clusters swaying and rocking. Finally, after Sheridan had rung and knocked again and again, a black-costumed, white-haired maid opened the front door.

She nodded at Sheridan. 'Good day to ye, Master Sherry,' she said as if she had only just seen him an hour before. 'I shall tell Miss Biddy you're here, I shall. We'm been very busy with last of the dustin', we'm have,' she murmured, and before either Sheridan or Celandine could step into the hall, she promptly shut the door in their faces.

Celandine clutched her beloved umbrella, which was threatening to turn itself inside out, and stared questioningly at Sheridan from under her hat.

'I thought you said your aunt was expecting us,' she said, raising her voice above the wind.

'She is. That's just Gabrielle – Aunt Biddy's maid. She's always like that, a bit forgetful and so on.'

Celandine continued to struggle between her hat and her umbrella. 'Let's hope she remembers us in due course.'

They waited, the wind seeming to grow colder and the rain wetter before the door opened once more.

'Miss Biddy says to come in, and I'll send the boy down to the pavement there to get your portmanteaux. Russo, Russo, boy, boy!' she cried urgently, turning away from them.

Not wanting a repeat of her previous performance, Sheridan quickly put his foot inside the front door just as 'the boy' came up from the basement, his white hair shining under the hall lamp, his faded grey wool-slippered feet sliding across the wooden floor in a manner that made Celandine immediately think of someone on skates.

Once they were inside the hall, however, away from the crying of the gulls and the pounding of the sea against the harbour walls, Aunt Biddy's house seemed reassuringly warm and welcoming.

'My dears!'

She stood at the entrance to her sitting room, her old-fashioned wide crinoline dress with its hooped underskirt swaying as she held out her arms in welcome to both of them.

'How delightful this is, how delightful.' She held Sheridan's bent head against her ample, plum-coloured satin bosom before turning to Celandine. 'The bride!'

Celandine too was held against the plump frontage, and then both of them were taken by the hand and led into a large room stocked with ornaments and tables, velvet armchairs and sofas. Indeed, so many and so varied were the furnishings that Celandine found herself looking nervously round, unable quite to respond to Aunt Biddy's command to make herself comfortable.

Meanwhile Aunt Biddy arranged herself with fascinating aplomb on a large buttoned sofa upon which she perched herself sideways, which was only practical, considering the size of her dress.

'Sit, sit, oh do!' she cried, her plump white hands clapping softly against each other, her large rings catching the light. 'This is so romantic,' she went on, as both Sheridan and Celandine finally elected to sit opposite her. 'My dear,' she said to Celandine, 'ever since Sherry sent me his letter to explain your situation, I have been so excited. Of course you will have to run away to Gretna Green, seeing that you are under the age necessary to marry in England without the permission of a parent, but run away you shall, and when you return we will arrange a delightful wedding party.'

Celandine swallowed hard. First Cornwall and now Scotland? 'Is that entirely necessary?'

'Oh yes, my dear, *de rigueur*. Everyone in your situation has to run away to Gretna Green. The Scots, you see, will marry *anyone*. You will have to be on your way tomorrow before your family catch up with you. So terrible of whomever it was that Sheridan wrote to me has threatened to horsewhip poor darling Sherry, and for no better reason than that he has fallen in love with you! Quite, quite shocking.'

Celandine shot a look at Sheridan, and quickly turned away, as he shrugged his shoulders and made a comical face to make her laugh.

'Really, I cannot understand it,' Aunt Biddy continued, unnoticing. 'Such violence in the world without civilised people resorting to threats. Oh good, here is Russo with the sherry wine and herbal biscuits, so fortifying before a meal, I always find. You must partake before you change for dinner – it will help to keep the tingle tangles away: so discomforting to feel hungry before a meal, I always think.'

Russo, who was as white-haired as the maid, and as bent as an aged dressmaker's pin, held out a trembling silver tray with the refreshments arranged on it.

'Your suitcases are in your rooms, Master Sherry,' he murmured, before wobbling back towards the door, his shoes making a strange sliding sound as if they fitted him not at all.

'No point in unpacking everything before Gretna, my dears,' Aunt Biddy instructed them through a mouthful of biscuit. 'Really there isn't. Good gracious, I have not known life to be so exciting since Russo took Gabrielle fishing for her birthday, some years ago now, you may imagine; at all events they were lost at sea for days and boats sent out to find them; so exciting. I quite despaired, of course, but you can imagine my delight when they were found. We had quite a celebration here at Rosewalls. And the relief for me, for I know I should never have found more devoted creatures than my beloved Gabrielle and Russo.'

As they excused themselves to change for dinner and were led up to their very separate rooms, Celandine whispered, 'What is all this about you going to be horsewhipped? What *could* you have written to Aunt Biddy?'

'Only the truth,' Sheridan murmured. 'I told her that you had been thrown from the family home because of our great love for each other, and we needed to take refuge from parental fury, which was why we had to come to Cornwall and seek refuge with her. I added that I feared being horsewhipped, which indeed I did, or do!'

'Well, really! And now it seems we have to go to Gretna Green, in Scotland, of all places, and all because of your letter.'

'It will be an adventure, you will see; and

afterwards we can honeymoon all the way back down to Cornwall. Besides, Aunt Biddy is right, my darling; going to Gretna Green is indeed the quickest way to marry, because as she says the Scots will marry anyone. You will see, it will all be all right. Everything will turn out to be for the best in the best of all possible worlds, or something to that effect, at any rate.'

Celandine sat down on the edge of her bed. Her bedroom, like the sitting room downstairs, was over-furnished to a degree, but it was warm, it was welcoming, and most of all it was comfortable. Nevertheless, when she had removed her still damp hat, she found herself putting her head in her hands and letting out a great shuddering sigh as she realised how uncertain her future might yet prove to be. If she had not said she would go to the summer school in Brittany with Sheridan, if she had stayed behind in Paris with her mother and Agnes, she would not now be in a strange place, far from everything familiar, and about to have to run off to Scotland of all places to be married of all things.

There was a scratch at the door. Without waiting for her to call out 'Come in' Sheridan darted into the room, and seizing her hands pulled her to her feet and kissed her.

'There,' he said. 'That's for being so beautiful. And here's my sketch to prove it.'

Seconds later he was gone, leaving Celandine to stare down at the water colour he had done of her on the boat, and remember just why she was there. The reason she was alone in a foreign country was six feet in height, dark-haired, hazel-eyed, and had just left the room. She started to change out of her travelling clothes knowing that there was no more point to remorse, and what was more, no turning back. Her destiny was set, for better or for worse, and she might as well accept it.

She dressed for dinner in a gown that her mother had chosen for her some months before, a memory which she now tried to push away, knowing that it would make her feel both guilty and melancholy. To drown these feelings she hummed the Wedding March to herself. She must think only of the future. It might be dark outside, and it might still be raining, but there was no reason not to think of blue skies to come, of sunshine, of the clear light of Cornwall, and all the joys of her new life.

When she rejoined Sheridan and Aunt Biddy in the drawing room Celandine was looking elegant and composed in grey silk, and she soon found herself feeling reassured by the many comforts of Rosewalls, her confidence returning as she agreed to everything Aunt Biddy was suggesting, from running off to Gretna Green, to coming back to a grand reception to be held later in the summer and to be arranged by Aunt Biddy herself.

'You will find Cornwall so friendly, my dear. There is nothing that people will not do for you,

I promise you, not just here at Porthrowan, but also at Newbourne, where I know Sherry here wishes to settle after the happiness he enjoyed there a year ago, before he left for Paris. It is just how it is. Nothing to be done about it. Friendliness everywhere you go.' Seeing Russo at the door she added, 'And now dinner, my dearest dears. Dinner.' She sighed happily. 'But only six courses, I am afraid. It is all Cook is up to nowadays – gout, you know; but we will take biscuits and milk up to bed to help us through the night.'

Sheridan glanced at Celandine and bossed his eyes at her to make her laugh, but she only turned away, remembering with some longing their impromptu café meals together in Paris and Brittany, the hilarious painting expeditions to the seashore where everyone's concentration had been frequently interrupted not by the call of the seagulls but by the cries of the painters as they lost their easels among the sand dunes. Those carefree days now seemed a lifetime away. Soon she would have a ring on her finger and the responsibilities of a wife. She would have to concern herself with laundry lists and the ordering of meals, and Sheridan would become used to her in the way that Agnes and her husband were used to each other. And yet it seemed to her that there was nothing to be done. She must submit to her fate.

She switched her attention back to the easy banter Sheridan was swapping with his aunt, her eyes wandering round the dining room in which they sat as she inwardly scolded herself for being so unappreciative. After all, if Sheridan had been a different kind of man, he might have abandoned her, and she would have been forced to join the long army of young women who, having had their reputations ruined for ever, had to resign themselves to spinsterhood, or worse.

If Gretna Green sounded far away when it was first mentioned, it proved to be only just over the Scottish border, but the journey there was so tedious that the whole idea of being married in haste and repenting at leisure returned once more to haunt Celandine. Sheridan seemed to understand this, because he spent most of the long train journey trying to raise her spirits until finally, perhaps tired out from his efforts, he allowed himself to become exasperated.

'If you don't start acting more like the happy bride-to-be, I will find someone else to run off with, see if I don't,' he threatened, waving his soup spoon at her.

They were staying the night at a hotel near the famous lovers' refuge, which should have meant that the wedding seemed excitingly close, and yet, despite her best efforts, bewildered loneliness had once more engulfed the future Mrs Montague Robertson, and it must have been showing a little too much for Sherry's peace of mind.

'What is the truth of your serious face, Miss

Benyon? I have never seen you so lacking in good spirits. Not changing your mind about your choice of husband, are you?'

In spite of his light tone the look in his eyes was worried.

'No, of course not,' Celandine replied quickly.

'What might be the matter, then?'

He took one of her hands and kissed the palm. It was a romantic gesture which was usually most effective, but he could now see it was not having the desired response.

'I haven't a dress to wear. I haven't a white dress. I have nothing suitable in which to be married,' she finally confessed after he had coaxed her yet again to confide in him.

'That doesn't matter, my love. I don't mind, I promise you. As far as I am concerned, you look beautiful in everything—' Sheridan stopped. 'Oh, no, it was wrong of me to say that, because you *do* mind. Of course you want to *look* like a bride, not just be one. Leave it to me, my darling. I will work a miracle, see if I don't.'

He looked thoughtful, but made no more mention of the subject until the following morning when they came downstairs from their separate bedrooms and he pointed to a small lady in a tartan cloak who was seated, very upright, in the dark brown reception hall of the hotel.

'Mrs McGregor is going to turn you into a bride before midday. Apparently she does it all the time,' he added airily.

Celandine looked from Sheridan to Mrs McGregor and back again, and mentally closed her eyes. After Paris and the chic shop windows of the rue de Rivoli for which the Parisians were so justly famous, the sight of Mrs McGregor in her plaid coat and bonnet was hardly encouraging.

'Follow me, if ye will. It's not far, thanks be. We'll have to hurry if we're to have ye clothed before the travelling parson comes. He'll nae stay more than a minute or two for anyone but the Almighty. For hasn't the mon six more couples to wed before he goes for his wee dram?'

Celandine, her head bent against the wind, followed Mrs McGregor to her house, a most respectable-looking establishment not far from the place where they were to be married.

'I fit up brides of all shapes and sizes and have done for many years.' There was a trace of self-importance in Mrs McGregor's voice, and when Celandine saw the choice of white gowns set about the sitting room, she had no trouble believing her. She stared round at the dresses ranged about the room, some spread on chairs and sofas, some hung against the cupboards. All the dresses were wide-skirted, quite obviously designed to be worn over a crinoline hoop such as Aunt Biddy wore. At the mere idea that she was going to be married looking about as fashionable as a teapot cosy, Celandine felt like catching up her cloak again and running back to the hotel; but realising, with a sinking heart, that she could hardly back out of the house without causing great offence, she pointed in vague desperation at a silk dress with small pearl buttons.

'I dare say that might fit me,' she said, a little hopelessly, and started to remove her bonnet.

The truth was that she had started not to care less what she looked like on her wedding day. So far from home, so far from anything familiar, with none of her family present, what did it matter now?

'Ah, now that is beautiful on ye, and doesn't it fit like a glove, wouldn't you say?'

Celandine stared helplessly at her reflection in the dressing mirror. It was really very little wonder that the gown fitted, since Mrs McGregor was standing behind her holding in the waist with both scrawny hands.

'I think it's a little big, wouldn't you say?' Celandine turned back to the older woman. 'Besides, I haven't managed a hoop in such a long while. I would not want to be embarrassed as one so often remembers ladies who could not manage their hoops were, or could be. The way they used to tip up unexpectedly was so mortifying for them. Without wishing to offend you, Mrs McGregor, I think I will just wear something of my own. I have a nice grey evening dress which I am sure will serve perfectly well . . .'

Mrs McGregor looked round the room in

desperation. 'A bride in grey! What will folk say? It will be terrible for my business, real terrible.'

Her eyes alighted on a large box, newly opened, the dress not yet hung out.

'Well, now, this is quite new, arrived this very morning. It came from a jilted bride; I bought it from her poor wee mother. She is a foreigner, from Northumberland, but it could be just what ye would be wanting, it could indeed.'

She held up a white silk dress, pristine, unworn. Celandine stared at it, wanting to know only one thing.

'It does not depend on a crinoline hoop, does it, Mrs McGregor?'

Mrs McGregor smiled for the first time. 'It does not, nae shall it!' she replied stoutly.

Not much later the two women, with Celandine's day dress safely boxed, hurried back towards the hotel, the future Mrs Montague Robertson dressed in white under her dark green cloak, with a pretty white rose-trimmed hat set on her dark hair, and a bouquet of white flowers plucked from Mrs McGregor's garden in her hand.

Sheridan was pacing up and down the cobbled yard in the usual state to be expected of a bridegroom, but when he saw Celandine he stopped pacing and stared. He had packed off a downcast young woman only an hour before, only to find her replaced by a beautiful bride.

'I must buy that dress for you, so I can paint you like that,' he cried over the wind and the rain as they hurried into the building where they were to be married at last.

The ceremony was quickly over, and they both bolted the wedding breakfast as fast as they could, anxious only to return to Cornwall, where Sheridan had once more rented his house at Newbourne.

'But what about Aunt Biddy? Didn't she say we were to return to her house, for a wedding party?'

'And so we shall, for a wedding party that will make the roof rafters shake with the sounds of our celebrations, but first we must honeymoon, my darling. A train is no place to celebrate a marriage.'

Sheridan kissed Celandine with passion. It was a long kiss, and the first of what proved to be hundreds, for, as his bride soon discovered, not only did Sheridan like to make love, but when he was not actually making love he was thinking of making love, and when he was not thinking of love in those first weeks of their marriage, he was painting it.

One languorous afternoon he climbed out of the bed, and painted her as she lay asleep, her long hair spread across a white pillow, her body relaxed and sensual – so sensual that it was all too obvious to the onlooker that the painting must have been modelled from real life, and there was no doubting that what had just taken place had been so fulfilling that the young woman whose body was only a little less white than the sheets upon which she lay would not be moving for some hours.

Unable to contain her curiosity about the progress of the painting Edith decided to confront Napier as they walked together to the studio.

'How is the painting going along, Napier?' she asked tentatively. Since he made no reply, she went on, 'I suppose I may not see it, even after all this time, may I?'

As he turned towards her the look in Napier's eyes confirmed her supposition, and Edith, who on this particular day, despite the cool early morning air, had felt unnaturally hot, realised that she was not going to be rewarded with an answer, and dropped her eyes.

Perhaps because of Napier's refusal to talk to her, the ensuing sitting seemed twice as long as usual. Edith, confused by her own feelings of curiosity and isolation, of loneliness and depression, not to mention a pounding head and a racing pulse, finally found she had to move her hand from the wretched harp. She was rewarded with the sound of a heavy sigh and the inevitable sight of Napier putting down his palette and walking away from his easel.

'Can you not sit still!' He turned away, throwing his brush into a corner, and folding his arms across his chest. 'Do you not know what it does to my concentration when you move like that? It does not just disturb the pose, it disturbs the muse.'

Edith had never quite grasped the idea of 'the muse' to which Napier had often referred, but seeing his fury she felt compelled to apologise.

'I am so sorry, Napier, truly I am. I would not disturb your concentration for anything. It is only that—'

She stopped, realising all at once that her pulse was beating far too fast and that her vision of the studio was definitely becoming blurred.

Napier, oblivious of anything but his own cares, walked off down to the other end of the studio and threw himself into an old, much worn library chair, staring into the fire that Mrs George always lit for her mistress's benefit.

'The painting has been going quite magnificently, up until now, that is,' he stated bleakly, a sulky look on his face. 'If only you would not *move*. I have told you time and time again that if you move it breaks my concentration.'

He himself stayed motionless in front of the fire, while Edith, for reasons she could not quite understand, went on sitting pointlessly still. Eventually she managed to run a quick hand across her eyes, blinking in desperation as she did so, trying to comprehend why the studio, normally so icy away from the benefit of the small coal fire, now seemed so airless.

Finally he stood up. 'Very well, let us try to go back to where we were, shall we?' He turned, a resigned expression on his face, a patronising tone to his voice. 'That is what we will do. We will assume there has been no break. We will go back to where we were and, if you have no objection, we will try to keep still for just a little longer; we will try to hold our pose and not break my concentration.'

He walked back towards his easel, frowning, and it was some few seconds before he glanced towards his model, only to find her collapsed on the floor.

Napier was in terrible trouble with Mrs George, and for once she was quite certain that he knew it, for as Edith's temperature soared and the doctor from the village arrived in his pony and trap to pronounce on her state of health, swiftly followed by the rector in *his* pony and trap, she was glad to see that Mr Todd's self-preoccupation faltered at last as he began to realise just how serious was his wife's condition.

'Not the rector as well?' Napier paled as he watched the dark figure with his Bible and bag walk solemnly up the elegant wooden stairs to Edith's bedroom.

'Dr Bennington recommended it, her condition is that serious, *sir*,' Mrs George told him, tight-lipped with suppressed anger. 'Sitting day after day in those freezing conditions in the studio, with hardly a stitch on – what on earth else did you expect to happen, Mr Todd, *sir*?'

The way Mrs George said 'sir' was as if she was boxing Napier's ears with the word.

'It is still summer, Mrs George. I never thought that Mrs Todd would feel cold in the *summer*.'

'It is never summer in your studio, *sir*. It is never summer in a vast stone edifice with only a small coal fire burning, and wearing a flimsy dress such as would be too little if you were going to your bed wearing it, *sir*.'

The rector, having visited the bedside and said prayers over Edith, shook his head sadly as he looked down at her feverish state before slowly descending the stairs once more, and proceeding with funeral tread to pay a call on the servants and the workers who were trying to enjoy their tea in the hall off the kitchens.

'I must ask for your prayers for the life of your poor young mistress,' he announced, having lightly banged the table in front of him. 'Mrs Todd's condition is so serious that we are now fearing for her life. As you go about your manual labour, praising God for His abundance, make sure that you include this virtuous young woman in your orisons.'

Mrs George, revelling in her authority over her patient, took complete charge, refusing to let Napier see Edith, and banishing him to sleep in his dressing room.

'A man has no business in a sick room,' Mrs George told him firmly, and she made it her business to stand by the bedroom door in such a way that Napier dared not push past her. 'I will let you know if her condition worsens. Dr Bennington believes just the sight of you could send her temperature up. No excitement with fevers, he says.'

She stared straight into her master's eyes and held his look in such a way that he was forced to read her unspoken words.

Thanks to your unrelenting selfishness she may well soon die, and nothing either the doctor or I can do to save her.

Finally, since Edith appeared not to be turning any sort of corner, and to his own astonishment, Napier found himself escaping the house to go to the nearby church and pray.

'I will of course be only too happy to attend your poor young wife in her last moments, Mr Todd.'

Napier stared at the rector, the realisation coming to him at last that he might well be going to lose Edith. He started to walk backwards down the church path, cramming his hat on his head, moving slowly away from the pale-faced cleric, before finally bolting back towards Helmscote, this time determined on seeing Edith, on telling her how much she meant to him.

He walked quickly up the shallow wooden stairs, and down the corridor to the bedroom just as Mrs George was emerging from it carrying a large bowl of water, with towels draped over her strong arms.

'I would like to see my wife,' he stated.

Mrs George did not smile. She looked at him gravely, as always blocking his path. 'You may see your wife now, Mr Todd, but only if you compose yourself. She is a very sick young woman. I do not want you upsetting her, especially not at this moment.'

Napier stared at the housekeeper, realising that the expression on her face was not unlike the one he had just seen on the face of the vicar. Mrs George's face was majestic in its solemnity. Edith, her expression seemed to be saying to him, was about to depart this world. For her part Mrs George was well aware that her own face was pale owing to sitting up all night and all day beside her patient, but as she looked at her master she realised that Napier's face was not pale, it was bloodless. The fear in his eyes was so real that she knew she would have to tell him the truth. She simply could not live with her conscience if she did not.

'Your wife, sir, has taken – your wife has taken a turn for the better, but I don't want anyone disturbing her, sir.'

'I shall endeavour not to do so.'

'That would be just as well, given the circumstances.'

Mrs George looked grim and stern but felt resigned, knowing that her words would have little effect on Mr Todd. She remained standing in front of the door.

'I don't want anyone bursting in on her. I don't want her upset. It could reverse her progress, bring her down, if you understand me, Mr Todd? We are very lucky to have her still, as you may very possibly have at last realised. You may go in,

213

but only for a minute, you understand. Only for the smallest of minutes, not more than that.'

She gave him yet another stern look before finally allowing him to pass her, and made her way down the corridor on careful tiptoe, as if to demonstrate to Napier just how she expected him to conduct himself in her patient's presence.

Edith opened her eyes just as her husband entered the room. She had no idea how dangerous her condition had been, or how high her fever, how delirious her state. All she knew was that a pale-faced Napier was now creeping towards her bedside, an expression of assumed calm on his face, anxiety in his eyes.

'Well, well, you have given us all a terrible turn, Edith. Mrs George and the rector quite feared for you,' he told her, clearing his throat, his heart beating faster as he realised, just from the look of her, quite how sick Edith had been.

'I don't know what can have been wrong with me . . .'

She moved her lips with difficulty for they were still dry and cracked from the fever, and seeing this Napier leaned forward and took a glass of water from her bedside table and offered it to her. She sipped at it.

'I am so sorry I have held you up, Napier,' she whispered, giving him back the glass. 'You must be so late with your painting . . .'

'Old Hollingsworth will wait for my masterpiece,' Napier told her. 'He will have to now, won't he? No matter he has finished the room in which it is to hang, no matter that he has chosen the frame, he will just have to wait until you are better and it is finished.'

Edith smiled bleakly and then closed her eyes again. If she had had the strength she knew she would have cried at his words. For it seemed to her that the reality behind them was that Mrs George and the rector had feared for her, but Napier had only really feared for his painting.

The truth was that he had not missed Edith at all; that was really quite certain. It seemed that nothing had changed.

Within a week or so Edith was allowed downstairs and able to sit in the small morning room off the main hall. She felt too weak to do more than sit in front of the fire and stare into it, but Mrs George was so assiduous in her attentions that even if she had been able to do more, the housekeeper would not have let her, fussing around her as if she was still in danger, instead of well on the way to recuperation, which Edith was certain she must be.

Napier on the other hand was obviously at a loose end, and without perhaps realising it made this quite plain. He could not finish his great painting without Edith, but at the same time he was finding it impossible to get on with anything else.

'She's not coming back to the studio until the doctor says she can, Mr Todd,' Mrs George told her master, her ultimatum emerging so tightly that the words appeared to be squeezed out from between her thin lips. 'Not for anything is she going back to that studio of yours until Dr Bennington says she may, and at the moment I have to tell you, sir, he says she may *not*.'

It amused Mrs George to see Napier struggling with his feelings as he was forced to accept that until Edith was *quite* better he must obey the doctor's, and Mrs George's, orders.

'I feel some guilt about my wife's condition, you know, Mrs George.' He had walked off to the morning-room window, but now he turned to face his housekeeper.

'I am sure we all should,' Mrs George told him, careful to keep her tone as objective as possible. 'But least said soonest mended, I always think, and let us hope that we can come up with some way to speed Mrs Todd's recovery.'

'Do you think there is something else we can do?'

'I always think there is something else we can do, sir.'

'I must think of something then, I must really.'

Finally, some days later, Napier came into the morning room holding a letter, obviously newly arrived.

'This is from my friend Sherry Montague,' he announced.

Edith looked up at him, her expression remote, as it always seemed to be nowadays.

'Sherry has written saying that I must come back to Cornwall, and bring you too, that it will

216

be perfectly splendid for your health. He says there are plenty of lodgings in the villages around Newbourne and suchlike places. I know that from when I visited him last summer.'

Edith's expression did not change, and Napier went on in a rush, hoping to engage her interest.

'Cornwall is beautiful at this time of year. I am sure it will help you recover. You will feel quite different once we go to Cornwall, I know it. You will benefit from the sea air. I am sure that Mrs George and the doctor will be happy for you to travel now you are a little stronger.' He took up one of her hands and patted it, his expression optimistic as he imagined a rosier future. 'And once I see you settled and happy in our lodgings, I will be able to go off with Sherry and paint in the open air, something he is always only too anxious for me to try.'

Without waiting for Edith to say whether or not she wanted to go Napier left the room, humming happily to himself, not realising that Edith had said nothing in response to his pronouncements.

Edith stared after him for a few seconds before closing her eyes and surrendering herself to lassitude. Each time she saw Napier she longed to ask him why he had not yet loved her in the way men were meant to love their wives. She longed to ask him if her innocence put him off; if she was too young and too unsophisticated for him. And yet she dared not, because she had no idea how she should frame the words. Besides, there was something about the look in Napier's eyes that always stopped her. Since her illness, it seemed to her the look had strengthened in purpose, as if he was determined on something about which he could not, or would not, tell her.

Mrs George looked heartened by the news of the projected journey, and she too seemed to think that Edith would do nothing except benefit from sea air.

'You will be well out of this cold, damp climate here in the Cotswolds. Even at this time of year we are not as warm as we should be, and a lot less warm than we would wish to be, Mrs Todd, and if that isn't the truth I don't know what is. Besides,' she gave Edith a shrewd look, 'you need to get some colour in those pale cheeks of yours; need to put on some weight, too, or we will soon be seeing right through you, same as we can see through that windowpane over there, and that would never do.'

Edith nodded excitedly, only half listening.

'I've never been to the sea, you know,' she confided suddenly, dropping her voice as if such an admission was scandalous. 'I was always too busy working to be able to do anything like that. I could never be spared at home.'

Mrs George nodded. 'I know, my dear,' she agreed absently. 'I am the same, never been to the coast, nor seen the sea, but then my mother and father had never been to the next village until Father turned eighty last year!' She gave a sudden, rich laugh. 'We took him to Lower Broughton – he lives in Upper Broughton, mind – and he came back that shocked. Yes, he was that shocked. "Don't never want to go to them foreign parts again," he told Mother.' She gave another laugh. 'Now Mother only has to threaten him with going to Upper Broughton, and he'll set to and do as she wants soon as a knife goes through summer butter.'

'I dare say I will have to take warm clothes for the seaside,' Edith mused.

'You take just what you have, Mrs Todd, just what you have, and I am sure that will be perfect, seaside or no seaside.'

But Edith ignored her, knowing instinctively that she would need to take only the simplest outfits from her wardrobe, although she thought she would need a warm coat for walks along the seashore.

'You bring me back some shells from the beach, and yourself with a bonny look to you,' Mrs George commanded a few days later when they were all packed up, and Edith, with Napier waiting impatiently in the hall, was hurrying out of her bedroom. 'Maybe you will even bring us back some happy news,' she murmured, but only to herself.

Once on their way, and settled into their train carriage, Napier did not trouble to engage Edith in conversation but stared out of the window, watching for something at which she could only guess.

'You must have lived in a great many houses—' Edith began, determined on breaking the silence, no matter what.

Napier stared at her. 'What did you say?'

'I said, you must have lived in a great many houses.'

'Yes, I have, as a matter of fact. I was an only child, and as such able to travel a great deal with my father. After my mother died when I was hardly more than four years old, Father never did like to stay long in one place, and seeing that he was a master builder, happily his work took him to more places than most. He built a series of follies for Lord Branscombe at Puddleton, a Dower House for Cecilia, Lady Gasper, at Winson, and a Swiss Cottage with Dovecote for Mrs Arbutnot in Derbyshire. His last commission was Helmscote, but the owner died before it was finished; so Father bought it, and then he too died, and so it finally passed to me.' He stared out of the window again as they started to pass through the lush green countryside of the West Country.

'I expect it was on account of living near all those fine houses that you became a painter, was it not, Napier?'

'Do you know, I think it was. How perceptive of you.' Napier put his head on one side, frowning. 'Yes, it was seeing all the fine paintings in their beautiful settings. I am sure it was that, more than anything, that encouraged me from an early age to think of myself as a painter before anything else. Nothing matters more than art, you know, Edith – nothing.'

Edith, perhaps emboldened by Napier's compliment, ventured further. 'What will you paint when we are in Cornwall, Napier?'

'To begin with, the sea, the shore, anything but a model,' he said, blithely ignoring Edith's feelings. 'For the next few weeks, while you regain your strength, I shall embark on this new idea of painting in the open air, painting the strong faces of the Cornish people. I told you Sherry is determined on my changing my ways, and turning from the Pre-Raphaelites to the realities of fisherfolk. Sherry is all too enthusiastic, even more so now that he is married. Yes, you will have company at Newbourne. I believe his wife is a beautiful American girl. I know she also paints.'

Edith looked away from Napier and stared out of the window, trying not to feel daunted. A beautiful American girl who was also a painter would surely never want to be friends with someone like herself? She would be clever, and most likely a bluestocking too. She would look down on Edith as she knew Napier looked down on her for not knowing anything about art, or perhaps even about life. It was not a happy prospect, but at least she would see the sea.

In the event they had left Helmscote so early they were able to arrive at Newbourne before the sun had begun to set. The pony and trap that brought them from the station had been hired by pre-arrangement with Sheridan. The noise from the sturdy creature's hooves was drowned out by the insistent cries of the seagulls, but nothing, alas, could drown the smell of the fish that permeated the town at dusk.

'Welcome to Newbourne.'

Almost as soon as the trap came to a halt the front door of the house to which the driver had been directed was opened by a young woman, white-aproned, smiling, her hair caught back into a net.

'Mrs Harvey, it's Mr Todd from last summer,' Napier called up the flight of steps. 'Remember?'

'Of course. I remember you well, sir.'

Napier walked up the steps towards Mrs Harvey, leaving Edith to struggle out of the trap. The driver, seeing her difficulties, jumped down from his seat to help her over the debris in the road. Slightly out of breath, she gained the top of the steps and smiled at Mrs Harvey, who smiled back.

'Good afternoon, ma'am, and a truly fine one it has been.'

Napier walked ahead of them both into the house, followed by the driver carrying their luggage, one piece on his head, the other in his hand.

'I have supper prepared for you whenever you may wish it, ma'am, but a hot bath before might be what you would be wanting, I dare say.'

The idea of a hot bath after such a long journey

appealed to Edith as being near to bliss, but it seemed that Napier was determined on going straight out again to visit the Montague Robertsons.

'You can stay here, Edith. There is no need for you to come, I don't suppose.'

'I had rather go with you, Napier, really I would. I had rather not be left here.'

Napier looked surprised, as if he did not quite know what he would do with Edith if she did come with him.

'Oh, very well.'

He walked determinedly along the narrow streets, the houses of which seemed about to topple over on to them, so near to the passers-by did they appear to Edith. After her illness and convalescence she had a job of it to keep pace with her husband, but as she did so she made sure to keep on his inside, away from the fish scales and debris that littered the sides of the narrow streets.

It seemed that the town was divided into two, and they were lodged in Newbourne Town, whereas Napier's friends were living on the other side of the river in a place called Street-anlyne. Despite the pace that Napier had set, Edith determined on memorising everything they passed, until all at once it appeared that they had arrived, because Napier was knocking at the door of a pretty white-painted house.

To the side of the front door were fishing nets and easels, and all sorts of homely paraphernalia that spoke of a happy, industrious life, and once again the door was opened by a white-aproned figure, but this time an older woman, who nevertheless smiled her welcome, and turning back called to unseen people inside.

'Your friends are a-coming in, Mr Sheridan – Mrs Sheridan – here be your friends, and they're a-coming in to find you in the garden!'

'Hallo, Mrs Molesworth. You haven't changed an iota—' Napier began, but he broke off and frowned as the landlady curtsied to him. 'Come, come, Mrs Molesworth, let us have none of that. We live in a democracy.'

As she drew up from her courtesy Napier absentmindedly, or just rudely – Edith herself had not yet quite made up her mind as to which – went to walk in front of his wife, as was generally his habit, but the housekeeper gently caught his arm and held him back, making way for Edith to go in front of him.

'Nay, Master Napier, you're a married man now, you mun remember.' She nodded firmly at Edith to walk ahead of Napier. 'Make way for your little wife, Master Napier, or I shall want to know the reason why, I shall.'

'Gracious, Mrs Molesworth, seeing you there I confess I had almost forgotten I was married since I saw you last summer, I am sure I had,' Napier muttered, trying to pass the moment off with a laugh.

'Before you do away with bobbing and curtsying, Mr Todd, I've a mind to tell you to remember your wife's place. Anywhen you'm in my house, I'll be thankin' you to behave. Painters!' Mrs Molesworth clicked her tongue and shook her head firmly at his back. 'They know all about how the world should be run, but nowt about how it *is* run.'

Perhaps because it was the first time since her marriage that she had seen Napier out of his own environment, or perhaps because it was the first time she had seen him told off publicly, Edith found herself struggling to keep a straight face as she saw *him* struggle, albeit briefly, to find a suitable reply to Mrs Molesworth's robust put-down and, not really finding one, colouring in embarrassment.

'Did I hear Mrs M telling you off, Napier?'

They had emerged into the garden by now, and turned as a voice spoke to them from behind. Looking up, they saw Sheridan standing beside an easel on a large balcony above them.

'I'm coming down this minute,' he called, smiling delightedly at them both. 'How capital to see you, and earlier than we had hoped. Celandine will not be long; she is changing. Stay just where you are and we will join you in a matter of minutes, my dear friends. We have been so looking forward to this.'

Edith stared round the garden. It was not large but it had the air of being cared for, and the choice of flowers, the use of shells and exotics, made her feel as if she had travelled all the way from the Cotswolds not to another corner of

England, but to a foreign country. And of course, because of the clear, bright air of which Napier had already told her, the colours seemed more colourful, the blues bluer, the pinks pinker, even the sky above them, despite its going to be dusk quite soon, seeming to her to be more beautifully blue than any sky she had known. And then Sheridan, with Celandine moving quickly ahead of her husband and dressed in a charming sailor top and white skirt, an embroidered jacket and white lace-up boots, seemed to burst upon the garden scene, both of them smiling, arms out in welcome.

'My dear chap, I can't tell you, when we received your letter, how pleased we were!'

They had hardly finished their greetings and introductions before Edith had seen that there was no pretending that Sheridan was not everything to Celandine, and she to him. Despite the beauty of the garden, the clarity of the air, the feeling that evening was not quite upon them, they had brought their own aura of warmth and sunshine to the already romantic scene – as if there was not enough romance around them already! What was more, she could see that they turned and referred to each other often, while pretending not to take each other's conversation at all seriously.

And, too, she noted with a sinking heart that Celandine, seated now and pouring drinks for them all, had no need to wait or defer to Sheridan. She could be herself, allow her own character to shine. She could even tease him publicly, and still it seemed her husband loved her.

Edith sipped her drink, silently watching, trying to smile and laugh along with the rest, despite not being able to contribute much to the conversation; remaining, outwardly at least, the beautiful relaxed young wife while inwardly struggling with a misery so potent it seemed to her that she was filled with unshed tears. Her emotions were in marked contrast to the happiness she could see emanating from their hosts.

Finally, as they rose to go into supper together, and she realised just what she was missing, she allowed the sadness to overcome her, at which point she excused herself. Letting herself out of the front door, she vanished into the street outside, her rich auburn hair catching the last of the evening sunlight as she did so.

Chapter Six

Edith lay in bed absorbing the sound of the seagulls, the chugging of the boats coming into harbour, the early morning feel to the light coming through the curtains, and remembered Napier's coming to find her in the street outside the Montague Robertsons' rented house. He had looked puzzled but unworried as she begged to be allowed to return home.

'A slight nausea?' Napier appeared vague and disinterested, all at the same time. 'Ask Mrs Molesworth for something. She will be sure to have something that will help you feel better.'

'No, I would prefer to go back and rest. It's been a long day. I expect I am just tired after my illness.'

'Well, of course. I keep forgetting you have been unwell. It will take some time for you to get your strength back, I dare say.' He leaned forward and patted her arm in an avuncular manner. 'I also dare say Mrs George and Dr Bennington will be telling me off if I don't send you back to your bed,' he added, turning back to the house behind them even as he spoke.

Edith knew Napier well enough by now to recognise that particular look which had come into his eyes. He was ready to dine and wine, ready to let his hair down, as he had been sometimes at Helmscote when something happened to disturb the unrelenting artistic regime, such as when a neighbour called, quite unexpectedly, and Napier invited him to stay to dinner; or when a fellow painter, such as Alfred Talisman, had come to Helmscote for a night, and Edith was banished to the upper floor to have supper in her room and to fall asleep all too early, with only a book for company.

Napier turned and called to her from the top step of Mrs Molesworth's lodging house.

'I will make your excuses. I will also tell Celandine to be sure to call on you tomorrow, as Sherry and I are going to start on our open-air painting straight away. He has some splendid scenes all set and ready for us both. You two ladies can go off and do your little commissions, or whatever you wish; perhaps even some tasteful watercolouring on the harbourside?' Napier smiled. 'At any rate I will tell Celandine to be sure to call for you about eleven o'clock. You will be better by then, I know. As a matter of fact, since you are not quite the thing tonight, it is probably easier if I stay here, and set off with Sherry in the morning. That would mean we can take advantage of the light, which will be capital, and I can enjoy a late evening without too much thought of keeping you up.' He went to kiss his hand to her, but Edith had hurried off up the street. 'Oh, very well.'

Napier shrugged his shoulders, and hurried back up the steps and into the house and the welcome smell of Mrs Molesworth's excellent lamb stew, not to mention her fruit pudding and syllabub, last tasted the previous summer.

Edith hurried on, heading she hoped for the beach and the river that divided Newbourne, and promptly becoming lost. What with the sun setting out to sea, the dusk gently descending, and the narrowness of the streets, her feelings of dark despair seemed to be increasing and not decreasing, so that she found herself wandering further and further without caring too much if she was heading back to her lodgings or not.

Once or twice a drunkard would lean out from a doorway and try to catch her dress, but she managed to sidestep them, and hurried on until she found herself at the top of the town.

She had never contemplated such dark feelings before, not even when her mother had died, but now it seemed to her that she was losing out to some part of her nature that she had never before known existed. She felt dizzy and dry-mouthed, knowing with complete certainty that had there been some easy means for her to end it all, she would; knowing that when she had left Napier it was the river she had hoped to find, the deep stretch of water where she could finally escape her distraught feelings.

She sat down on a low wall, pulling her coat about her, and found herself staring round in increasing despair, not only because she had married someone with whom she had been sure she was in love, only to find that he cared nothing for her, but because she had no idea where she was, and it was quite probable that she would never find her way back to her lodgings until daylight came.

She put her head in her hands, feeling the tears dripping through her fingers, tears that suddenly seemed to be illuminated by the light of a lantern.

'Can I help you? You seem to be in some distress.'

Edith quickly ran an arm across her eyes, as she would have done when she was a child, trying to compose her face.

'No. At least, yes,' she said, in a half-whisper.

'Distress can come to us all, or is it just lost you are?'

'You are right, I am lost,' Edith admitted, raising her voice. 'You see, I am new to Newbourne . . .' She gave a faint smile because it sounded so stupid.

'So you're new and quite lost, is that what you are saying?'

Edith stared up into the kind, bearded face. 'Yes, yes, I am, in every way.'

'Do you remember your address, do you

think? Seeing that you are so new here you might be able to remember it.'

Dimly Edith remembered it, but as her throat once more felt constricted she shook her head wordlessly.

'Name of the person you're staying with, might that come to you, my dear?'

'Mrs Harvey.' That came out better.

'Mrs Harvey? I know Mrs Harvey – of Primrose House?' As Edith nodded, he went on, 'You'm on the wrong side of the Slip, my dear. You come with me, and we'll soon find our way.'

He swung the lantern encouragingly and Edith straightened up, knowing that she would have to go with him.

She did not know why, but as she followed the tall figure in front of her she felt as if she was leaving something behind on the low stone wall. What it was she could not have said exactly, except that she knew it was gone, because after a few minutes of walking at first behind and then beside the tall, bearded man, she began to be able to see in the dark, and it was not just because of the light of his lantern, not just because he talked gently to her of the sea and its ways, of fishing and boats, not really expecting her to reply – it was something to do with the gentleness and warmth that seemed to be coming from him.

'Here we are, my dear.' He held up his lantern and it swung a little too vigorously in the breeze as he did so, lighting his face. 'Mrs Harvey will be coming to the door any moment.' He nodded towards the owl doorknocker that he had dropped against the blue-painted door. 'You are no longer lost, my dear, but quite safe again, and here's herself, here's Mrs Harvey to take care of you.'

'Mrs Todd! Back again so soon?'

'Yes, I am afraid so – the bad penny and all that that entails.' Edith smiled at Mrs Harvey before turning at the door to thank her escort, but he had gone.

'I thought it too much for a little thing like you to go straight out a-visiting, and after a long journey like that; but that's Mr Todd all over, I'm afraid, as you must know yourself by now. You'm be as tired out as a bird in the spring coming back to Cornwall. You come with me, my dear, and I'll help you to your room.'

Mrs Harvey put an arm round Edith and helped her up the stairs to her bedroom where her visitor sat down on the bed, staring wordlessly for a while at nothing much, while Mrs Harvey fussed about her, taking the brass warming pan with its loose hot coals from her bed, and laying out her nightclothes.

'I was lost and a kind gentleman showed me the way home.'

Mrs Harvey nodded, not really listening. 'That's right, my dear. Now you undress yourself and don't stir until morning, and whoever it was that showed you home, he must have been a nice gentleman, because anyone can get lost in

233

Newbourne down the lines as we call them – the lines is that narrow and that crooked even us gets lost down them some of the time.'

Those had been the last words that Edith remembered. She appeared to have undressed and climbed into her wonderfully warm bed and fallen asleep before she could ask Mrs Harvey what the name of the kind gentleman who had accompanied her might have been.

Now she drew back the flowered curtains of her bedroom and stared out at the picturesque scene outside. With her despair quite fled, Cornwall seemed to her to be a paradise that morning, and she no longer felt haunted by the unhappiness that had been weighing her down the previous evening. She was in a new place, and new places it seemed held out their hands to you, grasped you by the fingers and whirled you round in such a way as to remind her of her birthday bumps at the Stag. Birthday bumps had always been a highlight of the year. The other maids would take hold of her hands and feet and swing her backwards and forwards before they bounced her up and down on the hard wooden floor until they had bumped her the same number of years as her birthday.

Remembering these and other happy times, and thinking that perhaps there was a chance that one day there would be more, Edith jumped out of bed, and hurried down the uneven corridor to the bathroom, determined on washing and dressing as quickly as possible before

taking a walk on her own to try to work up her
still feeble appetite for breakfast.

As Napier had promised the evening before,
Celandine did indeed call before midday. Edith
was seated in Mrs Harvey's front room reading a
book in a desultory fashion when she saw her
crossing the narrow street and coming towards
the house. Celandine saw Edith too, and waved
long before she reached Mrs Harvey's front door,
her face lighting up.

'I am glad you are up and about. I hope you
are quite recovered?' she said, as soon as she
realised that Edith was ready and waiting for her.
'I was so worried when Napier said you had to
go home on account of not feeling well. We
missed you. I have not been married so long that
I don't still find that *I* miss female company.
When on my own, alone and dining with gentlemen, I quite flounder, really I do. Either I sit there
silent as the grave, listening to their high-flown
ideas, or I start to argue against everything they
are lecturing me about, which is so tiring that I
wake up in the morning vowing never to do
anything so silly again. Gracious heavens, whoever changed the mind of a man over a dinner
table? It has never been known.'

Celandine laughed gaily. They were both out
in the street again, and she caught up the front of
her elegantly tailored coat and nodded towards
the harbour.

'I thought, as it is your first morning, we would
walk along to the old harbour and, just for a

game, watch out for the West Cornwall Luggers. Sometimes they can come back unexpectedly early, although not often, Mrs Molesworth tells me; but when they do, it seems it is quite a sight to see, at least so she says.' Seeing Edith did not understand what she meant, Celandine explained. 'The Luggers go to sea in the summer, sometimes for as much as three months at a time. It's a hard life, Mrs Molesworth says; but they enjoy being away from their wives, as so many men do. And of course the wives can get on with running their boarding houses and other such things without having the men coming in and out smelling of stinking *poisson*! Fish does smell so, as you probably noticed as soon as you arrived in Newbourne.'

Edith fell in readily with Celandine's plan, walking along beside this vibrant young woman with more vigour than she had brought to anything for what seemed weeks, all the while well aware that, perhaps because she was still feeling tired after her illness, she was feeding off Celandine's buoyancy, just as she had fed off Mrs Harvey's concern the previous evening. It was as if Celandine was the sun, and Edith her earth, desperately in need of her warmth after a long, hard winter.

Since it was a beautiful morning filled with perfect sunshine they walked at a leisurely pace towards their goal. Celandine, sensing that her companion was not yet feeling as well as she was perhaps pretending, kept up a one-way flow of conversation, until they eventually came to a stop on the waterfront.

'This is the old harbour,' Celandine explained. 'Sheridan is always painting it.' She turned to Edith, and pulled a face. 'At least, I say Sheridan – I should say Sheridan and *Mrs* Sheridan, because he very generously allows me to fill in the background, the sky and those roofs over there – he hates roofs, so monotonous he always says, tile after tile. So good for your technique, I always say, but of course he will not believe me. After all, not all tiles are the same. Some have mossy bits, some have chips, some are redder or browner. Detail, boring detail, he murmurs, unimpressed, and leaves it all to his poor wife.'

'He lets you paint on his canvases?'

'No, Edith, he *makes* me paint the dull uninspired bits on his canvases, the bits that he does not wish to bother with, while he gets on with the figures in the foreground!' Celandine gave a light laugh.

'Do you like doing that?'

'As long as he doesn't touch *my* canvases I am perfectly happy to paint *his* roofs and his sky. Although of course I can't help ribbing him about it. "Do you think Turner would have done this, Sheridan?" I ask him. But Sheridan being Sheridan merely says that Turner did not paint with the square-brush technique, he did not attack his canvases in the *modern* manner, but had he been alive of course he would have done, or so Sheridan says.' She laughed again, obviously not believing her husband, and not caring that she didn't. 'And you? Does Napier make you daub? Or is he still firmly and shockingly a Pre-Raphaelite, as he was so busy assuring Sheridan last night?'

Edith shook her head, feeling suddenly ignorant and exposed by the question.

'I don't know what Napier is,' she confessed. 'I have no idea how he is painting at the moment. I sit to him in his studio for his new painting, that is all I know. He does not like me to comment. I just sit to him, for this new painting he has had in his mind for so long,' she finished in a suddenly low voice.

'You sit to him?' For the first time Edith could see that she had shocked Celandine. 'You *sit* to him? In that case you are a martyr. I *refuse* to sit to Sheridan. If he wants models he has to go into the village and find them for himself. I can think of nothing worse than hour after hour spent in holding a pose, but the fishermen and women here don't seem to mind at all. In fact they are so long in patience it makes me weep. I tell them they should charge Sheridan, but they seem to be flattered by the attention, and of course Sheridan plies them with drink and food before or after, I forget which. I suppose it all depends on the time of day, but whatever the time, and for however long they sit, they are quite touchingly grateful. Fishing is such a hard life, but knowing nothing else, and belonging as they do to a small community, they seem to want for nothing, not even hope.'

Celandine frowned, staring out to sea while thinking over what she had said.

'The next haul is always going to be the one that brings them in their hearts' desires, and if it does not, well, there is always the next, and the next after that, and so on. But enough of that. It is surely time we went back to our house, and I gave you luncheon in the garden? Ever since leaving my mother's house and marrying Sheridan I have become assistant cook to anyone who will let me help them. Happily Mrs Molesworth is too good a cook to need me, but I like to watch. Not this morning, however. We will have far too much to talk about this morning, will we not?'

Once back in the garden with Celandine serving them glasses of Mrs Molesworth's delicious home-made wine, Edith, feeling herself to be under scrutiny from her companion, felt confident enough in her company to turn the tables on her.

'Were you married in Cornwall? Were you married in Newbourne?'

Celandine shook her head. 'No, I had to run away with Sheridan to Gretna Green to be married, would you believe?' She shook her head. 'What a thing! A young American woman running off with an Irishman of all people – and to Scotland of all places. Shocking, my dear, too *shocking*! Little wonder my mother refuses to have anything more to do with me.'

'Does she not like Sheridan?' Edith asked, wondering to herself if it was possible for anyone not to like such an instantly warm personality.

'She has never met him.' Celandine half closed her eyes, leaning back in her chair, remembering. 'She has only seen him, in a drawing I did of him.' She looked across at Edith, willing herself to shock her new friend.

'Was it a good drawing?' Edith asked, hesitantly, because she was longing to know more, but unwilling to reveal her longing.

'It was a *very* good drawing of Sheridan,' Celandine informed her, pride in her voice. 'The only trouble being that . . .' She held her head at the same angle, eyes still half closed. 'The only trouble being,' she repeated, 'Sheridan did not have any clothes on. He was as Mother Nature made him.'

Edith straightened herself, carefully replacing her glass on the table. 'Oh,' she said slowly. 'Well, I dare say if you are married that is not quite so shocking, surely?'

'Quite. The only trouble being that at the time of the drawing we were *not* married.' Celandine opened her eyes fully and stared at Edith, trying to keep a straight face, and finally failing.

'Can you imagine?' she asked, laughing helplessly. 'For a woman like my mother whose ancestors sailed to America on the *Mayflower*. Can you imagine her thoughts, or lack of them, when she saw my drawing? Such was the shock I thought she might pass out.'

240

Edith too began to laugh, but only really because Celandine's laughter was so infectious.

'I was turned out of the house, of course. Really rather lucky that Sheridan wanted to marry me, don't you think?'

'I suppose—'

'You suppose, Mrs Todd! But for Sheridan I would now be a fallen woman, and heaven knows that is not a position in Society that anyone sensible would choose. Women do not win at love.'

Edith stared at Celandine, whom she had from the first found delightful, but whom she now found fascinating, slowly realising that she had another less conventional side to her character, and one that was perhaps not really very susceptible to shock.

Encouraged by this discovery she opened her own large eyes wider, remembering the previous evening's despair, and how attractive a leap into the river had seemed – should she have been able to find the wretched stretch of water. Realising that, such had been her despair, but for finding herself lost and meeting the stranger she might well be dead, she took the verbal leap necessary to friendship, all of a sudden determined on being as candid as Celandine.

'I do not know whether women win at love, for the simple reason that I have never known love,' she confided.

Celandine was so busy pouring them both

another glass of wine that she seemed not to have heard her new friend.

'What was that you said?' she asked, for she had heard, but thought it only right to pretend that she had not.

'I said,' Edith repeated, 'I have not known love. I do not know what love *is*.'

'But you must do! You are teasing me, of course you are. After all, you are expecting *une petite quelque chose*, are you not?'

After a few seconds' pause Edith reddened as she slowly came to understand from Celandine's expression just what she was implying.

'No, no! No, that would not be at all possible, quite impossible, in fact. Quite impossible.'

'But that is why you left us, surely, last night when you left us feeling suddenly so unwell, because of your interesting state? At least, that is what Sheridan and I instantly imagined, although we said nothing to Napier. Nevertheless, we both thought it. We were quite sure. We were so happy for you. It is what we ourselves want so much,' she confided. 'It is such a happy outcome to the delights of love, don't you think? I myself find I look forward so much—' Celandine stopped as Edith shook her head.

'No, I am very much afraid I am expecting nothing. How could I? When I have not known love, how could I be expecting anything?' she asked, unable to keep the despair and the sadness from her voice. 'Napier does not love me. It

242

seems I do not please him, not at all. No, I do not please him,' she finished.

Celandine stared at the beautiful young girl seated at the table, for once lost for words.

'You have left me speechless,' she said, after a pause, adding with a swift retreat into humour, 'And believe me that does not happen often.'

Edith gave a faint smile. 'Well, if I were you,' she said, with almost ruthless honesty, 'and you had told me the same about your marriage, I confess I would be the same, I would not know what to say at all. Not that it would happen with your marriage,' she said sadly, as she remembered Sheridan and Celandine together the night before. 'It is very evident that your husband loves you very much indeed, and that you love him very much indeed. That at least is quite plain to see. Napier does not love me. To be honest, I do not know why he married me, except perhaps for some reason that he has now forgotten, or which he is trying to remember. I think that is why he decided to paint me, to take his mind off having married me, which he obviously now believes was a mistake,' she said, finally allowing her deep, long-held misery to surface. 'I am now convinced that he is repelled by me.'

'Oh, surely not?' Celandine sprang up from her chair and stared down at Edith before slowly sitting down again, such was the almost physical effect Edith's confession had had upon her. 'I am afraid I cannot believe that what you have just said to me is true.'

'It is true.' Edith looked down the garden, staring at the flowers, wishing that she could feel as she would like to feel, relaxed and happy, able to appreciate the beauty of her surroundings, as she knew Celandine must be doing.

Celandine allowed a minute or so to elapse before she continued.

'I think I know what the matter is. Napier is an *Englishman*,' she told Edith, in a low voice, as if she herself was now stating something really rather shocking. 'And I have heard that Englishmen are often afraid of women in the Biblical sense, that the men are too much incarcerated with their own sex when growing up, and as a consequence, unless they have sisters, or an enlightened mama, they are not well versed in the ways of women.' She frowned at Edith, her head on one side, before going on. 'The interesting thing is that from what you say Napier insists on your sitting to him, and that is not something that a man who is – forgive my using your words back to you – but that is surely not something that a man who was repelled by you would do? Indeed, I would say that he worships your beauty.'

'Yes, perhaps.' Edith nodded. 'He has admitted as much, several times. When we talk about when he first saw me, which is not often, he has said it was my looks that first attracted him to me. I think he feels that I should feel grateful for that. And I do see that I should. After all, I was on my hands and knees scrubbing floors when he first saw me. I dare say I *should* be grateful.'

'What about his painting? What about the masterpiece for which you have been sitting to him?' Celandine asked, a little too quickly, knowing that Edith had a point and at once realising the pain behind the statement.

'I became ill before Napier could finish it, which is so irksome for him, because the gentleman who commissioned it has finished the room into which it is destined to go. It was because my illness interrupted him that we had to come away, so that Napier could have a change, allow fresh breezes and the good ozone to help him back to the inspiration that he lost while I was ill.'

Celandine snorted lightly and prettily as Edith gave a small cough, as if talking about her illness had prompted one of the symptoms to recur.

'Oh, my. *You* are ill, and *he* has to come away! How that painterly all-male Hamlet behaviour brings about a flood of impatience in me. I suppose once *you* were ill *he* felt neglected because his inspiration had run out?' She laughed, and then held up a hand, shaking her head. 'No, you don't have to tell me. Believe me, I can guess.'

'Painting is so difficult, is it not?'

'Of course painting is difficult, but then so is everything interesting – cooking and marriage, having babies and riding horses – everything interesting is impossibly difficult if you are trying to do it well. Painting is no different.' Celandine breathed in and out just a little dramatically. 'And it is certainly not a reason, never should be a reason, to neglect your wife.' She stopped suddenly. 'Except that it could be.' She looked serious, then excited, before she widened her eyes. 'My goodness, of course! I see exactly. I see precisely. Indeed, I am sure I might be right.'

Edith waited, silent, not wanting to distract her hostess from what might be an inspired notion.

'Napier is trying to make a great painting of you not because he is repelled by you, but because he worships you. I am sure that he *must* have fallen in love with your *beauty*, but as yet, because the painting is not yet complete, you have not become a *human being* to him. You have remained as he first saw you – as his inspiration – which means that in a fervour of silly artistic activity he has neglected you for some reason – perhaps artistic superstition, who knows? Perhaps not even he does? But the truth is that he has neglected you and his marriage.'

Celandine sighed, and clicked her tongue in such a way as to suggest that it was nothing new.

'It is too sickening, but quite typical of someone like Napier, a painter first and foremost, in his own mind at least. Believe me, Edith, there is no such thing as an unselfish artist – I know because I am one of them! Selfish to the core, that is what we are – we artists who decide to call ourselves *painters*. Driven by some need to paint first and live second we fully expect the rest of the world to fall in step with us, while failing singularly to explain any of our motives for wanting such things. Happily Sheridan and I are both as selfish as each other.'

She put a hand on Edith's arm.

'My dear Edith, all this must have been too horrible for you, but down here, in Cornwall, you will see, everything will very soon change. Believe me, before we came to this place I was in despair at being cast out by my mother, at all the harm my love for Sheridan seemed to have brought upon everyone I loved. I was – ashamed; there is no other word for it. But since coming here that way of thinking has quite disappeared. I think you will find that Napier too will change. His reticence towards you can be nothing to do with his love for you, but everything to do with selfish egoism, with not thinking, with becoming caught up in his work, which is to say, becoming caught up in *himself*.'

'Yes, but when the painting is finished, what then? He might still not want me, he might still find himself – repelled.'

'We won't use that word,' said Celandine, severely. 'Of course I can only imagine how you must feel, most especially as you are so young, and innocent, not travelled as I am both in America and in Europe. You have only known first your father's and then your husband's house. Besides which you have no one whom you can have been able to ask about such things either, I don't suppose.' She shook her head, half speaking to herself rather than Edith. 'We must make a plan, Edith, a plan that will jolt your silly

247

husband into realising your worth, and not just as a model for his painting. We will change the way you behave towards him, and force him therefore to change towards *you*.'

'In what sort of way should I change?'

Celandine put her head on one side and stared at the picture of heartbreaking innocence opposite her. 'You will become more assertive, but that is only to start with. You will state your feelings, instead of hiding them for fear Napier will despise you for them. You will start to make sure that he knows that you have a right to your feelings and opinions – although I dare say you haven't had time to form many of those quite yet, but time and more experience of the world will help you in *that*.'

It was as if dark curtains had parted in Edith's imagination and she could suddenly see blue skies and hear birds singing as she realised just how afraid she had been of ever saying what she felt, of ever even holding an opinion which she could dare to express.

'Do you think Napier chose to marry me, as I was, because I was so – young and he could make me sit to him for as long as he wished? And so stupid that I would not question him?'

'You are, or were, innocent, not stupid. You are, or have been, due to your upbringing, all too innocent,' Celandine told her firmly. 'It is Napier who is stupid, not you. But as I say, we will help you in that. Or rather, I will help you. I will make your husband see how selfish he is being, selfish,

selfish, selfish. Oh, but here they are. The men are coming out intent on interrupting us – alas.' Despite her words, Celandine looked round with a feeling of relief at the sound of male voices, before turning quickly back to Edith. 'Remember, now, not a word to either of them about our conversation. My mother always said that the male of the species does *not* confide in each other except on the subject of politics or cigars, so they do not understand the necessity for women to confide in each other about their emotions, which is probably just as well!'

She waved up to Sheridan, who was once more standing on his balcony, promising to come down and join them as soon as he and Napier had washed their hands and made themselves respectable.

Celandine too excused herself to go to see Mrs Molesworth about the lunch, but as she did so she found herself wondering at the cruelty of life. Whatever her encouraging words to Edith, she knew that her new friend could be proved to be right. Napier might well have married Edith in some flurry of artistic fascination, worshipping at the shrine of her beauty, only to find himself repelled by her naïve personality. Edith, although stunning, was after all an innocent, unsophisticated to a degree, and Napier quite evidently the opposite.

Aunt Biddy's crinoline was swaying in the strong sea breeze and her voice was being drowned out by the crying of the seagulls as they swooped and flew, darted and cried, and posed on decking and rigging before flying off to chase incoming boats.

'Russo, Russo!' she finally screamed, trying to get through to the old servant as he slid about the beach in his slippers. 'Russo!'

Her hoop flew up, first in front and then behind, causing passers-by and people on the beach to stop and stare and finally to laugh and point. Happily oblivious of the spectacle she was making of herself, she caught Russo by the arm and tugged at it.

'We have quite enough shells to decorate the cloths, really we have, quite enough.' She swayed and staggered up the beach again, closely followed by the old man, who was carrying a bucket in each hand. 'Really,' she said, her voice sounding abnormally loud once they were back in the house and the front door shut behind them. 'Really it is too bad that you never hear what I say out there, Russo. And my crinoline! It is too bad of it to behave as it does. It's as if it has a life of its own, but there we are.'

She called up to Gabrielle, who came hurrying down from the first floor, a feather duster in one hand and a cloth in the other. Her mistress pointed at the shells.

'Russo has been collecting these all morning. Now we must wash them and make a centrepiece round the flowers and fruit in the middle of the dining table. You see, Gabrielle dear, with so many from Newbourne coming to the party we must be at pains to make everything look as artistic as possible, you understand, for all those people from the new artistic colony there, why, they will look at everything very closely, and we want to astonish them with our beautiful effects, really we do.'

Gabrielle nodded, picking up the buckets and wishing quite heartily that they were filled only with water, as they normally were, and that the celebrations to honour the marriage of Mr Sheridan and his young wife were over, for her mistress had been in a state of such extreme anxiety over the past weeks that she and Russo had become certain that she would soon take off for outer spheres, her crinoline dress acting as some sort of balloon-like conveyance and wafting her into the blue beyond.

'When Miss Biddy has the wind up 'tis worse than a storm at sea, 'tis really,' she had kept insisting to Russo some weeks before, but seeing that he was as deaf as he was slow, she had finally realised that there really was very little point in trying to warn her old suitor of the dramas that might be in store for them. 'The place will doubtless go up in smoke from the heat of all the candles she's planning, and guests die of food poisoning if the cook she has retained is the one I think 'tis.'

Despite Gabrielle's worst apprehensions, those rooms in the old house that had been set aside for the celebrations were now looking gloriously festive, to the point of being positively arresting in the intricacy of the details set about the tables, the flowers and the wax fruit centrepieces, and the large, yellowed candles in their sconces, as still as guardsmen on duty, waiting to be lit and thereby throw the rooms and themselves into party mood.

The vast flower arrangement in the hall had arrived that morning from the florist and very soon the cooks in the kitchen would be setting out the many courses around the scullery tables, carefully covering the jellies and the meats with lace covers and the wedding cake with a vast cage. All would be deliciously ready, only the guests needing to complete what was intended to be a most joyous occasion.

In order to prevent Aunt Biddy from feeling out on a limb, Celandine and Sheridan had decided to tell their friends to dress in costume, which meant that attics and trunks could be raided, rather than much needed money wasted on new clothes. The result was that as the sun started to set over the sea, painting its warm colour over the horizon in welcoming effect, the guests, stepping out of their carriages and pony traps, or arriving on foot from some local hotel or lodging house, might have been arriving for a delightful reception some twenty or thirty years before, when the Queen was young, and Albert her consort still alive.

And of course, because of the trouble to which Aunt Biddy and her team from the town had gone, the general effect was of such glamour that the moment everyone entered her house they gasped at the vast floral arrangements, the array of food, and the gorgeous table displays – every setting decorated with flowers and linen, with Russo's shells placed in such a charming way that even he could see that the time spent collecting them had been worthwhile.

Aunt Biddy, clothed from head to toe in ruched blue satin, stationed herself on the first step that led into the main room to greet her guests, while Russo, in starched white dicky front and starched white tie with black cutaway, knee breeches and stockings, yelled the names of each arrival from the front door.

'Mr and Mrs MONTAGUE ROBERTSON!'

'I do so wish that Russo was not quite so deaf,' Aunt Biddy murmured as Sheridan and Celandine, followed by Alfred Talisman, turned into the reception room.

'Now you are clean-shaven shall we expect to see you cut quite a caper at the celebration, Alfred?' Sheridan demanded of him, straight-faced.

Alfred smiled shyly before helping himself to the proffered wine cup. 'I hope you think it is an improvement, Celandine?' he asked tentatively.

Celandine nodded. 'I am afraid I am more than a little conventional when it comes to beards and moustaches,' she admitted, smiling.

'If I have done the correct thing by you, I am more than happy,' Alfred murmured, and bending over her gloved hand he kissed it briefly in the continental manner.

'Enough of those Frenchy habits, Talisman,' Sheridan commanded.

'It is most fascinating, do you know, Sherry, to study your Aunt Biddy's face, which I am sure you have. You have no doubt noticed that it has been left completely unlined, untrammelled by the misfortunes of marriage, the worries of a life spent in trying to placate a husband, in the dread of childbirth. In my opinion all women who wish to remain beautiful should remain unmarried.'

'Not quite the right thing to say to us, Alfred, since this is meant to be a celebration of *our* marriage; we are here to celebrate my great good fortune in being able to persuade the former Miss Celandine Benyon to become my wife.'

But his words were lost on Alfred, for shortly after Russo yelled, 'Mr and Mrs NAPIER TODD!' the named guests made their appearance at the door of the room in which the other three were standing, as yet alone, drinking their fruit cup.

'Ah,' Alfred murmured, glancing towards the door. 'I have not yet met Mrs Napier Todd. It seems that her husband keeps her locked up. It made me suspect that she was either very plain or very – beautiful.' He stopped, staring.

Edith was wearing a dress found for her in Newbourne by Mrs Harvey, whose mother, also now the proud owner of a lodging house, had, it seemed, before her marriage and motherhood, worked for a lady of some consequence. The dress, carefully stored in immaculate cloths well away from moth and sunshine, dated from twenty or thirty years before and was astonishing in its complexity and allure.

The underskirt was blue silk overlaid with large flounces of muslin caught up at intervals with flowers – flounces being so very fashionable in those days. Celandine, who in common with most American girls understood dress-making, and could estimate the yardage of a dress at a few paces, not to mention the blessing of a good dressmaker, knew immediately that the stunning gown must have been made for a very grand lady indeed, probably for the opera or a ball. The cut of the neck was low, and the spread across the shoulders of the whole décolletage inset with the finest lace, as were the under sleeves. Wisely, considering the grandeur of the dress, Edith had chosen to dress her hair into a simple chignon at the nape of her elegant, white neck. But of course if she had hoped that by affecting a simple style she would draw attention away from the lustrous auburn mass, she was mistaken. Indeed the vast chignon of Titian hair, with all its classical simplicity, was immediately arresting, so that it vied with the dress, the white-ness of her skin, and her large eyes, more than any jewellery could possibly have done.

Celandine turned to say something to Alfred and Sheridan, but they were both so busy staring at the vision in front of them that she shrugged her shoulders and turned back to do the same, knowing that although she herself was dressed in her wedding dress and looking as pretty as she had ever done, she was now far outclassed.

'Edith, dearest Edith, where did you find such a beautiful dress?' she asked, hurrying up to her.

Edith shyly kissed the air either side of Celandine's face. 'It was far too big for me,' she confessed, staring up at Celandine who was some inches taller, her expression as usual as touchingly frank and innocent as Celandine's was amused. 'Far too big, but Mrs Harvey's mother, Mrs Topsham, took it in for me on her sewing machine. I do hope no one will notice the tucks, for she could not, as she said, cut into the material. It is far too beautiful, and anyway she might want to lend it to someone else who is not quite so – thin.'

She half turned as if to try to see if Mrs Topsham's tucks were all that they should be, and, failing, looked up at Celandine with an expression of quite evident doubt.

'Of course no one will notice anything. You cannot see any of the tucks; all anyone will notice is how beautiful you look,' Celandine reassured her in a lowered voice.

'I hope you are right.' Edith looked anxiously round, and seeing Napier already busy talking to Sheridan she felt it safe to confide to Celandine: 'Napier laughed so much when he saw me. He said I looked like his spinster Aunt Desiree. His taste, as you know, is not for anything old-fashioned. He likes only the very modern.'

Celandine looked across at Napier. 'What a husband you have to be sure, Mrs Todd. So certain in his tastes, so frank in his attitudes – but not, we hope, going to stay that way.'

She did not add, as she could have done, that if Sheridan had laughed at her gown she would have pushed him into Mrs Molesworth's ornamental pond. Instead she summoned Alfred, who was standing a little apart from them, unable to keep his eyes off Edith in her beautiful if old-fashioned evening gown.

'Alfred! Alfred Talisman.' Celandine beckoned to him impatiently, because he seemed reluctant to move. 'Alfred – come and meet Mrs Napier Todd, do, please.' To Edith she said, 'I believe Napier made sure you avoided meeting Alfred when he came to Helmscote, which is just as well, because at that time he would have still had a beard. Now at least he is clean-shaven, which is not to say much, but you can at least have the dubious pleasure of making his acquaintance. Although I have to warn you that judging from his petrified pose when he saw you coming into the room, I would say that he is already mesmerised by you. May I present yours and my husband's friend, Mr Alfred Talisman? Alfred, this is the object of your fascination, Mrs Napier Todd.'

Edith's large eyes stared up into Alfred's, and it was her turn to catch her breath, because Alfred Talisman was staring at her with an intensity which made her drop her eyes and wonder if Mrs Harvey's mother should have left the décolletage quite so low.

'I was just remarking to dear Celandine that I hoped the alterations to my ball gown did not show,' she said, and then, raising her eyes to Alfred's, she added, 'but since so many people are staring at me, I am beginning to appreciate that the décolletage might be cut a little too low? I asked my husband, but he was too busy laughing at the absurdity of my old-fashioned dress.'

Alfred's own quite brilliant eyes stared into Edith's but he did not smile. 'I see now, all too clearly, why Napier would not let you join us at dinner when I came by for the night at Helmscote,' he said at last, his painter's eyes taking in Edith's perfect girlish form, how her small rounded breasts, showing demurely above the cut of her dress, were still a long way from maturity, and how her long neck set off the proud carriage of her head, as if she had long ago made up her mind to brave the world and its slights, to never let anyone know the secrets of her heart. 'To make up for what I missed, I am not going to leave your side all evening, Mrs Todd.'

'That will please Napier,' came the disarming reply. 'But I am not sure that it will please you. I cannot discourse on Mr Ruskin's essays, or the principles of the modern movement.'

'No lady should discuss Mr Ruskin's essays at a reception, Mrs Todd, they are far too sensational.'

Edith smiled mischievously at Alfred, knowing at once that he must be a fellow spirit.

Celandine could not help feeling amused when she saw that the introduction she had effected had made such an impact on Edith, not to mention on Alfred himself. It was probably far-fetched, but for a few seconds at least she had actually imagined that Alfred had lost colour when he saw Edith coming into the room. Certainly, many minutes later, he was still standing by the side of the vision Edith made in her old-fashioned blue silk and muslin ball gown, her glorious auburn hair glinting in the light of the dozens of candles that Aunt Biddy had insisted upon lighting long before the guests started arriving – with the result that they were now creating a heat which must be making the gentlemen envy their wives their low-cut dresses.

Once Russo had shouted the last of the guests into the room, he took it upon himself to announce dinner.

'Ladies and gentlemen, tea is served!' he bellowed.

This was almost the last straw for the already flustered Aunt Biddy. She had to take out her fan and wave it frantically, moving quickly between the guests.

'Please take no notice of Russo,' she kept saying. 'Take no notice of him, he actually means dinner, of course he does. We may live in Cornwall, but we do dine at eight along with the

259

London fashionables, really we do. We dine at eight, and we have dinner not tea. Gracious, we are not so old-fashioned not to dine at eight, really we are not.'

The guests, immediately feeling for her concern, and realising that their appetites were quite ready to be appeased, quickly moved in to dinner.

And what a dinner! It was a meal of seven or eight courses which, while being served at a fashionable hour, was served in a reassuring and sturdily old-fashioned manner by young girls from the town dressed in the traditional Cornish style with lace-edged aprons and stiff starched headdresses.

Aunt Biddy liked to eat and what was more she knew how everyone else liked to eat, if they were able, with the result that she had composed the menu herself, starting with such dishes as pigeons in jelly and oyster pies, and going on to turkey and lamb, and chicken and tongue, cabinet pudding and wine jelly, peaches and grapes, and any amount of Cornish cream to accompany the fruits and the puddings. And that was all before the magnificent wedding cake was wheeled in to cheers from all those in the room.

The musicians arrived at ten o'clock and the guests were encouraged to retire to the larger room where chairs had been placed along the walls and dancing began as the servants cleared the dining room in preparation for supper – consisting of small sandwiches, ham croquettes and tiny chicken pies, not to mention cut meats rolled into neat shapes and corner dishes of lobster and crab salads, and potatoes kept hot over dishes of boiling water. Fruit jellies and small cream puddings stood at the back and side laid *à la française*.

'You will dance with me, won't you? You will dance first with me, and no one else?'

Edith, who had been temporarily separated from her party and was trying gamely to make headway with an old, deaf sea captain from the town, turned, half hoping that it was Napier's voice she was hearing above the din of the musicians tuning up, the sound of the guests' voices laughing and talking, and the distant sea heard dimly through the windows whenever there was a lull in the conversation, such as when grace had been said by the parson.

'I should love to have a dance with you,' she agreed at once, concealing her disappointment that it was not Napier but Alfred Talisman who was asking her. She excused herself from her table, escaping from the old sea dog with some relief, and moved into the middle of the room.

Edith had always loved to dance. In the dear old days at the Stag, when her mother was still alive, Mama had used to play the piano for her daughter to dance with other young friends under the instruction of a dancing teacher. Later, when her father remarried and Edith joined the maids' dormitories in the attic rooms, in the long summer evenings when it was difficult for the young girls to sleep they all delighted in copying what they had seen their elders and betters do whenever there was a celebration at the old inn. Edith's ability to dance gained her considerable popularity among all the other maids, since she had a particularly fine eye for the details of a dance pattern.

'I am so much the better for that!' Edith smiled with delight at Alfred after the first two dances. 'You are the perfect partner, Mr Talisman.'

Alfred turned reluctantly as he felt a tap on his shoulder, and saw Napier standing at his elbow.

'It would be a courtesy, Mr Talisman, if you would allow *me* to dance with my wife—'

'I am sorry, Napier.' Edith glanced down at her dance card, which had been rapidly filled up in the short pause between the first and second dances by men who could not wait to boast that they had danced with the belle of the evening. 'I have not a dance free until' – she looked at the names on her card – 'until the seventh.'

Alfred smiled privately at the expression on Napier's face.

'My dear fellow, don't look so shocked. Your wife is the most popular young woman at the party. You will have to sit it out with the rest of us until it is your turn.'

Napier frowned. 'But I have precedence over everyone else. Edith is my wife.'

'Not at a dance, she isn't,' Alfred said affably. 'Etiquette is that you must give way to those on

262

her dance card, old chap. Just a fact, but a fact it is. And this one I think is mine to claim.'

Napier drew himself up. 'Alfred, I hardly think—'

But Alfred had led Edith away, and there was nothing much that Napier could do but sit down and watch and wait.

As it happened, Celandine and Sheridan had also elected to sit out and watch the rest of the party, and it was with some amusement that they sat beside a silent Napier watching him watching Edith dancing.

'I fear I have been overshadowed by Edith this evening,' Celandine murmured to Sheridan and Alfred, pretending to look put out, while fanning herself with one of Aunt Biddy's many hand-painted Spanish fans.

The truth was that the gas lighting would have made the rooms warm enough, but with Aunt Biddy's insistence on lighting the candelabra they had become excessively hot, even though the windows were open. Indeed, the air was so still that the curtains hardly moved, despite there being white tops to the waves far out to sea on the distant horizon.

Sheridan took Celandine's hand and kissed it. 'No one could overshadow you in my eyes, my sweet, *particularly* not in my eyes, particularly not since you are wearing your *wedding* dress. But certainly I will admit that young Edith Todd is turning all heads tonight. No wonder there are so many people lining up to claim a dance with her.'

'And they will boast of it for months, for there are not that many beauties in Cornwall.' Celandine nodded towards Alfred and Edith, who were dancing together again.

Napier stood up and left them, returning as the music finished, at last to claim his dance with Edith just as Celandine lowered her fan and turned her attention back to the dance floor.

'Do look, Sherry: wonder of all wonders, *Napier* is now dancing with Edith. It is his turn at last.'

They watched with interest as their friends danced, both noting that Napier for once seemed to be paying attention to Edith.

'Nothing like a little competition,' Celandine remarked, feeling rather pleased.

'Which Alfred seems quietly adept at providing,' Sheridan remarked drily. 'Now I am going to find our hostess and dance with her.' Sheridan turned to see Alfred standing nearby.

'And I am going outside to smoke a quiet cigarette and contemplate the beautiful moon,' Alfred announced. 'That after all is what bachelors are meant to do, are they not?'

'Not all bachelors. Some of them try to find a nice girl to marry.' Sheridan leaned forward and touched Celandine on the arm. 'Will you be all right on your own for a little while?'

'I will be perfectly all right, in every way.' Celandine smiled, and then seeing Captain Black making a beeline towards her she half closed her eyes, already knowing her fate. 'Although if I spy what I think I spy coming towards me, I shall not be alone for long, alas.'

Celandine had now turned the old sea dog away three times, so a fourth refusal was out of the question. Without Sheridan to whisk her back on to the dance floor she would have to agree to partner the old chap in the next dance.

'My dear lady, as I have already stated some few times,' Captain Black began, 'it would do me the greatest honour if you could partner me in this—'

'Of course.' Celandine sprang to her feet, smiling, her heart sinking as she noticed that the old dear had such an importance of a stomach, and such large feet, she was sure he was going to put at least one of them through her wedding dress, and that was before he tried to hold her, despite his well-fed protrusion.

Outside, Alfred sauntered down to the water's edge for a quiet smoke, and leaning against one of the friendly old boats that had already become part of the scenery to him he lit a cigarette. It tasted delicious in the open air, and he enjoyed it so much that not content with leaning against the beached vessel he daringly climbed into it and made himself comfortable against the sides, feet propped up, cigarette glowing in the darkness.

It was not long before he heard voices coming towards him on the evening air, voices that were raised above a whisper but kept lower than a normal conversational level, voices that he recognised, saying things that he knew he should not be hearing, that he was certainly not supposed to hear, but unfortunately he *could* hear because in the still of the summer night, with the seagulls quietened and the sea like a mill pond, even the inhalation of a cigarette sounded loud.

'You are my wife, Edith,' Napier was saying, a little too insistently.

'*I* am perfectly aware of that, Napier. It is just a little difficult for me to remember it when there are other men around.'

'How do you mean?'

'I mean that since I am not, and have never been, your wife in the true sense of the word, I cannot help but be pleased with the attentions of other men. It is just a fact, Napier: if a wife is neglected she will inevitably become flattered by others.'

'I do not think you should feel flattered by others, Edith. It is not seemly for a married woman to have her head turned.'

'Perhaps not, Napier, but the truth is that if your husband takes no interest in you, you will take interest in others. Now I must go in. I have to dance with Colonel Head; I promised him the waltz. Lady Alicia – his wife, you know – says he dances quite beautifully!'

Celandine had changed partners and was no longer dancing with the well-upholstered sea captain but with Napier. At least Celandine was *meant* to be dancing with Napier, but from the way Napier kept looking round for Edith, Celandine felt she might as well not be dancing with anyone at all.

'Gracious, Mr Todd, sir, will you please try to pay a little more attention?' she murmured in a lightly teasing voice. 'You just trod on my dance shoe.'

For a second Napier looked contrite. 'I am so sorry, Celandine, really I truly am.'

'You look severely troubled. Why not tell me your problem and I will try to help you, because it will be a great deal less painful than having my toes assassinated.'

'I can't see Edith anywhere. She was outside with me taking some air, and now—'

Celandine's eyes took on a sphinx-like expression, which happily Napier did not notice. 'If you wanted to dance with Edith, Napier, it might have been wise to ask *her*, and not me, surely?'

'I tell you I have not seen my wife since we came back into the house from the garden. We had an exchange of words, which we have never had before. She is usually so gentle.'

Napier looked so genuinely puzzled at the notion that anyone could disagree with him that Celandine found herself almost feeling sorry for him. Almost, but not quite.

'You can make it up to her later, I should have thought,' she said lightly. 'After all, you will still be taking her home with you, surely?'

There was a short silence during which Napier's handsome face seemed set and he actually appeared to be considering leaving his wife behind.

'Yes, of course I will be taking her home, which is why it would be a good notion to find her, I should have thought.'

'Have you considered that she might be in the supper room?' Celandine suggested, adopting the kind of voice you might use to a child. 'As soon as you came back in from the garden, Colonel Head took her on to the dance floor while you went to replenish your glass, but immediately the waltz was over Alfred claimed her again. Perhaps he took her in to supper?'

'Edith having supper with Alfred? Well, there will be little harm to that, I should have thought. Except—' Napier stopped, frowning. 'Except she might be stupid enough to believe him if he makes sheep's eyes at her – she is so young for her age, even now.'

'Edith,' Celandine stated, 'is not stupid. I grant you she is young, but being stupid and being young are two very different things, Napier.'

'No, really, Edith is stupid, most especially about her health and suchlike matters. I know, believe you me, I do.'

They continued dancing in an increasingly forlorn manner, while Celandine found herself struggling not to tell Napier that it was *he* who was stupid, and Napier found himself struggling with a new anxiety about his wife.

'I hope Edith has not been foolish enough to go for another walk, not on her own, and not along the seashore. She is only recently out of her sick bed—'

'Ow! Please mind where you put your feet, Mr Todd, sir!'

Napier looked contrite, and Celandine relieved, as the dance at last came to an end and Sheridan came over to claim her, at which point Napier left them.

Sheridan stared after him. 'I fear there might be going to be trouble between Alfred and Napier, Celandine. Alfred has hardly left Edith's side. For one so reticent he can make his feelings rather too plain.'

Celandine, trying not to laugh at the undoubted success of her plan, nodded her head towards the disappearing figure of Napier, rapidly weaving his way through the other guests and out towards the garden, the harbour and the seashore. 'Napier has gone in search of Edith in the garden. Silly fool thinks she has taken herself off for a walk along the seashore again. Let him look; I happen to know that Alfred and Edith have just gone into the supper room.'

Sheridan sighed. 'I fear there *is* going to be trouble.'

Celandine's expression was enigmatic. She would not tell Sheridan, who she was well aware could be over-sensitive in some ways, and not quite sensitive enough in others – she *could* not tell him that she had only that morning suggested to Alfred that he pay attention to young Edith, for the sake of her marriage, to make Napier jealous.

It would not be the kind of thing that Sheridan would understand.

It had been a good plan, and by intention a worthy plan, and one that was already working quite beautifully, except that she now thought that Alfred might have actually succeeded in convincing himself that he had really fallen in love with Edith. Certainly, watching him, Celandine was sure that from the moment Edith had caught Alfred's eye there had ceased to be anyone else in the room for him, but then that had been the case for most of the men at the party.

As she watched Napier disappearing into the night to try to find his wife, Celandine could not help thinking with some relish that Napier's anxiety as to her whereabouts could only be healthy for poor Edith's marriage.

'Six pennies, or even six shillings, for your thoughts, Mrs Montague Robertson.'

'You will need to lay out a great deal more money than that, Sherry. Now, how much for yours?'

It was Sheridan's turn to look enigmatic. He could not tell Celandine his thoughts; she would be too shocked. Instead, he took her by the hand, and led her on to the dance floor.

'I am a very lucky man,' he told her, holding her tight and determined to change the subject, and as Celandine looked up into his eyes she thought that after all she did not really need to guess his thoughts.

'Don't let's stop dancing,' she confided, the look in her eyes softening. 'After all, it is our night of celebration, and I do not think I have ever been happier, and nor do I think that I really deserve to be this happy, do you know that? But there you are, it must be borne!'

This, as it was meant to do, distracted Sheridan. It also distracted Celandine, so much so that she found it was not until after returning home, and a night of sumptuous love, that her thoughts once more reverted to Edith, by which time, although she did not know it, there was very little she could do to help Edith, whose life had taken yet another irrevocable turn.

Chapter Seven

Edith opened her eyes slowly, feeling the cool of Mrs Harvey's linen sheets against her naked body. She turned, and seeing the second half of the bed beside her empty, she smiled.

At last it had happened. Napier had loved her, passionately and completely, and she had loved him loving her. She propped up several of what she now thought of as *his* pillows behind her and thought not just about their lovemaking, but about the evening which had preceded it.

Napier had suddenly appeared, looking . . . well, as she had never seen him look before.

'Where have you *been*?' he demanded, taking her by the elbow and trying to guide her away from Alfred and out of the supper room.

'Napier, I had rather not be handled like a parcel.' Fortified by more than one glass of Aunt Biddy's wine cup, Edith determinedly backed away from him, intent on showing him that he could not take her away from her supper. 'I have been in here, taking supper with everyone else.'

She glanced around the room, embarrassed by Napier's overt attentions, and trying not to see the look in Alfred's eyes as her husband threatened to make her do as he wished, rather than let her finish her supper.

'My dear fellow, help yourself to supper, why don't you?' Alfred said, and seeing her embarrassment stepped in between Napier and Edith. 'Help yourself to some of these delicious dishes, and allow your wife to finish her supper. You will, surely?' he murmured.

'Edith. Come home at once, won't you?'

Napier was speaking to her as if he was an officer and she one of his men, but Edith did not care.

'No, Napier, I will not come home. At least not until I have finished enjoying myself.'

'Well, at least come away from this open window, in that low-cut dress. First you insist on going outside in the middle of our dance together, and now you— You have been very *ill*, remember? Very ill indeed.'

Edith had stared up at Napier, determined on continuing in the way she had begun the evening, in the way Celandine had advised.

'It might be best not to mention my dress, seeing that you ridiculed it earlier, Napier,' she told him, widening her eyes before nibbling at her pie.

'Yes, perhaps best not to mention your wife's

273

dress, Napier, really you should not, if what she said is true.'

Napier frowned at Alfred. 'If you don't mind, Alfred, I am talking to my *wife*—'

'Yes, and so was I, Napier, my dear fellow, I was talking to your wife, but I was not talking to her as if she was a subordinate, I was talking to her as if she was a human being,' Alfred said quietly. 'Besides, I really think Mrs Todd should stay. If she leaves now, if she is the first to leave, your hostess will think she has not enjoyed herself, and that would be such a pity, because I think she has enjoyed herself.' He looked at Edith for corroboration.

'Alfred, will you allow me to talk to my wife?'

'Yes, of course.'

Napier led the bemused Edith to one side of the crowded room as if she was a naughty little girl. As she looked up into his face, his young wife realised with some satisfaction that she had never seen him so infuriated, not even when she distracted him when he was painting.

'Edith,' he began, clearing his throat and pressing his hands together before he began, a gesture which strongly reminded Edith of the Helmscote vicar about to preach. 'I must make it clear to you, Edith, that I did not laugh at you – I laughed at the *dress*, because . . . because, well . . .' he floundered, 'well, because – being that it is so old-fashioned, Edith.' He dropped his voice as if this was somehow shocking. 'Being that your dress is so redolent of the olden days. You look even younger in such a wide crinoline skirt,' he added, dropping his voice even further as if to look younger was also shocking.

Thanks to the wine Edith managed to look interested although not startled by this information.

'One of the reasons I wanted to paint you the moment I saw you was because you looked so young, and untouched. It was that more than anything that I wanted to capture.'

'I don't really want to talk about your painting, not tonight, Napier, if you don't mind. No, what I *would* really quite like are some of those little patties over there.' She nodded towards the supper table, not really caring that he looked startled at the decisive tone in her voice. 'And then perhaps some jelly and a touch of cream. Fetch it for me, would you?'

To his own astonishment and his young wife's secret amazement, Napier meekly did as he was told while Edith seated herself on a cutaway chair, carefully setting her vast skirt to one side while Alfred settled himself on her other side.

'While your husband's back is turned, and the rest of the room is too busy choosing supper to notice, might I tell you how beautiful you are, Mrs Todd?' he asked, his face a picture of innocence. 'Your mouth so kissable, your eyes those of a beautiful tigress—'

'You might,' Edith agreed, deliberately widening her own eyes to match his in their innocence. 'But at this moment I would really rather prefer to think of enjoying a wine jelly with Cornish cream.'

'I am in love with you, Mrs Todd, and you know it.'

'I know nothing of the kind,' Edith said, still arranging her skirt in as decorous a manner as possible, while wondering briefly, and sadly, why she had not understood the ways of the world before, and why she had taken so much time to come to understand them.

'All I know,' she went on, 'is that you have made my husband jealous, and I have made him angry, but nevertheless he is fetching and carrying for me, which is novel, to say the least.' Then she added, louder, as she saw Napier returning from the supper table with plates piled high with food, 'I think Celandine is right; married women should have the same rights as men, don't you, Mr Talisman? Married women should—'

Napier sat down beside Edith, staring at her. 'I will not have you talking about such things with Alfred, Edith, really I won't. Besides, you know nothing about married women's rights, or anyone else's rights for that matter.'

'Napier.' Edith glanced down at the plate he was holding. 'Do you see what you are carrying?'

Napier glanced impatiently down. 'Of course. A plate of sandwiches for you.'

'And what did I ask you for quite expressly, Napier?'

'A plate of . . .' Napier hesitated, frowning, unsure, but unwilling to admit his mistake.

Edith sighed. '*Patties*. I asked you, Napier, for *patties*, not sandwiches.'

She gave him a purposefully reproachful look, then stood up and went back to the dining table, leaving Napier with his plateful of sandwiches while she helped herself to some small pies. She returned to sit beside him.

'What has happened to you, Edith? You have quite changed this evening. I don't like it at all. It must be the dress. The dress has changed your personality in a way that is not at all agreeable.'

Edith smiled, biting into her food with sudden appreciation. 'You are right. It must be the dress, Napier,' she told him. 'They always say costumes from the olden days can turn you into something different. That and the wine,' she went on. 'It was lovely wine, it *is* lovely wine, isn't it, Napier?' She held out her glass and nodded back to the table. 'Fetch me some more wine cup, Napier, there's a good feller,' she added, mimicking Napier's manner so accurately that Alfred started to laugh.

Napier breathed in and out a little like an impatient horse on a frosty morning. 'Don't you think you have had enough wine cup already, Edith?'

'If I did,' Edith said, imagining to herself that she was someone quite as haughty as her step-mother, 'would I be asking you to fetch me some more, Napier?' She stared coldly at her husband, acting out her part with verve.

The astonishing thing was that it worked. Napier returned dutifully to the table and did indeed fetch her another glass of wine cup, after which they sat together eating silently, Napier sullen, Edith's expression deliberately innocent.

'I'm taking you home, after you have finished,' Napier finally announced.

'I have promised one more dance to Alfred – to Mr Talisman. He does dance so beautifully.'

'But—'

'No, really, Napier, I have.'

She did indeed insist on one last dance with Alfred, and that, quite naturally, was the final straw, as Edith had hoped and prayed it might be, because she had hardly finished clapping her hands together to applaud the musicians, so that together with the other dancers she could show her appreciation of their playing, when Napier called for their carriage and they returned home, locked in each other's embrace.

'Don't you ever dance with another man for so long again,' Napier threatened her as he kissed her with long-suppressed passion in the back of the carriage. But as Edith responded most readily she could not prevent herself wondering, quite mischievously, what Alfred Talisman's kisses might have been like.

Now, Edith reached for her nightdress and her lace-edged wrap to make herself respectable, only minutes before Mrs Harvey, having knocked at the door, ushered in a delicious breakfast which her maid placed for Edith at the open window overlooking the gardens, and finally the sea beyond.

'We'm be a glorious morning,' Mrs Harvey said, smiling and nodding towards the window, but no sooner had she pronounced on the weather than she raised a hand to her lips. ''Tis a glorious morning, and I think I can see – I know I can see – look out there, Mrs Todd, look out there, if you have a mind to, will you?' She turned and hurried back to the door, which had just closed behind the maid. 'Mary! Mary!' she called. 'It's happened at last. I swear to goodness they're coming home. The men are back!'

Mary rushed back into the room, twisting her apron between excited hands. 'Never say so, Mrs Harvey, never say so!'

'I do say it, Mary, I do. Look!' Mrs Harvey pointed at the horizon. 'If that isn't a Lugger comin' home, my name is not Tilly Harvey.'

They both stared over Edith's shoulder, momentarily oblivious of their guest's concerns.

'Didn't I just say this is a glorious morning, Mrs Todd? I felt it in my water, I did really.'

The two women hurried out of the room, leaving Edith with her breakfast. As she ate she thought of how much anxiety the women must suffer when their men were at sea, never really knowing what might have happened to them. She knew that the conditions in which the deep-sea fishermen lived were tough in the extreme, but if they came home with a vast catch life was momentarily eased for everyone at home. Not that Mrs Harvey herself wanted for much in the way of comforts, she being one of the luckier ones, what with her lodging house and a husband who ran a pleasure boat; but for her maid, Mary, who was less fortunate in her circumstances, she was sure it must be a relief to see her husband come home again.

Mrs Harvey was back in the room again before too long, smiling, clearing the tray from the window sill, making everything straight, fussing over Edith, saying, 'Sit down, sit down, this is my job,' as she tidied and dusted.

The result was that Edith sat at the window, too enthralled by the brilliant vista in front of her to be able to tear herself away and wash and dress. 'The sea is so beautiful today.'

'The sea is what it is, my dear, that's what it is. It is what it is, as cruel as it is beautiful, as full of plenty as it can be empty as an old tin bucket pitted with holes. Still, today young Mary is at least made happy, with the return of her man. First, though,' she looked over to Edith, 'first she has to go and sit to *your* man, I heard say.'

She neatly flipped up a corner of blanket and sheet while Edith allowed herself to stare at the blue of the sea, the sky reflecting in it in a turquoise and emerald mix that swirled in ever-changing patches. Napier had said nothing of making Mary sit to him, but then Napier had left so early in the morning, as was his habit, that he would not have thought to wake his wife, most especially not since they had both been awake half the night making love.

'Of course, yes, I remember my husband saying.'

'Yes, Mary and some other girls, they're all posing out there, them and a heap of wet fish, apparently. Happy for 'em they're going to have no rain. There'll be no rain until this afternoon, the seaweed in the hall tells me.'

She left Edith, who immediately started dressing as fast as she could. She did not know why but she could not wait to see what was happening out there on the shore, how the girls were being posed, and what sort of painting Napier had decided upon. But when she reached the beach, search as she could she did not find Napier, or Mary, or anyone. She only found Alfred.

'I was looking for Napier.'

Alfred looked deliberately puzzled. 'Who is – I am sorry – Napier is . . . ?'

Edith smiled at his teasing, and clicked her tongue. 'My *husband*, Mr Talisman, Napier Todd, my husband.'

'Ah yes, I remember now. You are a married woman. And yet.' Alfred looked sly. 'And yet last night, I would have said you were most definitely *not* a married woman, however large the ring you happen to be sporting on your left hand. While I was *dancing* with you, while I was *talking* to you, I would most definitely have said that you were so young, so fresh, so innocent, you could not possibly also be – *married*.'

Edith stared at him, and as she did so the thought crossed her mind that Celandine might have betrayed her previous state of *unmarriedness* to Alfred, who was after all staying at the same house.

'Well, you are wrong,' she said, having finally rejected the idea that Celandine could have betrayed her. 'I am married, Mr Talisman, very much so,' she added, remembering how passionate had been Napier's lovemaking, how deliciously tender he had been, how quite obviously versed in the ways of pleasing women.

Alfred nodded, the expression on his face innocent.

'You realise that I have fallen in love with you,' he stated. 'You do realise that? I love you, and I knew last night, the moment I saw you, I knew at once that I will always love you. And I know it again this morning. I have never seen anyone as beautiful as you, but that is not the only reason I love you. I love you because you are as innocent as the day, which makes me want to show you how I can love, how love can be, as it is meant to be. As you have never known it.'

Edith stared at him. 'Mr Talisman,' she said, after a small intake of breath. 'I know we enjoyed ourselves together last night, but this morning is another matter. This morning you are obviously determined on continuing with your nonsense, in order to embarrass me. I see that. And you must congratulate yourself, for you have succeeded very well in your intentions. I am very embarrassed. More than that, I am upset.'

She started to walk off in the opposite direction, but Alfred called after her. 'If you are indeed looking for your husband, *Mrs* Todd, Mr Todd is at Sheridan's studio. They are sharing a life class together.'

Edith turned. She was not so innocent that she did not know what the mention of a 'life class' implied.

'I thought that was probably where he was,' she admitted, smiling in a determined fashion, having let hardly a second elapse. 'Mrs Harvey told me Mary is sitting to them. Poor thing,' she added, 'it is always so cold when one sits to a painter. I myself nearly died of it.'

Alfred decided to take ruthless advantage of Edith's hesitation, despite its being only a second or two, and quickly caught up with her.

'Come for a walk along the coast with me,' he urged her. 'Napier and Sheridan will not be much company today, but we could enjoy a walk together, even if you are a married woman. That at least you will be allowed.'

If Alfred had not been so handsome, his dark eyes so compelling, if he had not had a tall figure and long legs and an intense expression that seemed to be reserved only for her, Edith might have accepted his invitation, but as it was she merely stepped away from him, shaking her head.

'I would love to go for a walk this morning.' She did not attempt to keep the sudden sadness she was feeling out of her voice. 'But I can't. I told you, I am – a – married – woman.'

'I love you, you know that, Mrs Todd, don't you?'

Edith looked up at Alfred and realised with an awful sense of shock that what he was saying was true. He was not it seemed, after all, flirting with her; he was telling her the state of his heart.

'You can't love me. What is more I won't let you love me,' she said, and made the mistake of stepping quickly backwards which meant that she started to lose her balance.

He caught her quickly to him. 'I don't need your permission to love you, Mrs Todd. More than that, I don't care for your permission. I only know that you have set my senses spinning. I love you as I have never loved before.'

Edith pulled herself away from him, not flattered but shocked, only to turn and see Celandine coming towards them. She knew that she must have seen them, and the knowledge made her more than embarrassed, it made her mortified.

'We were just practising a love scene from Shakespeare,' Alfred joked as Celandine joined them, walking unevenly along the shore, the wind blowing her pale pink and white sprigged cotton morning dress and jacket.

'I am looking for Sheridan.' Celandine looked distracted and sounded breathless. 'I was told that he was sketching along the harbour, a bunch of girls with some fish, or some such, sketching with Napier. Have you not seen them, Edith?'

'No.' Edith looked down, unhappy and unused to the situation in which she was now finding herself.

'Not another lost wife coming to find comfort in my Shakespearian tuition?' Alfred asked of no one in particular. 'I am meant to be doing a painting of Sir Henry Irving, you know. For the Garrick Club, I believe it is destined. But you ladies will not be allowed to view it, I am afraid. The Garrick Club, along with our dear prime minister, does not allow for female emancipation.'

'Oh, fiddle the Garrick Club, Alfred, I must find Sherry. I have just had a letter from France. It is my mother. It seems she is taken very bad, and I must go to her at once.' Celandine turned to Edith, reaching out to hold one of her gloved hands. 'The letter is from my mother's doctor. He says she may be in great danger and that I must come at once, but I can't find Sherry to tell him, or even Napier.'

'They are—' Alfred stopped and somehow managed to look guilty as he caught Edith's eye. 'They are painting fisherwomen and a mound of fish, in some cove nearby. We were just about to go to find them.'

'Were you? Were you really?' The pressure of Celandine's hand holding Edith's was the only thing that betrayed her inner desperation. 'In that case you must tell Sherry that I am gone to France. I have to leave now. There is a boat which I can catch if I hurry, within the next half an hour, Mrs Molesworth says. I am already packed. Please, tell Sherry—' She leaned forward and whispered in Edith's ear. 'Tell Sherry I love him, won't you? That I must go at once. It may even now be too late.'

Edith nodded. 'Of course. Can I do anything else to help you?'

'No, I am quite all right. I have been to France so many times that aside from crossing the Channel, which is never pleasant, travel is never a trial to me.'

She hurried away as Edith turned to Alfred. 'It was very kind of you not to say what you knew to be the truth just at that moment. Not that it matters, of course. Celandine is as aware as anyone of the importance of the life class to painters, and their models clothed or unclothed mean little to them or her, I know.'

'Whoever told you that, Mrs Todd, was not telling the truth. No, that is never true. His models mean everything to a painter of any merit, believe you me. That is why some painters even make the mistake of marrying them.'

Edith stared up at Alfred, only slowly appreciating what he was saying.

'Now I think we should go for that walk, don't you?' he said, after a moment.

'You can go for what you call "that walk", Mr Talisman. I shall return to my lodgings and see

286

if there isn't something I can do to help Mrs Harvey, perhaps with a little light dusting.'

'I do not think I have ever been turned down before for a little light dusting, really I don't.' Alfred could not help laughing.

'A little light dusting is preferable to risking my reputation with you,' Edith told him in the voice she had been accustomed to use to the inebriates at the Stag and Crown who tried to force themselves on her.

'What a pity.' Alfred started to move away from her towards the path to the track that led to so many of the coves and inlets around the harbour. 'Shall I give your husband your best wishes? Or shall I send him your love? Tell me. I *know* he will be disappointed to hear that you did not want to come with me – he did after all send me to fetch you. He and Sherry have taken the most delicious picnic down to the cove, and by lunchtime they said they will be quite played out. Dead fish, fisher girls filleting fish, all fish out of the way, and only a picnic lunch on the sand, prepared by the redoubtable Mrs Molesworth to take their minds off the piscatorial theme. You *know* how Mrs Molesworth dearly loves a picnic. The moment the baskets come out she starts rolling the pastry and cutting the sandwiches and preparing the meats, not to mention the bottles of ginger and lemonade and . . .' Alfred was over-elaborating quite intentionally so that Edith had time to turn and stare at him.

'What are you saying?'

'Only that Sherry and Napier sent me to fetch you for a picnic lunch in the cove down there. Why else do you think I came across you the way I did?'

'But – but you said that – you said that they were sharing a life class.'

'Which is what they *were* doing. The girls are, after all, alive; only the fish are dead.'

Edith turned and stared after Celandine, longing to catch up with her and tell her that it would only be a short walk to find Sheridan and Napier, but Celandine was gone, and Alfred was already walking away from Edith so quickly that if she did not follow him at once she would lose him, and miss out on lunch, and Napier.

The Channel crossing to France was thankfully much less rough than the journey to Cornwall, which meant that Celandine was able to eat a little, and think a great deal. The fact that the letter had been written by the doctor must mean that her mother's condition was indeed serious, but unfortunately he did not state from what she was suffering. It was impossible to stop thinking about what might be ahead, to stop imagining Agnes possibly hovering about her poor mother's deathbed, perhaps privately gleeful that Mrs Benyon was dying, so that Agnes would finally be able to reign supreme in the family hierarchy. To distract her thoughts from time to time she took out the little water colour that Sherry had done of her in the first few days of their marriage. It was full of tenderness, as only a man who loves a woman can paint her. But inevitably her thoughts would return to the treadmill of her family's complicated relationships.

Agnes had always coveted everything that had come to Mrs Benyon from her marriage, something about which Celandine and her mother had often laughed, fantasising that in the unlikely event of Mrs Benyon's early demise, Agnes would tear down the doors and whisk everything back to Avignon. It was a fantasy in which they only occasionally indulged, for Mrs Benyon always enjoyed robust health, and was much younger than her husband when they married.

After Cornwall with its fresh blue skies and winding streets, its white-painted houses and the eternal cries of the seagulls and the sound of the ever-present sea, Paris was bound to seem confined, even overcrowded. Celandine was prepared for this, just as she was prepared for feeling almost impatient as she stared out of the hackney-carriage window at the wide avenues filled with people going about their pampered lives with an air of sophistication which now seemed so artificial compared to the hard lives of the Cornish fishing folk. What she was not prepared for was the look of the apartment as, having placed her key in the lock and pushed open the front door, she took in the shock awaiting her.

One of the things that had always been such a

comfort to her mother, and to Celandine, had been the hanging of her father's paintings in each new apartment in which – due to Celandine's perennial inability to find a sympathetic art professor – they would so often find themselves.

An oil painting of a long avenue framed by tall poplars had always been hung first, and always in the hall of whichever apartment they were occupying. Now Celandine saw that instead of that much-loved painting, there was only a grey gap. She turned from the dark marks outlined on the pale grey paint, to find another empty space where a smaller oil, this time of her mother seated under a cherry tree in their garden in America, had once hung. She looked round further, only to find wall after wall empty of precious paintings. Well-loved friends had fled, and only the outlines of the frames were now witness to where they had once hung.

She pushed open the door to the main salon, where her mother had always so enjoyed entertaining friends and acquaintances, and promptly stepped into a strangely dark, unlit space. The long windows that opened on to the courtyard below were tightly closed and the curtains drawn, despite its being only early afternoon. Celandine threw the curtains apart, opened the floor-length windows, and turned to look at the interior, only to discover that all the walls, as in the hall, were quite bare of paintings.

Her father having had a great capacity for friendship had inevitably enjoyed intense and much treasured friendships with other painters, both in America and in France. A consequence of this was that many of them had exchanged work with him, each happily swapping his unsold paintings in a genial, bohemian manner, so that at the time of her husband's death Mrs Benyon had been bequeathed a large number of modern paintings of what was becoming known as the Impressionist school. And now Albert Benyon's treasured collection of valued friends' works, much loved by his widow and daughter, had vanished.

With absolute certainty Celandine knew then that her mother must be dead, for how else could Agnes – and Celandine knew immediately that it must be Agnes who had taken them, and with what glee she could only imagine – have removed all the paintings from the walls?

She found herself, for no reason at all, moving from one wall to another, and much as a house-wife might find herself staring at damp patches that had suddenly appeared in her decorations, Celandine stared at the marks where the beloved paintings had once hung. There had been 'Tower Bridge' and there 'Picnic at Arles', and there 'Children of Avignon' – and now there was nothing but dark, empty wall.

A baby cried. Celandine turned, thinking that the sound must have come from the windows which she had opened in such desperation, eager to let in not just light, but air. She frowned and turned back to the bare walls, unable or unwilling to move. Again came the cry of a baby, and this time she realised that it was coming not from outside the tall windows that gave on to the courtyard area which the Parisian pigeons so enjoyed, but from along the corridor that led to the bedrooms.

Without knowing why, Celandine found herself tiptoeing down the corridor towards the sound, only to bump into Marie who was at that moment coming out of her mother's bedroom. Marie screamed, and suddenly there was a cacophony, what with the baby crying, Marie screaming, and Celandine trying to raise her voice above the other noises.

Celandine caught the maid by the shoulders. 'Where is my mother, Marie?'

'Mademoiselle Benyon!'

'No, Marie, not Mademoiselle Benyon—'

'*Mais oui*, you are Mademoiselle Benyon!'

'No, *Madame* Montague Robertson.'

Marie obviously found this too much, because she merely shook her head in despair as if she knew that Celandine was determined on confusing her. '*Mademoiselle, votre mère est morte! Elle est morte, la pauvre.*' She crossed herself reverently, closing her eyes as she did so.

In seconds Celandine's worst fears were realised, her fragile hopes, to which she had clung with such ferocity on the journey, shattered. She took a few steps backwards and turned away from the maid's tragic expression in order to cover her eyes with her hands, as if by doing so she could avoid seeing the truth of her situation.

'*Elle est mort* – last Thursday the English priest he has come, and she has had the sacraments, and now she is quite dead,' Marie continued in a stream of hysterical French. Seeing Celandine's understandable shock and distress, she tried to take her by the arm and lead her back to the salon, but Celandine resisted her.

'No, but I must know. What is that baby noise? Is there a baby staying here, Marie?'

'No, madem— no, madame.' At this Marie looked more agitated than ever. 'No, madame.' She hesitated, her hands twisting the corners of her apron. 'No, madame, the baby is Madame's baby.' As Celandine stared: 'Madame Benyon has had the baby, madame, that is why she is dead, *enfin!*'

Celandine stared at the maid, uncomprehending, silent, imagining that the poor woman was in such a state of hysteria because her mind had been turned by the death of her mistress.

'That is not possible,' she said slowly, and she turned and walked back down the corridor to the salon, where there was more light, before turning back to Marie. 'My mother,' she began to say, '*is far too old to have a baby.*'

No sooner had she said this than she realised that she had just announced something that was medically ridiculous. Her mother was – had been – only . . . she tried to calculate the exact age of her mother. She had been forty-three! There was no reason on God's earth why she should not have been able to have a baby. The wife of the vicar of Newbourne had apparently just given birth at the ripe old age of forty-eight; and while the vicar had found it necessary to pass off the event as a miracle of the kind normally associated with the Blessed Virgin, nevertheless his wife had managed without any difficulty to give birth to a healthy baby boy.

'My mother has had a baby? My mother has died giving birth to a *baby*? But she wasn't married, Marie. My mother was not *married*!'

'No, madame, she was not married, no, she was a widow.'

For a moment Marie seemed to think that she ought to look shocked, which she did, but perhaps remembering her own sometimes colourful love life, she finally merely shrugged her shoulders.

'No, Madame was not married. No, Madame fell in love with a younger man,' she continued, speaking rapidly and in a low voice as if her late mistress might overhear her. 'She fell in love, *passionately*, with a younger man. When we were in Munich. He came twice a week to teach her German, in which he was most proficient. That was why she was so sad to leave Munich for Paris, but before she left he . . .'

For a brief second Celandine wondered why the word 'passionately', which was really so similar in English and French, sounded so much more *passionate* in French. And then she wondered, almost as passionately, why she had never taken any notice of her mother's eagerness to learn languages at the hands of young tutors wherever they had lived in recent years. She had to face the fact that she had probably been too self-absorbed, too caught up in her own quest to find someone who believed that a woman's artistic vision was as valid as that of a man. She had been too selfish.

'Yes, Madame was passionately in love – but not so much as to want to . . . be pregnant!' Marie continued.

As she said it again Celandine almost winced. She hated to think of her mother doing anything passionately with a younger man, but it seemed she would have to, if for no better reason than that Marie wanted, just as passionately, to convey how their present situation had come about.

'He was a painter like her late husband, but younger and more handsome, and one day she tell me he took advantage of her. She did not want it, she told me when she was dying, and she did not know she was pregnant, not ever, not until the end. She thought, perhaps because of his taking advantage of her, she put it away from her.' The maid paused, waiting for the right words to come to her, and finally finding them. 'She thought she was becoming – as older women become – fatter . . .' she mimed an ever-expanding stomach, 'but not fertile, yes? It could have been. But it wasn't. Maybe she shut out the reality, perhaps? This happen to an aunt of my mother, but *she* was married.' Marie straightened her stiff collar, allowing herself a moment of family pride. 'She died, my aunt, poor creature; and now your mother too is dead, and we have this baby which is being fed by Madame Montellier opposite – you know the apartment near to the concierge?'

Celandine nodded, too stunned to speak.

'Madame Montellier, she has a new baby, her eighth. It make her very 'appy because she like the even numbers, huh? But she has too much milk. Madame Montellier is in there now, in your mother's room. It was lucky that she was in the habit of sitting at her window for that was how I noticed her, or the poor baby and I, what should we have done? How would we have known which way to turn with its mother so dead?'

Marie started to cry once more, throwing her apron over her head as she did so and rocking backwards and forwards, moaning.

'It is so much tragedy, madem— *madame*. I love your mother as my own whom I never knew. She was always so kind. And what if the baby dies too?'

Celandine held Marie by both her shoulders, shaking her gently. 'Stop it! Stop it!' she begged. 'Isn't it bad enough that we are in the position we are in without you having hysterics?'

Marie stopped crying instantly. 'I have to inform you, madame,' she said, with some dignity, after she had dried her eyes on the apron, 'I have to inform you that I am owed two months' wages.'

'So you would be,' Celandine stated, after a short moment. 'You, and I dare say anyone else who happens to have come to the apartment in the last few weeks. Everyone will be owed at least two months' wages, will they not? The butcher, the baker, the candlestick maker, they will all be sending in their accounts – suddenly and surprisingly unpaid by my mother who was always so meticulous in such matters. And not unnaturally, I dare say too that the bills will all be vastly larger than in previous months.' Celandine gave a great shuddering resigned sigh. 'Now lead me to my mother's body, and to the baby.'

'But it is not possible, madame. Madame, your mother's body is gone. Mademoiselle Agnes, she sent Madame Benyon away. Before Mademoiselle Agnes took all the paintings from the walls and had them transported back to Avignon, the undertaker come. Your mother, may she rest in peace, is in the chapel waiting for the funeral tomorrow, but Mademoiselle Agnes she has already told me, she can't come back for the funeral, because of the *children*. One of them has measles, and she fears she too might have caught it. The measles will last three weeks, so she will not be coming to Paris for the funeral.'

'Of course. Only to be expected that Mademoiselle Agnes and her boys should all be too ill to come to the funeral. Only to be expected. How happy for them though that, despite all these worries, she was still able to take so many of my father's paintings back to Avignon to be in her safe-keeping. Now let me see the baby, please.'

Celandine walked to the bedroom where the baby had stopped crying, probably because the obliging Madame Montellier had just finished feeding it. The large moon-faced woman stood up as Celandine came into the room, smiling sadly and greeting her in the low tones considered appropriate when someone is in mourning.

'He is a very beautiful boy,' she announced to her visitor, nodding towards the baby, and perhaps to save Celandine the trouble of asking. 'He will be very beautiful. Let us hope that he will live to be as handsome a young man as his mother would have wished, *n'est-ce pas*?'

The shock of the circumstances in which Celandine found herself was so great that she hardly knew what she was doing, or she might never have held out her hands and taken the small human being who was her half-brother into her arms; never have held him for so long staring down at his serenely sleeping face.

Celandine would not have been human if she had not found herself remembering that when she had last seen her mother the latter had been full of righteous indignation. She had looked at Celandine as if she had committed murder, not succumbed to love. Now her mother was dead because she too had fallen in love and finally, perhaps, if Marie was right, been made to succumb to it.

Celandine put her finger in the tiny hand, and feeling it grip her knew at once, with a sinking heart, that whatever happened in the future, her fate and that of the baby were now securely entwined.

Edith sat staring out to sea, realising with delight what a brilliant subject it was, what a friend to the imaginative, what a source of fascination. Soon the Lugger would be putting in to the harbour and, as Sherry had just said, half the town would be down to help pull in the nets and greet their men from whom they had been parted for many months. Napier had already sketched Mary and her friends in their aprons and bonnets with some fish laid out on the beach, but that would be nothing, she was sure, compared to the sight they were about to see.

'Of what are you dreaming?'

Edith turned and smiled at Alfred. 'I was not dreaming. I was thinking about the sea, and how it is possible to sit and watch it for hours on end – more than any landscape, I should have thought.'

'It can be a cruel companion—'

'Not today. Today the sea is in a brilliant mood, no white tops, the Luggers coming back to the harbour. The sea is ready to celebrate.'

'As you were last night?'

'I had rather you did not talk about last night.' Edith laughed. 'I drank too much wine cup, and that is always a shocking thing to do.

299

But . . .' her eyes wandered over to where Napier and Sheridan were seated talking to each other with unusual intensity, 'at least Sheridan and Celandine were able to enjoy their evening of celebration.'

Alfred leaned forward, forcing her to look into his eyes. 'You should be with me, and you know it,' he told her. 'Your husband does not love as I would love you, and that too you must know. Your husband does not love you!'

'My husband most definitely does love me,' Edith said with satisfaction, and at the memory of the previous night a mischievous look came into her eyes. 'In fact my husband loves me so much I doubt if there is another woman who has been loved *better* than I, Mr Talisman.'

'Brave try, Mrs Todd, but *I* know better.'

Alfred lit a cigarette, and as he did so he remembered enjoying a previous cigarette in the shelter of the boat the evening before. More important, he remembered hearing the exchange between Edith and Napier, how Edith had protested to Napier that since he did not wish to enjoy her, he should at least allow other men to appreciate her. He smiled almost sleepily.

'I shall have you whether you like it or not, Mrs Todd, and when I do I promise you that you will not have to pretend any more for your husband's sake,' he murmured to himself, after Edith had moved away from him. 'One day, Mrs Todd, you will know what it is like to be really and truly loved. A beautiful girl like you should be loved all the time, every day, and every hour of every day.'

He was interrupted. Sheridan and Napier were packing up the picnic baskets and standing up, preparatory to leaving the little cove.

'I think we should go and do some sketches of the incoming boats, don't you, Alfred?'

Alfred stood up, brushing down his immaculate trousers. He was a stark contrast, Edith thought, to his two friends who were already charmingly dishevelled: their collars loosened, their trousers covered in sand, their shoes dampened by the sea. But she was not concerned with Alfred. All she saw was Napier's eyes filled with the same look that she had only glimpsed for a few seconds the night before – before they fell into bed, and he, she hoped, at long, long last into proper love with her.

They strolled back towards the main concourse of the harbour. The sun was still bright and warm, and Sheridan's thoughts were on Celandine. He knew she would have dreaded the Channel crossing, and hoped the settled weather would ensure an easy journey; found himself hoping against hope that she would be back as quickly as she had gone. He was glad to set up his easel and start sketching the scene before him. The men, the nets, the waiting women – it was a scene full of human emotion, the kind of emotion which nowadays he was always, quite purposefully, striving to capture in his work. Never mind that Napier and painters like him would say the scene was sentimental; Sheridan did not care. Let them paint their vast canvases full of pompous import, let them depict their Biblical subjects; he was only interested in the working lives of the people among whom he now lived.

Edith made sure to stand a little apart from the rest, not just because she did not like to see the fish jumping and rolling so helplessly, gasping for air, still beautiful, still shining with all the delicate colours that God had given them, which would fade to nothing as they died, but also to witness dear Mary greeting her long lost husband home from the sea.

There she was, standing with Mrs Harvey and a few others, some of them already walking back arm in arm with their loved ones, some of them, like Mary, still waiting. And all at once one of the reunited couples stopped, and turning to Mrs Harvey took her aside.

Edith knew. She knew as soon as she saw the way the fishwife's bonnet bobbed and her arm went out to Mrs Harvey, from the way Mrs Harvey turned to Mary, that Mary's husband must have died at sea. She knew before she saw the older women trying to reach out and comfort her, and Mary's head sinking into her hands, oblivious of their sympathy, oblivious of anything except the ultimate price that her young man had paid to bring home the precious catch.

Edith quickly turned away, not wanting to witness someone else's grief, but as she did so her eye was caught by Sheridan, like her watching the scene on the quay, except that he was standing in front of his easel, and had already started sketching what they could all see but which Edith thought was none of their business.

'How *could* he?'

Napier looked startled by Edith's ferocity. 'He is a painter, Edith. Painters paint what they see.'

'Yes, but Mary was in – in an *extremis* of grief. How could he switch off as if she was not a human being? How could he stand in that cold-hearted manner, and paint what was happening? It is so . . . well, there is no other word for it, Napier. It is heartless.'

'To *you* it seems heartless, to Sheridan it seems the right thing to do. If he paints the scene the way it should be painted he will deepen human sympathy for the plight of the fishermen and their wives. Not to paint it would be cowardly. It would mean that he is careless of what the human heart is all about. More than that, it is what he wants to paint, dearest. If it was a war scene, would you object that much? I doubt it.'

Napier put a tender arm around Edith's shoulders and guided her away from the harbour, away from the leaping fish, the heartbroken Mary, back to bed with him, to afternoon love, and delights of a physical kind, well away from the pain of the scene they had just witnessed.

But afterwards as Edith pushed open their bedroom window and stared out to sea, remembering the excitement on Mary's face that morning, remembering the longing in her eyes, she knew that it would take more than love-making, however passionate and involving, to wash away the images the day had brought. It would take more than the noise of the sea to drown the sound of Mary's weeping.

'Now what are you thinking about?' Napier leaned over and kissed her.

Edith smiled. 'Nothing,' she said.

'It is always nothing with you,' he replied, but he looked more than happy with her reply, as if he would rather not think of her thinking about much at all; and Edith, knowing that she was lying, turned away from the view of the sea beyond the window. For once it gave her little comfort, for it seemed to her that the sea too knew she was lying.

Chapter Eight

The funeral passed quickly, as in retrospect funerals always seem to do, and Celandine travelled back to Cornwall with her heart full of sadness, trying to wrestle with the complications that her mother's death had brought about.

She struggled to reason with herself, trying hard to put the case for her mother. After all, she had not been an old woman when she was widowed, so why would she not be vulnerable to some handsome young man who flattered her? And she could not have known that she was pregnant when she disowned Celandine. Celandine was so preoccupied with the problem of how to explain the difficult situation in which she found herself that she quite forgot to feel seasick. She knew Sheridan would be waiting anxiously for her, expecting her to arrive as limp as yesterday's lettuce, shattered by the journey. As it was he ran to take her in his arms, as he always did.

'Oh – of course, you are in mourning, dearest.

I am so sorry, I should not have done that.'

'Yes, but *you* are not in mourning, Sherry.'

They walked arm in arm up to where the trap was waiting for them and climbed in, sitting down and at once holding hands tightly, as they always delighted in doing, while the lightly sprung vehicle moved smartly through the narrow, hedge-bound lanes.

'How was Paris, dearest? As you can imagine I have been in agonies for you.'

'It was deeply distressing, as it would be to *anyone* who loved their mother. Most especially since . . .'

She paused, about to tell Sheridan about the strange and deeply upsetting circumstances surrounding her mother's death, only to find herself quite unable to do so. There was something so sweet, so genuinely honest, in Sheridan's expression, the loving look in his eyes as he stared into hers, that she found it impossible to confess all, or indeed any, of the circumstances of her mother's death.

What was more, as she had to admit to herself afterwards, because Marie had hinted that her mother had been taken advantage of, her daughter felt too ashamed to want to talk about it.

The truth was that if her mother had been mortified by the drawing that Celandine had done of Sherry, indeed had given every appearance of being repelled by it, Celandine could not deny that she herself felt not a little revulsion at the thought of her mother's having enjoyed a romantic involvement, struggle as she might.

Then too there was the knowledge that, in the admittedly hypocritical eyes of Society, her mother had committed the ultimate sin. She had given birth to an illegitimate baby. She had given birth to a child who would grow up under a cloud, a blank by his name where his father's name should be, doomed to be set apart in school, stigmatised through no fault of his own, always a figure of either pity or fun, and for no better reason than the circumstances of his birth, over which he had, poor creature, no control.

So Celandine said nothing of the baby whom she had enjoined Marie and Madame Montellier to have christened as soon as possible, deciding instead to delight in Sheridan's welcome, in his vivid descriptions of how much he had missed her, and much else that is always so flattering to young wives, not to mention the passionate love-making that a return home so often engenders.

The following morning being sunny, Sheridan was carefully cleaning up his best square-tipped brushes in Mrs Molesworth's back scullery, ready to set off once more for his favourite place on the harbour, when he heard the landlady call down to him.

'I'm in here, Mrs Mole!' he called happily back to her, knowing that his spirits had never been higher, possibly because although Celandine was still sleeping after her journey he himself had been up for some hours and was feeling that uncommon sense of self-congratulation and pride which always seems to come to those who have risen before anyone else at an unusually early hour.

'A letter for you, Mr Sherry.' Mrs Molesworth stared at the hand on the envelope. 'It looks important. The postman thinks it so important that he brought it to you rather than leave it at the post office until Monday.'

Sheridan hated letters. They seldom brought anything but bad news of one kind or another, but he took it quickly, afraid that it might have a French stamp, that it might be more news of Celandine's family, that she might have to return to France once again, something which he actually dreaded.

What a relief therefore to see that the letter was only from London, from his father's lawyers, a firm that was always writing him tedious missives about his small trust fund, and then only so that they could charge him for so doing.

He tore the envelope and read the letter rapidly through. It seemed to be the usual clap-trap – dah dee dah dee dah – until he came to the second paragraph, when it stopped being dah dee dah and quickly became oh God!

He sat down slowly on the rickety scullery chair where Mrs Molesworth usually peeled potatoes, taking them carefully from one bucket and peeling them into another before placing them with equal reverence in a third. This was grave news. It was worse; it was news of the very gravest. It seemed that the allowance upon which they depended was about to cease for all time.

'What?' Celandine stared at Sheridan, turning quite pale as she realised the import of what he was saying.

His wife looked so lovely sitting up in bed, her face un-creased by sleep, her hair tumbling about her shoulders, that for a very brief second Sheridan nearly forgot what he was talking about, ripped off all his clothes, and climbed into bed beside her.

'Yes, dearest. It seems there was a fire, a very bad fire, somewhere up north, and the extent of the damage is such that the insurers are now bankrupted, and since that is where my small annuity comes from I am quite sunk, and alas not just me, my darling, we are both sunk.'

Celandine jumped out of bed. Plucking at her blue crushed-velvet wrap she dragged it round her and fastened the belt before seating herself beside Sheridan, who handed her the letter. She read it through, bit by bit. The tone was implacable. Worse than that, even though coming from lawyers, its tone was tragic.

'I do not know what we shall do now, dearest. We only have enough to last the month here with Mrs Molesworth. We will have to work every hour of the day and night if we are to live only on our painting, and your tiny allowance.'

Celandine started to walk about their bedroom,

pacing up and down as she had done in Paris, when she was wondering what to do about the baby, whether he should be put up for adoption as Marie had advised, whether she should bring him to England, or send him to America, when he was older and stronger. Now she was pacing up and down wondering what to do about Sheridan. How best they could help each other, and stay solvent; how Sheridan could best earn his living; how they might both do so.

'We will manage, dearest,' she finally announced. 'We will manage, because we are both talented. We will do *better* without the money from your trust. We will do so well that we will realise it has been nothing but a blessing that your annuity has dried up.'

Sheridan looked doubtful, then a little sullen. He had hoped that Celandine would have some rather more practical advice, or perhaps a more brilliant notion.

'Your mother's death has not brought you any . . .' he began uncertainly, trying not to sound eager or avaricious although quite unable to keep from being hopeful.

'My mother's death has brought me nothing but debts and quandaries,' Celandine told him, sounding unexpectedly bitter.

Sheridan stared at her, momentarily surprised by her tone. Thinking that her bitterness must have come from reading the lawyer's letter, he stood up to take her in his arms, seeking to reassure her.

'You are right, everything will be better. I will work twice as hard as I have been doing. No more of Mrs Molesworth's splendid picnics on the beach, no more dillydallying with Alfred and Napier and talking a lot of rot; enough of that. On with the toil. I will paint so hard and so fast that, no matter what, I will bring in enough. I will bring in enough to feather not just one nest, but many!'

'Yes, but how, Sherry? How?'

Sheridan looked at her. 'Why, with my paintings, dearest. They will start to sell, I am sure. When I am better known.'

'Yes, darling, when you are better known, but just now you are not better known and quite soon Mrs Molesworth will come to the door with her hand out, waiting for the rent and the money for our food, and the laundry, and everything else.'

Celandine stopped. Remembering some of the paintings that had been supposed to come to her from her mother, which Agnes was now probably either hanging or selling, she could not help feeling another rush of bitterness.

'My paintings will sell. The new reality is going to become popular, Celandine, really it is.'

'Yes,' Celandine agreed in a kind tone. 'But not by the end of the month, dearest.' She stopped pacing up and down, and stood in front of Sheridan. 'You are going to have to paint portraits, Sherry.'

Sheridan sprang up. 'Paint portraits!' He ran

his hands down the sides of his trousers. 'Paint portraits! Portraits are the last outposts of the desperately inartistic!'

'Either that or we shall be in the street, Sherry,' Celandine told him flatly.

Sheridan, more desperate than his wife, thought quickly. 'We could go and live with Aunt Biddy. She would have us. We could go and live with her.'

Celandine stared at her young husband as if he had gone quite mad. 'Sherry,' she said slowly. 'I love your Aunt Biddy, I love Gabrielle, and I even love Russo, despite the fact that the last time he changed his clothes was for the Duke of Wellington's funeral – but I will not burden them with our presence. Can you imagine? The poor creatures, landed with a couple more mouths to feed, having to air and make beds, do the laundry, peel more vegetables, dust our rooms. They can hardly look after themselves. No, it is to portraits we shall have to turn until such time as the new reality to which you are so devoted becomes fashionable.'

She did not add 'if it ever does', because that was not her way.

'I know for a certainty that, for instance, Captain Black, the old sea dog I danced with at Aunt Biddy's celebration, is only too keen to have himself portrayed sans stomach, sans wrinkles, in all his naval splendour.'

She stopped, because Sheridan had flung himself on their bed and buried his face in their pillows. She stared at his momentarily inert body. Really, he was such a child. She sighed inwardly, realising that it was not just Sherry who was a child at heart; they all were really. When it came down to it, very few human beings ever grew up, not really, not deep down, which was probably both a good thing and a bad thing.

'I shall send Mrs Molesworth's boy to take a message to him, and before too long, you will see, you will have a great big fat commission, Sherry.'

Sheridan pretended not to hear, because he did not want to hear. He wanted to throw himself in the briny. Just when he felt he had made a breakthrough, just when his new paintings were about to take off, he was going to have to sit flattering a great fat naval oaf who would want his epaulettes picked out in real gold, and doubtless an admiral's hat somewhere in the background – to signify his boyhood ambitions, or some such conceited nonsense.

He would not do it! He stood up to face Celandine, but seeing the look in her eyes he realised that his fate was sealed, at any rate for the moment.

A few days later he returned from sketching the old sea dog, who did indeed want an admiral's hat, not to mention a skull and crossbones against the statutory red velvet drape that was a basic requirement for all English oil portraits.

Sherry flung his sketchbook across the room.

313

'Hateful, hateful, hateful,' he muttered, in childish fury.

Celandine, who had quite expected such an outburst on his return, picked up the sketchbook with every appearance of calm.

'Very good, darling,' she told him, after a small pause during which she studied the sketch, because it *was* very good. 'Very good indeed.'

Sheridan flung himself into the armchair in their bedroom and stared into the small coal fire, his face dark with inner frustration, with the effort of trying to suppress all his longing for the wonder of his own creations, for everything for which he had striven over the past years.

He longed to paint not pompous old sea dogs, but the working people of Newbourne. He longed to perfect the struggle of their daily lives. The women's faces etched with pain as they struggled with their fishing baskets across the sands and the stones, up the steep streets. The men's faces worn from months spent at sea, their fishing hats somehow becoming part of their heads, left in place so long that on the rare occasions when they were removed from their foreheads, the latter appeared as white as the purest marble. He wanted to dip his paintbrushes in reality, not flattery.

Celandine too was feeling despair, but not for the same reasons.

She despaired because she knew that she faced day after day of just such behaviour as she was now witnessing. Day after day of Sheridan's

314

feeling that he was throwing his life away on worthless subjects just to keep their particular wolf from the door, a wolf that would not be baying perhaps – and the thought would keep recurring – if Sheridan had not married Celandine, if he had not taken on a wife.

'I have an idea, Sherry.' She knelt in front of him, trying to hold his attention.

Reluctantly Sheridan stared into his wife's eyes. 'Yes?'

'I have an idea. And I think it might work, if you will agree to it.'

When she had finished outlining her plan Sheridan looked unimpressed, but since he did not turn it down straight away, and since she finally succeeded in making him smile, and even laugh, at the vaguely outrageous notion behind it, they were able to go down to dinner with the Napier Todds at Mrs Harvey's house with hearts lightened by a future which now seemed a great deal more rosy at least to Celandine, if not to Sheridan.

Happy as she was that Celandine was back from France, Edith could not help feeling shocked that she was prepared to go out to dinner so soon after her mother's death. When the men finally left them alone to go for an evening walk, smoke cigarettes and drink small glasses of rough French brandy, Celandine, sensing her friend's confusion, took it upon herself to try to explain her situation.

'My mother as you know ceased all communication with me after – after she realised that Sheridan and I had fallen in love.'

Edith nodded, but remained silent. She quite understood that it must have been a shock to Celandine's poor mother; her own mother would have felt the same, had she lived.

'Despite the fact that we married, and I sent her a letter with our new address, I never heard from her again. She did not care to write to me and congratulate me – which I understood at the time, feeling nothing but guilt, as a good daughter must. But then when I arrived in Paris – when I arrived in Paris it was to find that—'

Celandine stopped, unable to continue as she remembered the dreadful scenes that had ensued when she arrived at the Paris apartment.

'You must tell no one.' She leaned forward and touched Edith on the arm. 'Promise me, swear, you will tell no one what I am about to tell you?'

'Of course. I have kept secrets before,' Edith reassured her, remembering that young Becky had told her at least two, which she wished she had not, since they still haunted her. 'But perhaps,' she added hopefully, 'you had rather *not* tell me. You know how it is. Sometimes it is better not to tell anyone rather than rake over past sorrows.'

'You told me your secret—'

'And I am very glad that I did. What a happy notion it was of yours to make Napier jealous that way. And what a happy outcome it has had!'

316

Celandine hardly heard her, thinking only of her mother. Try as she might, she could not deny feeling ashamed of her. Indeed, she had found herself over the past days wishing, again and again, that she was somehow someone else's daughter – Aunt Biddy's, anyone's, rather than her mother's.

'My mother died—' She paused, and started again, after clearing her throat quite needlessly. 'My mother died in childbirth, Edith.'

Edith's hand flew up to her pretty mouth to prevent any exclamation that might upset Celandine, while Celandine turned away, embarrassed both for herself and for her mother.

'I know, it hardly seems possible, does it? But it seems that my mother was infatuated with a young man in Munich, a younger man who took advantage of her, and she, having ignored her pregnant state, finally died in childbirth, leaving a baby. A baby who will by now, God willing, be christened Dominique Benyon, but who is *not* a Benyon, not by any means. He is someone else's boy, but what could I do? I have no idea of the identity of his father, and Marie, my mother's maid, refuses to tell me. She had rather go to the guillotine, she said, than reveal the name of the father. Apparently she promised my mother, as she was dying, that she would say nothing. And you know Catholics: once they make an oath they keep it. I have always been given to understand their sense of sin is very deep.'

'Yes,' Edith agreed, remembering some of the

317

Irish maids at the Stag and Crown. 'Catholics are very convinced by sin, are they not? As I am by the devil,' she added, remembering how some of the girls had ended up on the streets, earning a great deal of money that they faithfully sent home, but finally, all too often, paying a dreadful price for it.

'Can you imagine how I feel now, in mourning for a mother who refused to forgive me, and yet died giving birth to an illegitimate baby? I am tortured by many thoughts, Edith, but most of all by one that will not go away.'

Edith stared at her older, more sophisticated friend, realising suddenly that in some ways Celandine was perhaps more naïve than herself. Edith might have been innocent as to the mentality of painters, she might not have lived abroad, or read the essays of Ruskin, but she was all too aware of the exigencies of a woman's lot. She felt she might not have been so shocked by a mother's having an affair. Mothers lived. Mothers loved. Mothers died. However, she soon realised that she was mistaken, because within seconds she was being thoroughly shocked by Celandine's next announcement.

'You see, Edith, I do not think that this love affair of my mother's . . . I do not think it was her first. From the look in Marie's eyes, I think my mother might have had other affairs. I think that is why Agnes, my half-sister, treated my mother with such despite, doing as she wished whenever she wished, never bothering with my

318

mother's feelings, because she must have known what I did not, that Mother had been unfaithful to Father. That she had never been what Society calls a virtuous woman. That she had this weakness. I believe it is in revenge for this that Agnes has taken all Mother's paintings, and left me only with the baby. My mother's baby. I can only imagine how Agnes must be enjoying my plight, knowing that I will have to put the little fellow up for adoption. Sometimes, in the middle of the night, I even think I can hear her laughing.'

'Must you put the baby up for adoption?' Edith stared at Celandine, surprised that she could even think of such a thing. 'Could you not bring him to England? After all, there is nothing here to say that he is your mother's child, surely? Only you would know, and Sheridan, perhaps.'

Celandine shrugged her shoulders, trying to appear calm. 'I haven't even had the courage to tell Sherry yet, Edith. I have no idea how he will feel. Men feel so differently about these things. Of course I long to bring the baby here, but I must also be careful not to take him from his wet nurse before he has grown stronger. Imagine if I insisted on bringing him to England too early, and he died? Imagine if I tell Sherry and he refuses to let me bring him? It is perfectly possible, after all. I cannot tell you the confusion of my feelings, and if I seem heartless, believe me I do not feel it. I only seek not to do the *easy* thing, but the right thing.'

There was a small pause as Edith wondered at this statement, but then, seeing that there must be a certain truth to it, she nodded. 'I see now just how intolerable your situation is,' she conceded, feeling guilty that she herself had felt critical of Celandine's seeming lack of feeling. 'I know that babies should be breastfed for as long as possible – especially boy babies, Mrs George told me.'

'I pray every night that some solution will occur to me, but none does.'

The expression on Celandine's face was one of utter misery, so it was with relief that they heard the men returning from their walk. Rising, they picked up their shawls and made to leave the garden, Celandine wishing that she had not confided in Edith yet feeling a certain relief at having done so.

'I am so sorry you are leaving Cornwall,' she said, kissing Edith goodbye. 'But you will come back to us again soon? Before the summer is quite out, before the winter sets in?'

'Yes, of course,' Edith agreed, yet, for some reason that she could not name, not really believing it.

As soon as Mrs George saw Edith coming towards her through the elegant double front doors she knew that her young mistress's health had improved and she was on the road to recovery. Nevertheless, she was more than ever solicitous around her, for she had, as her housekeeper, a certain interest in Mrs Todd's continuing not just well, but blooming.

What she had not counted on, however, was that Napier would return to the usual routine of expecting his wife to pose for him in his studio.

'Now, Mr Todd—'

Napier had noticed that he was always 'Mr Todd' except on the few occasions when he was in Mrs George's good books, when he became 'Mr Napier'.

'I don't want you causing my poor little mistress another recurrence of her illness. She was as near to death a few weeks ago as I hope I'll ever see her.'

'And now she's as bonny as the peaches in the peach house, and you know it, Mrs George.'

'I'll not have you putting her in that studio without proper heating and ventilation. The gas must go on, and *both* the fires be lit, despite its being a good temperature outside, even though it is already September.'

'Anything you say, Mrs George, anything you say.'

Mrs George frowned after Napier's departing back. This was most unlike Mr Todd. Mr Todd was normally so caught up in his own ideas that he made a practice of laying down the law before he had even thought about what he was laying down the law *about*!

'Well, I don't know,' Mrs George said out loud, and she shook her head and hurried off to instruct the maids to lay the fires for the following morning. 'I'm sure I don't, really I don't. If I didn't know him better I would say that Mr Napier has become what I would call civilised.'

Edith on the other hand was actually looking forward to taking up her old pose. She was sure that it was all going to be different now that they had made love. She was so convinced of this that she could not wait to struggle into the once hated Grecian-style dress with its floppy sleeves.

'Ah, and here's my darling little harp,' she murmured, settling herself on the gold seat against the velvet backdrop.

In order to maintain her pose she had decided to bring with her into the studio all her memories of Cornwall. It would take her mind off the stillness that Napier demanded to think of the sound of the sea, of the patination and colour of the stones on the beach, of the hard-working fisherfolk, of the steep winding streets, of the whitewashed cottages, of the skies that seemed to hang over the sea as it tempted them to touch the top of its white waves, threatening to refuse, just once, to reflect them in its ever-changing colour. More than anything she was determined to be Napier's inspiration, to be everything to him in his life and work, just as he was everything to her in every way.

They began their new routine with great enjoyment, pursuing the cause of art in the studio, dining and making love in the evenings. It was a happy time, a time of learning, and appreciation, with Napier instructing Edith in poetry and even Ruskin's essays – rather too many of those but she tried not to mind – so that she would be able to converse with him on equal terms at dinner.

The atmosphere of the house changed, not just because of the Todds' new and open fascination with each other, nor because of Mrs George's hopeful expectation of a happy outcome to their lovemaking, but because Edith was, at last, able to claim a victory over the dining room.

'Napier?' She had chosen an exceptionally good time to ask him for something, since he had just made love to her. 'Napier, I want to ask you something which I don't think you will like, but which I find I *must* ask you.'

Napier, stretched out half asleep on Edith's side of the bed, looked at her out of lazy eyes. 'Ask me, my darling. You know I will do anything for you at this moment.'

Edith was brushing her long auburn hair in front of the mirror so that she could see Napier's head of thick blond hair reflected in it.

'Why do you think that the men, and their poor wives, want to eat with you?'

Napier frowned. 'Because like me they are artisans, they work with their hands, and they want to feel as one with each other under my roof, feasting together as the Anglo-Saxons did before a long day of toil.'

Edith looked thoughtful, and then, deciding that honesty must be the best policy – something with which she knew Celandine would never agree – she put down her hairbrush and turned towards her husband.

'Napier, I'm sorry to say this to you, but you are only thinking of yourself. The men, and their wives, do not I think you will find enjoy having to feast with you under your roof, as you so poetically put it. They would really rather be in their own homes, in their own cottages, with their children running about putting their sticky fingers over everything. They feel so . . . self-conscious here. They can hardly taste their food for thinking that they might have picked up the wrong knife or that Mrs George is going to give them something they don't like!'

Napier sat up, banging his head against the oak headboard. 'How do you know all this, Edith?' he asked, looking shocked.

'Quite simply, because I asked them, Napier. I asked them why they all looked so gloomy during mealtimes, and they told me. It was as simple as that. They want you to free them, Napier. They don't want to be the same as you, they just want to be themselves. By making them equal with you you are embarrassing them. They just want to make your furniture, the way you and Mr Ruskin have conceived that they should do it, joyously and beautifully, and then be allowed to be themselves.'

Napier jumped, naked as he was, from the bed, and started to walk up and down, which was such a funny sight that Edith rushed to get his gown and hand it to him. She did not mind making him think a little about how much he might be imposing on others, but that did not mean that she wanted to laugh at him.

'Edith,' he said, frowning but nevertheless accepting the gown, 'what you are saying is that by making the men and their families live with me on equal terms, I am in fact imposing on them? I can't believe what you are saying is true.'

'Why else do they look so miserable in the dining hall?' Edith asked simply. 'Have you not noticed that when they are outside making your furniture they are happy, they sing, they laugh, but when they come in here they have faces like a funeral, as if they are coming to church not to eat and be merry.'

'Did they *tell* you this? Or did you observe it, truly? Because – because if they told you this themselves they might have thought you wanted them to say they were miserable, that is all. They might be merely trying to please you. Going along with you to be pleasant.'

'Well, if I had told them what I thought, perhaps, but I have not expressed an opinion. Besides, you must have noticed yourself, Napier, surely? Or perhaps you haven't? They all look as gloomy as coffin nails seated around your dining table, whereas once they leave the house and go to the workshops they start laughing and smiling once more, purely because they have been freed from having to go along with your notion of equality. Try letting them eat at home in the bosom of their own families instead of forcing them to be part of your ideal, and you will soon see whether or not I am right.'

Napier did as Edith advised and to his chagrin saw his workforce turning up after meals looking a great deal more cheery than when he had forced them, in the name of equality, to do as he wished. Mrs George was triumphant.

'There is nothing so tiring as working for a man who spends the whole time insisting that he is not the master of the house; believe me, I know.' The housekeeper gave her young mistress a look that was so appreciative, it might as well have been a victory medal.

It was indeed a singular victory for Edith, but one that seemed to puzzle Napier, who turned it over and over in his mind, hardly able to leave the subject alone as he realised that Edith had been right and he had been wrong. He had finally, and reluctantly, to give in to the notion that equality had everything to do with freedom of choice and nothing whatever to do with imposing your notion of it on someone else.

'If you had been French, my darling, there would have been no revolution,' Napier assured her.

Two curious side effects resulted from Edith's suggestion. One was that the production of the furniture in the workshops actually went up, and the other was that Napier fell even more deeply in love with his wife.

*   *   *

'I cannot paint you!'

It was halfway through their normal working morning together, but Edith could not help noticing that Napier had hardly put a brush to the canvas. Now he threw one of his precious brushes – actually his most favoured – across the studio, and sighing mightily walked over to the fireplace to stare into the coal fire that was burning there, thanks to Mrs George and her solicitous eye for detail.

'Have I done something wrong, Napier?' Edith climbed down from her throne, and set her harp aside.

'Yes. Yes. You have. You have done something dreadfully wrong.'

Edith stared at him as Napier raised his head and sighed again.

'You have become a person!'

'Was I not always – a person?'

Edith frowned, feeling that she might be about to be hurt, but refusing to acknowledge it, knowing with a sinking heart that what was at stake was not just the painting.

Napier walked away from her down the studio, and sat down on the small gold throne where she normally sat.

'I have to tell you, Edith, that when I married you I married your beauty. I could not help myself. Your face when you looked up from the floor that day was something I will never, ever forget. Of course I have known many beautiful women, painters of my kind always do, but I

327

have never been so taken by a face before. Your face. But I didn't want you to be more than that. I wanted to keep you as you were, unknowable, an image that I had to convey to canvas. I did not want you to become human. I did not want you to become – Edith. But then when we were in Newbourne – no, later than that; when you were being so wooed by all those men, so admired by everyone, at that celebration at Miss Biddy Montague Robertson's – I – I gave in – because I realised just how much I loved you. No, not just how much I loved – how much I was *in* love with you. Horribly, dreadfully, in love with you. Never mind that I had struggled all the time since we were married to keep you from me. That night I thought I might lose you, and so I gave in, and I made love to you, something in which I have continued to delight. But . . . I know now I can no longer paint you. You are no longer the mysterious subject of a painterly notion of womanhood, you are my darling Edith, and as a consequence – I cannot put your likeness to canvas. The look in your eyes now is the one I see on my pillow. That funny sweet smile with which you turn towards me, that is the one I want to paint, but I can't. I have to finish this painting, and I can't do that either, because you are now *my* Edith. And what is more I don't want you any other way.'

Edith put out a hand and touched Napier's face. She no longer felt in danger of being hurt; she just felt for him. She realised that everything she and Celandine had talked about now made sense. The cold baths in the early morning, Napier's insistence on keeping his distance – everything made beautiful sense, and was thankfully no longer hurtful.

'I am sure we must be able to find a solution to all this,' she said tentatively. 'I could always – we could always cease intimacies, could we not? Until the painting is finished, perhaps? Would that help?'

'No.' Napier smiled. 'It would not help at all. Not in the least, alas. I have told you – you are my Edith now, and there is no going back. And besides – I don't want to go back.'

'Mr Napier?' Mrs George was standing by the outside studio door.

'What is it now, Mrs George? This is a very difficult time, really it is.'

'That's as maybe, Mr Napier, but you have a visitor to the main house, that Mr Alfred Talisman.' She made her voice purposefully accusing. 'He said that you had invited him when you were in Cornwall, but that you might have forgotten to tell me, or Mrs Todd.' Mrs George looked at Edith. It was the kind of look that might have passed between two martyrs who had been given the thumbs down by Caesar and were now hearing the roar of the lions.

Edith hardly registered the housekeeper's look. She was feeling totally confused, and the idea that Alfred Talisman, of all people, would be coming to stay with them was just what she did not at that moment want to hear.

'Is this true, Napier?' she asked. 'Did you ask Mr Talisman to stay?'

'I might have done. I don't know, really I don't.'

'No, well you wouldn't, Mr Todd, but here he is, and waiting for you in the main house. He does not seem to think that he was invited for one night, either.'

'Does he not? And how would you know that, Mrs George?'

'Why, sir, from the amount of luggage he has brought with him, how else?' Mrs George curtsied and went. Napier stared after her.

'I do wish she would not do that,' he said absently. 'Really I do. There's no need for her to curtsy to us as if we were royalty. God knows, we are all equal here.'

But then he caught the look in Edith's eye, and started to smile.

'We have talked about this, Napier. She *likes* to curtsy,' Edith reminded him. 'She takes a pride in being the housekeeper here at Helmscote and doing things what she sees as properly, and part of what she thinks is doing things properly is curtsying. That is Mrs George. She doesn't *want* to be your equal, she wants to be allowed to do her job as she thinks fit.'

'Oh, very well, have it your way. Now that the painting is not to be finished and your husband is not to be paid by that old devil Mr Algernon Hollingsworth, we shall probably have to let Mrs

330

George go anyway, but not, it seems, before Alfred has imposed himself on her, and you!'

Alfred's luggage was indeed splendidly prolific, encompassing not just a portmanteau but his many work cases and canvases carefully tied in their usual coverings, not to mention his favourite easel, which accompanied him everywhere.

'I thought this hall quite spacious until you arrived, Alfred,' Napier stated ruefully as he wrung his friend's hand in greeting. 'Imagine you coming to see us after all, and straight from Cornwall, I dare say?'

Edith too shook his hand, after which she looked away quickly, because as soon as she saw Alfred's tall figure in the hall, and heard his rich-toned mellifluous voice, she found she was forced to turn away from the men before they both noticed that she had coloured. She moved towards the door.

'Mrs Todd!' Alfred called out. 'I am most hurt. I have hardly arrived, and you are leaving?'

'I am going to find Mrs George, so that *she* can go and find Biff, the new boots boy, and tell him to take your easel to the – studio.'

Alfred turned to Napier, smiling. 'Am I again to be allowed to work in the studio next to yours? How very generous of you, my dear fellow.'

'You can set up your easel next door, and do as you please, Alfred. You know that. You are welcome to stay as long as you like, and in the house you can have the guest bedroom over-looking the garden.'

331

Napier was smiling so broadly and looking so relieved at seeing his friend that Edith suddenly realised he must be pleased at this distraction, at not having to keep concentrating on the problem he was having in completing the painting for Mr Hollingsworth.

'I shall be very quiet. I shall paint away, I promise you, without you even noticing my presence next door. I shall be virtually invisible, see if I am not.'

Napier nodded affably at his tall, handsome friend. 'My dear Alfred, it will be capital to have you here, really it will. You can spend the day as I do, coming back to the house in the evening.'

Alfred smiled but his eyes were not on Napier, who had anyway walked off to find the boots boy, but on Edith.

'You are looking almost impossibly beautiful, Mrs Todd, really you are, but why the old-fashioned cloak? Are you intent on leaving us? I do hope not,' he said quietly.

He looked puzzled as Edith, intent on tightening her grip on the cloak that she always wore between the studio and the house to cover the Grecian garb, dropped her eyes.

'No, I am not leaving. I am just going up to change for luncheon.'

Edith turned to walk away but as she did so, because it had been raining, she slipped slightly on the hall floor and once again, as he had on the way to the beach, Alfred went to her rescue, catching Edith's elbow just as the cloak dropped away.

He stared, mesmerised, surprised, as she tried to right herself, but it was too late. He had seen the Grecian dress, and what was worse he had seen *her* in the Grecian dress.

'What *is* it that you are wearing?' he asked.

'This is just the costume I sit to Napier in,' Edith replied, her colour deepening even more as she tried to snatch her cloak up and cover herself fully again. 'As I say, I am just about to go to change for luncheon.'

'Napier makes you sit to him in *that*?'

'It is for his painting, for Mr Hollingsworth. Mr Hollingsworth wanted a large painting in the Pre-Raphaelite style, and as you know, until he went to Cornwall, Napier was a determined Pre-Raphaelite, although less now, I think; much less now.'

'Yes, but making you, of all people, look as you do, in *that*.'

'How do I look?'

Edith knew that she should not ask, but she had done so, and nothing now to be done but to wait for the answer – or the laughter.

Alfred shook his head, but he did not laugh, or even smile. 'You look like someone else, not yourself at all. That sort of look does not suit your beauty at all. It makes you look – cold, and you are warm; you glow with warmth and life.'

'But that was the whole point,' Edith rejoined quickly, ignoring his compliments and feeling defensive of Napier while at the same time secretly agreeing with Alfred that she did look – as well as sometimes feel – very cold indeed. 'Yes, that was the whole point. Mr Hollingsworth likes women, in his paintings at any rate, to look like cold, marble statues, figures from the ancient world. He is, like so many older people, obsessed with the antique, or so Napier told me.'

'Have we a title for this painting yet?'

Alfred raised an eyebrow, but Edith did not notice, she was too busy tripping up the stairs, away from him, away from what she now knew was something she did not need, must not ever need, and which, although Edith did not know it, was encompassed very neatly in the title of Napier's painting.

'I don't know, I have never asked Napier. I have not even seen the painting yet.'

'You must surely know the title?'

Napier had returned with the boots boy, and was directing him to take Alfred's luggage to the best guest bedroom, and his easels and painting materials across the courtyard to the studios.

'I don't know the title, no.'

Edith was gone, so Alfred turned to Napier.

'Your beautiful young wife, whom I have just gathered you force to sit to you in Grecian garb, tells me that she has no idea of the title of the painting for which she is so busy sitting to you.'

'No? Well, she wouldn't have any idea,' Napier agreed cheerfully. 'I never allow my models to see the paintings for which they pose. As you know, all models are inclined to make remarks, remarks which at the time, although often well meant, are nevertheless very off-putting, or so I have found in the past. You paint the model, or models, over months of intense concentration, and if you allow them to see what you are doing while you are engaged on the painting they are inclined to come up with remarks such as "You've made my elbow bigger than it is". Or "I don't think my mother should see this, Mr Todd, really I don't." Mrs George has never forgiven me the painting I did of her – not a portrait, mind, a painting – she has never forgiven me for making her elbow look bigger than she thinks is its natural size. Never mind trying to explain to her that the enlargement of the particular elbow holding the basket of stuffs is to make a point, never mind that. As far as Mrs George is concerned, I am the vile debaser of her elbow.'

'That is exactly my experience. A few years ago, some stunner that I had discovered in the back streets of Whitechapel—'

'Does Whitechapel have any front streets, do you know, Alfred?'

They both laughed.

'At any rate, this particular stunner, once I had scrubbed her up, flew into a tantrum when she saw what I had done to her front prow, and bother me if she did not refuse to sit to me ever again! She preferred to go and work as a sales assistant in Whiteleys. Imagine choosing to sell doilies and dusters rather than be the subject of a

great painting by Alfred Talisman! And she herself nothing more than a streetwalker when I
discovered her. But that, she claimed, was a respectable trade compared to what I had done to
her, painting her as a goddess of the sea arising
from a shell, complete with fish tail.

'But Edith is your wife, Napier, old chap. She
will not put you off, will she? She is not the sort
to make a misplaced remark.'

Alfred knew at once that he was on to something because he had hardly uttered when
Napier turned away too quickly, and started to
help him carry his canvases from the hall.

'Edith is surely a help to you? If you are
making her pose in that Grecian gown, surely
she must be?' Alfred persisted.

Napier was still silent, walking ahead of his
friend towards the studio.

'Well, at any rate you must at least let me know
the *title* of your painting, even should you not let
me see it,' Alfred called after him as they both
crossed the courtyard.

'Oh, the title – the title is not exactly original. It
is called "Temptation".'

Alfred smiled, and although he did not say
How appropriate that might prove to be, if Napier
had seen the look in his eyes he might have sent
him packing. As it was he helped him set up his
easel in the studio, and seemed only too happy to
have his company.

Edith, dressed once more as herself, found
them in the drawing room, where they had at

once fallen into one of their usual animated conversations, arguing amicably about some finer point of brush work, something for which Edith could not help feeling grateful, for try as she might to avoid meeting Alfred's eyes she knew that he was yet again concentrating on her.

'Luncheon is served.'

Mrs George executed her usual defiant curtsy by the door, and opened it wider to allow the three of them to follow her to the dining room, where Alfred at once stared around him in theatrical disbelief.

'How is this, Napier? No crowded eating hall full of the honest faces of noble workers fresh from toying with your furniture designs?'

Napier shook his head, looking rueful. 'I am afraid not.' He smiled across at Edith. 'This was not my doing,' he added, pulling a wry face. 'This desertion on the part of the noble worker was all to do with my beautiful wife here, who is even now going to explain her theory to you.'

Edith spread her napkin over her knee as one of the maids came towards them with a dish poised and ready.

'It is perfectly easy to see that what was happening in the dining hall was quite wrong,' Edith murmured firmly, which made the maid holding out the vegetable dish to her simper. 'We could all see,' she continued, deciding to ignore the reaction beside her, 'that the men, and the women, were miserable, but most particularly the men. They did not like eating together like a

337

lot of school children on a day out. They were self-conscious about their manners, always looking around as if they were about to be told off by teacher. So it seemed to me to be a good idea to suggest to Napier that he did away with *his* ideas of equality and let them choose to do as *they* wished – which in truth is after all what equality is all about, surely?'

The two men laughed at Edith, who had widened her eyes over-dramatically to make her point.

'Bravo. So Mrs Todd has brought about a revolution at Helmscote?'

'More than a revolution,' Napier said quietly, and he looked across at Edith. 'There has been a climate change, a breath of fresh air, since we were in Cornwall. Ozone is now being breathed in this house where before there were only the musty, dusty ideas that come from too much time spent thinking, and too little time loving.'

Napier's look to Edith was so tender in its appreciation that Alfred could not help feeling puzzled. After all, some weeks before, he surely had not imagined that he had heard Mrs Todd saying, with some force, that since Napier obviously had no desire for her she could do as she wanted with whom she wanted?

'Mrs Todd?'

Mrs George was once more standing at the door.

'Yes, Mrs George?'

'There is a lady at the door who insists that she

is a friend of yours, and she would like me to tell you that she requests to – to see you.'

'Can you not see that we are at luncheon, Mrs George?' Napier asked impatiently, frowning round at the housekeeper.

'Could you ask her to call back later, Mrs George, or leave a card perhaps?'

'I think that might be difficult, Mrs Todd. She says she has walked all the way from Stowe, and she does not look like the kind of lady who leaves calling cards.'

'In that case, show her into the morning room, and tell her I will be with her as soon as I have finished eating luncheon with my husband and Mr Talisman.'

'Very well, ma'am.'

Mrs George shut the dining-room door again, and Edith pulled a little face at Napier.

'Mrs George only ever calls me *ma'am* if she is disapproving,' she said in a low voice, glancing from Napier to Alfred and back again.

Although luncheon was full of laughter, and the food delicious, Edith could not help wondering to herself who the visitor might be. She had after all made no friends locally, and the few that she had made in Cornwall would not possibly walk to see her, and certainly not all the way from Stowe. It could not be anyone rich, or even comfortably off, for they would have arrived in a carriage, or a pony trap, or ridden over.

Napier must have been thinking along the

same lines because he smiled at Edith as they neared the end of the meal.

'I think your visitor must be someone who, like Mr Ruskin, believes that walking promotes health,' he announced, because he too had obviously been puzzling as to who it might be, but was still determined that whoever it was would not be allowed to interrupt luncheon.

As it turned out it was not someone who would ever even have heard of Mr Ruskin. But it *was* an old friend of Edith's, and someone who was about to rescue Napier from his artistic quandary.

Chapter Nine

'Becky!'

Edith had to stare for a brief second at Becky before she recognised her. To say that Becky had changed was to say the least. She was dressed in the height of fashion; her long, sandy-coloured hair was caught up under a hat with a cheeky ostrich-feather plume decorating the front of it, and her travelling dress was richly sewn with lace edgings.

'Becky, come in, do!'

Becky stepped proudly into the hall, and looked around her with obvious appreciation, while nevertheless determinedly maintaining an airy expression as if she was now so used to big houses that she thought them two a penny.

'Bit like a church, innit?' she asked after staring at the stained-glass window of Queen Philippa and her Plantagenet king. 'Bit like St Peter's down the way from the Stag, wouldn't you say?'

Edith smiled. 'It's not just churches that use coloured glass for decoration, Becky, but I know what you mean. Come in here, and I will have some tea fetched for you. Come into what we call the "ladies' sulking room", and we can have a cosy conversation while the men go back to the studio.'

Edith was determined on locking Becky out of sight before Napier and Alfred emerged from the dining room, but Becky was equally determined on examining the spacious hall, the staircase, and the paintings, some of which were by Napier, naturally.

'I wouldn't want to dust that every day, thank you very much,' she said, staring at an overlarge statue in one corner. 'What do you do it with to keep it that glossy?' she demanded of her former companion in domestic arms at the old inn. 'You couldn't use a honeybee wax nor nothing like that, so what do you use? Soda and damp knitted cotton, I dare say?'

Edith who, since her marriage to Napier, had never yet raised so much as a duster to help the maids at Helmscote, nevertheless, while asking God's forgiveness for her lie, found herself muttering, 'Yes, that's right,' rather than explain that the Carrara marble had its own natural sheen and only needed a flick of a feather duster to keep it gleaming.

Hearing the door of the dining room open she found herself almost shooing Becky into the small sitting room where she liked to sit and read in front of the fire when Napier was out visiting potential patrons.

'Ah, the visitor! Introduce us, do.'

Alfred strode across the hall and Becky, seeing how tall and handsome he was, how beautifully, if artistically, dressed, instantly preened.

'Quite well, I'm sure,' she said, curtsying.

To Napier she said as she curtsied to him, 'You, I know, Mr Todd. On account of you marrying Edith here. That was a great day in the history of the Stag and Crown, and none of us what was there that day will ever forget what a beautiful bride Edith made, nor what a handsome groom you were, despite having a beard!'

Both the men laughed as they bowed in turn over Becky's hand.

'You surely did not walk across from Stowe dressed as you are, Miss . . . ?'

'Snape. And, no, of course I didn't, but I knows the ways of servants, I do, same as what Edith here does. I knows how to get them to go into the dining room, by saying you won't take nothing for an answer.' She smiled, showing surprisingly pretty teeth. 'So I says to the 'ousekeeper, you tell Mrs Todd I walked all the way from Stowe, knowing that neither she nor the 'ousekeeper could send me away then, see? But no, 'course I don't have to walk nowhere. I got me own carriage now, but I left it at the gate and walked up. No, I has me own carriage, same as what you have.' This last was directed to Edith. 'And having me own carriage I have to tell you makes all the difference to this particular lady of consequence. Yes, I have me own carriage, and me

343

own horses, and me own ideas about how to go on, as well, you may be sure. And since I was in the neighbourhood, and that, I decided to call on my old friend Edith, because apart from anything else, I promised Edith I would, and all.'

'Shall we let the gentlemen go about their work now, Becky? While we go to my little sitting room? I think we should.' Edith put a gentle hand under Becky's elbow, because, knowing her of old, she was aware that once you started Becky talking you could be all day listening to her.

'I don't mind if I do, but I will say this before I goes along with you.' She turned to Napier. 'You 'as a lovely 'ouse, you do, even if it is too modern for my taste.'

The door closed behind the two young women. Alfred stared at it for a second before turning to Napier.

'Very well, we must do as we are told, must we not, Napier, my dear chap? We must go and work, it seems, and by order of the lady of the house no less.'

The two men strolled in companionable silence across to the studio buildings, enjoying the feel of the autumn air, the smell of smoke on the breeze, and the sound of the maids laughing and singing in the kitchens.

'Ah yes, of course! I knew I knew that face, as soon as I saw it,' Alfred announced suddenly to Napier as they set up his easel together in the studio adjoining Napier's. 'It was only a few weeks ago I saw it, only a few weeks ago, but not in this part of the country, to be sure, no.'

'You were in the Stag and Crown near Richmond?'

Alfred shook his head. 'By no means. No, I was in Leicestershire finishing a commission for Lord Belton. His hunting *wife*, you know!'

They both laughed. Leicestershire was famous for the upkeep of so-called 'hunting boxes': small houses which were kept for the use of those gentlemen who followed the hunt; and of course their mistresses. The rules of hunting if not written into the legislature were nevertheless firm. Mistresses were allowed to mix with whomever they chose in the hunting field, just as they were allowed to follow the chase provided they rode fast and well, but because they would never be invited to any of the grand houses by the wives, the husbands were forced to find them alternative accommodation. Husbands might hunt with their mistresses, they might dally with them after the chase, but they would never, ever, be allowed to bring them home.

'Yes, it was in Leicestershire that I glimpsed Becky Snape. She is the new young stunner being kept by Belton's uncle, the Earl of Brinsmore. She doesn't hunt yet, but she will soon. I dare say that is why she is in this neighbourhood: to take lessons from Captain Joshua Plume. Her patron will have seen to that. Stunning she may be, but if she don't learn to ride like the devil, she will be yesterday's bread as soon as you like.'

345

Napier, who, unlike Alfred, had no interest in horses, looked questioning.

'Captain Plume,' Alfred explained, 'is the newest fad in riding. He can teach a lady to jump and hunt in a matter of weeks, and thanks to the new safety buckle on the sidesaddle he is, at this moment, having the success of his life. The ladies of the night are queuing up to learn from him, and the hunting field is fuller than ever of their kind. So much so that I have even trifled with the thought of following the chase myself. But funds being what they are, and having no time to go to Ireland where it is more exciting and less costly, I have put aside the notion, at any rate for the moment.'

He stared at the blank canvas he had just put up on his easel, and so did Napier. The blank canvas was always an exciting moment for both of them. They had often discussed the terror of it – the fascination of it – the challenge of it. The pull to put the first mark on it, the dread of putting the first mark, the holding back even as you were drawn forward.

'Well, my dear fellow, I know what I am going to put on this inviting canvas, with your permission, of course.'

Napier looked at Alfred, feeling almost before the two words were uttered that he knew exactly what they were going to be.

'Your wife.'

'Of course. What could be more natural than that you should want to paint my wife?'

'And you?' Alfred nodded in the vague direction of Napier's studio.

'Me? Well, my dear Alfred, I am hoping that Captain Plume will take some time to instruct Miss Snape in the equestrian arts, time during which, during just such an afternoon as this, I can paint her into "Temptation".'

Alfred smiled, yet again thinking of the appropriate nature of the painting. 'It must be difficult to paint one's wife, once one has married her?' he suggested.

'Impossible,' Napier told him, with some feeling. 'But not for you. How do you see her?'

'As herself.'

Alfred turned away, ostensibly to start unpacking his paints, but in fact to hide the depths of his feeling. How could he tell Napier what he felt for his wife? More than that, why should he tell him? After all, if Napier did not want her, he should not be surprised if Alfred Talisman did.

Celandine stared at all the sketches that Sheridan had made of the old sea dog, Captain Black. They were brilliant, and yet somehow defiant, as if he knew that he could paint the man in a flattering light, but hated having to do it with such a ferocity that he had determined to paint him as he saw him, which was as a bloated old bore.

'This will not please the subject,' she murmured to herself. 'In fact this will please the subject about as much as the artist has been pleased with the commission.'

She started to copy from Sherry's sketches on to her canvas, making sure to soften the lines and make the old gentleman look both younger and less conceited. She remembered how he had looked when he danced with her, so pleased with the fact that she had at last consented to step out on to the dance floor with him that the buttons on his waistcoat jacket threatened to fly off.

'Well, now here you are, Captain Black, in all your potential glory.'

She stepped back, her head on one side, feeling a strange excitement, for this was after all her first commission. Sheridan might despise the bourgeoisie and only want to paint the working population, to convey the harshness of their lives, but she was happy to paint Captain Black not just as he saw himself, but as she saw him – a man who had been to sea all his life and was now looking back on his adventures with a sense of wonder, and perhaps even of relief that he, unlike so many, had at least returned. His house, she knew from Sheridan, was very much a retired sea captain's place, full of the mementoes that such men treasure on their retirement, and, naturally, facing the sea. He could stand on his balcony with his telescope and pretend that he could see pirates, or the invading French, or – worse – Jesuits.

'What have you there?'

Sheridan was standing behind her, so close that she was forced to give way to him, and step aside so that he could examine her work.

'Mmm.' He looked thoughtful. 'If you continue in this way the old boy will like it, that much is certain.' He looked at Celandine. 'Don't forget he wants the skull and crossbones.'

'No, I won't.'

'If you continue as you are, he will be pleased. I told him that I had no need of any more sittings, for the moment, and he did not seem to mind. Knows nothing of art, thank God, just wants to stare at a painting of himself the way he has never looked.'

'He's a goodly type, Sherry – at least, that is how I see him – even if he is not a fisherman.'

Sheridan nodded, already uninterested because it was after luncheon and he did not want to lose the light.

'Have it how you will. He will probably like it better for what you are doing.'

Celandine realised at once, and only too well, that the inference was that Captain Black might like it, but Sherry certainly did not, but she did not mind. She smiled at the closed door before turning back to the portrait.

'Never mind, Captain Black, dear,' she told her canvas. 'We will make a good painting, no matter what Sherry thinks of it!'

In the event Sheridan was so caught up in his own work that he did not bother to examine the portrait very closely until it was finished.

'Do you know, you are really making a quite fine job of it,' he told Celandine when she showed him how she was progressing.

It was nearly Christmastime, but the weather having continued fine, if colder, Celandine was able to work with the windows open and the sound of the sea in her ears. It made her think of the lives of people like Captain Black, the history of places such as the one in which she now lived. Mrs Molesworth had told her that the Blacks had been a naval family in previous centuries, eventually turning to piracy and preying on ship-wrecks, as so many Cornish families did.

'The whole of this coastline was nothing but piracy,' the landlady often explained, waving one of her many heavy irons towards the open window. 'And even now, if there should be a shipwreck, the beaches will be swarming with scavengers. It's a sight to see, believe me. But the Blacks were like most of the families round here: they turned from waging war for His Majesty to waging war for themselves. The lighthouse was not popular when she went up, as you can imagine. The locals didn't want ships getting safely to port and no wrecks to pick to the bone!'

Perhaps it was Mrs Molesworth's stories, or perhaps it was her own recollection of the gentleman in question, but the portrait was finally finished – with Sherry going backwards and forwards to Captain Black to show him its progress – far more quickly than if Sheridan had undertaken the commission.

'You work fast, Mrs Montague Roberton, I'll say that for you.'

'Has he told you the kind of frame he wants?'

'Nothing too extravagant, nothing too poor, something gold, but not too costly, I dare say.'

Sheridan was mimicking the rich tones of the old salt, which was very funny in a way because Sherry was an accomplished mimic, but Celandine, for no reason that she could think, felt hurt, possibly because she had put so much into painting Captain Black that she now felt that in some way, through the painting, he belonged to her, just as a person who has painted a view might afterwards feel that in some way its beauty has become a part of them, something that has changed them.

Hardly had they finally settled for choosing Captain Black a handsome frame in gold leaf, when a letter arrived for Celandine from France.

'Oh, not France . . .'

Sheridan handed Celandine the letter with a worried look. He knew nothing of Mrs Benyon's dying in childbirth, nothing of his wife's agonising situation; he only knew that he dreaded a letter from France out of habit, because it might presage Celandine's having to return to Paris for one reason or another.

'Well?' He moved restlessly about the room, trying not to look at either her or the letter.

'It's from Marie, my mother's maid. I must go at once.'

'I don't see why, when a letter is from France, it is always so urgent that you return,' Sheridan complained, but he spoke to an empty room because Celandine had already hurried off to pack.

'Mrs Molesworth will look after you better than anyone else can, most of all your wife,' Celandine told him when she finally reappeared, already in travelling clothes and preparing to leave.

Sheridan looked sulky and irritated, but when Celandine touched him on the cheek to reassure him, he smiled.

'If you let me catch the boat this morning, I will promise to be back as soon as you can possibly imagine.'

Sheridan nodded. He had no idea why she should be needed by her mother's maid, but since she had also muttered about wanting some of her father's paintings to be returned to her, he imagined, in his vague artistic way, that there must be family business to do with wills and suchlike. Since their finances were as always precarious, he knew that it would be best to let her go without too much fuss.

On the boat, and then the train to Paris, Celandine thought over what she knew she would soon have to face. Should she adopt her mother's child? As a daughter was it her duty to adopt and bring up her own half-brother? And if she did what would Sheridan say? He would be understandably furious that she had not mentioned the situation before. And that would be only the beginning . . .

'Mademoiselle Celandine?'

Marie was as ever perfectly turned out, sharp of eye, and pretty.

'Madame?' Seeing how pale and worried Celandine looked the older woman's tone became conciliatory. 'You have had a long journey, *n'est-ce pas*? You must bath and rest yourself. Marie has made you your favourite dinner, *salade de tomates, filet mignon avec sauce béarnaise, une tarte normande* . . .' She murmured the names of various dishes soothingly as a nurse might sing a lullaby to a baby.

'Where is the baby, Marie?'

Marie's face lit up. 'Ah, *bébé* is in with Madame Montellier opposite. You must come and see him. He is so handsome. He love her milk, he take more than her own baby!' She laughed gaily, seeming to find this funny, as if it made the baby cleverer than his rival. 'He put on *kilos*.'

Celandine smiled at the pride in Marie's eyes. 'That *is* good.'

There was a small silence.

'I'm longing to see him,' Celandine confided. 'Does he look like anyone in particular, do you think?'

'He look just like a baby always does: some time he look like one person, some time another. That is babies!' Marie smiled the smile of a woman who was obviously feeling, since his mother had died, that this particular baby owed his life to her. 'We have called him Dominique, for the moment. But if you take him to England, he will maybe be called something else, perhaps?

Come, we must go and see him at Madame Montellier.'

Since the look in Marie's eyes told Celandine that to call the child anything except Dominique would be to court the most terrible danger, she followed the maid across the courtyard to Madame Montellier in a suitably humbled state. She was, however, allowed to pick up the handsome little bundle that her half-brother had already become.

'Isn't he beautiful?'

Both women, watching her with careful eyes, nodded. Yes, he is beautiful, their eyes seemed to be saying, thanks to us!

Celandine rocked him in her arms, feeling the stirrings of maternal emotion for the first time, and only reluctantly finally handing him back. 'You have done so well,' she told Madame Montellier, who smiled and stroked her ample front with pride.

'He is a fine child,' she said simply, her eyes not leaving the cot.

Celandine turned away reluctantly, wishing to goodness that she had plucked up the courage to tell Sheridan.

'He looks really rather like Madame Montellier, doesn't he?'

Marie shrugged her shoulders, but she nodded as they crossed the courtyard to go back to their own apartment.

'It 'appen with babies when they take the milk from the other mothers,' she said, her tone philosophical. 'Sometimes, if the milk is from a Chinese, or an Algerian, then the baby will soon have the look. Or if from a singer then he will have the voice of an angel. It has always been said that mothers' milk is very strong, huh?'

Marie had cooked Celandine exactly the dinner she had described, and there was no doubt that it achieved the desired mellowing effect. The true taste of Marie's French cooking was, as it was meant to be, soothing to a degree, the meat cooked to perfection, the sauce subtle and piquant, and the home-made tart with its buttery pastry of a lightness which Celandine had quite forgotten was even possible. Yet mellow though she might feel, Celandine knew that she could not give Marie the news she wanted.

'Marie. It is very difficult for me to take the baby back to England at this precise moment, because my husband has lost all his money. Not that he had a great deal, but that which he had has, alas, been taken from him, I'm afraid. A fire that was so bad that the company had to pay over all their assets. Nothing was left.'

'*Tiens.*'

Marie looked thoughtful, but impressed. She understood money very well; or rather she understood the lack of it only too well.

'A baby is very costly in that it takes up all your time, Marie, as you probably well know. I have brought you some money, enough to keep him with Madame Montellier for the next few months, until he is grown bigger, but I can't take him back, not just at this moment. I am having to work, to paint portraits, and although I have been paid my first commission, it is not enough, yet, for me to be able to take the baby back with me. Besides, I have to prepare my husband for the idea of adopting him. At the moment he knows nothing about the baby. I will tell him, on my return, but for the moment Dominique will have to stay where he is.'

Marie nodded. She understood, but the expression in her eyes was one of disappointment, as if she felt that Celandine, having eaten her exquisite dinner, was somehow now cheating her.

'I tell you in my letter, Madame Montellier cannot keep feeding the babies, not even her own; she too must return to her former occupation soon. She 'as no 'usband, as you know. She calls herself Madame because it is much more *convenable* for a concierge in an hotel. She need money.'

'Therefore,' Celandine said firmly, 'the money I have brought you will bring her some relief. She will be able to put off returning to her job, just until the moment when I can tell my husband of my new situation. Then you can bring the baby to us, yes? Or I will come over once again, and fetch him.'

Marie nodded, outwardly in agreement, but Celandine had the feeling that she was truly a little put out; that the money, although very welcome, was not quite what she actually wanted from Celandine.

'I do not want the baby to stay for too long with Madame Montellier,' she murmured, leaving Celandine in no doubt at all that she would soon have to tell Sheridan the truth, something to which she could only look forward with dread.

Her arrival home was, however, a supremely satisfying contrast to the unhappy state of affairs at the Paris apartment.

'Oh, Sherry, you shouldn't have! But I am so glad that you did!'

Sheridan had filled the whole of their suite of rooms with flowers, extravagant, rare and beautiful flowers that perfumed the air with such subtlety that they set Celandine thinking that their rooms were not in Mrs Molesworth's house but a part of heaven.

'I have missed you so much.'

'I was not gone long.'

'To me, unless I am painting, five minutes away from you is too long.'

'You flattering Irishman.'

Mrs Molesworth had prepared a welcome dinner, beautifully presented as well as being utterly and rather satisfyingly English.

'So what was the sudden hurry to return to France about, may we ask, Mrs Montague Robertson? What is your news?'

Sheridan was leaning over the harbour wall, smoking a late-night cigarette, while Celandine, only too happy to be home and standing beside him, stared at the faraway lights, wondering how to tell him what she knew she had to tell him. Or, rather, how to ask him what she knew she had to ask him.

She turned to him. He turned to her and, having thrown his cigarette away, took her in his arms. She returned his passionate embrace with fervour, realising that if there was one moment to ask your husband if you could adopt your half-brother, this was most definitely not it.

Edith looked at Napier. Seeing the detached look in his eyes, she should have suspected that he had already made a plan to which she was going to have to adhere.

'You will be sitting to Alfred, while he is staying,' he announced.

Edith did not know why, but she felt as if Napier had hit her.

'Is that what you want?' she asked, her confidence draining from her.

'Otherwise why should I ask you, Edith?'

'I don't like sitting to people as much as I thought I might.'

'You will not mind sitting to Alfred. He is more patient than I am.'

'Well, perhaps that is something after all.'

'It is impossible for a man to paint his own wife. It is nevertheless surely possible to paint someone *else's* wife. Which is why I thought you might not mind sitting to Alfred, since you are not *married* to him. He does so need a model at the moment. He very much admires your beauty.

358

And you are in full beauty at the moment, truly you are, Edith, since Cornwall. I think you cannot have ever looked more beautiful.'

Edith thought for a moment. 'Oh, very well, Napier. If that is what you wish. I will sit to Alfred, but you must understand that I am not going to wear a Grecian gown, or pose with a harp. I will never do that again. I will wear something of *my* choosing.'

'No, of course, you must wear something of your own choosing, and that I am sure would be Alfred's wish too. He simply wants to paint your portrait, because he finds you beautiful.'

Edith's thoughts went to her wardrobe and she started to wonder what dress she would wear, in her mind's eye turning over each of her fashionable outfits – the grey with the black velvet trim, the blue with the high-necked lace collar – which meant that Napier was able to deliver his *coup de grâce* just as he reached the door and started to turn the handle.

'Meanwhile I have to finish old Hollingsworth's painting, because, apart from anything else, if I don't, he will spread the word that I am not to be relied upon. Miss Snape has agreed to sit to me for that. Granted her hair is not exactly the same red as yours, but she will do very well for the arms and hands, not to mention the forehead. We will meet at dinner. For the moment, *au revoir.*'

He was gone before Edith had registered exactly what he had said. In fact the full import of what was implied, of what might be about to happen, only came to her when she turned to her wardrobe to try to pick out the most flattering dress in her possession.

She was to sit to Alfred, who had already confessed his attraction to her, and Becky Snape, of all people, was to sit to Napier? It was all becoming like a game of artistic musical chairs, but there was a part of her that was naturally quite curious to sit to someone besides Napier. It would be very different, as Napier had hinted. Perhaps, unlike Napier, Alfred Talisman would find her inspiring? Hard on the heels of this question came others. Why would Napier consider Becky Snape, of all people, *inspiring*? Or was her husband's inspiration dependent on something that he was not telling her?

Celandine had awoken early for her – although late for Sherry, whom she had just heard leaving the house for the harbour to sketch one of the old fishermen before the poor fellow set sail.

It was pleasant to be left not just to sleep, but to tussle with the question that, since her visit to France, had haunted her. The truth was that even after several weeks had passed she still had not plucked up enough courage to ask Sherry the question she needed to ask. She kept feeling that if she had only just a little more peace and quiet she would most definitely be able to come up with the best possible way of asking Sherry if he would mind adopting her half-brother.

The truth was that she was fast coming to the conclusion that there was no good or tactful way of putting what she had to put to Sheridan except in good plain American English, and she was bracing herself for the shock of his reaction. She had barely convinced herself of this, when there was a knock at her bedroom door.

It was Mrs Molesworth, and she had brought up Celandine's breakfast on a beautifully laid tray, complete with embroidered cloth and hot coffee. One glance told Celandine that the landlady had carefully placed on it everything that Celandine enjoyed, such as newly baked hot cinnamon buns, and fresh Cornish butter.

Celandine skipped out of bed and, after donning a warm night robe, seated herself at the table by the window.

'Join me, oh do,' she begged, and seeing that she really meant it Mrs Molesworth quickly disappeared back to her kitchen, to reappear moments later with a fresh cup and saucer.

After Celandine, feeling unusually hungry, had eaten several of the cinnamon buns, Mrs Molesworth having made sure that they were lavishly spread with yellow Cornish butter and pale Cornish honey, the two women, already well versed in each other's ways, fell to companionable silence, sipping their coffee and watching the sea, which was, as always, a gloriously enriching sight.

'Mr Montague Robertson is to collect the painting from the framer this afternoon, and tomorrow it will be off to Captain Black's house, I hear?'

Celandine, still thinking over the problem of little Dominique, nodded absently, only turning back to her companion's conversation after a short pause. She hoped that Captain Black would like the painting. Indeed she *prayed* that he would like it, for he had only paid for half of it, and the other half of the commission, although vital to their security, was dependent on his approval.

'Yes, as I understand it, it is off to Captain Black now, and no delay, Mr Montague Robertson said,' Mrs Molesworth reiterated, but this time her eyes left the sea despite the fascination of its intense winter blue and she stared at Celandine in a concentrated manner. 'And now that you have finished the portrait of Captain Black, which Mr Montague Robertson has *signed*' – her voice had become uncharacteristically sarcastic – 'now that you have finished that portrait on behalf of your husband, I wonder would you consider painting my granddaughters and myself, Mrs Montague Robertson? Or are you always to have to do your husband's work for him?'

Celandine stared at Mrs Molesworth, thinking that she had never before realised that she was quite so observant. It was stupid of her, because if she examined the life of a landlady, it was clear that the day-to-day running of a lodging house was not simple. The constant watching that no one slipped out of the back door with any of her silver, or out of the front door without paying their dues. If a landlady was to succeed she had to be among the most observant of people.

'My husband is not interested in painting portraits,' Celandine said finally, careful to keep a defensive note out of her voice. 'It is not that he *cannot* paint portraits, he does not *want* to paint portraits. He wants to paint the working people of Cornwall. He wants to show how they live, the grim details of their lives. He is part of the new movement of realism, the Newbourne school as they are now calling it. It should be very exciting, the new movement, if it succeeds, which I am sure it will, but for the moment there is no public for it, although I am sure there will be quite shortly.'

'No doubt,' Mrs Molesworth agreed. 'No doubt at all, but the truth is that you have to eat. I would say that is the reality of your situation, Mrs Montague Robertson, no doubt at all. Men allus likes to fill their mouths with words, but we women know you can't eat words, nor fill your stomach with 'em. No, food is what does that, and food has to be bought.'

The expression on Mrs Molesworth's face became momentarily grave as she turned back to the view.

'However that mebbe,' she said, once more gazing diplomatically out to sea in order to take the heat off the moment. 'However that mebbe, it may also be that you want to paint the reality out

363

there, Mrs Montague Robertson, and ignore the reality in here.' She patted her stomach in a small significant gesture.

'No, I don't want to paint any other reality than my own, Mrs Molesworth. I just want to paint for my living in the same way that you let your houses and your rooms for yours. My attitude is . . .' Celandine paused, as she also found herself gazing diplomatically out to sea to avoid putting too much emphasis on their conversation. 'My attitude is,' she continued, lowering her voice as if what she was going to say was shocking, which perhaps it was, 'that my art is, or should be, at the *service* of what I am commissioned to paint. Never mind what the subject might be, I will paint it, if commissioned; provided always, of course, that the subject is not distasteful. I want to work and be paid. I want to be a professional painter. But it is much more difficult, Mrs Molesworth, for a woman to be a painter than a man. Men, you see, can spare the time to go to art galleries, and they have control of the purse strings, most especially in England; which means that it is the men who buy the paintings, and the paintings they buy are inevitably by – men. This is why, if we are to be paid, my husband has to sign the portrait. What is more, it seems that with few or no exceptions men do not want a female signature on the bottom of a painting that is about to hang on their wall, whereas a woman does not mind the sex of the painter, only the subject.'

Mrs Molesworth considered this quite complicated thought in silence for a while, turning it over in her mind, waiting in her usual Cornish way before giving her verdict.

'I knows what you mean,' she said, breaking what turned out to be quite a protracted silence. 'I knows indeed what you are on about, for my Albert, when he was alive, he never would give a second look even to a book if it was by a woman. *Women's palaver* is what he called it. I put it down to his being naval. Always at sea with men, he knew no better than to think his sex ran the world, same as what they run ships, poor souls.'

'No, it's not just naval, I'm afraid, Mrs Molesworth.' Celandine smiled. 'It's general. But, see here, I would love to paint you and your grandchildren. How would *you* like to be painted?'

'In my best frock with my cameo brooch,' came the prompt and proud reply.

'And how would you like your grandchildren to be?'

'Seated about my chair, their heads on my knee, like a story book of old. I have a mind to thinking that's allus a nice picture. I saw one like it, many years ago, of a Lady St Probyn, I think it was, a local lady; but she looked graceful, to my mind, very ladylike, very elegant.'

'I know just what you want. And I would love to do it, believe me, Mrs Molesworth.'

Celandine leaned forward impulsively and kissed Mrs Molesworth's soft cheek, for they both knew that, one way or another, the commission was Mrs Molesworth's way of saying that for the next few months Mr and Mrs Sheridan Montague Robertson would be living rent-free.

Alfred took a step back, his handsome face impassive, which meant that, when he did finally utter, what he had to say proved to be all the more shocking to Edith.

'The grey tone does not suit your skin,' he announced, his voice cool, his expression still impassive.

Edith stared at him, about to protest, and then, realising that it would not be the best way to start their sitting, she sighed. It was not the large sigh that Napier would give if she moved so much as a muscle when sitting to him, but it *was* a sigh none the less.

'This was chosen for me by one of the most chic and fashionable establishments in Richmond,' she said, after she had made her point with the little sigh.

'From a painter's point of view, Mrs Todd, I would not care if the grey had been chosen for you by Tintoretto himself, the fact of the matter is that it does nothing for your skin.'

'But there are other colours here too!'

Alfred stared at her, left a pause, and then said, 'May I come up to your dressing room and see what is in your wardrobe?'

The look in his eyes was purposefully compelling, and they both knew exactly why. If Edith said *no* it would mean that she was frightened of what he would say; if she said *yes*, it would mean that inevitably their relationship would change. After all, a man viewing your wardrobe was next to a man choosing your clothes, and once a man chose your clothes it was only a short step to his paying for them, and eventually for – you.

'Why, of course you can come up to my dressing room, Mr Talisman.' Edith smiled. 'Follow me, please do.'

Alfred did indeed follow her, his face still expressionless, until, as they entered the house, Edith paused in the hall and rang the bell for Mrs George. The housekeeper appeared all too promptly, which immediately made Edith wonder if she was always crouching under the stairs listening to the goings-on in the hall.

'Mrs George, Mr Talisman doesn't think that this grey silk dress suits the colour of my skin—'

'Oh, he doesn't, does he?' Mrs George stared at Alfred. She had never liked him, and for some reason she could not name she liked him even less now.

'No, he doesn't. So I wonder if you could be awfully obliging and take him up to my dressing room to show him the contents of my wardrobe, so he can choose the colour he thinks is most fitting.'

'Painters!' Mrs George said under her breath.

Edith pretended not to hear and promptly turned on her heel and returned to the studio, satisfied that she had in some way she could not really explain won the first round. Alfred

Talisman might want to go through her clothes, but he was not going to do so with her as a witness, if she had anything to do with it. If he wanted to take stock of her wardrobe he could do so with Mrs George as a witness. The idea of watching Alfred sighing and shrugging his shoulders in painterly fashion at her poor little outfits was far from enticing.

But she had counted without Alfred, who finally returned twenty minutes later, closely followed by Mrs George carrying a stack of dresses in her arms, and looking like a fury.

'Not the yellow, no. I don't like women in yellow, they make me think of custard—'

'We don't want to know that, thank you,' Mrs George cut in quickly, looking shocked, as if custard was not a ladylike subject, which perhaps it wasn't. 'Just choose a dress, Mr Talisman, and let me go back to my work, would you, please? I have a great deal to do, as you will no doubt appreciate – or perhaps you will not?'

Alfred did not say anything, leaving the housekeeper to wonder, for perhaps the thousandth time, why it was that she had ever had anything to do with painters.

'The trouble with you painter people,' she murmured from under the stack of dresses she was still supporting, 'is that nothing is good enough for you. And, if you ask me, it never will be. Always on about something or other, you painters, but when it gets down to it, what is the result, may I ask?'

'The result is that I have chosen the blue jacket with the white dress. Yes, I have most definitely chosen the blue jacket,' Alfred announced, interrupting the housekeeper, and he stood back, holding up the jacket first to Edith's face, and then to the light. 'The blue is shot through with a little mauve, so that should be most suitable for the subject.'

'As I was saying, the trouble with you painters is that you must have everything perfect, and what is the end result – just a painting that hangs on the wall that most people stand in front of for little more than a few seconds. Just a wall cover finally, that is what a painting is, just a wall cover. Just a bit of paint arranged in a frame, and hanging over another bit of paint on a wall—'

The rest of Mrs George's theory was lost to posterity as Alfred once more piled up the dresses in her sturdy arms, turned her forcefully towards the door, opened it for her, and showed her back out to the courtyard.

'You are quite right, Mrs George, no doubt of it, but happily for us there are people prepared to pay a great deal of money for those bits of framed paint to hang on their walls.'

'Nothing better to do with their money, and no sense to go with it, neither—'

She was still grumbling as she crossed back to the main house. For a second Alfred watched her go, and then he closed the door.

'Mrs George is just like my late mother,' he told Edith. 'My mother was always saying just those things to my father, which is probably why he left her for the South Seas, and never came back. Now. Where are you going to change, Mrs Todd, may I ask?'

Edith was aware that by constantly addressing her as 'Mrs Todd' Alfred was being, in some way that she could not put her finger on, vaguely flirtatious. It was the way he said 'Mrs Todd' as if he did not believe that she was really married to Napier.

'I will change in the room off my husband's studio, thank you, *Mr* Talisman.' She snatched up the blue jacket and white dress, which was actually her own favourite, and passing Alfred, who was already starting to prepare his canvas, she left the room and went next door.

'Come in!'

Napier had probably expected to see Alfred standing in the doorway. Certainly he did not bother to look up but stood wrapped in perfect concentration staring at Becky, who was now wearing the hated Grecian robe and holding the harp that had once been Edith's dreaded prop.

Edith put her finger to her lips and started to tiptoe across the studio, but she need not have bothered, because Becky too was wrapped in concentration, unmoving, her hand, which now looked surprisingly graceful, holding the harp, her eyes gazing straight out at Napier.

Edith changed into the dress, tiptoed back across the studio, then quietly closed the door, and it was only as she settled herself in front of Alfred that she realised that there had been something missing in the scene she had just witnessed in the next-door studio. Napier had not been heard to give one of his great sighs. Not once!

In the time it had taken her to struggle out of the grey costume and into the blue jacket and white dress, he had not made a *single* sound. Edith was sure that if it had been she who had been sitting to him, he would have heaved a sigh that could be heard across at the house. Whereas Becky had stayed still as a statue, looking suddenly and magnificently suited to the wretched Grecian gown, and Edith could almost hear him humming delightedly as if he had at long, long last found his true inspiration.

'Anything the matter, Mrs Todd?' Alfred asked, after a moment, when she walked back into the smaller studio, dressed in his choice of clothes. He was gazing at her with sudden sympathy, looking so guileless, and to such a fetching degree, that Edith found herself thinking that the expression on his face must be precisely the one that the devil would use when at his most Machiavellian.

'Nothing at all, no, Mr Talisman. Why should there be?'

'There should not be. It was just that you looked suddenly unhappy.'

'I am not unhappy; I am just thoughtful. When another woman is sitting to your husband for the same painting for which you have sat, it makes you – thoughtful.'

'Of course. Now if you wouldn't mind my arranging you?' He started to walk towards Edith, innocence personified.

Edith had not planned for this, as why should she? She had not sat to anyone besides Napier before. Now she found that it was one thing for Napier to rearrange her, putting her hand this way or that on the harp, or plucking at a sleeve, but for Alfred Talisman to put his hands on her, doing up a button in the middle of her jacket, a button that she certainly had not realised had somehow loosened itself, smoothing the shoulder lines on the same jacket, tucking a tendril of hair back into place – for Alfred Talisman to do that to her was somehow very different.

Quite against her will she found herself falling into an unexpected trancelike state, as if what was happening to her was not truly happening; as if she was being transported to another world, a world where she was no longer 'Mrs Napier Todd', but just – Edith. And then he started to paint her.

Napier always worked in – indeed demanded – a concentrated silence, but Alfred, she discovered, was quite different. It seemed that, while working at a terrific pace, he loved to talk incessantly, even as, using the new, more modern technique favoured by the Newbourne School, he stabbed at the canvas in front of him, his normal reserve fled.

He also demanded a contribution from his sitter, constantly posing questions to her, and, to Edith's amazement, actually *listening* to the answers. As the days passed he entranced her with his travel stories – he seemed to have spent more time abroad than in England – and his gossip, which seemed to touch on everyone and everything in Europe; and of course, being a painter, he was mildly if engagingly risqué. The most surprising feature of his personality was that, unlike Napier, he was sensitive to how his model was feeling.

'You must want to get down and walk around?'

He held out his hands to her, smiling down at her, and Edith, not wanting to, but wanting very much to, placed her hands in his. As she did so she made the mistake of looking into his eyes, and immediately dropped her own, purposely avoiding the expression in his, not wanting to see what they were saying to her.

'There.' He let go of her hands. 'Why not take a turn or two around the room? And shake your hands about a little, it will help the blood to keep chasing around your frame.'

Edith had grown used to his looking at her as if he knew exactly what she would look like if she was sitting to him stark naked, but once he set her down she walked quickly away from him, putting up what she hoped was a good show of pretending not to see and feel what she knew Alfred was seeing and feeling.

'You won't always be able to run away from me, Mrs Todd, you must know that. I have seen into your soul; more than that, my canvas has become the mirror of it.'

Edith turned. It was true he had seen into her, and she would find it difficult to run away from him. Worse, she now knew that she could not run away from the realisation that Alfred might love her in a way in which, it seemed, Napier was incapable. It seemed he loved her for herself.

Chapter Ten

Mrs Molesworth adjusted the cameo brooch at the neck of her maroon silk gown. She had been a widow for many years now, but still took great comfort from the lock of her husband's hair which nestled inside the brooch. Celandine had left her to choose her own gown, and she had plumped for the maroon silk, which she had read in her favourite periodical was once again a fashionable colour, and one much favoured in Court circles, although not of course with the Queen, who had not been seen out of black since the death of her beloved Albert.

Mrs Molesworth felt she understood and sympathised with the intensity of the Queen's feelings at the loss of her consort, although she herself would not have chosen to stay in perpetual mourning for her own husband, Mr Molesworth, since he had really been too much the black sheep of his otherwise eminent family. He had been a source of some considerable trouble to herself and their son, who happily had not taken after his father, except in his love of the sea, and was now in the Navy sailing the seven seas. His father was now in the churchyard, unable to gamble any more of their precious money away, which meant that Mrs Molesworth could continue to be prosperous and live a life free of fear. So all in all, it could be said that even a much-loved one's demise could bring some benefits.

'Crowd into my skirt,' she instructed her two granddaughters. 'And lean on Grandma the way she told you.'

Her granddaughters did as they were told, with every show of reluctance, because sitting still and cuddling up to Grandma was essentially, as far as they were concerned, not just one punishment, but two.

Celandine, who had no real experience of children, beyond Agnes's two arrogant sons, leaned forward and rearranged the children's dresses while they rested their blonde heads on the maroon silk.

She knew she had to work quickly, because that was the nature of the commission. She also knew that bribing the children was out of the question, for not only was their grandmother present, but any suggestion of plying them with cake would be vetoed if only because of Grandma's best dress.

'I don't like the frocks that my daughter-in-law has insisted on them wearing,' Mrs Molesworth announced, seeming not to care if the children informed their mother of their grandmother's opinion of her taste. 'I would have preferred them both in pink, myself, I would. I allus prefer a girl in pink; you knows where you are with pink.'

'I think you will like the look of the sprigged cotton once I have put it on the canvas,' Celandine told her, determined to be diplomatic.

Once conveyed to canvas, after only a few weeks' labour, the two children came out looking angelic, and finally, it seemed, rather too angelic for Sherry's taste.

'Mmm, dearest, I see your point,' he announced before dinner one night when he was allowed to view Celandine's painting at last. 'But to my mind you have not conveyed their personalities. They look too alike.' He stared at the painting as if he were a dealer. 'In fact, I find that there is rather too much detail in the painting overall. Really far, far too much detail. The toy pony placed to the side of this child's shoe, the doll being held by the other child, and then Mrs Molesworth's lace cap, and her cameo brooch, not to mention the background that you have chosen – it is all much too much detail. Why could you not hang a curtain behind the good lady? A velvet curtain is traditional in portraiture, and the curtain that I used in the Captain Black portrait serves admirably, I think. Much better than all those objects on the chimneypiece. That's her diary, is it? And the cooking utensils, not to mention the cake on the stand on that table to the side of her. It is all too much detail, dearest, really too much detail.'

Celandine breathed in and out very slowly. She knew that Sherry was having a hard time of it trying to sell his paintings, which were too local for London, and too London for the locals, and she also knew that he had been painting in difficult conditions, having chosen to go to the harbour rather than stay in his studio on the coldest day of the winter, but even so she felt that she would have appreciated it if he had kept his opinions to himself.

'To begin at the beginning, which is always a good place to start,' she said, after taking a sip of wine to steady her emotions, 'the children look alike, Sherry dearest, because they are in real life actually twins. There is no curtain as a backdrop, as in *your* portrait of Captain Black, because Mrs Molesworth wanted me to paint in the details of her everyday life, the household effects to which she has to pay such attention. The diary where she notes down the people who are coming to stay, the cake—'

'You should never pay attention to sitters' whims, dearest, really you shouldn't. Mark my words, if you do, believe me you will be there all day, really you will. They always want flattery and their demands can be truly astounding. No, you must never pay attention to the sitter. Paint the truth of what you see, not what they want.'

'But you paid attention to Captain Black. You made sure that I put in the blessed skull and crossbones and the admiral's hat, and brought out the gold on his epaulettes, even though he was only the captain of a trading vessel!'

Celandine could hear Mrs Molesworth calling them to dinner, so she turned away and went to the door, still carrying her glass of wine, rather than take the argument any further.

'That was only your first attempt, dearest. I judged it better to leave you to your own devices, but if you are to make portraiture your chosen path—'

They were going down to dinner, so Celandine fell silent rather than protest that she would never, ever have chosen portraiture as her artistic path, but that she *did* choose it, *had* chosen it, because she did not want either Sherry or herself to starve.

Nor did she say how much she longed to paint what she wanted, to express her own artistic vision, because she knew, for the present anyway, that there was not even a remote possibility of its happening.

The Japanese style of painting which had so impressed her when she was in Paris, the art of Degas and many others that she longed not to imitate but to become *part of*, had once been her vision of the future, but no longer. For the moment she must be practical. Portraiture was the boat she was frantically rowing to keep Sherry and herself afloat; her own painting was the far horizon, a beautiful dream that she might, one day, realise.

Edith could not prevent herself from looking forward to sitting to Alfred every morning with all the happy enthusiasm that she had never felt when she was sitting to Napier. Alfred did not seem to look on her as an *object*. He looked on her as a woman to be painted as she was; as herself. And what was more, unlike Napier, Alfred not only allowed her to see the painting as it progressed, he positively encouraged her to do so.

It was always a most satisfying moment at the end of the day. The moment when they stood together to look at the painting.

'So. How do you like what I think of you, Mrs Todd? Do you think I have read your character correctly, or do you think I have merely painted just another woman?'

He had never asked that question before. He had only ever asked the kinds of questions that were, perhaps, uppermost in his mind in the early stages. Questions such as 'Do you think there is too much mauve in the jacket?' or 'Do you think the Titian in your hair is coming out as it should?'

Edith glanced up at him, and then at the painting again, before answering.

'I like it very much, but – it is very strange, when I look at it,' she said. 'Most strange.'

'And what is *most strange*, Mrs Todd?'

He still seemed to love to use formality to discomfit her, while always employing the slightly raised eyebrow to underline the fact that he was not laughing *at* her, but with her.

'I see it is me, but I also see that you have made me look very innocent.'

'You are the most innocent person I know. You certainly should be.'

He did not add that he *knew* she was innocent, because he had overheard the conversation between Napier and her on the night of the party.

'I am not innocent, Mr Talisman,' Edith retorted, laughing. 'No young girl brought up in an inn can be totally innocent, I do assure you.'

'You are as innocent as the day is long, and I must tell you that I like your innocence more for the fact that you are so convinced that you are nothing of the kind. Now, back to work, Mrs Todd.'

He put his hands around her tiny waist and lifted her as effortlessly as a father lifting a child on to the chair, automatically rearranging her skirt as he did so.

'Ah, you ladies, you must all thank heaven for the health bustle,' he remarked lightly. 'The dear little health bustle, snapping back and forth into place, an invention too long in arriving, and what a relief it must be to you all, relieving you as it does of the heat of the dreadful old horsehair.'

Edith was becoming so used to Alfred's easy attitudes since sitting to him that she hardly registered the fact that he had such intimate knowledge of female underclothing. His love for women, and his appreciation of their clothing, not to mention their attributes, was so much part of his character that she now accepted that he knew all about such intimate matters as health bustles, not to mention the relieving effect they had on the female body after the over-use of the old-fashioned kind.

'Snip snap,' he murmured, as he now always did when he finished adjusting her clothing to his satisfaction.

Edith stared up at him, feeling happily dreamy, knowing that the hours ahead would be all too entrancingly restful.

'You have a very bad effect on me,' she murmured, as she repositioned her arm how she knew he liked it.

'Why is that, Mrs Todd?'

'I think,' Edith announced, after a small pause, 'I think it is because you are such easy company.'

She did not need to add that Napier did not have the easy bohemian manner that Alfred possessed. Napier did not, at least when Edith sat to him, seem to appreciate a woman's need to be treated as a person.

Nor, in the way that seemed to come so naturally to Alfred, did Napier appreciate the need to understand that women were not put on this earth to represent some high-flown ideal of womanhood, but longed, as did men, to be allowed to be able to be themselves, neither all male, nor all female, but *human*; not to be for ever straining towards some sort of extreme virtuous

382

state that would turn them into either saints or goddesses, far beyond the reach of men.

'Are you not used to easy company, Mrs Todd?'

Edith reflected on this. 'Sadly, it seems to me now that a husband can never be as easy with his wife as another man can be,' she finally announced.

'And a wife?'

'Wives are different. Since you are still a bachelor you might not have noticed that wives are not expected to have opinions, only duties.'

'You make marriage sound as grey as the dress in which I refused to paint you, Mrs Todd.'

'Oh no, not grey exactly. But I do think that marriage is a state in which everyone seems to be in just that – a state. Most of all those outside it!' she added, staring straight at him.

Alfred jabbed at the painting in front of him. 'Oh me, oh my.' He shook his head before turning round and staring at Edith in some admiration. 'It is truly said that it is always the innocent of heart who say the most wounding things.'

Edith stared straight ahead, unmoving as she had to be, but unable to stop herself thinking of the impossibilities of relationships. Now that Napier was once more caught up in his painting he seemed to be considerably less than passionate. He was kind and thoughtful at meals, to be sure, but so tired at night that he could hardly keep his eyes open to climb the stairs to bed, which was, to say the least, disappointing.

Perhaps taking account of her continued silence, Alfred decided to move their conversation to a different subject.

'Your husband seems to be roaring ahead with this most difficult of his paintings, doesn't he?'

Alfred managed to sound both innocent and artless at the same time while continuing to attack his canvas, but for once Edith pretended not to hear him and continued to stare ahead.

It seemed somehow so different when someone was painting a portrait of you, rather than for ever seeking to be *inspired*. She had failed, dismally, to inspire Napier, and it was not something that either of them could perhaps forget, for not only had she failed, but so had he, which meant that every time he looked at her he surely saw only – failure.

'I myself have to go away for a few days,' Alfred went on, pausing to stand back and view his work. 'I am trusting that you will miss me most dreadfully. But more than that, as you must know, I am going away in the express hope that you *will* miss me.'

Edith laughed. 'You are incorrigible, Mr Talisman. Quite incorrigible.'

'You may see the painting now that you are not sitting for it, dearest, if you wish?' Napier announced to Edith a few days later.

But Edith, because she was not sitting for the painting, and because she *had* sat for it, and disliked doing so, looked puzzled by the idea.

384

'I would really rather not see it, Napier, because I don't want to put you off. After all, the slightest word can put a painter off his stroke. Alfred told me only the other morning that a friend of his remarked that the lady's hat reminded him of a saucepan, and he was not able to finish the painting. He slashed the canvas, and could not work for weeks.'

'Ah yes, the little matter of the saucepan hat. I remember that. It was when Alfred was having one of his many affairs with a famous Parisian cocotte – she of the hat. Yes, I do remember.'

'What *is* a cocotte, Napier?'

'Something we would not wish you to become. Now you will please come and view,' Napier told her, so abruptly that Edith was forced to follow him into the studio and stand in front of his easel.

She stared at the painting. She did not like it at all. In fact, try as she might, she hated it straight away; happily Napier was staring at it with such ferocious attention that she had plenty of time to hide her feelings.

'It is beautiful, Napier. Truly beautiful. Really it is,' she said.

It was true. It was beautiful, but that did not stop Edith from hating it. She hated it as much as she adored Alfred's painting of her.

'It is much better, wouldn't you say? I truly hope that I have found the kernel of it. "Temptation" has to be cold on the outside, but here, up here, with the depiction of the same face, done several times, the coldness ends, don't you see?

There is a change of emphasis. I think I am starting to get to the heart of it. Indeed, I hope so, for I am sure that old Hollingsworth is about to hang up his boots on the whole subject.'

'You must be pleased. You should be pleased.'

Edith turned away, struggling with her feelings. Napier had found it so difficult to paint her, and yet now it seemed he had no difficulty painting *Becky* of all people. He had been spending his days painting Becky Snape's face over that of Edith. Becky who had undoubtedly become one of the people about whom he would privately use that word – what was it? Ah yes, cocotte! Becky was undoubtedly a cocotte. Edith knew that, if only from the way that all the men around the place looked at Becky, as if they knew about women like her; but most of all from the way that Mrs George, in the nicest possible way of course, set her face against her presence in the house. No matter what the weather, or how late her carriage, Mrs George always made it quite clear that she could not wait for Becky Snape to be on her way.

'I hope Miss Snape is progressing with her riding lessons. Ladies of her kind do need to ride well, especially in the hunting field,' she had murmured the previous afternoon, after seeing Becky into her carriage.

'I hope so too,' Edith had agreed, watching the smart conveyance drive away. 'I must say Becky Snape has come a long way from the Stag and Crown, Mrs George.'

'That at least is obvious,' Mrs George had agreed, and she smoothed down her starched white apron, inspecting it as she did so, as if she suspected that Becky might have made a mark on its pristine surface.

'And so have I,' Edith had added, not wishing to divorce herself from her own background.

But Mrs George had walked off, making a light 'puh' sound. 'You, Mrs Todd, are a different *type*,' was her parting comment.

Edith, while not wanting to agree with the housekeeper, nevertheless knew what she meant. She had indeed always been a different sort of person from poor little Becky. Becky had been thrown into work at a too young age by necessity, and by the fact that her stepfather worked at the Stag and Crown and resented having to feed her. But now, by what means Edith did not like to think, Becky was in their neighbourhood complete with fashionable clothes and a smart carriage, and taking riding lessons, at whose expense Edith also did not like to think; and what time Becky was not bent on improving her seat in the side saddle was now spent posing for Edith's husband, something which Edith felt was somehow very wrong, although as usual she could not have said why.

Then the reason came to her. Becky Snape should not be sitting for 'Temptation' for the simple reason that, it was now obvious to Edith, Becky Snape might *be* temptation. How could she be anything else given that she had obviously become a cocotte?

Napier was quite open about the fact that he adored her form, that she was now his inspiration, in the same way that Edith had once seemed to be the same. All in all it seemed that by some strange twist of fate Becky Snape was now in Edith's place, a place where Edith had not wished to be, but now wondered if she should have stayed.

Edith snatched up her coat and hat and her fashionable fur muff and walked off to the garden. She would have to get good and cold to stop herself from thinking too much about her situation.

'Never tell a man too much, Edith, not ever. And never let him know what you really think. A man likes to feel he is free to do exactly as he wishes. If he feels you're putting a fence round him he will only want to jump it. It's in the male nature.'

Edith stared at the snow that was beginning to fall, remembering Celandine's words in the summer. She had not put a fence round Napier, who would never have countenanced such a thing anyway, with the result that he had felt quite free to put Becky in Edith's place, a fact about which Edith was becoming increasingly unhappy.

She looked up at the sky. It was as dark as her thoughts, and the snow was now coming down fast. Inside the studio, Becky Snape was once more posing for Napier, surrendering herself to Napier's inspiration. It made Edith feel wretched, and for once she knew just why it made her feel so. It was because she herself was now caught up in Alfred's painting. She had moved from failing as Napier's inspiration to succeeding as Alfred Talisman's, and neither role was comforting to her.

'I am really rather afraid that Miss Snape's carriage will not be able to get back to Stowe,' Napier announced loudly, emerging momentarily into the garden, his blond hair awry, his artist's smock covered in oil paint. 'The snow has come too quickly. She will have to stay the night. Will you go and tell Mrs George to arrange to have a bed made up and a fire lit in one of the spare rooms, Edith?'

The snow was piling up on Edith's hat as she stared at her husband's departing figure.

'Mrs George will not like that,' she muttered, but she returned to the house and confronted the housekeeper.

'I don't usually countenance the likes of her staying *here*, Mrs Todd, really I don't. I don't like it at all. I will make up the bedroom above the studios. I'm not having the likes of her in the house. We have the likes of her in the house no one decent will call on you again, that I can tell you. And if you think they will, you are wrong, for if *I* didn't tell no one one of the maids *would*, that is certain, and you will not get no callers, and Mr Todd no commissions. Having the likes of her staying the night in the house, I ask you!'

Much as Edith had, at least at the start, felt a certain loyalty to Becky, a loyalty based on their shared experiences at the Stag, she could not help seeing the housekeeper's point of view. There was something vaguely threatening in Becky's new manner, as if with every pace she took she was challenging Society to stop her having what she now considered to be her due.

'There is nothing else we can do, I'm afraid, Mrs George. We must offer her a bed for the night. We cannot turn her out in the snow.'

Mrs George sighed. 'Well, let's hope the blessed Lord sends a thaw as soon as maybe,' she murmured piously, looking up to heaven as she turned on her heel. 'But in the studio she goes, make no mistake; not in the house.'

As it turned out the blessed Lord did not send a thaw and Napier, eager to get on with his painting, found the fact that Becky could pose for him indefinitely most convenient for his needs, if not for his wife's peace of mind.

The thaw finally came after a week's long interment, during which, in the absence of Alfred Talisman and her own consequent inertia, Edith became increasingly unable to keep her mind off her husband's seeming obsession with Becky. She felt herself burning up with jealousy, an emotion that up until then had been quite alien to her. She was sure that she could smell Becky's scent on his clothes, convinced that when he slept he dreamed only of her. Why wouldn't he, after all? Why wouldn't he, when he was so obsessed with painting her?

Celandine, on the other hand, by rising early and going to bed late, found that she had completed Mrs Molesworth's portrait in a matter of a very few weeks.

'You work hard, Mrs Montague Robertson, and that is the truth,' her landlady told her in admiring tones. 'I like a hard worker. I have always worked hard myself, and that is what keeps the good ship afloat, I always tell my son – not that he needs to be told, being that he takes after me rather than his father, thank the good Lord – I always tells him that hard work never killed anyone, but boredom did.'

'I thought it as well to paint quickly, Mrs Molesworth, seeing that your granddaughters might tire of coming here and having to sit still. Besides being tedious for you.'

'Not tedious at all.' Mrs Molesworth raised her head, her nostrils flaring slightly. 'It's a privilege to be with you, Mrs Montague Robertson. You allus treat everyone the same, and I like that. You don't talk down to a person the way my husband used to talk down to me, like as if I had been born with half a brain, just because I wasn't a Molesworth. A grand Cornish family, the Molesworths, though my husband only came from them right far back. But it stays, you know, that manner of being, it stays. It's in the blood, and no more to be said. Now that you are finished, I dare say you would like another commission, wouldn't you?'

Celandine blushed. It was difficult not to feel that she had somehow become a charity case, someone to be pitied, at any rate in Mrs Molesworth's eyes.

'My dear friend Mrs Dunstan, she's not from round these parts, but she is a widow, as I am, and I know she would like a portrait of herself and her dog Cimmy to hang above her chimney-piece. That would make her so happy.' She leaned forward conspiratorially. 'She's lonely is Mrs Dunstan, lonely and rich, and it would help pass the time for her, I know that.'

It somehow seemed too hard-hearted to turn away a commission from a lonely widow. Moreover, Celandine knew, as Mrs Molesworth must know, that she simply could not afford to refuse it.

'I should love to meet Mrs Dunstan,' she admitted. 'It is most kind of you to recommend me, as I am sure you did.'

'No, Mrs Montague Robertson, I did nothing of the sort. She saw the portrait for herself.'

Celandine looked surprised.

'Why, did you not know, Mrs Montague Robertson?' Mrs Molesworth smiled. 'You are very talented.' She paused. 'Yes. You are a very, very talented woman.'

'Yes, but a *woman*. Artistically speaking that is to be born a cripple, as I have found out to my cost, Mrs Molesworth.'

Mrs Molesworth breathed in and out, reminding Celandine oddly of one of the carter's ponies that brought the firewood and the coal to the house, trotting through the narrow streets with blinkered faces and docked tails.

'Well, I know enough about the plight of women to fill a book, so I do, Mrs Montague Robertson, and I allus say to anyone who will listen that as if it's not enough to be a woman, with all that that entails, the Bible has to blame us for all the evils of the world too. It had to be a woman who made up to the snake and ate the apple first, didn't it, not a man, if you please, but a woman! No wonder we're allowed less rights than a common criminal. I ask you.'

Celandine burst into laughter. 'I see I am not the only supporter of the suffragist movement in Cornwall.'

'That's as maybe, Mrs Montague Robertson, but nevertheless it's allus best to keep your opinions under your hat with your brains, if you know what's good for you, really it is. But to get back to this other matter, women like Mrs Dunstan, they like paintings of themselves as much as the likes of Captain Black. Yes. When we have the money, Mrs Montague Robertson, we women can spend it quite as well as the men, I allus say that too!'

They both laughed.

'When would Mrs Dunstan like me to meet her?'

'As soon as maybe. If the winter weather

continues this bright you will still have plenty of daylight, I should have thought.'

'Yes, but as you know, my letter from France this morning means that I must go back again within a few weeks. The portrait might be interrupted.'

Mrs Molesworth looked serious, and was silent for a while.

'Family matters can be like a stone in your shoe, I allus think. You keep stopping to take it out, and then a few minutes later another jumps into its place.'

'My mother died leaving a rather complicated matter.'

'And you have Mrs Todd coming to stay first, I know that, poor creature, allus looks as though a breath will take her away. I told Mrs Dunstan that, though, told her you will have a visitor to look after afore you can set her on to a painting.'

Celandine watched the tall, big-boned and pleasantly rounded figure of Mrs Molesworth leaving the room. She knew that Mrs Molesworth could have no idea of her problems, but she also realised that the good woman must have guessed that whatever took Celandine to France so frequently was not an easy matter. What neither of them knew, however, was why Edith had suddenly written to ask herself to stay.

Celandine waited on the platform of the winter-bright station, longing to see Edith, but at the same time unable to suppress her feelings of anxiety about the situation in France. To say it haunted her day and night was to say the least. She had written to assure Marie that she would be back in Paris as soon as her current commission allowed, but she also knew, only too well, that if she was to keep the commissions coming, she would have to at least start Mrs Dunstan's portrait. It was Marie's last letter to her, written in an urgent hand, that had given her real cause for concern.

Madame, I have to tell you the situation here is becoming grave. You must, madame, make up your mind about the matter which must concern us both, before it is too late. Madame Montellier and myself are unable to continue as we are, but please believe me, madame, your most loyal and humble servant, Marie Depardieu.

Celandine believed the urgent tone in the letter. In fact she believed everything in the letter, aside from the fact that Marie could never, would never, be humble. Part of Marie's undoubted fascination was that she was neither humble, nor really a servant. She was, and always had been, *Marie*. Celandine was well aware that her mother had loved her, that they must have shared many secrets as mistress and maid, that they had in some way been a partnership, with Celandine, when they were out of sorts, going between them, an uneasy messenger. She herself had never really been part of the serious business of

395

running the house, never known quite what they both thought of her as she induced them to move from America to Holland, and from Holland to Munich, and from Munich to Paris, in search of sympathetic tuition. All Celandine knew was that she had disgraced herself by falling in love; most of all, perhaps, because she had fallen in love too soon for their own plans.

'Edith . . .'

'Celandine!'

The two young women kissed, holding each other carefully because of their hats.

'You have no snow?'

'No snow, only bright, cold sunshine. It is so beautiful here, even in the winter.'

'And daffodils out already in the hedgerows. And flowers in the fields, and look! I am sure I can see blossom on the trees.'

'No, no blossom.' Celandine laughed and helped Edith up into the trap.

Edith's foot slipped for a second and she paled, looking round at Celandine. 'Oh, dear. I'm always doing that. I am so clumsy,' she murmured.

'You are far from clumsy,' Celandine reassured her, staring up into the lovely face and momentarily taken back by the fear in the strangely coloured eyes.

'Oh, I am, I am. I seem always to be slipping when I shouldn't.'

'You run and skip everywhere, you know you do,' Celandine teased her, settling herself down beside her, as the driver touched the pony with his whip and the animal seemed to jump forward from standing still into an instant trot. Edith looked paler than ever. 'Are you all right?'

'Yes, perfectly,' Edith murmured, but since she gave a little cough, and remained pale, Celandine, although she looked away, nevertheless immediately started to feel concerned. She knew from Napier that, before coming to stay in Cornwall, Edith had been very ill, and that she still had an intermittent cough, although Napier had reassured her that the cough was only a result of the fever, and not serious or contagious in any way.

Once out of the vehicle and installed in Mrs Molesworth's front parlour, Edith seemed to recover herself. She sipped her tea and made Celandine and Mrs Molesworth laugh about all the revolutions that had been going on at Helmscote.

'I knew that you would soon turn everything on its head once you found your feet there,' Celandine assured her finally.

Edith was silent for a second, staring into the fire. Now that Mrs Molesworth had left them she felt able to be truthful with Celandine.

'I have not altogether found my feet, as you put it, Celandine,' she admitted in a rush. 'There are some new developments at Helmscote about which I really couldn't tell anyone but you.'

Celandine suddenly felt she had enough troubles of her own without having to listen to poor Edith's, but she couldn't say so. As soon as she was in Edith's company she found herself feeling protective towards her. The truth was that Edith, because she always put on such a brave and independent air, virtually imploring the world not to feel sorry for her, always succeeded in achieving quite the opposite.

'You lost your mother so young,' Celandine murmured. 'Having just lost my own I know how you must have been feeling all this time. Even at my age one misses one's mother.'

'And now *I* am to be a mother,' Edith murmured quietly, more to the fire than to Celandine.

'I beg your pardon? Did you say you are expecting *quelque chose*, Edith? But that is such lovely news.'

Edith nodded, still staring into the fire. 'It is lovely news,' she agreed. 'And I should be so happy, but the truth of the matter is that I am so muddled I hardly know which way to turn.' She looked round at Celandine. 'You see, Napier does not know. In fact, he will not even speak to me at the moment. He will have nothing to do with me. Nothing at all. Our marriage is at yet another standstill, but this time I think it is all my fault.'

Celandine stared at her. It did not seem possible, after all their previous troubles, that Edith and Napier should be yet again at odds with each other.

'Tell me,' she said simply, thinking that whatever her own troubles – their lack of any steady income, her continuing worry over whether to adopt her mother's baby, Sherry's seeming determination not to take on any commissioned work, but to go his own sweet way – judging from Edith's expression they were as nothing compared to hers.

Edith found it hard to explain herself, as is normal when a person has to explain the unexplainable. The fact that she had become seized with jealousy over Napier's painting out her own face and replacing it with that of Becky Snape; that he seemed to have no trouble using Becky as his inspiration, whereas he had always seemed so irritated by his wife.

'But, dearest, you know we talked about that. His difficulties were because he *desired* you. Seeing that he was holding back from you all the livelong day and night, it was only normal that he should be in a permanent state of irritation!'

'I know that now, but when I found the footprints in the snow – I don't know why, but I became convinced that they were Napier's footprints, and I faced him with it. I am afraid I did. I faced him with it.'

There was a long and dreadful pause.

'Edith.' Celandine looked stern. 'How many times have we discussed the fact that no woman should ever attempt to face a man with his sins, or her suspicions? You may act upon your suspicions, you may subtly try to find out more, even with stealth, perhaps, but you never ever *face* him with them. If you do that he will immediately say that you are suffering from delusions, that you are mentally disturbed, that you are not the person he thought you were.'

Edith nodded sadly. 'That is exactly what did happen. Worse than that, I made a scene, and you know Napier is not the kind of person who relishes any kind of scene. But at least I had Alfred to turn to.'

'You had – *Alfred*? Alfred Talisman? *Our* Alfred?'

'Yes, your Alfred – Napier's Alfred.'

'I despair of you, Edith,' Celandine stated, but her tone was light, and she stood up to pour them both some tea. 'Really, after all our talks when you were here, you go and ignore all my good-hearted advice and face your husband with your suspicions. Really, it is too bad.'

'Perhaps . . . perhaps it happened because I am in an interesting condition, wouldn't you say?'

'Very likely, dearest.' Celandine handed her a fresh cup of tea, not believing a word. 'I do believe – that is, my mother told me—' She stopped speaking momentarily, remembering her mother's own condition, and the ensuing result. 'I do believe that being in a state of interest can make one lose—' She was about to say 'common sense', but she stopped and started yet again. 'I do believe it is most *affecting*. The only thing *I* am producing at the moment is a portrait of Mrs Molesworth's good friend Mrs Dunstan.'

They both laughed.

'I did not know that you had started to paint

400

portraits. I thought you always wanted to remain a free spirit?'

'So I did, and so I will once again I dare say, but for the moment, my dear Edith, necessity just has to be the mother of invention. Poor darling Sherry's annual income, his precious annuity, has been cut off for ever, and we must find ways of keeping the poorhouse at bay.' She shuddered, momentarily distracted. 'Poverty is a terrible thing, dearest. I have seen too much of it in Europe ever to be fooled into thinking you can be truly poor and happy.'

'I know exactly what you mean. When I was in London I walked past the poorhouse in Putney many times, and the faces of the women were terrible, all of them just sitting in rows, waiting, looking out to where the food might be coming. It was a terrible sight. No, you never want to be truly poor, Celandine.' She stopped, realising just how brave Celandine had been, and how hard she was trying to make light of her situation. 'Oh, but there, I have been running on when I should have been listening to your troubles, not making you listen to mine.'

'I am solving my troubles, I promise you. Besides, I am happy. Sherry and I have come to an understanding. He is pursuing his ideals, and I am dedicated to trying to keep the wolf from our particular door.'

To hear Celandine stating that she was happy made Edith feel even more miserable, because it put her own state into stark contrast.

401

'At any rate, why do you not continue with your story? You confided in Alfred, you were saying?' Celandine widened her eyes, intent on putting on a good listening face, while at the same time she tried to push away her own memories of Alfred taking her on long walks in Brittany; tried to forget how sympathetic and interesting he could be, and how dreadfully engaging.

'Yes, I did confide in Alfred, I admit, Celandine. It was all too easy, after all. I was sitting to him.'

Now Celandine's eyes widened of their own accord.

'You were sitting to Alfred Talisman at the same time that this Miss Snape was sitting to Napier? No wonder there has been trouble brewing at Helmscote. What a pretty kettle of fish! Could you not see that this would all become – that it would be, undoubtedly, a recipe for some kind of disaster?'

'No. You see, I was so grateful finally *not* to have to sit to Napier, what with his sighing and finding everything so difficult, that I quite happily said I would sit to Alfred, who had come to stay. And it was only later, when I realised that Napier had somehow just slipped in that Becky Snape was going to sit to *him*, that I started to find the situation increasingly intolerable. I am so stupid. I should have put up with Napier, except he could not put up with *me*. I think he knew how much I hated that silly gown and holding the harp. People do feel things, don't they, without one's having to say anything?'

Celandine nodded slowly in agreement, but she could not help remembering that Napier had said, more than once, although only jokingly, that Edith was stupid, while she herself had defended Edith as being innocent rather than stupid. Now it seemed she might be both.

'How did this all end in a visit to Cornwall?' she asked, determined on finding some solution to the whole muddle, while Edith fell silent, hesitating to go on.

'Because after I had confronted Napier and he had thrown me aside, saying that I was mad, and that he could not care less what my suspicions might be, because he only cared about finishing the painting, Mrs George, suspecting my condition I think, and not wanting me to be further upset I believe, packed up my suitcases and sent me down here. She does not like having Becky Snape in the house. She is not the type that we should have to stay, she says. But she likes it even less that she is sitting to Napier, as you can imagine.'

Celandine leaned forward to put another log on the fire. It was probably only a small matter, a slight ripple rather than a storm at sea, but a bit of a stiff breeze none the less. It was only when she turned round and saw Edith's face that she realised that there was more to come, that she had not yet been told the whole story.

'There's something else?'

'Yes—'

'I don't think I want to hear any more,' Celandine told her, with sudden firmness. 'I think this is all a terrible misunderstanding and that you must go home as soon as you are well enough, go home and tell Napier that you are sorry.'

Edith looked astounded. 'But I have done nothing wrong except to confess that I was jealous.'

'No, of course you haven't done anything wrong, Edith. You must understand, however, that men can only ever *accept* apologies. Do not ever expect them to *make* them, will you?'

'Is that true?'

'Why else do you think they used to constantly fight duels? Why do stags clash their antlers? Why do – well, never mind. The male of the species would rather die than admit he is at fault. Once you have accepted this, you will live happily ever after, see if you don't.'

Edith sighed sadly as she realised that her journey to Cornwall had really been for nothing. She had to face the fact that in her heart of hearts she had hoped that Napier would follow her, full of understanding. But, if Celandine was right, and she had no reason to doubt her, then the only thing she could now do was return to Helmscote. It was a bleak prospect.

'I suppose I had better get straight back on another train?'

Celandine shook her head. 'You will do no such thing. No, you will stay and get some ozone into those poor old lungs of yours. Another journey so soon would be bad for you. So tiring. No, you must stay on, for as long as you like.'

Celandine had actually meant to set off for France a few days after Edith's arrival, but since it was obvious that to do so would seem more than heartless, she decided to go later than she would have wished.

The truth was that Celandine felt torn between wanting to shake Edith for being so stupid as to show her feelings to Napier, and wanting to mop up the tears she had overheard her shedding in the middle of the night. Whatever her own emotions, she could not leave straight away.

As usual the solution to Celandine's problems seemed to be ready and waiting, thanks to Mrs Molesworth and her observant eyes.

'You can leave Mrs Todd in my safe-keeping, believe me, Mrs Montague Robertson.'

Mrs Molesworth was looking all too four-square. Indeed she was looking so reliable, so trustworthy, that Celandine had the feeling that what her landlady was really telling her was that Edith would be *better* left in Mrs Molesworth's care, better kept away from Celandine for a short while, because it might be that Celandine was actually too sympathetic, and too much sympathy can be weakening.

'I will feed her up, and we will go for nice short walks along the beach. You will be surprised when I tell you just what a difference the company of someone quite other will make to a young woman like Mrs Todd. I will have Mrs Harvey over to tea. That allus does a body good, to have another person over. And perhaps I will teach her to make a few baby garments, because it's never too late to learn, is it, Mrs Montague Robertson?'

Celandine thought the idea of learning to sew baby garments might be a little too lowering for Edith in her present emotional condition, but seeing that the expression on Mrs Molesworth's face was as firm as her corseted body, she thanked her from the bottom of her heart and went straight away to pack.

'I hope that this visit to France will really be the last, dearest, won't it?'

Celandine stared up at Sherry for a short moment. She had tried hard to bring herself to tell him exactly what had happened in Paris, but had finally failed. Perhaps it was Edith's visit, illustrating as it did the dreadful repercussions that could come about when you faced a man with the truth, or perhaps it was the news that Edith was in the very state that Celandine herself so longed for. Whatever it was, she had found it impossible to tell Sherry that she had quite made up her mind to adopt her half-brother.

'I will be as short a time as possible, dearest, really I will. I am not going to be away from you longer than is perfectly necessary.'

Sherry looked momentarily reassured by this, before turning back to his painting of the old fisherman. The hat was giving him a great deal of trouble and he did not want the paint to dry.

The journey to France did not pass uneventfully as Celandine was extremely unwell, with the result that she arrived in Paris, at the old apartment whose lease she knew was just about to expire, feeling like a piece of chewed string.

Marie was waiting for her, and as always had cooked her a magnificent dinner, but it was a dinner that Celandine could not face, try as she might. This did not find favour with Marie.

'I am sorry, Marie. I was so ill on the boat – unlike last time the sea so terribly rough – I am afraid to eat at this moment.'

'Very well, madame.'

Marie was tight-lipped. She picked up the beetroot soup and marched it straight back down to the kitchen as a teacher might frogmarch a naughty pupil out of the classroom. Celandine sighed, and, picking up her glass of water, she sipped at it, hoping for the queasiness to pass.

Marie returned from the kitchen, and sat down opposite Celandine. 'You have received my letter, no?'

Celandine nodded, thankfully feeling the colour gradually returning to her cheeks. 'Yes, I did, thank you. I am sorry I could not come straight away, but a friend arrived who was not at all well, at least not at all happy, and I could not leave her until yesterday.'

'A pity.' Marie looked haughty and at the same time sad, which was something at which she had always been a bit of a past mistress. 'Yes, a great pity. Had you come earlier you might have been able to take Dominique.' She shrugged her shoulders. 'As it is, he has gone.'

Celandine stared at her. 'He has gone? What do you mean, he has gone? You mean he has gone from here, from Madame Montellier?'

'Ah yes, he has gone from Madame Montellier, yes. But he has also gone to 'is new 'ome. A very good 'ome. He has been adopted by a beautiful couple, and he has gone.'

She looked momentarily tragic. Celandine could have reached across the table and slapped her, but instead she wiped her lips on her napkin.

'Could you not have waited, Marie?' she asked, feeling both relieved that she no longer had the burdensome responsibility of the baby, and disappointed that she no longer had the pleasure of him either.

'No, I could not wait any longer. Madame Montellier has a new *bébé* come in – a girl.' She could not keep the contempt out of her voice. 'So she must give Dominique to a new family, but it is a very splendid family. They have a château and many servants. They are an old family. He will be their son. They have taken him and made him their son.'

'I must know where he has gone!'

'No, madame. He is not your *bébé*, and you will never know where he has gone.' Marie rose to her feet with great dignity and taking off her apron she flung it aside. 'You will never know where he is. It is a secret.'

'But I must know! Marie.' Celandine tried to calm herself. 'Marie. Tell me at least a little more.'

But Marie was walking away from her, down the corridor to the kitchen, where the remains of Celandine's supper was still waiting to be brought through, but Marie went straight past it, on to her own room at the back.

'Good night, madame. We will say our *adieux* in the morning.'

She shut her door, and turned the key in the lock as if to emphasise her refusal to discuss the matter of Mrs Benyon's unwanted baby any further.

The following morning, Celandine having slept not at all, the maid once again presented herself in the salon where Celandine was attempting to drink a cup of coffee. She eyed the maid's smart travelling clothes.

'Marie, you are leaving?'

'Yes, madame. I am going back to Burgundy, where I come from, and where I have a fiancé with a farm. We will be married in time, when the summer comes and the vines have ripened. He will not know of you, and I will not know of you again. It will be as if we have never been here in Paris, which is perhaps the will of God.'

Marie walked ahead of Celandine, and as if they had changed roles Celandine found herself opening the front door for the ex-maid. As she passed through it Celandine felt herself filled with an awful panic. It was all her fault. If she had come to Paris earlier, if Edith had not delayed her, everything would be so different. She closed the door and went back to the salon, which had once been so cheerful, hung with paintings and filled with pretty furniture. It seemed that Agnes must have come back for that too, because the room was now emptier than ever. Not that Celandine cared, really. The fate of the baby seemed more important, even though it was not her baby, nor even a baby that she could be sure that Sherry would welcome. To announce to your husband that you wished to adopt his mother-in-law's baby seemed somehow to be asking of him something that he should not have to do.

She sat down miserably on a small side chair. The kind of chair that used to be drawn up for evenings at home, when on first arriving in Paris they would sit round the table, her mother sewing, and Celandine reading to her from one of her favourite books.

Celandine did not know why, but perhaps because the room was so terribly empty she found herself once more filled with guilt. The truth was that she could see now that had she not fallen in love with Sherry, everything would have been so different. She could have *waited* to fall in love with him, couldn't she?

She sighed, thinking back to the heady, forbidden days of love in Brittany, and the way they still were so passionate about each other, and

410

remembering how she had felt she realised that she could never have waited. Love, when all was said and done, was, after all, irresistible. It was the greatest force in the world, and for good reason. And yet how does true love differ from attraction, from what she had, however fleetingly, felt for Alfred Talisman on their walks, or from what, to her dismay, she could see that Edith too felt for him? She could hardly say. She only knew that love was as different from attraction as the ocean from a shallow puddle, and she hoped that it was truly able to look on storms and never be shaken, because if it were not then she would have made a great many people unhappy for no good reason.

She stood up quickly, having come to some sort of conclusion, and realising as she did so that all she wanted now was to get back to Sherry, and Cornwall, and her painting as quickly as possible. She adjusted her large hat, picked up her small suitcase, and quietly closed the apartment door behind her.

She was crossing the courtyard, disturbing the pigeons momentarily with her footfall, when Madame Montellier leaned out of her first-floor window and called to her to come up and have some coffee.

Celandine hesitated. She was still feeling unwell from the journey over, and now, knowing that she had to face yet another journey, she did not want to risk feeling sick once again. However, there was something about Madame

411

Montellier that made her stop. Something urgent and yet secretive in her face that induced Celandine to risk missing her train and turn back to the older woman's apartment.

'Marie has gone, no?'

Celandine stepped inside. Hearing the new baby crying, she stood firmly by the front door, not wanting to stay too long, but also not wanting to see the baby, in case she reminded her all too tellingly of her own brother.

'Yes, she has gone. To Burgundy, to be married, apparently.'

'That is good, huh?' The older woman looked equivocal and yet at the same time not unsympathetic. 'She has not had a very good time. It is as well that she is to be married. Most particularly since she . . .'

Celandine was still standing resolutely by the door.

Madame Montellier looked back at her, and perhaps realising that Celandine still had a mind to leave, she quickly completed her sentence.

'Most particularly because she has had a baby.'

'Marie *too* has had a baby?' Inevitably, Celandine now followed her hostess into her sparsely furnished sitting room, her voice rising.

'Sit down, madame. Please, sit down.' Madame Montellier nodded her head in answer to Celandine's question, as authoritative as any knitter by the guillotine. Celandine sat down slowly and nervously, placing her small suitcase

412

carefully beside the worn, lumpy chair offered to her. 'Yes, madame, Marie has had a baby. Your baby, Dominique? The baby, he was not of your mother. He was of Marie, not of your mother at all. Your mother, she died of something which grow inside her, but not a baby,' she finished discreetly.

Celandine, already weakened by sickness and only a few hours' sleep, slumped forward. Madame Montellier moved quickly to her side and held her head for her, before fetching a glass of water.

'Madame, my sincere apologies. But seeing you out there, I felt I had to tell you the truth, lest you feel guilty for leaving in France what you thought was your brother, when he was nothing of the kind!'

Celandine straightened up. She always forgot just how sick fainting made you, and how black the world became as you started to pass out.

'No, no, you did quite right,' she said eventually. 'Truly, madame, you did quite right. Is the family suitable who have adopted him?'

'Oh yes, they are suitable, madame. I know. I found them. And they are very eminent. He is a very lucky little boy. I often do this for my babies, if they are not in the way of having two parents.' She coughed, again at pains to be discreet.

'So why did Marie not tell me the truth?'

'Marie, she did not want to admit that it was her baby. Your mother, she was getting so . . .' she demonstrated with her hand an enlarging stomach, 'that when she died the same week as Marie had the baby, Madame Bonneville—'

'Not *Agnes*—'

The older woman nodded. 'Madame Bonneville suggested to Marie that she made out that the baby was of your mother. She thought that you would take it to England with you, and that would be that, mmm?'

'But I didn't.'

'No, madame, you did not.'

'Why could you not have told me the truth, you yourself?'

'I could not, madame.' An opaque look came into her eyes. 'I have not licence for the babies, and the Préfecture . . .' She shrugged. 'They will make me stop if they know I take money, and maybe I could go to prison. Besides, your sister—'

'My half-sister—'

'It is her idea, and I know she wanted you to take the baby thinking it was your mother's. She is like that, no? She doesn't like you, yes?'

'No, she doesn't like me.' Celandine stood up. She was feeling better in every way, if weak and bewildered. She turned to Madame Montellier with a look of profound gratitude. 'Thank you so much for telling me the truth. I am so grateful, really I am.'

'I can imagine, madame.'

'As it is, if what you say is true, he will be brought up in a beautiful house, with everything he could want. I have to admit it *is* a relief.'

414

'Of course, madame. But you will not want to talk again with your half-sister, I think?'

'No, of course not. I will never want to communicate with her again. Not that I would have done, but now, with this – I could not, ever, have anything to do with her, ever again.'

Celandine knew that she was being over-emphatic, but she did not care.

'That is good.' Madame Montellier smiled. She touched Celandine lightly on the shoulder. 'God is good, *n'est-ce pas*?'

'God *is* good,' Celandine agreed, suddenly seeing the reality of what could have happened. She could have taken the baby home and Sherry could have made her have it adopted in England. It could have all been so difficult.

'God is good,' Madame repeated.

'Yes,' Celandine agreed. 'Now I must hurry. My train, you know. It is probably on the point of leaving even as we speak.'

'I have already told the concierge to hold the hackney waiting for you, madame.'

'That is good of you. Why – you think of everything!' Celandine leaned forward and impulsively kissed Madame Montellier on the cheek. 'I am so grateful you called to me. I could have gone on thinking bad things about my mother, or bad things about myself, for not adopting little Dominique. It could have been all so truly bad, could it not?'

'But now it is not, huh?'

'No, it is not,' Celandine agreed. 'Now I can go home with a peaceful conscience.'

'Which is all that is necessary for a good night's sleep, huh?'

They parted at the outer door, and Madame Montellier watched Celandine being guided to her hackney carriage by the old concierge.

The older woman paused for a moment, watching the pigeons ducking, clucking, making up to each other, moving away again. They were really very like human beings, wanting to love and be faithful, but all too often finding life more difficult than they expected, with partners dying, eggs shattering, cats and rats preying on the little squabs. It was a struggle for them too.

She closed the outer door and walked up the stairs to her own cheaply furnished apartment. She earned her money how she could. She had her own babies, she took in other people's babies, and sometimes she helped out in other ways. She pushed open the front door and walked down the narrow, dark corridor.

'Marie!' she called. 'Marie! You can come out now, my dear. Mademoiselle Celandine, she is gone.'

Marie, still dressed in her travelling clothes, emerged from the darkness of the corridor, and she too, like Celandine, was carrying a suitcase.

'How was she?'

They peered at each other in the low light of the Parisian lamp.

'She was relieved, my dear Marie, as who

416

would not be? She has gone home thinking the baby is yours, and not that of her mother, which is much better than the truth, I think, huh?'

The two women moved back to the front door and for a moment they stood staring at each other in the better light. There was a slight pause as, with a dawning sense of relief, they realised that the plan they had conceived together looked as if it was going to prove to be successful.

'How fortunate that you thought of this story—'

'And how much more than fortunate, Marie, that you found a good family for him.'

They both smiled before Madame moved away from the front door, touching Marie briefly on the arm and guiding her back into the apartment once more, and towards the salon.

'Let us have *un petit coup* to celebrate, eh?' Madame Montellier moved to the small tray where she kept a bottle of brandy and other fortifications.

'Madame Benyon, she was a nice woman, but she had a fatal weakness for the young men. And the young men, they love her because she always make them feel good. She listened to them, and she loved them very generously,' Marie said, having taken a good slug of her drink. Despite the early hour she found herself, to her own surprise, relishing it. 'When she die, what to do? We were in a terrible state, were we not, my friend?'

Madame Montellier nodded as she topped up

their little brandy glasses. 'We were, Marie, we were. We might have been blamed for her death. Happily the doctor is a cousin.'

'We try to hide the truth from Mademoiselle Agnes, but she is too clever.'

'She want Mademoiselle Celandine to have the baby, while she take the paintings—'

'And the furniture – disgusting one!'

They both nodded in agreement.

'But now, it is better that Mademoiselle Celandine think that the baby is *not* that of her mother. She will think, "Well, poor Marie, she has had *her* baby adopted, and that is good." She will not think for the rest of her life, "I am a bad woman. I should have taken my mother's baby."'

'We are so good at our acting.' Perhaps because of the effects of the brandy, Madame Montellier started to laugh. 'We should be at the Comédie Française, yes?'

The glasses yet again refilled, they fell to discussing, at some length, the wonder of the baby's new home, the château, the servants, the delight of his new parents. He would be christened with a name as long as that of a French king. He would become the heir of a great house. And no one but them would know his true story, and the two women would never let on.

Brandy at that time of the morning was powerful stuff, but not as powerful as the knowledge of their own wisdom and foresight, their brilliance and sagacity.

'Now I must leave to catch my train.' Marie kissed Madame Montellier, and took up her suitcase.

The older woman watched her from her window. Marie, like her mistress, as her friend well knew, had used to have a weakness for young men, but now she was going home to Burgundy, and a suitable marriage. She would put her former life behind her. She would be châtelaine of a small vineyard. She would have children; and since the vineyard was so near to the château where Dominique would be brought up, she would be able to keep an eye on the young man. All in all, it had to be said, it was, or should be, a happy outcome to the whole sorry affair.

Mrs George was looking implacable.

'I don't like the sound of her cough, and what is more I'm not standing for it,' she told Napier.

Napier looked apprehensive, as well he might. He knew that Mrs George was in that particular state of mind which could bring about that dread of all dreads, a reliable housekeeper's handing in her notice.

'I know, I know, Miss Snape's cough does not sound good,' he admitted.

'Does not sound good? It sounds fearful, Mr Todd, and if I was you I would certainly give her the marching orders that are so necessary. The snow has melted, and she has no business staying on in the studio room. The way she has been going on, she should not stay anyway, Mr Todd. Anyone but myself would have left your service by now, housing a woman of that nature in a respectable establishment!'

Napier was hardly listening to her. He knew that Mrs George must know that he had quarrelled quite terribly with Edith and that as a result she had left Helmscote and gone to stay with the Montague Robertsons in Cornwall.

'We were not housing her, exactly, Mrs George, and anyway she has now left the studio room, and is only coming here for a few hours each day, so that I can finish my painting for Mr Algernon Hollingsworth.'

'You are housing a woman who is taking riding lessons at Captain Plume's establishment, Mr Todd. Many sorts of people, some of whom are far from healthy, I can tell you, Mr Todd, many what you could call diseased people, frequent Captain Plume's establishment. If you care to risk your health, I do not care to risk mine, nor that of Mrs Todd. It is one of the reasons why I encouraged Mrs Todd to go to Cornwall. Not just because she has become pale and tired sitting for that Mr Talisman' – she practically spat out Alfred's name – 'but because it was not good, not for a young lady in her condition, to risk her health. Not if it were ever so, it was not.'

Napier, who was intent on putting a last few finishing touches to his painting, was still not really listening, so it was not until Mrs George had left his studio, leaving her hidden threat

420

behind her, and closing the door rather more loudly than he would have wished, that the penny finally dropped. He flung down his brush and burst out of the door after her.

'Mrs Todd's condition? She is not feverish again, is she?'

'No, Mr Todd, she has a cold. But perhaps you had not noticed? That is why I thought it wise for her to go to stay in Cornwall, where the weather is warmer, and she will have the benefit of the sea air.'

Mrs George stared at Napier. If she had not known him so long she might have despised him, but as it was she found herself always excusing his ignorance and selfishness as being the direct result of his involvement with his work, and trying to ignore his shortsighted egomania. But now, with his entertaining this Miss Snape all the livelong day in his studio, and quarrelling with his poor young wife, she felt that she had just about had enough.

'Something I have come to realise about you, Mr Todd, over the years, is that you artistic people never do seem to notice much, do you? Yes, I am afraid that outside of your painting, and that, you really don't notice much. I find myself wondering if that painting you're on about at the moment was taken away from you, whether you might not notice a bit more, perhaps?' She turned away. 'But knowing you, Mr Todd, it wouldn't make any difference, I don't suppose.'

Napier ran round her, standing in her way so that she could not move ahead on the path that led back to the house.

'Are you really telling me . . . are you really telling me that my wife – that she might be . . . that she could be in an interesting condition?'

'Yes, I am, Mr Todd, even though it is not my place to do so. Why, even Mr Talisman noticed. But you, no, you didn't notice. Too busy painting that Miss Snape and she smitten with that Mr Talisman all the time anyway, and not with you at all.'

Napier stared after his housekeeper as she walked past him towards the house. 'I don't understand,' he said slowly.

Mrs George turned and shook her head. 'No, well, you wouldn't. That's what I just said, Mr Todd. That is you all over, and always has been. You are too busy staring at your painting to notice real life, which is what you're meant to be painting anyway, as I understand it. Too busy looking at the noses on other people's faces to see the nose on your own face.'

The side door of the house closed behind her.

Napier stared at it. He knew that Alfred was a ladies' man; everyone knew that. Why had it not occurred to Napier that he would work his charm on Becky Snape?

But of course it made sense, now he could bring himself to think about it. Alfred had always been in the wings, if not at Helmscote, then elsewhere. Napier suddenly remembered that he

422

had made Sheridan furious with his attentions to Celandine when they were at the summer school. It was all too obvious – if Mrs George was right – that Alfred would have taken advantage of Becky Snape, particularly if she had a crush on him. After all, Alfred had immediately recognised Becky Snape when she arrived to visit Edith so unexpectedly.

Napier frowned. It suddenly seemed all too coincidental that Becky had turned up so suddenly at Helmscote.

Very well, the man under whose protection she was living had sent her to take riding lessons, and he supposed it was natural for her to have known where Edith lived, but even so it seemed almost too coincidental, especially now that Napier remembered how Alfred had confessed to knowing *the Snape*, as he always called her, in Leicestershire.

'Alfred! My dear fellow! Luncheon is served.'

'Capital.'

Alfred did not know Napier well enough to know that Napier at his most affable was Napier at his most dangerous.

'Lamb cutlets for the entrée, one of the maids told me. The first of the spring lamb, heralding not just spring but summer too, I always think. And, because I am now quite done with "Temptation", I find I must open a bottle of champagne. Indeed we must both celebrate the completion of our paintings, although you seem to have finished your portrait in a shorter time than even Reynolds himself!'

'Reynolds, my dear Napier, took only a few hours. Dashed 'em off, the dear man did, you know; but it don't mean they aren't good, does it?'

They drank and gossiped, and if Alfred had been able to see into Napier's heart he might have felt daunted, but he could not. Nor did he see that when they had finished their champagne, and he turned away to move towards the luncheon table, Napier's eyes, following him, were uncharacteristically cold.

Nevertheless, because Alfred as usual was full of stories of the Continent, and they had both finally finished their paintings, as always Napier found himself beguiled by his friend's company.

Perhaps because of the champagne, and then the wine, and the delicious food, Napier found himself starting to question Mrs George's judgement. He was well aware that she would welcome an addition – if not many additions – to the household, if only because it would mean that she would be continuously employed through yet another generation. But he was also aware that because of her extreme loyalty to Edith, a loyalty that amounted almost to fanaticism, Mrs George was quite capable of mounting a campaign to make him feel guilty about his treatment of his pregnant wife, in order to bring about a reconciliation. On the other hand, it might be that she was wrong about Edith's condition. The wine and the pace of the talk only served to make him more confused.

'You know that Mrs Todd has gone to Cornwall because she is – as my mother would put it – in an interesting condition, of course?'

The lunch over, they were both smoking large cigars and generally celebrating as if they were officers in the field who had come to the end of a long campaign, which in a sense they had.

'Edith has a cough, Alfred, not a cold,' Napier said, his tongue firmly in his cheek as he sent up the usage of the day. The convention of calling a pregnancy 'a cold' had doubtless arisen in order to preserve the ladies from embarrassment. 'Mrs George, who as you know watches over my wife's health like a hawk, most particularly since her illness, told me she has a *cough*, and that is why she has gone to Cornwall.'

Alfred's eyes widened and his voice took on a falsely charming tone. 'No, Napier. Edith has a *cold*!'

Napier stared at him. From the moment Mrs George had hinted at Edith's condition he had been determined to keep it a secret from his friends until such time that he himself knew exactly what her condition might be. After all, Mrs George might be wrong, or Edith might have made a mistake.

'My dear Napier, it is a fact. She told the Snape, before she left in such a hurry. She said that feeling as she did, having been frequently sick in the mornings, *she* believed that she must be expecting a baby, but that the baby would not be yours.' Alfred stared at Napier, and as he watched the colour draining from his face he found that it was difficult not to feel that particular excitement which jealousy of a close friend so often engenders. Why should Napier have all the luck?

'I don't think you can be right, Talisman, really I don't,' Napier said. 'Edith is not the kind of girl to make the sort of mistake that would bar her from Society for ever. Nor is she the kind of girl who would turn against a loving husband. She is the kind of person who would come to me, and tell me personally what she hoped might be wrong with her. Edith is pure, and good, but over all Edith is honest. She is incapable of dishonesty. I really believe that.'

Alfred looked intently into Napier's eyes and hated him for loving Edith and at the same time not making love to her.

'I know how you must feel, my dear fellow, but really, it happens in the best of families. Girls slip up, often girls who are perhaps *too* innocent. Edith is too innocent, don't you think? She might believe that, with your fascination with Becky—'

'No, no, surely Edith knows me too well to suspect me of—' He stopped, remembering Edith's jealous outburst about Becky Snape.

Much as Napier tried to play down the artistic fascination that he had undoubtedly felt for Becky, he was all too aware that Alfred might have happened on something too near to the truth for

426

comfort. He had to face the fact that Alfred might be right: Edith might not have wanted to tell him that she was expecting a baby.

'I hate to ask the question, but it has to arise. We have to wonder which fascinating man's baby is it that Edith is perhaps expecting?' Alfred pulled on his cigar, and then dipped it, slowly and judiciously, into his brandy.

Chapter Eleven

Celandine had arrived home to find Edith gone, and a note from her confirming that she had decided to take Celandine's advice and go back to Helmscote and ask for Napier's forgiveness.

Celandine felt the usual regret that a person must feel when she finds a friend gone before an agreed departure date; a fleeting conviction that she could not have had enough of Edith's company, but also a feeling of relief that she could once again be alone with Sherry.

It was also a relief not to have to tell Sherry about the baby, now that she knew that Dominique had not been anything to do with her mother. She therefore settled down to delightfully hard-working days, painting first Mrs Dunstan, and then Mrs Dunstan's friend, and then, to her surprise and delight – Mrs Dunstan's friend having been really rather well connected – she was asked to paint the portrait of none other than Admiral Belitho.

'He wants *you* to paint him?'

'He certainly does, Sherry!'

Celandine was positively glowing with the triumph of bringing off such an important commission. She held out her arms, not to Sheridan, but to demonstrate just how large the portrait was to be.

'And he wants it *this* big!'

There was a long silence as Sheridan poured himself a pre-dinner drink.

'Are you sure he wants *you*?'

Celandine stared at Sheridan, wanting to say something, but not sure what.

'Why, yes, he does want me, Sherry,' she said finally. 'He wants me because of the portrait I did of Lady Trererice. The last one I did, remember? Oh, no, you never saw it: I had to go to Trego Place to do it, because she is quite crippled with rheumatism – the climate here is not kind to rheumatism – and you never saw it, did you, Sherry? I was quite pleased with it, but she was *very* pleased with it. So she recommended me to the admiral. It was most kind of her, don't you think?'

'But has he seen your portrait of Lady Trererice, Celandine? I mean has Admiral Belitho actually seen it? Because if he hasn't you might be in for a difficult time of it, dearest, really you might. He might not like your style, seeing that you're a woman and so on. He might find your style too soft, and your talent not suited to him.'

Celandine stood up and walked to the window, her heart beating slightly too fast.

'Sherry,' she said eventually, turning back to him. The beautiful view of the sea had quite calmed her, as it always seemed to do. 'Sherry, I have to remind you that when I painted Captain Black, and you put your name to it, you were more than happy with that situation, were you not?'

'Yes, I have to confess I was.'

'So if Captain Black was happy with his portrait, why would not Admiral Belitho be happy with his?'

Sheridan thought this over for a minute, and finally found that he could only come to one conclusion.

'I think, dearest, that whatever the quality of the work, a man is always more at ease if he is sitting to another man for his portrait, even if it is only for the preliminary sketches, as with your first commission. It is just a fact. And I fear that Captain Black would not have enjoyed the portrait you did of him should you have signed it, rather than me. For a man it is like having his hair cut. He would not want his hair cut by a woman, d'you see?'

'Yes, I do see. So what you are saying is that I should let you do the preliminary sketches as before, and that you should put your name to it when I have finished it?' Celandine breathed in and out. 'I see.'

'We do need the money, dearest, really we do,' Sheridan reminded her.

'Precisely, Sherry! And I have been given the

430

commission. If you wish for such commissions you should go out and paint portraits too, but you had rather not do that, because you would rather risk our security by following your own particular vision. And that is perfectly fine, I am sure, Sherry, but what is not perfectly fine is that you should cast doubt on the strength of my abilities. I have obtained this commission on the strength of my portrait of Mrs Dunstan's friend, Lady Trererice. The admiral is well aware that I am a woman, and he, unlike yourself, does not seem to think that it matters in the least. Quite the contrary, he told Mrs Dunstan that Mrs Angelica Kauffmann was one of his favourite painters, and that he believed women brought more sympathy to their portrait work than his own sex.'

'I don't see why you are becoming so heated, dearest, really I don't. I merely stated that I could see that being a woman painting a man could present some difficulties.'

'It could, but it will not!'

Celandine seldom became furious, and she had never really felt angry with Sheridan before, but at that moment she could see exactly what he was up to, and it was called – in nursery language – having your bun and eating it.

Sheridan wanted to pursue his own course, which was not going to pay for two-day-old bread, not to mention anything fresh from the bakery, let alone Mrs Molesworth's charges for their board and keep, and at the same time he wanted to cast doubts on Celandine's talent, and lower her confidence to the point when she would give in and put *his* name on the bottom of her work.

'I am a painter in my own right, Sherry. You are a painter in your own right. We might not be equal in the eyes of the wretched English law, but when we face a blank canvas we are equal in the eyes of Art. I will paint the admiral, and he will be pleased, see if he is not.'

At that moment the sitting-room door opened slowly. Celandine knew at once that Mrs Molesworth had overheard every word that had just been said, because she stared momentarily at Sheridan with a look that said, 'Well, you asked for that, young man!'

'Mrs Montague Robertson, may I have a word?'

Celandine could not wait to leave Sheridan to his thoughts and so she quickly followed Mrs Molesworth out into the corridor.

Alfred had been most reluctant to tell Napier the truth of his wife's condition, but when he asked himself afterwards whether he should or should not have done so, the second truth of the matter, if it could be called that, was that he always came to precisely the same conclusion.

He had, as a friend, surely, to tell Napier? It was his duty. After all, if Napier had never even touched his wife, then Napier surely only had it coming to him when she turned to someone else?

In fact it could be said that he had forced the poor girl into a situation where she would be less than a woman if she did not.

'Why do you suspect that the baby is not mine?'

Alfred could not say, *Because, my dear Napier, I heard your poor young wife, innocent that she is or was, upbraiding you for neglecting her.* Instead he had just stared soulfully at Napier, relishing the fact that if he himself could not have her, it was only fair that Napier, who did not want her, should lose out on her too.

It had been a bitter blow to him to realise that if Edith was pregnant the likelihood of her ever giving herself to him would be remote, to say the least; but it must be a more than bitter blow for Napier, who had, after all, married her.

'It was when I was painting her the last few days that it gradually dawned on me that her skin condition was changing and she was filling out, almost imperceptibly of course; that despite that irritating little cough she was changing, her skin blooming, her hair growing more lustrous. Of course . . .' Alfred was careful to laugh in order to hide his bitterness. 'Of course, for a wonderful moment I thought that this might be because she was falling in love with her portrait painter, that she was so pleased with the picture that she had fallen for the artist, but, alas, that was not apparently the reason.'

Napier had started walking up and down the dining room, looking and feeling as if he was in a nightmare. Mrs George had suggested to him that Edith was in an interesting condition, and now it seemed that Alfred too was telling him the same thing, but hinting at an altogether different outcome.

'I would not normally pay any attention, but Mrs George has just mentioned the very same thing. But why do you think that it might not be mine, Alfred?'

'Let us say . . .' Alfred sighed. 'Let us say I *know* that it could not be yours, Napier. Let us just say that I overheard certain things that mean that it could not be yours. It might be anyone's, my dear fellow, but you and I know that it can't possibly be yours.'

Napier groaned and leaning forward he wrapped his arms across his body as if in sudden pain.

'But I love her, Alfred. She is my wife!'

'Of course she is, but first and foremost, as we both know, you married her because she was your inspiration, and that isn't always what a woman wants, or understands, unless perhaps she too is an artist, like Sherry's wife. You know the ladies well enough, Napier my dear fellow. They have their own ways of expressing resentment. Mrs Todd could have fallen in love with her doctor, with her groom, with her gardener; there is no possible way that you will ever find out, except to ask her yourself, which of course I suppose you will have to do.'

'But Edith seemed so jealous of Becky Snape.

That was one of the reasons that we quarrelled so badly, because of Becky Snape. She hated the fact that I had painted over her face in favour of the Snape. It seemed that it maddened her; and then of course she saw two sets of footprints in the snow, and came to the wrong conclusion. Would she indulge in such jealousy if she herself was being *unfaithful*?'

'Perhaps that was what, I believe, is called a feint, my dear fellow. You ever watch a bird building a nest? I used to watch them all the time when I was young. They are full of the most cunning feints. The ladies, God bless them, make awful asses of us men, which for the most part we really rather enjoy. It is only when it comes to these other matters that we are pulled up short by our boot straps and wonder if we are not what they wish us to think we are; if they are not at pains to hide the fact that we are, in fact, their playthings, their baubles.'

'Would that be the reason she went away to Cornwall so suddenly? To go to see Sherry and Celandine, because she was in a quandary about her state, and hoped that I would be distracted by her accusations? Accusations which I may say are, and were, completely without foundation, I do assure you.'

'Oh, I know, my dear fellow. If only she had not run off that way, I could have reassured her that the Snape is not at all your type. My type perhaps, but not yours at all. You are too fastidious.'

Alfred lit another cigar. He had always been jealous of Napier, not just because he had inherited a good income from his father, or because he was able to follow his artistic principles to such a narrow degree, but because he was, finally, and Alfred knew it, a gentleman. Alfred was not a gentleman. He might be a member of an exclusive London club, if not two exclusive London clubs, but gentlemanly he was not.

Alfred had always enjoyed his life, and he had always looked out for moments of indulgence for which he found it all too easy to forgive himself. What he had never done before was fall in love. He had been careful never to do so, but now that it had happened, and he had found that the object of his undoubted passion had been taken, he was damned if he wanted Napier, who had after all neglected the beautiful creature, to take her back again. If Edith, as she must have done, had been unfaithful to Napier because he had neglected her, that was one thing, but in pursuing her own ends it seemed to Alfred that she had also been unfaithful to his own vision of her. To him Edith had been innocence personified, loving and giving, always anxious to support, to help. Now that that vision of her had been destroyed he wanted nothing more than for Napier to desert her. He only thanked God that he had finished the painting; that he had completed 'Friday's Girl', as he had called it.

'Let us go for a ride, and then let us come back

and get drunk again,' he suggested, a little thickly, to Napier, who, confused and wounded as he was, agreed.

'I feel how Othello must have felt,' Napier confided to Alfred after a good, long stiff canter during which he had a hard time of it staying on, such was his lack of sobriety.

'It only took a handkerchief to turn his insides to fire, not a pregnancy,' Alfred reminded him. 'And Iago, of course, was on hand to help,' he added slyly, looking sideways to see if Napier had picked up his nuance, but he was only staring miserably ahead.

'I really love Edith, you know, Alfred. I really do. I know I married her for her beauty, but I have grown to love her for her character. She is so insouciant, so impish, so mischievous on occasion, but with it all, I hoped – I *believed* – so innocent. And to think that she accused *me* of dallying with the Snape.'

'It is best to forget that time, surely? The footprints in the snow, they were undoubtedly those of Mrs George making sure that the Snape had her door locked – from the outside, I dare say!' Alfred laughed.

'Yes, yes, of course.' Napier suddenly pulled up his horse. 'Well, of all the damn developments this is surely the most damned!' He turned to look at Alfred, pointing ahead with his riding whip. 'Behold Mrs Todd climbing out of a hackney carriage, and due to get straight back in again, I do assure you.'

'Give her a chance, my dear chap, give her a chance to explain herself,' Alfred pleaded, becoming attacked by conscience, if a little too late in the day.

'I'm damned if I will!' Before Alfred could reason with him further, Napier rode up to the side of the carriage and leaned down to the driver. 'Take Mrs Todd back to the station, if you please, Mr Jeffrey. Tell her, if you would, that she is not welcome here, not ever again. She must go straight back to where she came from.'

'But there isn't another train until the morning, Mr Todd.'

'In that case make sure that she stays at the station hotel overnight, and see her on to the first train to Cornwall, or wherever she wants to go, in the morning.'

'Yes, Mr Todd.'

Napier turned his horse and urged it into a canter. 'Where the devil are we going now, Napier?' Alfred called after him, following him nevertheless.

'Who the hell cares?'

Celandine stared at Edith's pale face. She had large black shadows under her eyes. All the bloom of early pregnancy seemed to have deserted her, and she looked frailer than ever.

'I am sorry to return so quickly, Celandine. I know that it will not be at all convenient, either for you or for Mrs Molesworth here, but I did not know where else to go. Well, I did think of going

438

to the Stag, to my father, but the truth is that my stepmother would receive me with about as much enthusiasm as a bout of the measles.'

'I will take her to the spare room,' Mrs Molesworth stated, eyeing Celandine over the top of Edith's head. 'And I will bring her supper, and put a warming pan in her bed, and everything will seem quite different in the morning, I am sure.' The look that once again came Celandine's way was so significant that she knew that Mrs Molesworth must have overheard the argument between herself and Sheridan.

'I am so sorry, Celandine, but I did not know which way to turn.'

'Well, you would not, dearest Edith.'

Despite all the warning looks from Mrs Molesworth Celandine found herself following Edith upstairs.

When they were alone, Mrs Molesworth having lit the fire and bustled off to fetch all the usual comforts, Celandine turned to Edith, who was now sunk in a chair staring ahead of her as if she did not quite know where she was, but, worse, as if she did not care either.

'I did as you suggested and returned to Napier, all ready to apologise and explain myself and my condition, but the hackney had hardly stopped in front of the steps at Helmscote when Napier appeared from nowhere, with Alfred of course' – she said the last name almost bitterly – 'and went up to the driver and told him to turn round and take me back to the station, at once.' She looked up at Celandine. 'The poor man, Mr Jeffrey, was so embarrassed. As well he would be, because he and I know each other well now. He is quite a friend of Mrs George. There was talk at one time of them even—'

'Yes, yes,' Celandine interrupted, feeling and showing her impatience, because really she could not care less what Mr Jeffrey was like or whether he had ever intended to make an honest woman of Mrs George. 'But why would Napier turn on you like that? He must have taken leave of his senses, he truly must.'

She paced about the room for a little while, thinking. There was only one explanation possible. When a man took a turn into madness, when he changed character to such a degree, when he turned his wife from his own front door, it was always because of another woman. When Edith had become frenzied with jealousy, it might actually have been with good cause. Napier was obviously now obsessed with Becky Snape, the way he had once been with Edith. Why else would he be painting her? She looked across the room to where Edith was seated in front of the fire and felt the utmost pity for her situation.

'There can be only one answer to the situation in which we find ourselves,' she announced finally, by the careful use of the word 'we' tactfully putting herself in the same situation as Edith. 'There is only one answer, and I think, dearest Edith, that I have it.'

*　　*　　*

Celandine looked around Aunt Biddy's drawing room, savouring its old-fashioned fittings, its oval miniatures set about the fireplace, its long-skirted cloths covering tables that held more ornaments than she would have thought it possible for any one table to hold. It seemed so long since the summer when they had all danced in the bigger room across the hall and eaten their supper to the sound of the sea outside the open windows. She remembered how Sheridan and she had felt, and how they had finally run home to make love.

'My dear Celandine!' Aunt Biddy, as always in a crinoline skirt with a tight-waisted jacket, a high-collared blouse and a large cameo brooch, issued forth from the door, neatly avoiding her own crowded tables in such a dexterous fashion that Celandine had the feeling that when they were young, ladies such as Aunt Biddy must have been given private lessons in how to move through a crowded room in their large skirts. 'Well, well, well.' She smiled, taking Celandine's hands, her head on one side. 'It is so long since I saw you, or Sheridan. How is dear, dear Sherry?'

'We are both very well.'

Celandine tried not to look either guilty or embarrassed as she realised that this was her first visit to Aunt Biddy since the party. It was too terrible really. Rosewalls was not so far away that Sherry and she could not have come before, but now that they wanted something, well, here was Celandine, all dressed up to the nines and putting on her best smile.

'I am sorry I have not been to see you before, Aunt Biddy, but I have been so busy, painting portraits, you know. And Sherry has been trying so hard to sell his paintings, there has hardly been a free moment.'

'Do not you fret. Whatever you want, I shall certainly consider it,' Aunt Biddy said, and seeing the look in her eyes Celandine realised at once that she must have heard – perhaps from some other member of the family – that Sherry's annuity had been terminated.

'It is not something that *we* want particularly,' Celandine said, beginning slowly, 'it is something that we want for someone *else*. A young friend. She is in terrible difficulties.'

Aunt Biddy reached for her handbag and took out a lace-edged handkerchief. 'Gracious, Celandine dearest, is this going to make me lachrymose?'

'I hope not, Aunt Biddy, but it is certainly making *me* anxious. You see, she is married and—'

Celandine stopped. Mrs Molesworth had told her that there were many unmarried ladies living in Cornwall who had no knowledge of married life, and that they were always most anxious to stay as ignorant as possible.

'It seems the poor innocent has had the misfortune to find herself married to a poor sort of creature who glories in believing the very worst of her.'

Aunt Biddy promptly pressed her handkerchief to the side of her mouth. 'This is terrible. And who is this unfortunate person?'

'It is my friend, Edith Todd. Do you remember she came to the party in the old-fashioned – in the *beautiful* crinoline? You took to her at once, I know you did.'

'Of course I did, of course I remember. Yes, and she was quite the belle of the evening, after you, of course, my dear. Am I therefore to assume that that nice Mr Todd is the wretch to whom you just referred, Celandine?'

'I am very much afraid so, Aunt Biddy. He can no longer expect our friendship. He has been too harsh on his poor innocent wife. Our friendship with him has to be considered to be at an end.'

Aunt Biddy removed the handkerchief from its emotional position near her mouth, and put it back in her handbag. 'My dear, I have heard . . .' She leaned forward and lowered her voice. 'I have heard that a man can change horribly once he is married, and that everything one fears about the opposite sex becomes true.'

Celandine considered this for a moment. She still felt that she must be at pains not to upset Aunt Biddy, but on the other hand she did not like to think that anyone would think badly of Sherry. Sherry might be irritating at times, but he was quite incapable of being unkind.

'It seems,' she said, choosing her words with care, 'that what you have said about *some* men has turned out to be true, in this case.'

443

'But how am I to help?'

'I wondered, at least Sherry and I wondered, if you would mind terribly having Edith to stay? She would be more than happy to contribute to the household in any way that you should think appropriate. She is very good with her needle—'

'But of course! What could be more charming than for her to come here? She will act as the most delightful companion to me.'

'She would be more than happy to help Gabriel and Russo.'

'Oh, Celandine, I doubt that anyone could do that, outside of the angels, that is.' Aunt Biddy sighed. 'No, that would be asking too much. They have their little ways, you see, and I doubt that even the good Lord understands them, for I certainly never have. I always hoped that one day they might marry, but it seems Russo is not that way inclined. So Gabrielle has become and stayed her own mistress, because she has certainly never allowed me to have much say here at Rosewalls.'

In light of the fact that neither she nor Sherry had visited Aunt Biddy since the party, Celandine felt that she had progressed with her mission faster and better than she could possibly have hoped; and yet she knew she still had one last, very delicate hurdle to leap, and that was the little question of Edith's interesting condition. It was a particularly difficult subject to broach since Aunt Biddy was a spinster, and moved in a society that had never been known to

444

acknowledge the pregnant state, referring to it always, as Celandine had been repeatedly told by Mrs Molesworth, as a 'cold'.

'There is one more thing, Aunt Biddy, that I know I should mention.' Celandine braced herself to face Aunt Biddy with the facts of life. 'Edith Todd has a cold. It is not a particularly advanced cold, but it is a cold all the same.'

Aunt Biddy blushed, and at once reached for her handkerchief again. 'My dear, of course. I understand. I have great sympathy for young married women who contract colds,' she said, faintly, after a small, significant pause. 'And I dare say I speak for both Gabrielle and Russo too.' She paused. 'When might the cold be over, do you think?'

'I think a cure should be effected by the spring.'

'Things always do look up, as far as colds are concerned, once the spring comes. Spring and early summer in Cornwall is just what we all long for, and it is certainly the best time to be rid of a cold.' She stood up. 'Now, my dear Celandine, I must go for my rest, and you may tell your dear little friend, beautiful Mrs Todd, that she can come to stay here as soon as she likes, and for as long as she likes.'

Celandine leaned forward to kiss the air around Aunt Biddy's head, but Aunt Biddy outwitted her and she found herself being enveloped in the old lady's ample bosom, breathing in the smell of lavender and camphor, her face rubbing against the silk of the blouse.

'You have made an old lady very happy, trusting her this way, Celandine. Really, very happy.'

She left the room in a quietly euphoric state, her lace-covered head held high, so that Celandine could also return home feeling as happy about poor Edith's situation as Aunt Biddy was obviously happy to receive her.

There was something about helping Edith to pack up the few clothes that she had brought with her, to sort her boxes and brush the mud from her travelling clothes, that lowered Celandine's spirits.

'It could all have been so different,' she kept saying later that evening and the following morning to Sherry, who while maintaining a patient expression could have been forgiven for finally feeling bored.

'Since you are so busy with the admiral's portrait, dearest, why don't I go over to see Edith?' he asked, once Celandine had settled Edith into Rosewalls.

Celandine agreed at once. The admiral's portrait was an ambitious project, and one that she had at times wondered if she was really competent to undertake. But in the past few days it did seem to be progressing, to be stating something not just about him, but about England, about an island people who were always facing and as often repelling invasion.

'Did you know the admiral was nicknamed

Old Redoubtable when he was only twenty-eight?'

Sheridan nodded. 'Yes, dearest. You did tell me that.'

He turned away. Celandine was really so caught up with this commission, she seemed to be living in a different world from him. They still loved each other as passionately as ever, but during the day he knew she was not really with him, even when they were together – and just at a time when his own progress was very intermittent. It was partly because of the weather – the storms of the past weeks had seemed incessant – and partly because of his own lack of inspiration.

'Perhaps painting inside doesn't suit you?' Edith suggested when he called in on her at Rosewalls one morning.

Sheridan stared moodily at his feet. He liked visiting Edith, partly because he liked talking to her, and partly because Aunt Biddy gave him such a capital luncheon, fussing over him as much as she had when he was a small boy in short trousers.

'I will admit that being in the studio all day is confining, and I will also say that I miss Celandine a great deal. She is out painting this admiral fellow. I expect she told you about him?'

Edith nodded. 'Yes, she did,' she admitted, adjusting her decorously cut jacket over her enlarged waistline. 'She told me that it is the largest commission she has yet undertaken, and she was worried about it at first—'

447

'She was worried about it? She said that? She never said that to me.'

'She would not have wanted to tell you.' Edith smiled, her head on one side, and picked up a small baby garment that she was sewing.

'Why would she not have wanted to tell me?'

Edith looked across at Sheridan. He was tall and handsome, and it always seemed to her that his generous nature shone from his eyes, but he did not seem to understand women, and made no pretence of it.

'She would not want you to see that she was afraid of the undertaking, at least that is what I would feel if I were her. Women do not want to show men fear. They want to seem brave, as men do, most particularly when they do not feel anything of the kind!'

Sheridan looked at Edith, the thought gradually dawning on him that she was not just talking about Celandine and her painting of the admiral, but was doubtless also talking about the ordeal in childbirth that she must be gradually becoming all too aware lay ahead of her.

'I wish that Celandine was looking forward not to finishing a painting, but to *your* happy outcome. I wish she was in the same state as you,' he confided suddenly.

Edith did not take her eyes from her sewing. 'I appreciate that you think you would like that very much,' she said quietly, 'but you would not want darling Celandine to be in my situation. Who after all would want to be expecting a child by someone who would not communicate with them? Who would want to be alone in the world and in my position? If Celandine was in the same state as me,' she said, still sewing, 'she would be happy, and you would be happy, and so, finally, she would *not* be in the same state as me. Therefore, you would not wish her to be in my situation now, really you would not, when you really think about it. Truly not.'

Sheridan knew that it was not a reprimand, yet at the same time he felt that he had been put in his place, that he had been tactless, which was why he thought it a good moment to take his leave.

When he arrived home Celandine had fallen fast asleep in front of the sitting-room fire. It was Mrs Molesworth's night off, and it took Celandine for ever to put together a cold collation.

As he waited for her to assemble the meal Sheridan thought back to the slap-up luncheon he had enjoyed at Rosewalls, and sighed inwardly. The truth of the matter was that if a woman was out fulfilling a commission, instead of being in supervising the house, it was inevitable that she neglected her husband. It was only the memory of Edith's words that prevented him from complaining. Edith was unlucky. He was lucky. He had to remember that.

The following week when Sheridan again visited Edith in Celandine's stead he brought up the subject of the women's vote, something about which Celandine always became most emotional.

'Would you like to have the vote, Edith?'

Edith looked at him over the top of her teacup, her large eyes momentarily amused. 'Of course. Every woman wants to have the same rights as a man, without having to become one, that is.' She smiled. 'After all, as Celandine said the other day, it is surely a truly sad state of affairs when a man who is a common criminal, a man who has committed some dreadful crime, can come out of prison and have a say in the running of his country, and a woman who has the command of a large estate and runs a business with as much efficiency as anyone has no rights in the eyes of the law! It makes no sense.'

'But surely a woman, being so much more sensitive, gentle and kind than a man, is best left in the home, where she finally has more power than her husband? It is surely more important for women to set an example there? A virtuous married woman is after all the person who is finally in charge of the future of the country. Women ennoble us men.'

'I hope you never suggest as much to Celandine!' Edith looked at Sheridan, and smiled mischievously. 'To suggest that women should not have the vote because they are *married* means that only single women such as teachers, and street walkers, will have a say in the running of the country. That makes no sense.'

Sheridan looked thoughtful. He had hoped that Edith with her sweet face and feminine manners might be more on his side. 'I find it very difficult to see how men and women can ever be equal,' he confessed.

'No one can be equal; the very notion is silly. Equality is an ideal, but an ideal which nature defies. Poor darling Napier wanted everyone at Helmscote to be his equal, and it made them miserable, because he was forcing *his* ideas of freedom on them.' She paused, looking sad. 'The truth is that Napier made me miserable in the same way, trying so hard to keep me as his muse, not wanting me to be his wife until such time as his painting was completed.'

'How strangely hurtful.'

Edith was silent for a moment. 'So much to do with men and women is hurtful, don't you think?' she asked eventually. 'Mr Talisman says that most men want to be looked up to by women, to be flattered by them, but not to have to see them as they really are, which results in everyone being unhappy, because no one is really being truthful about their situation, or their feelings.'

At that moment Sheridan was too preoccupied with his own feelings to really hear Edith, most particularly the discomfort he felt about the success that Celandine was enjoying locally with her portraits, and the fact that the money that was coming in, although paid to him, was earned by his wife.

'I'm sorry? Who did you say said what?'

'Alfred Talisman, your friend. Napier's friend. He says that men want to be flattered by women, but not to have to see them as they really are.'

'Alfred has been staying with you?'

'Oh, yes. Napier asked him, and then he suggested that I sit to him for a painting. He has finished it, I believe, and is submitting it for the Summer Exhibition.'

Sheridan frowned as the memory of just how jealous he had felt of Alfred when they had been at the summer school in Brittany came to him. 'I am sure if *you* are his subject his painting will be delightful, but I have to tell you that if I had known Alfred was staying at Helmscote I would have told Napier to throw straw in front of the door!'

Since Sheridan was careful to keep his tone light, Edith assumed that he must be teasing her, so she smiled; but when he had left her to her own thoughts, waving to her gaily from the pony carriage before it set off back to Newbourne, she found herself worrying about his reference to the still current custom of throwing straw in front of the front door to warn of disease or death.

Nor would she have been comforted if she had been able to follow Sheridan back to Newbourne and overhear the subsequent conversation between him and Celandine.

'No wonder there has been trouble at Helmscote, if Alfred has been staying.'

'But, Sherry, I told you that Alfred was there—'

'I understood that he was just passing through, not that Edith was sitting to him.'

'Such silly nonsense,' Celandine said, turning quickly away to cover her embarrassment as she

452

remembered how she had encouraged Alfred to flirt with Edith to make Napier jealous. 'As if Edith, who is after all a married woman, would not be able to cope with Alfred.'

Sheridan frowned at his wife's back. 'Your voice sounds tired, dearest. Why not go and change?'

Celandine knew this was his way of getting rid of her. 'I will go and change, Sherry, but I am not tired, I promise you.'

When she came back down again, nevertheless feeling refreshed, Sheridan had obviously come to a decision, because he was looking both masterful and excited, as if he had been wrestling with a problem for some time but finally solved it.

'I am going to go up to London, Celandine. I think I should. I can sort out a few things at the gallery, and better to do it face to face. I have written to Napier at Helmscote hoping that he might be in town at the same time. I shan't tell him I have been seeing Edith, or talk of her condition, but I believe I may find out more about the situation if I go to London.'

Celandine would have liked to talk Sherry out of sending his letter, and out of going to London, but the memory of her mischievous dealings with Alfred and Edith held her silent. She realised with a sickening intensity that she might have made the great mistake of making mischief with an arch mischief-maker.

'Never take on the devil at his own game,' her beloved mother would have said.

Celandine looked across at Sherry, who was still talking of his plans for his journey to London, how he would go to such and such exhibition, how he would visit Devigne at the gallery and show him some of his new canvases. Unable to unravel the tangle of her confused thoughts, she hurried out of the room, leaving Sheridan to sip his pre-dinner drink in solitary splendour. It was only with the best intentions that she had sought to make Napier love his wife, who so loved *him*. She had really only wanted to make him see how selfish he had been in neglecting Edith in pursuit of his art.

'Anything the matter, dearest?'

'No, not at all, Sherry. Of course not. Why should there be?'

They had gone through to dinner and were seated opposite each other in the window of Mrs Molesworth's dining room overlooking the cobbled street outside. People were hurrying by in the winter darkness, stooped shapes of different sizes and colours lit by the street lamp, but all bent double against the weather. Suddenly it seemed to Celandine that it was not just the winter that was dark, it was the future. Unable to bear the guilt of what she had done any longer, she turned to Sheridan.

'Sherry, I have to tell you, I think I might have done something rather foolish.'

Sheridan stared across at Celandine, silenced, which was unusual for him. 'Well?' he asked at last. 'What have you done, Celandine, that you think is foolish?' He was now looking rather serious and much older, which made it more difficult to confess.

'I encouraged poor little Edith to flirt with other men, at our celebration party at Aunt Biddy's, because Napier was so neglecting her, you know? I felt so sorry for her, so young and so innocent really, and Napier not really appreciating how much she loves him, in my opinion, not appreciating it at all, as a matter of fact, but at least he did after that.'

Sheridan was silent for a few moments longer, considering this. 'I have heard of worse things, dearest.' He paused, his expression one of tempered relief. 'As a matter of fact I think if *you* had not done so, *I* would have!'

Celandine sighed with relief as the guilt slid off her. 'You are a saint, Sherry, do you know that? A real and golden saint, and I shall paint you as one, see if I don't.'

Sheridan smiled. He had only spoken the truth, but if it made him even more lovable in Celandine's eyes, who was he to quarrel with that?

Chapter Twelve

Despite his usual reluctance to leave home and Celandine, Sheridan could not help feeling excited as the train steamed into the station. The journey had been long, but anything but tedious, his mind preoccupied by the constant twists and turns of his confused thoughts.

He had always been more than happy for women to be allowed to practise their art, indeed he had actively encouraged their presence at the summer school in Brittany, but now that Celandine was enjoying a certain success with her portraits, and bringing home much-needed money, he realised that his principles had run up against his masculine pride.

Worse than that, Mrs Molesworth had been so pleased with her portrait that she had persuaded him to bring it up for possible admission to the Summer Exhibition of the Royal Academy. It was even now, framed and varnished and safely packaged, sitting in the guard's van under the supervision of the good guard who had taken it under his wing. However, what Mrs Molesworth had not noticed, but Sheridan had, was that Celandine had not signed it – yet.

'I will leave that to you, Sherry,' she finally said, half mockingly, half serious. 'We need to have someone exhibit, if we can, and the London public are not yet ready for your hard-worn sailors or your fisherwomen striding across the sands with baskets on their hips.'

Sheridan had loved Celandine for not signing the painting, which was, he now had to admit, superb, but at the same time he had felt shamed both by her practicality and by her modesty. They both knew that the painting would have a better chance of being chosen by the hanging committee if Sheridan signed it – and yet, if he signed it would he not be conducting some kind of fraud? Worse than that, would he not be conceding to some kind of prejudice, a prejudice to which he had thought himself immune?

'My dear fellow, how perfectly delightful to see you.'

Sam Devigne, Sheridan's London art dealer, stood in front of Sherry, smiling broadly. Sheridan, who had made his way to his premises with his usual mixed feelings of suppressed excitement and dread, shook his hand.

'How long since we had the pleasure of seeing Sheridan Montague Robertson in London?'

'Cornwall is not an easy place to leave, Sam, you must know that.'

'I take your word for it, my dear Sherry, I take your word for it.' Sam laughed with good humour. 'More than that I delight in taking your word for it. I believe you too. But as you know I am famous for rarely having been caught without my gallery.'

Sheridan laughed. It was true. Everyone in the art world knew that Sam Devigne was his gallery, and his gallery was Sam Devigne; so much so that it was a running joke among artists that even if his own mother passed Sam in the street, without his gallery, he would go unrecognised by her.

'So.' Sam ran expert eyes over the packages that the hackney-cab driver had deposited inside the gallery room for Sheridan. 'So, Sherry, my dear fellow, what have you for us today? The hanging committee sits pretty soon, but I think nevertheless that I will be able to forget the niceties if you have something special for me.'

He nodded to his assistant to sally forth with scissors and carefully begin to unwrap Sheridan's small collection of canvases.

'I think I will leave you to it, Sam. I am feeling the journey a little and I would dearly love to go in search of some lunch. Besides, I have a horror of seeing the expression on your face when you view. You either look as if you have just swallowed a rat, or you look as if you have just met your future wife. Neither expression is conducive to my comfort.'

Sherry turned to go, but as he did so his eye

was caught by a large painting leaning against the wall behind him. It was of a young red-haired girl sitting in a Grecian robe, holding a harp. Pre-Raphaelite in the execution, Pre-Raphaelite in the subject, he knew at once that it would become a talking point at the Summer Exhibition. He also knew the artist without even looking at the signature.

'Napier is in fine form, wouldn't you say?' Sam's voice came from behind him.

Sheridan turned back briefly to the art dealer. 'He certainly is, and so is his painting,' he agreed. 'It should cause quite a stir . . . quite a stir. Sure to be picked, don't you think?'

'Certainly it should be picked,' Sam agreed, looking critically at it. 'It will sell for a fortune.' He snapped his fingers lightly, and then gave Sheridan a quizzical look. 'You have no liking for the style any more, Sherry, have you?'

'Art reflecting nature, it is not, Sam. Art reflecting art, it most certainly is! And of course it is perfect.'

They both laughed, and with some affection Sam watched Sheridan bounding happily out of his gallery. Sheridan was one of those painters who was at ease with his talent. Determined to follow his star, he would never make the living that artists such as Napier Todd would make, but perhaps for that very reason he was finally, to his dealer at least, infinitely more endearing.

Outside the gallery Sheridan stepped into the path of an immaculately dressed figure.

'Napier!'

'Sherry, my dear fellow. I never thought to see you here, and in London?' Napier stood back, holding up his hand to his face in mock horror. 'Never did I think to see you within walking distance of Piccadilly, not ever again, really I didn't.'

'You are a shocking tease, Napier, really you are.'

Seeing Napier in London was a shock for Sheridan too, since Napier had not responded to his letter, and Sherry himself had, of late, been spending a great deal of time with his poor pregnant wife, and been a reluctant witness to her suffering. He knew Celandine would expect him to distance himself from the fellow, but Sheridan being Sheridan he decided to try to hear Napier's side of the story – and preferably over a slap-up luncheon.

As they walked along together it seemed to him more and more that he should give Napier a fair hearing. After all, as he understood it, women, particularly if they were in an interesting condition, could get themselves into the most terrible twist over the most trivial incidents. There might well be a good and hearty explanation for Napier's turning his wife out of his house.

As the waiter pulled out his chair and he sat down Sheridan made up his mind to grasp the emotional nettle and get straight to the heart of the matter, with no shilly-shallying, but only once they had been good to their inner men. No sense in trying to say anything on an empty stomach.

'I am so terribly sorry about Edith, Napier.'

They had lunched off mutton and puddings, and cheese and fruit, and were agreeably wined, or despite his firmest resolve Sheridan would never have had the courage to bring up the subject of poor Edith.

Napier held up his hand. 'I am sure you are quite right to be sorry, Sherry my dear friend. But believe me, *I* am not sorry. You must agree, surely, that it is better to discover that a wife has deceived you before it is too late. I certainly feel grateful to Alfred. But for him I might have brought up someone else's child, left Helmscote to someone else's offspring, and never known the truth. That might have been my fate. Whereas now, as it is, I know that I can never, will never, set eyes on Edith again.' He stopped speaking, lighting a cigar and staring across the table at the astonished Sheridan.

'Is that the cause of your behaviour, Napier?' Sheridan found himself spluttering, after a considerable pause. 'You think that Edith's condition is not caused by you, but by another? And you believed *Talisman* when he told you that this was so?'

Sheridan's expression spoke of so many mixed emotions that Napier found himself staring at him. It was not like the easy-going Sherry to look both indignant and appalled – worse than that, repelled by his old friend.

'Why, Napier, if I was half a man, the first thing I should do is call you outside. I should call you outside so I can hit you.'

'That is usually why people call each other outside, Sherry,' Napier told him, attempting a soothing voice.

'Second,' Sheridan continued, determined not to be soothed, 'I think I should have you sent to the lunatic asylum. Do you really, truly and honestly believe that dear, beautiful little Edith is anyway anything but the most *innocent* of women?'

'I know that Alfred must have been telling me the truth. I am sure that after sitting to him – as she did for days on end – Edith must have confided in him. Alfred is not such a good actor that he could fake the information confided to him.'

'Alfred Talisman is the most awful meddler. When we were in Brittany he kept going for long and purposeful walks with Celandine. I tell you, it nearly drove me mad with jealousy. He went about everything so quietly too, always pretending that he was talking about art, holding intelligent conversations, when all the time I knew he was secretly lusting after my girl, and not even Celandine could see it.'

Napier shook his head. 'While I am sure you are right that Alfred is a womaniser, he is also one of my oldest friends. He was good enough to confirm Edith's condition. He need not have done so, but since she was sitting to him she felt quite able to confide in him.'

'You are such a duffer, Napier,' Sheridan stated, after a short pause during which he yet again tried to control his fury, finally allowing a humiliating amount of pity to enter his voice. 'Like so many of our sex you don't know when you have found a pearl.' He stopped, his voice changing. 'I know this because I too am a duffer, I too have not appreciated the pearl in the oyster of my life.'

'You cannot be guilty of that, Sherry. Why, your devotion to Celandine is already legendary. And look how you are devoting your talent to the life of the working men and women of Cornwall when you could be enjoying a glorious income from painting for the rich and the famous. No, you are a dear sentimentalist, wanting only to follow your heart.'

'I may be sentimental, Napier, but I am also a realist. If you have done your poor young wife a wretched harm, if you have suspected someone who is innocent, *you* will not forgive *yourself*.'

Napier paused, pulling on his cigar. 'If Edith was not guilty why has she not tried to plead her case with me?'

'Can you not see that Edith is so innocent she would not think it necessary? Besides, Celandine would not let her. Celandine knows the truth of your relationship. The truth is, and she assured me of this, the truth is that she knew of your using Edith's beauty as your muse, of your, let us say, neglect of her, in favour of your painting.'

Now Sheridan fully expected Napier to take him outside and hit him for his effrontery. Instead he only looked mortified.

'It is true, I did marry Edith more as a springer to my art than as a potential wife. That is true.' He looked reflective, trying to search for the right words to explain his lack of feeling. 'I had been moribund for months. The moment I saw Edith's face that morning, the way was cleared. I knew I could paint "Temptation" – and everything was going brilliantly with the work, until we had made love.' Napier sighed. 'After that I could no longer paint her. I had fallen in love with her. She was Edith, and I could no longer see her as anything else.'

'She still *is* Edith. Damn the painting, Napier, truly, damn it. Edith is your *wife*, she is expecting your child and no one else's. I have hesitated to interfere in this painful matter, but I have been spending some time with Edith – and believe me I know her to be as innocent as the day. Truly, she is. She talks of nothing but you, thinks of nothing but you.'

Napier stood up and flung down his napkin. 'I think you should have told me that you knew of Edith's whereabouts,' he said tightly.

'How could I?' Sheridan also stood up. 'To do so would be to betray her, and Celandine. However, if you want to hit me, I will follow you outside.'

Napier sighed. They both knew that he was incapable of doing such a thing. 'I am as incapable of hitting you, Sherry my dear fellow, as – as—'

'Edith would be of deceiving you.'

Napier walked off, not wanting to hear this last affirmation of his wife's innocence.

Sheridan followed him with a sinking heart. His sex were so stubborn. His sex were so sure of themselves. His sex were so quarrelsome. Really, it was no good mincing words – he despaired of his sex. He knew that he was right about Edith, and while he could never tell Napier that Celandine had encouraged Edith to flirt at Aunt Biddy's party, he also knew that Celandine had acted from the purest motives. He walked out into the street. Despite the warmth of the day, London was at its best: the smart ladies and gentlemen in their carriages, the luncheon – such good wine and such good food . . . he had already started to miss her, damn it.

They returned together to the gallery, where Sam was striding about, smoking a cigar and beaming from ear to ear, closely followed by a retinue of adoring female assistants.

'Napier my dear fellow, this is your finest. Everyone has said so, before and after luncheon!' He winked and nodded towards some expensively dressed ladies and gentlemen. 'We have hooked them, my dear fellow, we have hooked some really big fish. Never mind that old

Algernon Hollingsworth could not wait for you to finish and bought one of Leighton's instead, never mind that. No, we have a ready-made audience, dying for your every painting. Dying for them, simply dying for them.'

It was that word 'dying' that hit Napier amidships. Despite his outward demeanour, despite everything that he had said to Sherry at the end of luncheon, the walk from the hotel to the gallery had been murderous for him. Every step of the way, above the sounds of the streets, the carriages and the people, he could only hear Sherry's voice insisting on Edith's innocence.

Supposing Sherry was right? Supposing Edith was innocent, and Alfred just a meddler? What would he do if Edith died? Women died in child-birth all the time. It was a commonplace. How would he live with himself if his baby was born, his wife died, and he subsequently discovered that he had falsely accused her?

'Are you all right, old fellow?' Sheridan stared at Napier, who had started to mop his brow.

'Perfectly, thank you, Sherry. It is just a little hot in here, don't you find, after the country, that is?'

Sheridan leaned forward and whispered, 'Napier. How can you feel hot when you know that it has never been known for Sam to light a fire, not in all the years we have been coming here. All those lady assistants of his over there' – Sheridan nodded over to where they were busying themselves – 'it is well known that they all

466

have to under-dress in the thickest Highland wool, for once the public go home the place is an ice box.'

Napier stopped mopping his brow. 'How do you know that they have to wear wool, Sherry?' he asked, sounding childishly curious.

'Because Alfred told me. You know the Talisman – he never can resist a lady in a shop. He is notorious in Burlington Arcade, I tell you, quite notorious.'

Sheridan wandered off to view other paintings, and Napier followed him.

'Burlington Arcade, did you say? Alfred frequents Burlington Arcade? But who told you this? And what does it mean?'

Sheridan nodded across to Sam, who was busier than ever laughing and talking the *beau monde* into spending more money than they wanted to at his gallery.

'Who do you think knows more about everyone than they know about themselves – Sam Devigne. Alfred and he have been huggermugger since they were at school together. Ask Sam anything about anyone and he will tell you. He told me last time I came up to London. All the gentlemen love the Arcade, do they not? First they interest their wives in some little trinket, then they send them off down the Arcade, and then they slip into the back of the shop and meet some willing young lady. *Et voilà*, the wife is happy, and the gentleman is happy, and so they make their respectable way home. It is the

467

way of the world – not mine but that of so many of the fashionable set who find it difficult to avoid temptation in any form, even on a polite shopping trip.'

'Well, I dare say Alfred can do as he wants. He is unmarried, after all.'

'Certainly, of course he can do as he wants . . . This is quite a fine painting, would you not say?'

Sheridan tapped Napier on the arm because he was paying no attention to the work of his rivals, work that they were meant to be viewing, but Napier had the emotional bit between his teeth.

'Alfred can do as he wants,' he repeated. 'I know he had a little brush with the Snape when he was staying at Helmscote . . .'

'Precisely. He has little brushes everywhere, not just with canvases. That is all I am trying to tell you, that Alfred is a certain kind of man. Not one I would call a gentleman, but' – Sheridan stood back and gave an admiring sigh as he nodded towards the painting in front of which they were standing – 'but, gracious me, Napier, Alfred can paint, can't he?'

Napier was still paying no attention. 'What did you say?'

'I said, Alfred may not be a gentleman, but he can paint, can't he? Look at this.' Sheridan leaned forward the better to read the title of the painting. ''Friday's Girl''. How does the phrase go? Oh yes. Friday's child is loving and giving, and so is Friday's girl is she not?'

They both stared up at the large painting. It

468

was Edith, but not as Napier had tried to paint her, symbolising some false depiction of womanhood, rather as a young, vibrantly beautiful woman. It was Edith as Alfred had seen her, innocent and loving. Edith painted by a man who was clearly besotted by her.

Sheridan stared from the painting to the subject's husband and back again.

'I think we have got to the bottom of this particular matter, my dear Napier, don't you?' he asked in a suddenly sombre tone as the excitement and emotion of the painting swept over him.

Napier backed away from the canvas as if it was a person intent on crowning him, and then stood staring up at it.

It was all too clear what the painting was saying. It was saying what he, in his conceit, had refused to acknowledge. He was about to speak, when Sam came up and stood between himself and Sheridan.

'Your painting, Sherry,' he told Sheridan, in delighted tones. '"Mrs Molesworth with Loelia and Pansy". I can sell it ten times over! But my dear fellow, typical of you, you have forgotten to sign it!'

Napier continued to stare wordlessly up at 'Friday's Girl', oblivious, as Sheridan turned to Sam Devigne.

'My – er – my painting? Don't you mean "Women on the Shore", Sam?'

'No, no, "Mrs Molesworth with Loelia and

Pansy". Delightful, quite delightful, just what is wanted.'

'What about "Women on the Shore", though, Sam? And the others? "Fisherman and His Pipe"?'

'Both delightful, of course, but a little too realistic for my clientele, Sherry, just a little too realistic. They want to think of fisherfolk as being a great deal more noble than you have depicted them, but "Mrs Molesworth" is just their cup of tea, really she is. You must sign it for me. Set the ball rolling.'

Sheridan looked rueful, and sighed. Finally, having struggled momentarily with his feelings, he shrugged his shoulders.

'It is not by me, Sam. It is by Celandine Benyon.'

'Who?'

'Celandine Benyon. A very talented woman to whom I happen to be married. I brought the painting to London on her behalf.'

Sam sighed heavily. 'By a woman, you say? Oh dear, Sherry. What a pity.'

'A pity, you say?'

It was Sam Devigne's turn to shrug his shoulders. 'Yes, Sherry. Men don't want to buy paintings by women; not even women want to buy paintings by women. It is just a fact. Watercolours by friends may be hung in bedrooms, but not oils by women in drawing rooms. Women painters are not considered.'

'Ridiculous!'

'I agree, my dear chap, I agree. But no matter how many male painters admire feminine talent, the public regard a professional painter of the female sex somewhat in the same way as they regard an actress, and they don't want them on their walls either!'

'When I was in Paris—'

'No, Sherry, no good trying to make a case for it. The French, the Germans, Europe in general, although America less so, do not feel that a woman with a painting talent should be encouraged. It is against their finest principles.'

Sam's eyes, as always, were full of mischief, but the tone of his voice was rueful. Finally he leaned forward and said in a low voice, 'You could sign the painting, since it is by your wife. It would sell in seconds.'

'No, I could not do that, Sam.' Sheridan shook his head. 'As a matter of fact I would rather drink hemlock. Celandine is a fine painter, and soon, if not today, she will be recognised as such. I know it.'

'Put her name to it then, my dear fellow. What you will.'

Sam patted him on the shoulder, and moved quickly off. Of course the painting would finally sell with a woman's name on it, but not for the sum that it would have fetched had it been signed by Sheridan Montague Robertson.

Edith had started to enjoy the even tenor of Aunt Biddy's household. The slow routine suited her state of health. Neither Celandine nor Sheridan had been able to visit her recently, but this did not appear to her as being in any sense a desertion, for the truth was that while she was more than grateful to Aunt Biddy, she had managed to induce in herself a peace of mind that was by far the best thing for her condition. Or perhaps her condition had brought about peace of mind?

Lately she had found herself thinking a great deal about her own mother, and wondering how it would have been had she not died. She liked to imagine that they would have sewn baby garments together, would have talked excitedly of the time when the baby would arrive, and what its sex might be. Most of all she could have benefited from her advice, and enjoyed her sympathy.

'Mrs Todd?'

Gabrielle stood at the door of the little sitting room, her worn old face flushed with confusion and anxiety. Her hand trembled slightly as she pointed behind her.

'Outside there,' she said, 'is Mr Todd, and he is asking to see you.'

Edith laid aside her sewing, and stood up. It was a moment that she had imagined many times, Napier come to see her, to fetch her, to tell her why he had cast her so cruelly aside, but now that it had arrived she wanted nothing of it. She could not believe it. She did not want to see him. All the cruelty and despair that she had suffered over the last months, all the nights awake and wondering, flooded over her, and she suddenly knew, with complete certainty, that she could not, would not, see him.

'Tell Mr Todd, if you would, Gabrielle, that if he has anything to say to me, he must put it in a letter. Tell him I will not see him, not today, nor any other day.'

Gabrielle nodded, her hearing suddenly perfect, and for a second it seemed to Edith that the older woman looked relieved.

'Very well, Mrs Todd.' The old maid paused by the door. 'If I was you,' she said, lowering her voice, 'if I was you, Mrs Todd, I would take the back stairs, right away from him.'

Edith nodded, and catching up her sewing she swiftly exited through the other sitting-room door.

'For myself, I think I will call the mistress and Russo,' Gabrielle went on, talking out loud to herself, and she too exited through the door to the back of the house, circuiting the other rooms until she found Aunt Biddy.

'Go and tell him, by all means, Gabrielle, and I will position myself in the hall.'

Gabrielle went, and, as she had suspected, Mr Todd, not content to be left on the doorstep, moved past her into the hall, only to be confronted by the imposing figure of Aunt Biddy dressed in one of her more elaborate crinolines.

'Mr Todd?'

Aunt Biddy's voice was uncharacteristically

cold, and her best and most cutting drawing-room manner was to the fore. It stopped Napier, as it was meant to do. He stared at her for a few seconds, as if he could not quite believe that it was the same Aunt Biddy at whose party he had danced.

'Mr Todd, I will ask you to leave this house. You are not welcome here, as you must realise. As you should realise. Your behaviour towards your poor young wife has been reprehensible, and understandably she has no wish to see you. If you wish to communicate with her, do so by all means, but in writing.'

Napier had been so involved in his painting, so involved with 'Temptation', that he had not had time, and perhaps before his confrontation with Sherry never would have had time, to take account of how his actions towards Edith had affected *other* people.

Certainly he had taken account of what Sherry had said to him over lunch, and when he had seen Alfred's painting of Edith the truth of Sherry's words had come home to him at a fast gallop. Alfred, being unable to seduce Edith, had taken care to work Napier up into precisely the same state as he had obviously worked Edith, but finally it was his painting that had given him away. He had painted her looking as innocent, as kind and as loving as Napier now realised, in his heart of hearts, he must have always known her to be.

Now, facing Aunt Biddy, the true realisation of

the nature of his behaviour towards Edith came home to Napier. The expression in Aunt Biddy's eyes told him that what he had done to his wife was unforgivable. The question that now remained was whether Edith felt the same.

I do not look for you to forgive me, I only wish that I had not been so involved with 'Temptation'. I saw neither to the right nor to the left of me, and seeing nothing I have, deservedly, been left with nothing. It was only when I saw Talisman's finished portrait of you in London the other day that it came to me that he loved you. It is a portrait of such insight into your lovely nature that it made me feel shabby to a degree. I have been in hell ever since, and I dare say I shall remain there, again deservedly.

Edith put the letter in her dressing-table drawer. Napier was right. She could not forgive him the hurt he had done her. Moreover, she *would* not forgive him: to do so would be bad for her, and much worse for him. She had been too hurt by him for too long. He would have to remain wherever his particular hell was, at any rate for the moment.

Chapter Thirteen

The unmistakable and strangely piercing cry of a newborn baby rang through the old house. It was as startling a sound as any that could have been heard in that particular establishment.

Aunt Biddy heard it first, and reached once more for the sherry bottle. Downstairs Gabrielle and Russo heard it, and they reached for the port bottle. Upstairs Celandine reached for a glass of water and handed it to Edith.

'He's a beautiful, big, bouncing, bonny boy,' she told Edith, and her smile had never been wider. 'A beautiful big bouncing bonny boy.'

Edith stared down at the infant, and then up at Celandine. 'He looks just like his father,' she said eventually, and although there were tears on her cheeks, her smile was such that both Dr Bellingham and Celandine could not help laughing with delight. In fact they all laughed. Not that Dr Bellingham knew of the complications preceding the birth, but he certainly knew joy when he saw it, and even more certainly he had never felt more relieved.

'Thank you so much for everything you did to help me,' he told Celandine as she followed him downstairs.

'Is there someone who can come and help Mrs Todd with the baby, Dr Bellingham?'

The doctor nodded. 'I will send someone from the village. There are many women with nursing experience who will be eager and willing.'

Celandine turned towards the drawing-room door, and pushed it open slowly. She suddenly felt so tired she could have collapsed. Once inside the room she realised that Aunt Biddy already had.

She touched her on the arm.

Aunt Biddy stopped snoring and woke up with a start, looking indignantly up at Celandine as if she had no idea who she could possibly be. 'What is it? What is it, my dear?'

'It's Edith, Aunt Biddy. She has been delivered of a bonny, bouncing baby boy.'

Aunt Biddy stood up, her crinoline swaying. 'Well, I never. I felt sure that the doctor would make nonsense of it all and we would be going to a funeral, instead of a christening.' She walked unsteadily back towards the table bearing the now sadly depleted sherry decanter. 'I felt sure of that,' she announced. 'Sherry wine, my dear?'

Celandine shook her head. She glanced over at Aunt Biddy's clock. She was meant to be back at Newbourne before nightfall and it was already five o'clock. 'No more sherry wine, thank you, Aunt Biddy.'

'Must wet the baby's head, surely?'

'No, thank you very much. I think it has been quite dampened enough already,' she murmured, smiling. 'I will go and make sure that Edith is quite comfortable, and then I really must return to Newbourne.'

'What does the baby look like, my dear? If you know what I mean?'

Aunt Biddy's tone was conspiratorial, and of course Celandine knew just what she meant.

'Just as a boy should. The image of his father, there can be no disputing that.'

'Well.' Aunt Biddy's smile was triumphant. 'Well, that is good.'

On Celandine's return Mrs Molesworth opened the door to her with a worried, disapproving expression.

'We have a visitor, Mrs Montague Robertson, and not one I think you will wish to welcome, really I doesn't.'

Celandine stared at the sitting-room door, thinking at once that she knew who it must be. She went into the room fully prepared to find Alfred Talisman there, and then paused just inside the door, unable to quite believe whom she was actually seeing.

'Why is Mr Todd here, Sherry?' she asked in a cold voice, turning to Sheridan.

It was difficult to say who was looking more

478

guilty at being caught together – Sherry or Napier.

'He is here,' Sheridan said, 'because I asked him to supper with us, Celandine. And where have you been? I was just about to become worried.'

The moment was irresistible to Celandine.

'I have been delivering Mrs Todd of a baby.' She looked across at Napier's instantly paling face. 'Yes, Mrs Todd has been delivered of a fine healthy baby boy, and she is quite well, you may be delighted to hear.'

She turned away from the men, who were staring from her to each other and back again, and Celandine took the opportunity to pull off her gloves, wondering why it was that so many men looked so strangely helpless at just the mention of a baby.

'Can I see her? If she is safely delivered of the baby now? Will she see me now, do you think?'

Celandine looked up at Napier, who had moved to stand in front of her.

'I have no idea. I cannot speak for Edith, Mr Todd,' she said, but her voice was a little less cold because the expression on his face was so haunted. 'It would be impossible for me to say. What I can say is that the baby looks exactly like his father, which is all to the good, most especially in these circumstances. Now I must go and change.'

Sheridan followed Celandine out of the room. 'You must tell Napier who the baby looks like, Celandine! You can't be that cruel.'

Celandine turned at the staircase. 'I am in no position to speak for Edith, Sherry, and you know it.'

Napier too came into the hall. 'Are they really all right?' he asked, looking up at Celandine, who was at the top of the stairs by now. 'Are you quite sure they are all right? Edith is so frail, such a frail little person.'

Celandine relented. 'Not only are they all right, Napier, they are very well.' She looked down the stairs, trying to avoid the pleading look in Sherry's eyes. 'Not only are they very well, but as I told you the little boy is bonny and bouncing and looks—' But she could not do it. 'He looks, as I said, just like his father.'

Napier and Sheridan turned away, defeated.

'I should try your hand tomorrow, old fellow, really I should.' Sheridan put a brotherly arm round Napier's shoulders. 'You know mares and foals – best to leave both to get on with it until the straw's a bit flattened around them, my father used to say. Least disturbed, less to be mended.'

Napier sighed and walked off into the gathering dusk, looking as if the weight of the world was on his shoulders.

'I am very sure it will all turn out for the best in the best of all possible worlds.'

Napier turned back at the gate that led to the road. 'I wish I had your certainty,' he said in a low voice, before walking off down the narrow winding street.

*　　*　　*

Edith stared down at the baby. She had fed him and laid him beside her in the crib brought in by Gabrielle. A ruddy-faced nurse had been sent up from the village and was hovering proudly around the bed as if she had just delivered the baby herself.

The baby moved his head slightly, only a vague shifting, but to his mother it seemed enormous, a whole stride of a movement.

'If there is nothing more I can do, I will fetch me a cup of tea.'

Edith nodded without looking up. It was odd that she had loved her son the moment she saw him. More than just odd, it was *most* odd – most particularly since he looked just like Napier. She stared towards the closed velvet curtains, remembering. When he was first laid in her arms Napier's face in miniature had stared up at her, and yet it had not upset her. Napier's face looking up at her had only filled her with devotion. Did that mean that she still loved the baby's father?

Sheridan could not leave the subject alone.

'She must allow Napier to see her now surely, Celandine?'

'I hardly think there is a must about it, Sherry.'

It had been two weeks since the birth and while agreeing to disagree about her duty to Edith, Sherry still seemed determined to take Napier's part.

'We could arrange it, couldn't we?' he pleaded. 'It could be so romantic. Napier surprising her—'

'That idea is not one I would recommend, Sherry.' Celandine could not help laughing. 'Gracious heavens, imagine the scene. Napier surprises Edith, Edith drops the baby, tragedy ensues and it is all our fault!'

'You know what I mean.'

'Of course I know what you mean, dearest. But truly there is only one way out of this muddle. We must pray that Edith gives in to the idea of seeing Napier, of letting Napier see the baby, so that he may discover who is the father for himself.'

'He loves Edith so much, wants her back so much, I truly don't think he minds *who* the father is now,' Sheridan said ruefully. 'He only wants to have Edith *back*. He keeps saying that, cares for nothing more than that she should forgive him for his selfishness. He can't paint, can't even draw, he is not eating. He has suffered enough, surely?'

'I am sure he has, Sherry, but what can I do? I am not Edith. Now I must rush off to the admiral or I shall be late.' Celandine glanced up at the clock. 'Oh dear, I think I must know more about the battle of Trafalgar than anyone now. Goodbye, darling, and don't worry about Napier. I am sure he will be forgiven, eventually.'

Sheridan watched Celandine from the window of the sitting room. He knew he should be outside painting, but the truth was that since Napier had arrived at Newbourne his friend's misery had become his own unhappiness, and he found he could not settle to anything. He waved to Celandine, because she had suddenly turned and waved to him. For a second he tried to imagine life without her, and knowing that it would be unbearable he turned away from the window.

Mrs Molesworth stood at the door. Sheridan thought that she was going to shoo him out of the room so that she could clean it, but instead she announced a visitor.

'There's a gentleman to see you, sir.'

Sheridan stared at his visitor, feeling vaguely uncomfortable.

'Alfred?'

Edith was up and about, eager to push the baby down to the sea front, but fearing to meet Napier she had remained in the garden of Rosewalls, enjoying the sunshine and the feeling of well-being that comes from being restored to health.

The baby woke her every night, and every night she fed him with delighted attention. She was sure that she would never need anyone else in her life now, that she would become everything to him, although the precise origins of these feelings were not entirely clear to her. What *was* clear to her was the familiarity of the figure coming across the lawn towards her.

She quickly started to push the baby in the opposite direction, aiming for the safety of the house, but it was too late.

'No, don't go, Edith, please don't go. Please. Don't run away from me. I am not here to harm you.'

'Napier.'

Edith's voice sounded flat, unenthusiastic, unwelcoming, not at all as it normally did, but there was little she could do to colour it with more warmth. Just seeing Napier walking across the lawn towards her brought back such cruel memories. The way he had sent the carriage away when she had gone to see him to ask his forgiveness for falsely accusing him. The way he had refused to have anything more to do with her, the punishments that he had inflicted on her when she had done nothing more than love him. She saw, all too clearly, that she could never forgive him for how he had behaved to her, that to do so would be to give in to the lowest emotion. She would not be craven. She would hold on to the dignity which she had finally recovered, after it had been taken from her in such a cruel fashion by Napier.

'Edith, please, don't back away from me.'

'I had rather you went away. I am only just recovering from my confinement and I really must be left in some peace. My life has been so good without you, everyone here so kind. I really want nothing more to do with you. Although I wish you no harm, I just don't want to see you any more. Not ever.'

For the first time in his life Napier was able to look at the undoubted result of his own selfish behaviour. He had lost Edith's love, and he could see it. Worse than that, he had lost her respect. If he went down on his knees to her he could see that in all probability she would remain indifferent. Worse again, she would despise him.

'Edith.' He began again. 'I know that how I have been in the past has made me seem despicable in your eyes.'

Edith continued to push the pram away from him, weaving in between the trees. 'I understand now just how badly you have treated me, with what indifference to my feelings you married me and ignored me, taking advantage of my innocence.'

'Stop!'

They had somehow reached the terrace of the house, albeit by different routes, but since Edith had won their strange erratic race she was able to snatch up the baby and hurry indoors with him. She handed him to the nurse. 'Take the baby, please. His father is here, visiting unexpectedly.'

The nurse did as she was told, and Edith returned to the terrace to find Napier leaning in despair against one of the rose-laden pillars that bordered it.

'Won't you please leave now?'

'No.'

Now that she was close to him Edith could see that Napier was looking shocking. He was pale and thin, with black lines under his eyes, and his clothes were hanging off him.

'Aunt Biddy and the vicar are due back for luncheon very soon. They will not want to find you here, most especially not Aunt Biddy.'

'No, the old gorgon hates me, doesn't she?'

'What do you expect? She has seen how cruel you have been. How can she respect or like someone who has treated his wife the way you have treated me?'

'Was everything my fault? Truly, ask yourself, was everything that has come between us my fault?'

Edith turned away. 'No, not everything.' She paused, and then said with dreadful simplicity, 'I realise now that *I* should never have married you. It was the mistake of a foolish innocent, although that is no excuse, for foolishness and innocence of purpose are never, finally, forgivable, even in the very young. I did not know you. I hardly even knew what you did, and yet I agreed to marry you. When I look back, I think I married you to get away from the Stag and Crown as much as you married me in an effort to recapture your wretched muse.'

Edith's honesty made Napier feel as if she had stabbed him in the side, and yet it was this, more than anything perhaps, that made him realise just how incapable she would always be of any kind of infidelity.

'So. So – neither of us really loved the other, is that what you are saying?'

Edith lifted her large eyes to his. 'Oh, I loved you all right; yes, I loved you. But not in the way

486

that I *should* have loved you. Not in an honest way, but in a passionate all-giving way that is not healthy. I should have spoken up for myself when you neglected me in that unkind way, instead of which I suffered in silence, always thinking that you were repulsed by me in some way, or that I was simply not good enough to be anything except your model. But there, I was young and foolish, and you – you were mature and selfish.'

'Is there no hope for us?'

'Not that I can see. Can you?'

Napier summoned every inch of his waning emotional strength, straightened his back, and after a few seconds during which he felt he might lose control, he spoke.

'I – er – I can see – *some* hope.' His voice was on the verge of breaking. 'I think one *should* see hope for – for – two people who have been through so much together. For two people who have a child as proof of their passion, there surely must be some *hope*?'

'You don't yet know the child is yours.'

Napier smiled at her, the sudden tenderness in his eyes tempering his forlorn appearance. 'Of course the child is mine, Edith dearest.'

'How do you know?'

Napier took her hands. 'Because despite everything I think you still love me. That is why I know the child is mine. I know that you love me, despite everything you have said, perhaps because of everything you have said. I also know that you are incapable of dishonesty, or deception. I am sure that I am the only man to have made love to you. Edith. Please try to love me again. Please?'

Edith freed her hands. 'No, Napier, I can't.'

'You mean – you won't? You mean you won't even try?'

Edith hesitated. How could she say she would not even try to love him again without sounding at best stubborn, and at worse hateful? Her hesitation proved to be fatal.

Napier moved closer to her, dropping his voice because he thought he could hear sounds of Aunt Biddy returning.

'Let me call on you, let me woo you again, and again, until time has taken the dreadful hurt I have inflicted on you away for ever. Please, please, Edith. I love you, and only you, and I will only ever love you. You are the centre of my life, the captain of my soul.'

'Very well, you can visit me – perhaps next week.'

'I can't wait that long.'

'You have no alternative!'

'Edith! Edith dear! The vicar is here!'

Aunt Biddy's voice floated across the garden as Napier seized Edith, trying to pull her towards him, trying to kiss her, but Edith pushed him away from her, frowning.

'You shouldn't have done that, Napier,' she said in a voice that surprised even her by its unnaturally firm tone.

'How can I not want to love you? How can you know how I feel? Look at me, do, I have become ill with longing for you—'

Edith could see the truth of his words, because Napier did look quite ill, but she was not prepared to be moved either by his looks, or by him.

'You must go before Aunt Biddy sees you, truly you must.'

She looked at him in a detached manner. She felt sorry for him, but not so sorry that she was prepared to forgive him. She might try to do so, but she could not put away the harm he had done her.

Napier backed off down the lawn. 'I will go, but only in order to come back.'

Edith shook her head. 'No, don't come back, Napier, not yet. If you come back too soon I will never change my mind, I promise you.'

Even at a distance she could see that he had lost what remaining colour he had.

'Do you hate me that much?'

Edith turned away from him so that her words seemed to come floating back down the lawn. 'No, I don't hate you, Napier, but I confess I do keep wondering if I can ever love you again. Something has gone from me these last months, shut down, perhaps never to return.'

The luncheon with the vicar and Aunt Biddy passed as all such luncheons must, with equanimity, a feeling of everyone doing the right thing, and without any undue excitement beyond the vicar being pressed to some more pudding.

'Poor man, he is never fed properly at home. The Church's stipend to him is so modest, he has hardly enough money to pay for the starch in his collars.' Aunt Biddy watched the man of God making his comfortable way down her steps, the wind blowing his hat so that he had to hold it tight to his head. 'Now, dear, what about you, and the baby?' she asked. 'I hear tell – Gabrielle and Russo, you know – I hear tell from them that this morning we had an unexpected visitor.'

Edith turned back towards the drawing room, towards the steady existence to which she had become strangely accustomed.

'Yes, we did have an unexpected visitor, Aunt Biddy, but I have sent him on his way.'

Aunt Biddy sighed with satisfaction. 'Unexpected visitors should always be sent on their way,' she said, reseating herself in her favourite chair and nodding to Edith to sit herself down opposite. 'Tell me, did he make himself a nuisance, my dear?'

Edith stared into the fire. 'Yes, I am afraid he did make himself a nuisance,' she admitted, flushing slightly.

Aunt Biddy looked at her and her eyes brightened. 'This is good, dear, very good. So now you must keep him at bay, like the poor old stag in the painting, for the next few weeks, if not months, which will give you time to make up your mind as to whether you want to go back to him, or not, as the case may be. For myself I shall not wish for either you or Baby to go away. You have both become as much part of my house as the old dears who look after me, and the roses outside; as much as the sea view, and the velvet drapes. But I have to say that a boy should have a father, and if you should resolve the matter satisfactorily I myself will be the first to congratulate you.'

On hearing this, Edith went up to Aunt Biddy and kissed her warm, rounded cheek. 'You have been too good to me and little John Napier, Aunt Biddy.'

'My home will always be your home, dear Edith. Truly I have found in you a dear, dear companion.'

She sighed, and minutes later was sound asleep, as was her habit after luncheon.

Celandine was filling in the background of a new portrait. Not, thank heavens, as she explained to Edith, either a red velvet curtain, or a maritime view of some sort, but a beach scene with children playing.

'Mrs Alfred Woodcock, the Mayor of Newbourne's wife, wants a painting of herself with her children on the beach. Oh bless Mrs Woodcock, if only I could tell her how much it means to me not to have to paint a curtain!'

Edith, who had left the baby and his new young nurse outside the house, waved to them both as the young girl patiently pushed him up

and down, the fringed canopy of the pram swaying gently in the breeze.

'Ah, such a pretty sight.' Celandine sighed
happily, peering over her friend's shoulder. 'So,
now,' she said, peering at Edith, 'what can I do
for you, Mrs Todd? No, don't tell me. First let me
fetch us a nice jug of lemonade.'

She returned with the lemonade jug and some
glasses, and beckoned Edith to follow her outside.

'Let us go and sit outside while we may, before
the sunshine goes. It does go so quickly from the
garden, I always find.'

Edith sat down, and as she did so she remembered when she had confessed her untouched
married state to Celandine in the same garden in
which they were now sitting, what seemed years
before. She sighed inwardly for the pain she had
felt, and sighed again as she realised that it
had been nothing compared to the pain she had
subsequently endured. Long months without a
husband, with only the consolation of friends,
giving birth with the almost certain knowledge
that the baby was to all intents and purposes
fatherless.

'It seems I always come to you for advice,' she
told Celandine. 'And now here I am again.' She
paused. 'You see, Napier came to Aunt Biddy's
house yesterday. I confess I was shocked by
his appearance.' She sighed, looking uncharacteristically restless, but Celandine was too tactful
to say anything, so she went on. 'He wants to

visit me, to try to persuade me to return to him, but I am reluctant to encourage him. He has, after all, rejected me not once but twice, Celandine. The trouble is – the trouble is – in so many ways, I must confess I am happier now. I do not pine for the excitement which Napier once brought to me. In many ways I am better now; and calmer too. With the arrival of the baby I feel I have reached a plateau of contentment which I could never have anticipated. But yesterday, when Napier called so unexpectedly, the sight of him did not make me happier, it made me less happy, and that is not because I have not forgiven him, it is because I have changed – these last months I have been happier without him.'

'Well, you would be,' Celandine said in a reasonable tone, but she sipped at her lemonade with a thoughtful expression, not looking at her friend. 'The question of the male in one's life is much more complicated than our society will choose to admit, most particularly for strong-minded women. I have to say I always enjoy a feeling of great calm once Sherry has left the house. He does not need to utter a word, he can remain completely silent and yet I will feel I am on call all the time; but once he is out of sight I can settle down to working, and generally not being fatigued by him; and yet, if I am honest, I am aware that all the time I am listening for his step outside the front door, his key in the lock, his voice calling to me, and that should I never hear it again, my life would be really quite over.'

Edith stared at her. She knew exactly what Celandine meant, and yet she did not know whether she could or had ever applied such emotions to Napier; since she had been quite sure that he would not return to her, she had grown used to the idea that she had nothing to look forward to other than the safe delivery of her child.

'And then again,' Celandine went on, dreamily, 'there is a great deal to be said for the annoyances that a man in your life brings with him, not least the realisation that, alas, you yourself are not always in the right, which is so irritating; most especially for me, since I am always quite sure, as you know, that I am right, and dislike intensely the idea that I am not perfect.'

'You are saying, are you not, that you think I should let Napier visit me, at least *visit*?'

Celandine's eyes widened. 'I am saying nothing of the sort, dear Edith. I am merely telling you how I myself feel. You, on the other hand, may feel quite differently.'

Edith frowned and then stood up and walked down the garden, staring about her as if seeking inspiration, or consolation.

She came back to the table and sat down again.

'Perhaps human relationships are like the sea, Celandine? They are sometimes still, sometimes stormy, but without them – there would be no life?'

'Perhaps they are.'

'So it is up to me to discover whether the

storms to which I have been subjected have wrecked our marriage, or whether it can be brought into harbour and repaired? I think that it is up to me, not even Napier, wouldn't you say?'

'Yes, I would, Edith. Only you can say whether you have been too hurt by what Napier has done to you. After all, here in Cornwall, we know that you already have an independent existence. You can stay with Aunt Biddy, as her companion and helpmeet, or you can return to your old life.'

Celandine stood up. She herself had to return to her painting. And besides, dearly though she loved having conversations with her own sex, she did not like to dwell too much on sensitive subjects. Sometimes words were truly not the answer, and really, they both knew only time would tell.

But as Celandine kissed Edith goodbye she could not help feeling sorry for her, but also thankful that she could only imagine the terrible hurt her friend must still be feeling. It was all very well for Napier to come bursting back into Edith's life again, but he had to be brought to understand the terrible pain he had caused, not once but twice. If Edith could not take him back immediately, or never took him back, that would be only his just deserts. At best he had been selfish and stupid, at worst he had been negligent and cruel.

Russo had been told not to admit any gentlemen, aside from the vicar on Thursdays, of course; so the first time Napier attempted a call, he was turned away abruptly, and allowed only to leave his card. On the second visit he was admitted, but only after Edith had written to tell him the conditions of his being allowed to call again.

In her note to him Edith wrote out the conditions most precisely.

Napier could call at teatime once a week, and he could view the baby, but only if Aunt Biddy and herself were present, not to mention the young nurse, Gabrielle and Russo. He could stay for an hour, but then he must go away again, and return the following week. He must not attempt to call at any other time. He must not call if he felt ill or had a cold. He must not make a scene. He must remember his manners at all times, or he would be immediately asked to leave.

If Napier had felt that exhibiting a painting was nerve-racking, he found it was as nothing compared to having five pairs of eyes watch his entrance into Aunt Biddy's drawing room that first Tuesday afternoon.

'Good afternoon!' he said, attempting to speak to the assembled company in a clear, firm voice, and failing miserably.

He bowed first to Aunt Biddy and then to Edith, not daring even to attempt to kiss the mother of his child, his perhaps soon-to-be-former wife.

'My, my, he is looking fine,' he said, clearing his throat, as the young nurse picked John

Napier up and displayed him proudly while being sure to hold him closer to her than to his father, as if she had been instructed not to let his father too near.

'Do sit down, please,' Aunt Biddy instructed Napier. He sat on the chair indicated, which was considerably lower than the sofas upon which his hostess and Edith were seated.

Napier stared around him, filled with unease and dark feelings of despair. He knew he was being punished, and he accepted it, but since he was a proud man he found it more than hard – he found it intolerable. And that was before the heat of the room began to make itself felt, and beads of sweat had to be wiped from his forehead with a large silk handkerchief.

Many such Tuesday afternoons followed, until one day he turned to Edith as he was leaving the house and said, 'I cannot visit next week as I have to go to London to see Devigne about the hanging of "Temptation".'

Edith nodded, the look in her eyes opaque as she remembered Napier painting over her face in favour of that of Becky Snape.

'Of course, "Temptation." How does it look?'

'Oh, I think everyone is pleased with it.' He did not feel it would be right to say that Devigne was treating it as a masterpiece. 'Devigne has found a rich nabob newly returned from India to buy it. He is mightily pleased with himself, and of course the sum paid will help to keep

Helmscote – and you and baby John,' he added quickly, for it was difficult for him to think of his home without a wife, and now a son; yet he knew from the implacable expression on Edith's face that he still might have to.

'I hope that everything goes well for you, Napier.'

Edith turned back from the front door, closing it behind her, and as she did so she felt the sadness of those days at Helmscote return to her. Remembering Napier's neglect, she did not kiss the tips of her fingers in saying goodbye, as she had used to do, but left him to continue down the steps towards the sea front, feeling no more for him than she had the week before. The truth was she knew herself to be still dead inside, and it seemed that nothing would wake her.

Once he got to London on that Tuesday, Napier could not help feeling like a freed prisoner. The relief of knowing that he would not be going before judge and jury in front of a roaring fire to eat crumpets and drink hot tea on a fine summer afternoon was intoxicating. If Devigne's gallery had not beckoned after his long journey from Cornwall, he thought he might have retired to his club and become more than a little inebriated, but, happily for his head, he had business to which to attend – visiting his bank, making a new will, and going to see Devigne.

'Ah, my dear Napier, how good to see you, but—' Devigne stepped back, shocked. 'But are you quite all right, dear fellow? You look positively wraithlike. Been working too hard, have you?'

'I have been working very hard, in Cornwall, as it happens, but not quite in the way I would have wished. To tell you the truth, I would give anything to be back at Helmscote painting in my studio, but at this moment it is not possible.'

Devigne frowned. 'Not taking to the New-bourne School, I hope?'

'No, more what you might call the School of Life.' Napier laughed sardonically. 'No, you have no need to worry, my dear Sam, I shall never abandon the Pre-Raphaelites. After all, I have sacrificed so much to the movement, I am quite sure that for me there can be no turning back now.'

'I am very glad to hear it. The compliments I have received from people viewing "Temptation" would have pleased you inordinately.' Sam lit a cigar and smiled benignly. 'So. What can we expect next from Napier Todd?'

Napier stared at him blankly. He could not tell Sam that he had come to a virtual standstill, that all ideas of where to turn next had deserted him since the birth of his son, and Edith's refusal to return to him.

'Something soon, I hope, Sam, but just at the moment I am resting, waiting for the Muse to visit.'

Sam patted him on the shoulder. He knew just how to treat painters like Napier Todd. It was important never to hurry them, just let them take their time, pretend it didn't matter when the next paintings were coming along, and that way they relaxed, and before long produced something quite beautiful like 'Temptation'.

'Come and see your work. As I told you, it has been much admired. Besides,' he nodded towards the upper end of the gallery, 'besides, there is your old friend Alfred Talisman. He will be delighted to see you.'

Napier stared between the backs of the prosperous men and women pacing the gallery, chatting to each other, and sometimes even looking at the paintings. Alfred Talisman was not just in the gallery, he was staring up at Napier's painting. Napier hurried towards him determined on facing him down, although with what he had no real idea, for he knew that he had been more at fault than Alfred had ever been.

Alfred turned as he heard someone behind him.

'Napier, my dear fellow.'

'Hallo, Talisman.'

Alfred took a few steps backwards. He, like Napier, despite his elegant appearance, was not looking as robust as he had in days gone by. He pointed towards the face in the painting.

'That is very good, Napier, really it is.'

Napier stared up. It was good. It was very, very good. He had managed to capture something of the nature of Eve in Becky's perfect face with its almost blank eyes, as if even should she succeed in tempting Adam she would truly have known quite why.

'Ah, the Snape,' Alfred mused, still staring up. 'She left me, you know.'

'Women like the Snape always leave you, Alfred. You should know that. They are all ambition, and no feeling. They use us as mere stepping stones upon which to climb upwards. You would never do for the Snape. She would always have much richer game in her sights.'

'How true, my dear Napier, how true.' Alfred smiled ruefully. 'Unhappily, though, she has left me with something more than pleasant memories and a successful season's hunting.'

'I am sorry to hear that, Alfred.' Napier looked at him. 'That is bad luck.'

'You did not partake of the forbidden fruit?'

'I love my wife, Alfred, it would not be an answer. Unfortunately, now, thanks to my insensitivity, and your meddling, she no longer loves me.'

Napier turned and began to walk away from Alfred. It was just his luck to bump into him; but Alfred followed him, determinedly keeping pace.

'You are not alone in loving Edith, Napier. I love her too. I loved her the first time I met her, but unlike you, I would have loved her passionately, as a woman should be loved. And I would have gone on loving her the way you have never loved or appreciated her.'

Napier turned and faced Alfred. 'I admit I

treated Edith abominably, and now she is making me pay for it, which is only right.'

Alfred paused, his eyes opening slightly wider. 'Edith has left you?'

'Yes, Alfred, Edith has left me, and will not return to me until such time as she feels she can love me again – if ever she feels she can love me again, which I am beginning to doubt.'

Alfred groaned. 'But for the Snape she could have been mine.'

'She could never be yours, Alfred. You would never have loved her as I do.'

'You didn't love her, Napier. You bought her with a wedding ring, and then you neglected her. You don't love her now, you're incapable of loving anything except your art, and you know it.'

Napier held Alfred's despising look for a few seconds, and then said in a quiet, determined voice, 'Very well, Alfred, I will prove to you just how much I love Edith.'

Alfred laughed at the seriousness of his face and tone. 'That is a very safe statement, since you know as well as I that you can't prove to someone that you love them.'

'Follow me.'

Napier pointed to 'Temptation'.

'To prove how much I love Edith I will destroy this painting which I still own – I will destroy it here and now – if—' He pointed across the room to Alfred's completed painting, 'Friday's Girl'. 'I will destroy this, if you will destroy your painting of Edith.'

Alfred paled. 'You can't do that, Napier. Good God, that painting means everything to you.'

Napier's expression was implacable. 'It is mine to destroy. Sam has not paid me for it. I shall do it to prove how much I love Edith. Do the same to "Friday's Girl" as I shall do to "Temptation" and I will know you love Edith.'

'Oh dear me, Edith, terrible news, I am afraid.'

Aunt Biddy sat down, forgetting to sit sideways, so her crinoline flared up too high and she had to bat it down and rearrange herself.

'Such terrible news,' she went on, fanning herself. 'The fact is that Napier has caused a scandal, and what a to-do! It is all in here.'

Edith put down her sewing and stared at Aunt Biddy as the older woman held up her copy of *The Times*.

'Shall I read it to you to lessen the shock, my dear?'

'No, no, please don't concern yourself, I will read it for myself.'

Edith turned the newspaper towards her, and read the item with growing incredulity.

Well-known society painter Napier Todd caused a sensation yesterday at the Devigne Art Gallery by publicly destroying his masterpiece 'Temptation'. It is as yet unclear as to what his motivation may have been. When speaking to us, Mr Samuel Devigne, owner of the gallery, said, 'I cannot understand the reason for his extraordinary behaviour, whether his action was prompted by dissatisfaction or by some sort of wager. Whatever the reason, the buyer, who happily for him had not as yet paid for the painting, is understandably furious. For a painter of Mr Todd's reputation to behave in this manner is utterly uncharacteristic. I have the highest regard for Napier Todd's work. I also know that he has not been well lately, and I only hope that this is not symptomatic of some sort of nervous collapse. Naturally, since he still owns the painting, no charges will be pressed, and I hope that a return to health will swiftly follow.'

Edith looked across at Aunt Biddy. 'Oh dear, oh dear.'

'I know, my dear. Oh dear, oh dear indeed, and whatever next? Oh dear, oh dear, oh *dear!*'

Edith stood up. 'I shall have to go to him,' she announced. 'He must be terribly unwell.'

Aunt Biddy watched her young companion hurry from the room, and picked up her fan and began rapidly to fan herself. Perhaps it had taken this violent action of Napier Todd's to bring Edith to realise that she loved the man? Or perhaps she would hurry up to London and find that she loved him even less? Whatever the outcome, there would be no more shilly-shallying.

Celandine stared at her nearly completed painting. Since taking up portrait painting she had greatly improved her technique, not to mention widening her circle of acquaintances in

Newbourne. What had begun as a reluctant pursuit to help pay the bills had ended in an output that was both demanding and pleasing. She knew that Sheridan was most relieved now not to have any part in her world, and she herself had no longing to share his constant quest, his daily struggle to paint the reality of life in present-day Cornwall.

At that moment she heard the pleasant sound of Sheridan's key turning slowly and erratically in the old front door, followed by a brief murmur from the narrow street outside, and the door shutting behind him.

'Celandine!' Sheridan stood at the door of the room that was now her small studio and waved a newspaper. 'The most awful drama, dearest. Too terrible. What can have happened to Napier to do something so frantic?'

Celandine stood up. She always looked forward to Sherry's afternoon return from his own studio with a purposefully subdued excitement, and now he was there, no matter what the news, she could not help smiling. He was, after all, her dear, dear Sherry.

'Well, something was bound to be the outcome of so much emotion during the past weeks,' she said in reasonable tones, taking the newspaper from him. 'As long as no one has died—' She glanced at the newspaper. 'Only a painting – then the world will go on spinning, I think.'

Sheridan looked at Celandine as she calmly read the item to which he had pointed. He was always grateful for her sanity, but at that moment he was more than grateful for it, he was entranced by it.

Edith had managed to find out from Sam Devigne that Napier was staying at Brown's Hotel. As soon as her train brought her into Paddington from Cornwall, she was able to take a hackney cab and hurry round to see him, but not before she had called in at the gallery to see Devigne.

'It seems,' Sam told her, his eyes dark with patient sorrow, 'that he was trying to prove something to Alfred Talisman.' He stopped, frowning, and stared a little closer at Edith. 'Ah, but I know you, don't I, Mrs Todd? Yes, of course I know you. You arrived ahead of yourself, only a couple of weeks ago, and have been very much admired, I have to tell you.' Sam's gaze immediately brightened as he recognised the beauty in front of whom he was now standing. 'Well, this is really quite delightful, I do assure you. I have two of you now!'

He marched her down to Alfred Talisman's painting and stood her in front of it.

Edith gazed up at Alfred's painting of her, and felt an almost physical shock as she saw how much Alfred had understood and even loved her.

'You, I am afraid, Mrs Todd,' Sam told her, humour coming into his voice for the first time, 'you are the cause of all the trouble, but I

506

will leave your poor demented husband to tell you the full story. As it is, I do assure you, since both painters will, in the fullness of time, become not just famous but immortal, this scandal will only enhance their reputations, believe me. Scandals are *always* good for art, Mrs Todd – and, naturally, business!'

He lit a cigar and smiled. After all, his gallery had just received more press attention than the National Gallery and the Royal Academy combined.

Edith, shocked by the violence of Napier's feelings for her, not to mention his willingness to sacrifice his painting to prove his love, eventually consented to return to him. Celandine and Aunt Biddy were pleased for her, but especially happy that Napier and she decided to sell Helmscote to a quickly formed co-operative group of workers, and return to Cornwall and their circle of loving friends.

For a while it seemed that the trauma of the scandal concerning 'Temptation' had indeed had an adverse effect on Napier, and he had returned to that same artistic state in which he had first encountered Edith scrubbing the floor of the Stag Inn; until one day she happened to mention the man with the lantern who had led her to safety through the streets of Newbourne.

Inspired by her description, Napier painted her rescuer as he imagined him. The painting, entitled 'Here I am, Child', depicted a bearded figure with a lantern. It became one of the most reproduced paintings of all time, and made Sam Devigne the happiest of gallery owners.

Celandine and Sheridan founded the Newbourne Art School, where Celandine made sure that the intake of female artists was at least as great as the male. She continued to paint local personalities, as Sheridan continued to promote his ideals of naturalism. Today their paintings hang side by side in the school's gallery at Newbourne. They are greatly admired by the kind of people who would never have visited Sam Devigne's gallery, but are quite sure that they know a good painting when they see one.

'Friday's Girl', on the other hand, hangs in the new National Gallery at Newbourne. It is a speaking portrait of a young girl at a certain moment in her life. A great many people think it sentimental. Only those who knew the sitter know the truth of it.

If you enjoyed Friday's Girl, *look out for Charlotte Bingham's next novel*, Out of the Blue.

Charlotte Bingham would like to invite you to visit her website at www.charlottebingham.com

THE MAGIC HOUR
by Charlotte Bingham

When Alexandra goes to stay with her cousins at Knighton Hall she is made to feel the poor relation; the daughters of the house are both beautiful and wealthy. She is not to meet the handsome stable lad, Tom O'Brien, until much later.

When Alexandra returns home, her father remarries and she is forced to become a maid-of-all-work. Alexandra makes a success of her new life and meets the lovely Bob Atkins. Meanwhile, Tom O'Brien has become impassioned by the beautiful Lady Florazel Compton who introduces him to the sophistications of 1950s London. Sadly, Alexandra's contentment with Bob is short-lived and Tom comes back into her life.

But the past seems destined to wreck the happiness of the present, as the still-beautiful Lady Florazel is determined to re-capture her former love and destroy the magic hour of Tom and Alexandra's meeting.

0 553 81592 X

BANTAM BOOKS

THE MOON AT MIDNIGHT
by Charlotte Bingham

It is late autumn, 1962, and darkness is falling, but not just over the idyllic fishing port of Bexham. The threat of atomic warfare is so real that people are taking their children to work, or staying home with their families as they face what they think might be the end of the world. For some, the threat is all the more bewildering as they struggle to understand the new generation of the Sixties, a generation for whom they had made so many wartime sacrifices, for whom they had such high hopes.

No sooner has the threat of nuclear war seemingly passed than Judy, Mathilda and Rusty are facing a new, personal crisis brought about by their teenage children. Much as Waldo Astley would like to remain on the sidelines, he finds it impossible, and this too brings about bitter opposition from those caught up in the near-tragedy. Still grieving for his lost wife, he tries his best to help his three friends, only to find himself falling in love with one of them.

Meanwhile the younger generation have their own problems, all of which involve their families. That all the generations find themselves once more united in a battle, this time to save the village they love, is both an irony and finally, a saving grace. Once more an enemy has to be defeated, once more they must arm themselves, but this time for a war of a very different kind.

The Moon at Midnight is part of the Bexham trilogy, which begins with *The Chestnut Tree* and continues with *The Wind Off the Sea*.

0 553 81399 4

BANTAM BOOKS

THE HOUSE OF FLOWERS
by Charlotte Bingham

It is 1941, and England is at its lowest ebb, undernourished, under-informed and terrified of imminent invasion. Even at Eden Park, the lovely country estate where Poppy and Kate, Marjorie and her adopted brother Billy have all become part of the rich tapestry that is being woven around them, confidence is at an all-time low. And that is before the authorities discover there is a double agent operating within the MI5 unit based there.

Lily volunteers to be dropped into France, only to discover that her partner is Scott, Poppy's fiancé. Meanwhile, Kate's lover Eugene is in Sicily to sabotage the bombers besieging Malta. As further lines of agents are wiped out and even Billy's life is threatened, Jack Ward, the spymaster, is forced to take desperate measures to uncover the identity of the traitor in their midst.

Meanwhile, Poppy, unable to stand idle, leaves Eden Park to train as a pilot. As she closes the wooden shutters at the House of Flowers, the old folly where she and Scott first found happiness, she realises that they were made over a century ago to repel another invader. England survived then; she will again.

The House of Flowers is part of the Eden series, which begins with *Daughters of Eden*.

0 553 81400 1

BANTAM BOOKS

A LIST OF OTHER CHARLOTTE BINGHAM TITLES
AVAILABLE FROM BANTAM BOOKS

THE PRICES SHOWN BELOW WERE CORRECT AT THE TIME OF GOING TO PRESS.
HOWEVER TRANSWORLD PUBLISHERS RESERVE THE RIGHT TO SHOW NEW
RETAIL PRICES ON COVERS WHICH MAY DIFFER FROM THOSE PREVIOUSLY
ADVERTISED IN THE TEXT OR ELSEWHERE.

40163	7	THE BUSINESS	£6.99
40497	0	CHANGE OF HEART	£5.99
40890	6	DEBUTANTES	£6.99
40895	X	THE NIGHTINGALE SINGS	£6.99
17635	8	TO HEAR A NIGHTINGALE	£6.99
50500	9	GRAND AFFAIR	£6.99
40296	X	IN SUNSHINE OR IN SHADOW	£6.99
40496	2	NANNY	£6.99
40117	8	STARDUST	£6.99
50717	6	THE KISSING GARDEN	£6.99
50501	7	LOVE SONG	£6.99
50718	4	THE LOVE KNOT	£6.99
81274	2	THE BLUE NOTE	£6.99
81275	0	THE SEASON	£5.99
81276	9	SUMMERTIME	£5.99
81387	0	DISTANT MUSIC	£6.99
81277	7	THE CHESTNUT TREE	£6.99
81398	6	THE WIND OFF THE SEA	£6.99
81399	4	THE MOON AT MIDNIGHT	£6.99
81591	1	DAUGHTERS OF EDEN	£6.99
81400	1	THE HOUSE OF FLOWERS	£6.99
81592	X	THE MAGIC HOUR	£6.99
05440	7	OUT OF THE BLUE (Hardback)	£12.99

All Transworld titles are available by post from:
Bookpost, PO Box 29, Douglas, Isle of Man IM99 1BQ
Credit cards accepted. Please telephone +44(0)1624 677237, fax +44(0)1624 670923,
Internet http://www.bookpost.co.uk or
e-mail: bookshop@enterprise.net for details.
Free postage and packing in the UK.
Overseas customers allow £2 per book (paperbacks) and £3 per book (hardback).